A Mad Love

by

Charlotte M. Brame

A Mad Love
by Charlotte M. Brame

ISBN: 978-93-62760-97-5

Published by

DOUBLE 9 BOOKS

2/13-B, Ansari Road
Daryaganj, New Delhi – 110002
info@double9books.com
www.double9books.com
Tel. 011-40042856

ABOUT THE AUTHOR

Charlotte M. Brame was a prolific and diverse Victorian author who wrote novels, short stories, and serialized fiction throughout her career. Among her outstanding works is "A Fair Mystery: The Story of a Coquette," a riveting story that exemplifies Brame's ability to weave intricate plots and engaging characters. In "A Fair Mystery," Brame expertly builds a story centered on the intriguing character of the coquette, a beguiling yet elusive creature whose actions and reasons propel the plot along. Set against the backdrop of Victorian society, the novel delves into themes of love, betrayal, and atonement as the coquette navigates the complexities of romance and mystery. Brame's literary style is distinguished by vivid descriptions, emotional depth, and subtle character development. She vividly describes the vibrant world of the Victorian era, engaging readers in a compelling narrative of love, passion, and deception. "A Fair Mystery" demonstrates Brame's storytelling prowess and ability to attract audiences with intriguing narratives. With its sophisticated narrative twists, compelling characters, and wonderfully drawn landscapes, the novel is a timeless masterpiece that continues to captivate readers today.

CONTENTS

CHAPTER I
A DISCONTENTED BEAUTY

"Leone," cried a loud voice, "where are you? Here, there, everywhere, except just in the place where you should be."

The speaker was a tall, stout, good-tempered looking man. Farmer Noel people called him all over the country-side. He stood in the farmyard, looking all the warmer this warm day for his exertions in finding his niece.

"Leone," he cried again and again.

At last the answer came, "I am here, uncle," and if the first voice startled one with its loudness, this second was equally startling from its music, its depth, its pathos.

"I am here, uncle," she said. "I wish you would not shout so loudly. I am quite sure that the people at Rashleigh can hear you. What is it that you want?"

"Have you made up the packets of wheat I asked you for?" he said.

"No," she replied, "I have not."

He looked disappointed.

"I shall be late for market," he said. "I must do them myself."

He went back into the house without another word. He never reproached Leone, let her do what she would.

On Leone's most beautiful face were evident marks of bad temper, and she did not care to conceal it. With a gesture of impatience she started forward, passed over the farmyard and went through the gate out into the lane, from the lane to the high-road, and she stood there leaning over the white gate, watching the cattle as they drank from the deep, clear pool.

The sun shone full upon her, and the warm, sweet beams never fell on anything more lovely; the only drawback to the perfection of the picture was this: she did not look in harmony with the scene—the quiet English landscape, the golden cornfields, the green meadows, the great spreading trees whereon the birds sung, the tall spire of the little church, the quaint little town in the distance, the brook that ran gurgling by.

She looked out of harmony with them all; she would have been in perfect keeping had the background been of snow-capped mountains and foaming cascades. Here she looked out of place; she was on an English farm; she wore a plain English dress, yet she had the magnificent beauty of the daughters of sunny Spain. Her beauty was of a peculiar type—dark, passionate, and picturesque like that of the pomegranate, the damask rose or the passion-flower.

There was a world in her face—of passion, of genius, of power; a face as much out of place over the gates of a farm as a stately gladiolus would be among daisies and buttercups. An artist looking for a model of some great queen who had conquered the world, for some great heroine for whom men had fought madly and died, might have chosen her. But in a farmyard! there are no words to tell how out of place it was. She stood by the gate holding the ribbons of her hat in her hand—beautiful, imperious, defiant—with a power of passion about her that was perhaps her greatest characteristic.

She looked round the quiet picture of country life with unutterable contempt.

"If I could but fly away," she said; "I would be anything on earth if I could get away from this—I would not mind what; I would work, teaching, anything; the dull monotony of this life is killing me."

Her face was so expressive that every emotion was shown on it, every thought could be read there; the languid scorn of the dark eyes, and the proud curves of the daintily arched lips, all told of unconcealed contempt.

"A farm," she said to herself; "to think that when the world is full of beautiful places, my lot must be cast on a farm. If it had been in a palace, or a gypsy's camp—anywhere where I could have tasted life, but a farm."

The beautiful restless face looked contemptuously out on the green and fertile land.

"A farm means chickens running under one's feet, pigeons whirling round one's head, cows lowing, dogs barking, no conversation but crops——"

She stopped suddenly. Coming up the lane she saw that which had never gladdened her eyes here before; she saw a gentleman, handsome and young, walking carelessly down the high-road, and as he drew near, another gentleman, also handsome, but not quite so young, joined him.

They came laughing down the high-road together, but neither of them saw her until they reached the great elm-tree. The sight of that wondrous young face, with its rich, piquant beauty, startled them. One passed her by without a word, the other almost stopped, so entirely was he charmed by the lovely picture. As he passed he raised his hat; her beautiful face flushed; she neither smiled nor bowed in return, but accepted the salute as a tribute to her beauty, after the same fashion a queen acknowledges the salutes and homage of her subjects.

With one keen glance, she divided him from his companion, the man who had *not* bowed to her. She took in that one glance a comprehensive view. She knew the color of his eyes, of his hair, the shape of his face, the peculiar cut of his clothes, so different to those worn by the young farmers; the clustering hair, the clear-cut face, the delicate profile, the graceful ease of the tall, thin figure, were with her from that moment through all time.

The deep low bow gratified her. She knew that she was gifted with a wondrous dower of beauty. She knew that men were meek when a beautiful face charmed them. The involuntary homage of this handsome young man pleased her. She would have more of it. When he rejoined his companion, she heard him say:

"What a wonderful face, Euston—the most beautiful I have ever seen in my life."

That pleased her still more; she smiled to herself.

"Perhaps I shall see him again," she thought.

Then one of the girls from the village passed the gate, and stopped for a few minutes' conversation.

"Did you see those gentlemen?" asked the girl; and Leone answered:

"Yes."

"They have both come to live at Dr. Hervey's, to 'read,' whatever that means. The young one, with the fair hair, is a lord, the eldest son of a great earl; I do not remember the name."

So it was a great lord who had bowed to her, and thought her more beautiful than any one he had ever seen. Her heart beat with triumph.

She bade the girl good-morning, and went back. Her beautiful face was brilliant with smiles.

She entered the house and went up to her glass. She wanted to see again, for herself, the face he had called beautiful.

Mirrored there, she saw two dark eyes, full of fire, bright, radiant, and luminous — eyes that could have lured and swayed a nation; a beautiful, oval face, the features of which were perfect; a white brow, with dark, straight eyebrows; sweet, red lips, like a cloven rose; the most beautiful chin, with a rare dimple; an imperial face, suited for a queen's crown or the diadem of an empress, but out of place on this simple farm. She saw grand, sloping shoulders, beautiful arms, and a figure that was perfect in its symmetry and grace.

She smiled contentedly. She was beautiful, undoubtedly. She was glad that others saw it. If a young lord admired her, she must be worth admiring. Her good humor was quite restored.

How came it that this girl, with the beauty of a young princess, was at home in the farmhouse? It was a simple story. The farmer, Robert Noel, had only one brother, who loved romance and travel.

Stephen Noel, after trying every profession, and every means of obtaining a livelihood, at last decided on becoming a civil engineer; he went to Spain to help with a rail-road in the province of Andalusia, and there fell in love with and married a beautiful Andalusian, Pepita by name.

Dark-eyed Pepita died on the same day Leone was born, and the young father, distracted by his loss, took the child home to England. The old housekeeper at the Rashleigh farm took the girl, and Robert Noel consented that she should be brought up as a child of his own.

The two brothers differed as light and darkness differ. Stephen was all quickness and intelligence, Robert was stolid and slow. Leone always said it took him ten minutes to turn around. He had never married, he had never found time; but he gave the whole love of his heart to the beautiful dark eyed child who was brought to his house sixteen years ago.

CHAPTER II
"WHAT, MARRY A FARMER!"

One can imagine the sensation that a bright, beautiful eagle would produce in a dove's nest; the presence of that beautiful, imperious child at the farm was very much the same. People looked at her in wonder; her beauty dazzled them; her defiance amused them. They asked each other where all her pride came from.

Uncle Robert often said in his slow fashion that he retired from business when Leone was seven. At that early age he gave the management of everything into her baby hands. From the chickens in the yard to the blue and white pigeons on the roof. She could manage him, big as he was, with one stamp of her little foot, one flash of her bright eyes; he was powerless at once, like a great big giant bound hand and foot. She was a strange child, full of some wonderful power that she hardly understood herself—a child quite out of the common groove of life, quite above the people who surrounded her. They understood her beauty, her defiance, her pride, but not the dramatic instinct and power that, innate in her, made every word and action seem strange.

Honest, stolid Robert Noel was bewildered by her; he did his best in every way, but he had an uneasy consciousness that his best was but a poor attempt. He sent her to school, the best in Rashleigh, but she learned anything and everything except obedience.

She looked out of place even there, this dark-eyed Spanish girl, among the pretty pink and white children with fair hair and blue eyes. She bewildered even the children; they obeyed her, and she had the greatest influence over them. She taught them recitations and plays, she fired their imaginations by wonderful stories; she was a new, brilliant, wonderful element in their lives. Even the school mistress, meek through the long suffering of years, even she worshiped and feared her—the brilliant, tiresome girl, who was like a flash of light among the others. She had a face so grand and a voice so thrilling it was no unusual thing when she was reading aloud in the school-room for the others to suspend all work, thrilled to the heart by the sound of her voice. She soon learned all that the Rashleigh governess could teach her—she taught herself even more. She had little taste for drawing, much for music, but her whole heart and soul were in books.

Young as she was, it was grand to hear her trilling out the pretty love speeches of Juliet, declaring the wrongs of Constance or Katherine, moaning out the woes of Desdemona. She had Shakespeare almost by heart, and she loved the grand old dramatist.

When she was sixteen her uncle took her from school, and then the perplexities of his honest life began. He wanted her to take her place as mistress of the house, to superintend the farm and the dairy, to take affectionate interest in the poultry and birds, to see that the butter was of a deep, rich yellow, and the new laid eggs sent to market. From the moment he intrusted those matters in her hands, his life became a burden to him, for they were entirely neglected.

Farmer Noel would go into his dairy and find everything wrong, the cream spilled, the butter spoiled; but when he looked at the dark-eyed young princess with the Spanish face he dared not say a word to her.

He would suggest to her meekly that things might be different. She would retaliate with some sarcasm that would reduce him to silence for two days at least. Yet she loved, after a fashion of her own, this great, stolid man who admired her with all his heart, and loved her with his whole soul.

So time passed until she was seventeen, and the quiet farm life was unendurable to her.

"Uncle," she would say, "let me go out into the world. I want to see it. I want something to do. I often think I must have two lives and two souls, I long so intensely for more than I have to fill them."

He could not understand her. She had the farm and the dairy.

"Be content," he would answer, "be content, my lady lass, with the home God has given you."

"I want something to do. If I did all the work on this and twenty other farms it would not touch my heart and soul. They are quite empty. People say it is a battlefield. If it be one, I am sitting by with folded hands. Inactivity means death to me."

"My lady lass, you can find plenty to do," he answered, solemnly.

"But not of the kind I want."

She paced up and down the large kitchen, where everything was polished and bright; the fire-light glowed on the splendid face and figure— the face with its unutterable beauty, its restless longing, its troubled desires.

Some fear for the future of the beautiful, restless, passionate girl came over the man, who watched her with anxious eyes. It began to dawn upon him, that if he were to shut a bright-eyed eagle up in a cage, it would never be happy, and it was very much the same kind of thing to shut this lovely, gifted girl in a quiet farmhouse.

"You will be married soon," he said, with a clumsy attempt at comfort, "and then you will be more content."

She flashed one look of scorn from those dark, lustrous eyes that should have annihilated him. She stopped before him, and threw back her head with the gesture of an injured queen.

"May I ask," she said, "whom you suppose I will marry?"

He looked rather frightened, for he began to perceive he had made some mistake, though he could not tell what; he thought all young girls liked to be teased about sweethearts and marriage; still he came valiantly to the front.

"I mean that you will surely have a sweetheart some day or other," he said, consolingly, though the fire from those dark eyes startled him, and her scarlet lips trembled with anger.

"I shall have a sweetheart, you think, like Jennie Barnes or Lily Coke. A sweetheart. Pray, whom will it be, do you think?"

"I know several of the young farmers about here who would each give his right hand to be a sweetheart of yours."

She laughed a low, contemptuous laugh that made him wince.

"What, marry a farmer! Do you think the life of a farmer's wife would suit me? I shall go unmarried to my grave, unless I can marry as I choose."

Then she seemed to repent of the passionate words, and flung her beautiful arms round his neck and kissed his face.

"I hate myself," she said, "when I speak in that way to you, who have been so good to me."

"I do not mind it," said Robert Noel, honestly. "Never hate yourself for me, my lady lass."

She turned one glance from her beautiful eyes on him.

"When I seem to be ungrateful to you, do remember that I am not, Uncle Robert; I am always sorry. I cannot help myself, I cannot explain myself; but I feel always as though my mind and soul were cramped."

"Cramp is a very bad thing," said the stolid farmer.

She looked at him, but did not speak; her irritation was too great; he never understood her; it was not likely he ever would.

"I will go down to the mill-stream," she said.

With an impatient gesture she hastened out of the house.

The mill-stream was certainly the prettiest feature of the farm—a broad, beautiful stream that ran between great rows of alder-trees and turned the wheel by the force with which it leaped into the broad, deep basin; it was the loveliest and most picturesque spot that could be imagined, and now as the waters rushed and foamed in the moonlight they were gorgeous to behold.

Leone loved the spot; the restless, gleaming waters suited her; it seemed to have something akin to herself—something restless, full of force and vitality. She sat there for hours; it was her usual refuge when the world went wrong with her.

Round and round went the wheel; on sunlight days the sun glinted on the sullen waters until they resembled a sheet of gold covered with white, shining foam. Green reeds and flowers that love both land and water fringed the edges of the clear, dimpling pool; the alder-trees dipped their branches in it; the great gray stones, covered with green moss, lay here and there. It was a little poem in itself, and the beautiful girl who sat in the moonlight read it aright.

CHAPTER III
THE MEETING AT THE MILL

In the depths of the water she saw the reflection of the shining stars; she watched them intently; the pure, pale golden eyes. A voice aroused her—a voice with tone and accent quite unlike any other voice.

"I beg your pardon," it said, "could you show me the way to Rashleigh? I have lost myself in the wood."

Raising her eyes she saw the gentleman who had raised his hat as he passed her in the morning. She knew that he recognized her by the light that suddenly overspread his face.

"Rashleigh lies over there," she replied. "You have but to cross the field and pass the church."

"Even that," said the stranger, with a careless laugh, "even that I am not inclined to do now. It is strange. I am afraid you will think me half mad, but it seems to me that I have just stepped into fairy land. Two minutes since I was on the bare highway, now I see the prettiest picture earth has to offer."

"It is pretty," she replied, her eyes looking at the clear, dimpling pool; "prettier now even than when the sun shines on it and the wheel turns."

She had told him the way to Rashleigh, and he should have passed on with a bow, but this was his excuse. The moon was shining bright as day, the wind murmured in the alder trees, the light lay on the clear, sweet, fresh water; the music of the water as it fell was sweet to hear. Away in the woods some night bird was singing; the odor of the sleeping flowers filled the air; and there on the green bank, at the water's edge, sat the most beautiful girl he had ever seen in his life.

The moonlight fell on her exquisite southern face; it seemed to find its home in the lustrous depths of her dark eyes; it kissed the dark ripples of her hair, worn with the simple grace of a Greek goddess; it lay on the white hands that played with the tufted grass.

He was young and loved all things beautiful, and therefore did not go away. His mind was filled with wonder. Who was she—this girl, so like a young Spanish princess! Why was she sitting here by the mill-stream? He must know, and to know he must ask.

"I am inclined," he said, "to lie down here by this pretty stream, and sleep all night under the stars; I am so tired."

She looked at him with a quick, warm glow of sympathy.

"What has tired you?" she asked.

He sat down on one of the great gray stones that lay half in the water, half on the land.

"I have lost myself in the Leigh woods," he said. "I have been there many hours. I had no idea what Leigh woods were like, or I should not have gone for the first time alone."

"They are very large and intricate," she said; "I can never find the right paths."

"Some one told me I should see the finest oak-trees in England there," he said, "and I have a passion for grand old oaks. I would go anywhere to see them. I went to the woods and had very soon involved myself in the greatest difficulties. I should never have found the way out had I not met one of the keepers."

She liked to listen to him; the clear, refined accent, the musical tone; as she listened a longing came over her that his voice might go on speaking to her and of her.

"Now," he continued, embarrassed by her silence, "I have forgotten your directions; may I ask you to repeat them?"

She did so, and looking at her face he saw there was no anger, nothing but proud, calm content. He said to himself he need not go just yet, he could stay a few minutes longer.

"Do you know that beautiful old German ballad," he said,

> "'In sheltered vale a mill-wheel
> Still tunes its tuneful lay'?"

"No; I never heard or read it," she answered. "Say it for me."

> "'In sheltered vale a mill-wheel
> Still tunes its tuneful lay.
> My darling once did dwell there,
> But now she's far away.
> A ring in pledge I gave her,
> And vows of love we spoke—

Those vows are all forgotten,
The ring asunder broke.'"

"Hush," she said, holding up one white hand; "hush, it is too sad. Do you not see that the moonlight has grown dim, and the sound of the falling waters is the sound of falling tears?"

He did not seem to understand her words.

"That song has haunted me," he said, "ever since I heard it. I must say the last verse; it must have been of this very mill-wheel it was written.

"'But while I hear the mill-wheel
My pains will never cease;
I would the grave could hide me,
For there alone is peace.'"

"Is it a love story?" she asked, pleased at the pathos and rhythm of the words.

"Yes; it is the usual story—the whole love of a man's heart given to one not worthy of it, the vows forgotten, the ring broken. Then he cries out for the grave to hide himself and his unhappy love."

She looked up at him with dark, lustrous, gleaming eyes.

"Does all love end in sorrow?" she asked, simply.

He looked musingly at the moonlit waters, musingly at the starlit sky.

"I cannot tell," he replied, "but it seems to me that it ends more in sorrow than in joy. I should say," he continued, "that when truth meets truth, where loyalty meets loyalty, the ending is good; but where a true heart finds a false one, where loyalty and honor meet lightness and falsehood, then the end must be bad."

Leone seemed suddenly to remember that she was talking to a stranger, and, of all subjects, they had fallen on love.

"I must go," she said, hurriedly. "You will remember the way."

"Pray do not go—just this minute," he said. "History may repeat itself; life never does. There can never be a night half so fair as this again; the water will never fall with so sweet a ripple; the stars will never shine with so bright a light; life may pass, and we may never meet again. You have a face like a poem. Stay a few minutes longer."

"A face like a poem." Did he really think so?

The words pleased her.

"Strange things happen in real life," he said; "things that, told in novels and stories, make people laugh and cry out that they are exaggerated, too romantic to be real. How strange that I should have met you here this evening by the side of the mill-stream—a place always haunted by poetry and romance. You will think it stranger still when I tell you your face has haunted me all day."

She looked at him in surprise. The proud, beautiful face grieved at the words.

"How is that?" she asked.

"I saw you this morning when I was going to Rashleigh with my friend, Sir Frank Euston. You were standing against a white gate, and I thought— well, I must not tell you what I thought."

"Why?" she asked, briefly.

"Because it might offend you," he replied.

He began to perceive that there was no coquetry in this beautiful girl. She was proud, with a calm, serene, half-tragic pride. There would be no flirtation by the side of the mill-stream. She looked as far above coquetry as she was above affectation. He liked the proud calm of her manner. She might have been a duchess holding court rather than a country girl sitting by a mill-wheel. The idea occurred to him; and then his wonder increased— who was she? and what was she doing here?

"Do you live near here?" he asked.

"Yes," she said, "behind the trees there you can see the chimneys of a farmhouse; it is called Rashleigh Farm; my uncle, Robert Noel, lives there; and I am his niece."

"His niece," repeated the young man, in an incredulous voice. She was a farmer's niece, then, after all; and yet she looked like a Spanish princess.

"You do not look like an English girl," he said, gravely.

"My father was English and my mother a Spanish lady; and I—well, I fear I have more of the hot fire of Spain than of the chill of England in my nature; my face is Spanish, so is my heart."

"A Spaniard is quick to love, quick to hate; forgives grandly and revenges mercilessly," he said.

"That is my character," she said; "you have described it exactly."

"I do not believe it; neither hate nor revenge could exist with a face like yours. Then your name is Noel?"

"Yes, my name is Leone Noel," she replied.

"Leone," he repeated, "that is a beautiful name. I have never heard it before; but I like it very much; it is musical and rare—two great things in a name."

"It is a German name," she said. "My uncle Robert hates it; he says it reminds him of Lion; but you know it is pronounced Leon. My mother read some German story that had the name in it and gave it to me."

"It suits you," he said, simply; "and I should not think there was another name in the world that would. I wonder," he added, with a shy laugh, "if you would like my name? It is Lancelot Chandos. My friends call me Lance."

"Yes, I like that. I know all the history of Sir Lancelot. I admire him; but I think he was a weak man—do not you?"

"For loving Queen Guinevere? I do not know. Some love is strength, not weakness," he replied.

Leone looked up at him again.

"Are you the son of a great lord?" she asked; "some one told me so."

"Yes; my father is Earl of Lanswell; and people would call him a great earl. He is rich and powerful."

"What has brought you, the son of a great earl, down to Rashleigh?" she asked.

"My own idleness, to begin with," he said. "I have been at Oxford more years than I care to count; and I have idled my time."

"Then you are studying?" she said.

"Yes, that is it. I am trying to make up for lost time. I have some examinations to pass; and my father has sent me down to Dr. Hervey because he is known everywhere as the cleverest coach in England."

A cloud came for just one half minute across the face of the moon; the soft, sweet darkness startled Leone.

"I must go now," she said; "it is not only getting late, but growing dark."

"I shall see you again," he cried, "do promise me."

"Nay, you have little faith in promises," she replied; and he watched her as she vanished from among the alder-trees.

It was an unexpected meeting; and strange and startling consequences soon followed.

CHAPTER IV
AN INTERESTING TETE-A-TETE

"Where have you been, Leone?" asks Farmer Noel.

She had begun a new life. It seemed years since she had left him, while he sat in the same place, smoking the same pipe, probably thinking the same thoughts. She came in with the brightness and light of the moon in her face; dew-drops lay on her dark hair, her beautiful face was flushed with the wind, so fair, so gracious, so royal, so brilliant. He looked at her in helpless surprise.

"Where have you been?" he repeated.

She looked at him with a sweet, dreamy smile.

"I have been to the mill-stream." And she added in a lower tone, "I have been to heaven."

It had been heaven to her—this one hour spent with one refined by nature and by habit—a gentleman, a man of taste and education. Her uncle wondered that evening at the light that came on her face, at the cheerful sound of her voice, the smile that came over her lips. She was usually so restless and discontented.

It was a break in her life. She wanted something to interrupt the monotony, and now it had come. She had seen and spoken to not only a very handsome and distinguished man, but a lord, the son of an earl. He had admired her, said her face was like a poem; and the words brought a sweet, musing smile to her face.

When the sun shone in her room the next morning she awoke with a sense of something new and beautiful in her life; it was a pleasure to hear the birds sing; a pleasure to bathe in the clear, cold, fresh water; a pleasure to breathe the sweet, fragrant morning air. There was a half wonder as to whether she could see him again.

The poetical, dramatic instinct of the girl was all awake; she tried to make herself as pretty as she could. She put on a dress of pale pink—a plain print, it is true, but the beautiful head and face rose from it as a flower from its leaves.

She brushed back the rippling hair and placed a crimson rose in its depths. Then she smiled at herself. Was it likely she should see him? What should bring the great son of an earl to the little farm at Rashleigh? But the blue and white pigeons, the little chickens—all fared well that morning. Leone was content.

In the afternoon Farmer Noel wanted her to go down to the hay-fields. The men were busy with the newly mown hay, and he wished her to take some messages about the stacking of it. She looked like a picture of summer as she walked through the green, shady lane, a red rose in her hair and one in her breast, a cluster of woodbine in her hand. She saw nothing of Lord Chandos, yet she thought of nothing else; every tree, every field, every lane she passed she expected to see him; but of course he was not there; and her heart beat fast as she saw him—he was crossing what people called the Brook Meadow—and she met him face to face.

They had met for the first time on a moonlight night; they met for the second time on a sultry summer afternoon, when the whole world seemed full of love. The birds were singing of love in the trees, the butterflies were making love to the flowers, the wind was whispering of love to the trees, the sun was kissing the earth that lay silent in its embrace.

"Leone," he cried; and then he flushed crimson. "I beg your pardon," he said, "but I ought to say Miss Noel; but I have been thinking of you all night as Leone. I did not think of it before I spoke."

She laughed at the long apology.

"Say it all over again," she said. "Begin at 'Good-afternoon, Miss Noel.'"

He repeated it after her, then added:

"I think my kind and good fortune sent me this way. I was longing for some one to speak to—and of all happiness to meet you; but perhaps you are busy."

"No; I have done all that I had to do. I am never busy," she added, with regal calm.

He smiled again.

"No; I could not fancy you busy," he said, "any more than I could fancy the goddess Juno in a hurry. To some fair women there belongs by birthright a calm that is almost divine."

"My calm covers a storm," she replied. "My life has been brief and dull; neither my heart nor my soul has really lived; but I feel in myself a capability of power that sometimes frightens me."

He did not doubt it as he looked at the beautiful, passionate face; it was even more lovely in the gleam of the sunlight than in the soft, sweet light of the moon.

"You cannot stand in the sunshine," he said. "If you are not busy will you go with me through Leigh Woods? I shall remember the way this time."

She hesitated one half minute, and he saw it; he raised his hat and stood bare-headed, waiting for her answer.

"Yes, I will go," she said at length. "Why should I not?"

They went together to Leigh Woods, where the great oak-trees made a pleasant shade, and the ground was a mass of wild flowers; great streams of bluebells that stirred so gently in the wind, violets that hid themselves under their leaves, cowslips like little tips of gold, wild strawberry blossoms that looked like snow-flakes.

How fair it was. The sunbeams fell through the great green boughs, throwing long shadows on the grass. It was a beautiful, silent world, all perfume and light. The poetry of it touched both of them.

Lord Chandos was the first to speak; he had been watching the proud, beautiful face of Leone; and suddenly he said:

"You look out of place here, Miss Noel; I can hardly tell you why."

"That is what my uncle says; he is always asking me if I cannot make myself more like the girls of Rashleigh."

"I hope you never will," he cried, warmly.

"I do not know how," she said. "I must always be what God and nature made me."

"They made you fair enough," he whispered.

And then he owned to himself that she was not like other girls.

She drew back proudly, swiftly; no smile came to her lips, no laughing light to her eyes.

"Speak to me as you would to one in your own rank, my lord," she said, haughtily. "Though fate has made me a farmer's niece, nature made me——"

"A queen," he interrupted.

And she was satisfied with the acknowledgment. They sat down under one of the great oak-trees, a great carpet of bluebells under their feet.

Leone looked thoughtful; she gathered some sprays of bluebells and held them in her hands, her white fingers toying with the little flowers, then she spoke:

"I know," she said, "that no lady—for instance, in your own rank of life—would walk through this wood with you on a summer's afternoon."

A laugh came over his handsome, happy young face.

"I do not know. I am inclined to think the opposite."

"I do not understand what you would call etiquette; but I am quite sure you would never ask one."

"I am not sure. If I had met one in what you are pleased to call my rank of life last night by the mill-stream, looking as you looked, I am quite sure that I should ask her to walk with me and talk with me at any time."

"I should like to see your world," she said. "I know the world of the poor and the middle class, but I do not know yours."

"You will know some day," he said, quietly. "Do not be angry with me if I tell you that in all my world I have never seen one like you. Do not be angry, I am not flattering you, I am saying just what I think."

"Why do you think that some day I may see your world?" she asked.

"Because with your face you are sure to marry well," he replied.

"I shall marry where I love," said Leone.

"And you may love where you will," he replied; "no man will ever resist you."

"I would rather you did not speak to me in that fashion," she said, gravely; and Lord Chandos found, that seated by this farmer's niece, in the wood full of bluebells, he was compelled to be more circumspect than if he were speaking to some countess-elect in a Mayfair drawing-room. Leone, when she had set him quite straight in his place, as she called it; when she had taught him that he was to treat her with as much, if not more courtesy, than he bestowed on those of his own rank; Leone, when she had done all this, felt quite at home with him. She had never had an opportunity for exercising her natural talent for conversation; her uncle was quite incapable of following or understanding her; the girls who were her companions lost themselves in trying to follow her flights of fancy.

But now there was some one who understood her; talk as she would, he appreciated it; he knew her quotations; no matter how original her ideas were he understood and followed them; it was the first time she had ever had the opportunity of talking to an educated gentleman.

How she enjoyed it; his wit seemed waiting on hers, and seemed to catch fire from it; his eyes caught fire from hers. She described her simple life and its homely surroundings in words that burned.

It was in her simple, sweet, pathetic description of stolid Uncle Robert that she excelled herself; she painted his character with the most graphic touches.

"Do you know, Miss Noel," said Lord Chandos at last, "that you are a genius, that you have a talent truly marvelous: that you can describe a character or a place better than I have heard any one else?"

"No, I did not know anything about it," she said. "I am so accustomed to being looked upon as something not to be understood, admired, or imitated that I can hardly believe that I am clever. Uncle Robert is really a character; nowadays men and women are very much alike; but he stands out in bold relief, quite by himself, the slowest, the most stolid of men, yet with a great heart full of love."

It was so pleasant to talk to him and see his handsome young face full of admiration; to startle him by showing her talent, so pleasant that the whole of the summer afternoon had passed before she thought of the time; and he was equally confused, for Dr. Hervey's dinner-hour was over. And yet they both agreed it was the most pleasant hour they had ever spent.

CHAPTER V
THE RECONCILIATION

It was, of course, the old story; there were one or two meetings by the mill-stream, a morning spent together in some distant hay-field, an afternoon in the woods, and then the mischief was done—they loved each other.

> "Alas, how easily things go wrong—
> A sigh too deep or a kiss too long;
> Then follows a mist and a weeping rain—
> And life is never the same again."

It soon became not merely a habit but a necessity for them to meet every day. Farmer Noel understood perfectly well the art of tilling the ground, of sowing the crops, of making the earth productive, but he knew less than a child of the care and watchfulness his young niece required. He contented himself by asking where she had been; he never seemed to imagine that she had had a companion. He saw her growing more and more beautiful, with new loveliness on her face, with new light in her eyes, with a thousand charms growing on her, but he never thought of love or danger—in fact, above the hay-making and the wheat, Farmer Noel did not think at all.

She had gone into the glowing heart of fairyland—all the old life was left far behind; she did not even seem to remember that she had been restless and discontented; that in her soul she had revolted fiercely against her fate; that she had disliked her life and longed for anything that would change it; all that was forgotten; the golden glamour of love had fallen over her, and everything was changed. He was young—this brave, generous, gallant lover of hers—only twenty, with a heart full of romance. He fairly worshiped the proud, beautiful girl who carried herself with the stately grace of a young queen. He had fallen in love after the fashion of his age—madly, recklessly, blindly—ready to go mad or to die for his love; after the fashion of his age and sex he loved her all the more because of her half-cold reserve, her indomitable pride, her haughty rejection of all flattery.

Young girls do not always know the secret of their power; a little reserve goes further than the most loving words. Leone's pride attracted Lord

Chandos quite as much as her beauty. The first little quarrel they had was an outburst of pride from her; they had been strolling through the sunniest part of Leigh Woods, and when it was time to part he bent down to kiss the warm, white hand. She drew it quickly from him.

"You would not have done that to one of your own class," she cried; "why do you do it to me?"

"You are not really angry, Leone?" he cried in wonder.

She turned her beautiful face, colorless with indignation, to him.

"I am so far angry," she said, "that I shall not walk through the woods with you—never again."

She kept her word. For two whole days Lord Chandos wandered through the fields and the lanes, through the woods and by the river, yet he saw no sight of her. It was possible that she punished herself quite as much as she did him; but he must be taught that, were he twenty times an earl, he must never venture on even the least liberty with her; he must wait her permission before he kissed her hand.

The fourth day—he could bear it no longer—he rode past the farm twenty times and more; at length he was fortunate enough to see Farmer Noel, and throwing the reins on his horse's neck he got down and went up to him.

"Have you a dog to sell?" he asked. "Some one told me you had very fine dogs."

"I have good dogs, but none to sell," replied the farmer.

"I want a dog, and I would give a good price for a good one," he said. "Will you let me see yours?"

"Yes, you can see them, but you cannot buy them," said Robert Noel; and the next scene was the handsome young lordling going round the farm, with the stalwart, stolid farmer.

He won the farmer's heart by his warm praises of the farm, the cattle, the dogs, and everything else he saw; still there was no Leone.

"I am very thirsty; should you think me very impertinent if I asked you for a glass of cider?" he said; and the farmer, flattered by the request, took him into the little parlor. He looked at his visitor in simple wonder.

"They say you are a great lord's son," he said; "but if you are, you have no pride about you."

Lord Chandos laughed; and the farmer called Leone. There was a pause, during which the young lord's heart beat and his face flushed.

"Leone," cried the farmer again.

He turned to his visitor.

"You will wonder what 'Leone' means, it is such a strange name; it is my niece. Here she comes."

The loveliest picture in all the world, trying hard to preserve her usual stately grace, yet with a blushing, dimpling smile that made her lovely beyond words.

"Leone," said the farmer, "will you bring a jug of cider?"

"Pray," cried the lord, "do not trouble yourself, Miss Noel. I cannot think——"

She interrupted him by a gesture of her white hand.

"I will send it, uncle," she said, and disappeared.

The farmer turned with a smile to the young lord.

"She is very proud," he said; "but she is a fine girl."

The cider came; the visitor duly drank his glass and went; his only reward for all that trouble was the one glance at her face.

That same evening a little note was given to her, in which he begged her so humbly to forgive him, and to meet him again, that she relented.

He had learned his lesson; he wooed her with the deference due to a young princess; no word or action of his displeased her after that, while he loved her with a love that was akin to madness.

So through the long, bright, beautiful summer days, in the early morning, while the sweet, fragrant air seemed to sweep the earth, and in the evening when the dew lay upon flower and tree, they met and learned to love each other.

One evening, as they sat by their favorite spot—the mill-stream—Lord Chandos told her how he had learned to love her, how he had ceased to think of anything in the world but herself.

"I knew you were my fate, Leone," he said, "when I saw you sitting here by the mill-stream. I am quite sure that I have loved you ever since. I do not remember that there has been one moment in which I have not thought of you. I shall always thank Heaven that I came to Rashleigh—I found my darling here."

For once all the pride had died from her face; all the hauteur was gone from her eyes; a lovely gleam of tenderness took its place; a love-light in the shy, sweet eyes that dropped from his.

"My darling Leone," he said, "if I lived a hundred years I could only say over and over again—'I love you.' Those three words say everything. Do you love me?"

She looked up at him. Then she raised her dark eyes to his and a little quiver passed over her beautiful mouth.

"Yes, I love you," she said. "Whether it be for weal or for woe, for good or ill, I know not; but I love you."

There was unutterable pathos, unutterable music in those three words; they seemed to rhyme with the chime of the falling waters. She held out her white hands, he clasped them in his.

"Why do you say it so sadly, my darling? Love will bring nothing but happiness for you and for me," he said.

She laid her white arms on his neck, and looked earnestly in his face.

"There can be no comparison," she said. "Love to you is only a small part of your life, to me it is everything—everything. Do you understand? If you forget me or anything of that kind, I could not bear it. I could not school myself into patience as model women do. I should come and throw myself into the mill-stream."

"But, my darling, I shall never forget you—never; you are life of my life. I might live without the air and the sunlight; I might live without sleep or food, but never without you. I must forget my own soul before I forget you."

Still the white hands clasped his shoulders and the dark eyes were fixed on his face.

"You and your love are more than that to me," she said. "I throw all my life on this one die; I have nothing else—no other hope. Ah, think well, Lance, before you pledge your faith to me; it means so much. I should exact it whole, unbroken and forever."

"And I would give it so," he replied.

"Think well of it," she said again, with those dark, earnest eyes fixed on his face. "Let there be no mistake, Lance. I am not one of the meek Griselda type; I should not suffer in silence and resignation, let my heart break, and then in silence sink into an early grave. Ah, no, I am no patient Griselda. I should look for revenge and many other things. Think well before you pledge yourself to me. I should never forgive—never forget. There is time now—think before you seal your fate and mine."

"I need not think, Leone," he answered, quietly. "I have thought, and the result is that I pledge you my faith forever and ever."

The earnest, eager gaze died from her eyes, and the beautiful face was hidden on his breast.

"Forever and ever, sweet," he whispered; "do you hear? in all time and for all eternity, I pledge you my love and my faith."

The water seemed to laugh as it rippled on, the wind laughed as it bent the tall branches, the nightingale singing in the wood stopped suddenly, and its next burst of song was like ringing laughter; the mountains quivered over the mill-stream, the stars seemed to tremble as they shone.

"Forever and ever," he repeated. The wind seemed to catch up the words and repeat them, the leaves seemed to murmur them, the fall of the water to rhyme with them. "Forever and ever, sweet, I pledge you my love and my faith; our hearts will be one, and our souls one, and you will give me the same love in return, my sweet?"

"I give you even more than that," she replied, so earnestly that the words had a ring of tragedy in them; and then bending forward, he kissed the sweet lips that were for evermore to be his own.

"You are mine now forever," he said, "my wife, who is to be."

She was quite silent for some minutes; then, looking up at him, she said:

"I wish you had never sung that pretty ballad of the mill-wheel to me; do you know what the water always says when I listen?

"'Those vows are all forgotten,
The ring asunder broken.'"

"My darling," he said, clasping her to his heart, "no words that have any ring of doubt in them will ever apply to us, let the mill-stream say what it will."

CHAPTER VI
AN IMPATIENT LOVER'S PLANS

There had been no mistake about the wooing of Lord Chandos. He had not thought of loving and riding away; the proud, beautiful, gifted girl whom he loved had been wooed and pursued with the ardor and respect that he would have shown to a princess.

There came another day, when something had prevented him from seeing her; and unable to control his impatience, he had ridden over to the farm, this time ostensibly to see the farmer, and ask for another glass of his famous cider; this time, under the farmer's eyes even, he stopped and spoke to Leone.

"You will be at the mill-stream this evening?" he whispered, and her answer was:

"Yes."

When he had drunk the cider and ridden away, Farmer Noel turned to his niece.

"A fine young man that, Leone; but what did he say to you?"

"Nothing particular; something about the mill-stream," replied the proud lips, that disdained a lie.

"Because," said Robert Noel, slowly, "you have a beautiful face of your own, my lady lass, and a young man like that would be sure to admire it."

"What matter if he did, uncle?" she asked.

"Harm would come of it," replied the farmer; "what a man admires he often loves; and no good would come of such a love as that."

"Why not?" she asked again, with flushed face and flashing eyes. "Why not?"

"We reckon in these parts," said the farmer, slowly, "that there is too great a difference between the aristocracy and the working-people. To put it in plain words, my lady lass, when a great lord or a rich man admires a poor lass, as a rule it ends in her disgrace."

"Not always," she answered, proudly.

"No, perhaps not always; but mostly, mostly," repeated Robert Noel. "You have a beautiful face, and, if you are wise, you will keep out of that young gentleman's way. I should not like to offend you, Leone; you will excuse me for speaking plainly."

"It does not offend me," she said, simply; "although I do not think that you are right. Why should not a lord, great and rich as this one, marry a girl who has no drawback but poverty? I do not see such a great difference."

"I cannot tell you, my lady lass, either the why or the wherefore," he replied. "I know that rich men do not marry poor and obscure girls; and if they do, there is sure to be something wrong with the marriage. We will not talk about it, only if he seems to admire you at all, do you keep out of that young man's way."

She made him no answer; his care for her touched her, but then there was no need. Lord Chandos was unlike other men; besides which he loved her so well he could not live without her.

So, when the sun was setting in the western sky, she went down to the mill-stream, where her lover awaited her.

The crimson clouds were reflected in the rippling water, the birds were singing in the trees, the flowers were all falling asleep; the fair, fragrant world was getting ready for its time of rest.

"Leone," he cried, seizing her hands and drawing her toward him, "my darling, I thought to-day would never come. How many hours did yesterday hold?"

"Twenty-four," she replied.

"Only twenty-four? Why, it seemed to me it was a day as long as a year, and I asked myself one question, sweet."

"What was it, Lance?"

"This: that if one day seemed so terribly long, what would become of me if I had to pass a week without you?"

"What would become of you?" she said, laughingly.

"I should die of my own impatience," he said, his handsome young face flushing. "Fate may try me as it will," he added, "but it must never separate me from you. It is because I have found this out that I have asked you to meet me here to-night. I cannot live without you, Leone; you understand that the hours are long and dark; life seems all ended, I cannot feel interest or energy; I am longing for you all the time, just as thirsty flowers are longing for dew. Leone, I should long until the fever of my own longing killed me—for you."

He drew the beautiful face to his own, and kissed it with a passion words could never tell.

"Why should I not be happy in my own way?" he said. "If I want the one only thing on earth that could bring me my happiness, why should I not have it? Of what use is money, wealth, position, rank, anything else on earth to me, unless I have you. I would rather lose all I have in the world than lose you."

"It is sweet to be loved so well," she said, with a sigh.

"I have had letters from home to-day," he said, "and I—I am half afraid to tell you lest you should say no. I am to leave Rashleigh in one month from now, and to go to my father's house—Cawdor, it is called. Leone, I cannot go alone."

She looked at him with wondering eyes; the ardent young lover who believed his love to be so great and so generous, yet who, in reality, loved himself best, even in his love.

"Darling, I want you to consent to be my wife before I leave Rashleigh," he continued. "I know it will be the best and easiest plan if I can but win your consent."

Her loving heart seemed almost to stand still; the crimson clouds and the rippling waters seemed to meet; even in her dreams she had never imagined herself his wife.

Lord Chandos continued:

"I know my parents well; my father is inflexible on some points, but easily influenced; my mother is, I believe, the proudest woman in the wide world. I know that she expects something wonderful from me in the way of marriage; I hardly think that there is a peeress in England that my mother would deem too good for me, and it would wound her to the heart should I marry a woman beneath me in rank. Indeed I know she would never forgive me."

She uttered a little, low cry.

"Then why have you loved me?" she asked.

Her lover laughed.

"How could I help it, my darling? In you I have found the other half of my own soul. I could no more help loving you than a bird can help singing.

But listen, Leone; it is as I say, if I were to go home and pray all day to them it would be useless. I have another plan. Marry me, and I can take you to them and say, 'This is my wife.' They could not help receiving you then, because the marriage could not be undone, and my mother, with her worldly tact, would made the best of it then. If I ask permission to marry you, they will never grant it; if I marry you, they will be compelled to forgive it."

She drew herself half proudly from him.

"I do not wish any one to be compelled to receive me, nor do I wish to be the cause of unpleasantness," she said.

"My darling, all lovers have something to suffer. The course of true love cannot run smooth. Surely you would not desert me, or forsake me, or refuse to love me because I cannot change the opinion of my conservative parents. I know no lady, no peeress in England, who is half so beautiful, so clever as you—not one. I shall be more proud to take you home as Lady Chandos than if you were a queen's daughter. You believe me?"

"Yes, I believe *you*," she replied.

"Never mind any one else, Leone. My father admires beautiful women; he will be sure to love you; my mother will be very disagreeable at first, but in a short time she will learn to love you, and then all will be well."

The little white hand clung to him.

"You are quite sure, Lance?" she said, with a sob—"quite sure?"

"Yes, sweet, I am more than sure. You will be Lady Chandos, of Cawdor, and that is one of the oldest and grandest titles in England."

"But will your mother forgive you and love you again?" she asked, anxiously.

"Yes, believe me. And now, Leone, let me tell you my plans. They are all rather underhand, but we cannot help that; everything is fair in love and war. About twenty miles from here there is a sleepy little village called Oheton. I was there yesterday, and it was there that this plan came to me. Oh, my darling, turn your sweet face to me and let me be quite sure that you are listening."

"I am listening, Lance," she said.

"No, not with all your heart. See how well I understand you. Your eyes linger on the water, and the falling of it makes music, and the rhyme of the music is:

"'These vows were all forgotten,
The ring asunder broken.'

A Mad Love | 35

When will you trust me more thoroughly, Leone?"

She glanced at him with something of wonder, but more of fear.

"How do you know what I am thinking of?" she asked.

"I can guess from the tragical expression of your face, and the pathos of your eyes as they linger on the falling water. Now, you shall not look at the mill-stream, look at me."

She raised her dark, lustrous eyes to his face, and he went on:

"Over in this sleepy little village of Oheton, Leone—it is a sleepy village—the houses are all divided from each other by gardens and trees. Unlike most villagers, the people do not seem to know each other, you do not hear any gossip; the people, the houses, the streets, all seem sleepy together. At one end of the village is a church, one of the most quaint, an old Norman church, that has stood like a monument while the storms of the world raged around it; the vicar is the Reverend Josiah Barnes."

"Why are you telling me all this?" she asked.

"You will soon understand," he replied. "The Reverend Mr. Barnes is over sixty, and he, together with the people, the houses, and the streets, seems sleepy; nothing would excite him, or interest him, or startle him.

"Now, Leone, I have taken lodgings for myself for three weeks in this sleepy village; no one will take any notice of me; I shall go and come just as I will; then I shall have the bans of our marriage published. The dear old vicar will read them in his sleepy tones:

"'I publish the bans of marriage for the first time between Lancelot Chandos and Leone Noel.' No one will hear the names plainly, and those who do will not know to whom they belong, and there will be no impediment; will there, Leone?"

The water laughed as it hurried over the stones.

"No impediment," it seemed to say; "no impediment, Leone."

CHAPTER VII
A FRIEND'S ADVICE

"But," asked Leone, anxiously, "will that be safe, Lance? Supposing that any one should hear and recognize the names, what then?"

"There is no fear. Nothing can ever be done without risk; but there is no risk there—at least, none that I fear to run. I guarantee that not one person in that church hears those names clearly. Then you will see that I have arranged every detail. Then, when the three weeks have expired, we will meet there some fine morning and be married. I have a friend who will come with me as a witness. After that I propose that we go to London, and there I shall introduce you to my father first; then we will go down to Cawdor to my mother. Do you like the plan, Leone?"

"I should like it much better if they could know of it beforehand," she replied, gravely.

His face grew grave as her own.

"That cannot be," he replied. "You see, Leone, I am not of age; I shall not be twenty-one until September: and if my parents knew of it, they have power to forbid the marriage, and we could not be married; but done without their knowledge, they are of course powerless."

"I do not like it," she said, with a shudder; "I would rather all was open and sincere."

"It cannot be. Why, Leone, where is your reason? If even your uncle knew, he would interfere to prevent it. In his slow, stolid, honest mind he would think such a marriage quite wrong, you may be sure; he would talk about caste, and position, and all kinds of nonsense. We must keep our secret to ourselves, my darling, if we wish to be married at all. Surely, Leone, you love me enough to sacrifice your wishes to me on this point?"

The beautiful face was raised to his.

"I love you well enough to die for you, and far too well to bring trouble on you, Lance."

"My darling, there is only one thing that can bring trouble on me, and that would be to lose you; that would kill me. You hear me, Leone, it would not make me grow thin and pale, after the fashion of rejected lovers, but it would kill me. Do not ask me to leave you an hour longer than I need. Ah, my love, yield: do not grieve me with a hundred obstacles—not even with one. Yield, and say that you will agree to my plan."

There was no resisting the pleading of the handsome young face, the loving eyes, the tender words, the passionate kisses; she could not resist them; it was so sweet to be loved so well.

"You must keep our secret from that honest, stolid, good uncle of yours," said Lord Chandos, "or he will think himself bound to call and tell Dr. Hervey. You promise me, then, Leone, my love, to do what I ask, and to be my own beloved wife, when the three weeks are over?"

"Yes, I promise, Lance," she replied.

Her voice was grave and sweet, her beautiful face had on it the light of a beautiful and noble love.

"Then kiss me, as the children say, of your own accord, and let that kiss be our betrothal."

She raised her lips to his for the first time and kissed him.

"That is our betrothal," he said; "now nothing can part us. Leone, I waited for your promise to give you this."

He opened a small jewel-case, and took from it a diamond ring.

"This is what ladies call an engagement-ring," he said; "let me put it on your finger."

She shrank back.

"Lance," she said, "do you remember the words of the song,

"'A ring in pledge he gave her,
And vows of love he spoke.'

How strange that by this stream you should offer me a ring!"

"You seem to think there is a fatality in the water, Leone," he said, quietly.

"I have an idea that I cannot express, but it seems to me that story is told in the falling water."

"If the water tells of a golden bright life, all happiness, with the most devoted and loving of husbands, then it may tell you as much as it likes. Let me put the ring on your finger, Leone."

She held out her hand—such a beautiful hand, with a soft, pink palm and tapering fingers. As he went to place the ring on her finger, it fell from his hand into the water below, and Leone uttered a low cry.

"It is not lost," he said; "it has not fallen into the stream, it is here."

Looking down, she saw the flash of the diamonds in the little pool that lay between two stones, Lord Chandos wiped it and dried it.

"You will prize it all the more because it has been dipped in your favorite stream," he said. "Give me your hand again, Leone; we shall have better fortune this time."

He placed the ring securely on her finger, then kissed the white hand.

"How angry you were with me the first time I kissed your hand," he said; "and now I have all your heart. There will be neither broken vows nor a broken ring for us, Leone, no matter what the water sings or says."

"I hope not," says the girl, brightly.

"I shall take possession of my lodgings at Oheton to-morrow," he said. "I shall have to spend some little time there; but you must promise that I shall see you every evening, Leone. Will you find your way to the mill-wheel? When we are married, I shall try to buy the mill, the stream, and the land all round it; it will be a sacred spot to me. In three weeks, Leone, you will be my wife."

"Yes," she replied, "in three weeks."

The wind fell, the ripple of the green leaves ceased, the birds had sung themselves to sleep, only the water ran laughingly on.

"Lance," cried the girl, suddenly, "do you know what the water says—can you hear it?"

"No," he replied, with a laugh; "I have not such a vivid fancy as you. What does it say?"

"Nothing but sorrow, nothing but sorrow," she chanted.

"I cannot hear that; if it says anything at all, it is nothing but love, nothing but love."

And then, as the shades of night were coming on, he saw her safely home.

That same evening Lord Chandos and Sir Frank Euston talked long together.

"Of course," said Sir Frank, "if you put me on my honor, I cannot speak, but I beg of you to stop and think."

Lord Chandos laughed; his handsome face was flushed and eager.

"The man who hesitates is lost," he said. "All the thinking in the world cannot alter matters, nor make me love my darling less."

"There is an old proverb I should like to recommend to you," said Sir Frank Euston; "it is this—a young man married is a young man marred."

"I am quite as willing to be marred as to be married," said the young lord, "and married I will be if all the powers on earth conspire against me."

"I know how useless all arguments are," said his friend, "when a man determines to be foolish; but do think for one moment of the terrible disappointment to your parents."

"I do not see it; they have no right to be disappointed; my father married to please himself, why should I not do the same?"

"You are outraging all the laws of your class," said Sir Frank. "However beautiful a farmer's niece may be, we cannot suppose even a miracle could fit her to take the place of the Countess of Lanswell."

A hot flush came over the young lord's face; a strange quiet came into his voice.

"We will discuss what you like, Frank, but you must not touch the young lady's name, we will leave that out of the question."

"You have asked me to be the witness of your marriage," said Sir Frank, "and that entitles me to speak my mind. I do speak it, frankly, honestly, plainly, as I should thank God for any friend to speak to a brother of my own if he felt inclined to make a simpleton of himself."

"I call myself a sensible man to marry for love, not a simpleton," said Lord Chandos grandly.

"My dear Lance," said his friend, "you make just this one mistake; you are not a man at all, you are a boy."

He stopped suddenly, for the young lord looked at him with a defiant, fierce face.

"You must not say that again, Frank, or we shall be friends no longer."

"I do not want to offend you, Lance; but you are really too young to think of marriage. Your tastes are not formed yet; that which pleases you now you will dislike in six or ten years' time. I assure you that if you marry this farmer's niece now, in ten years' time you will repent it in sackcloth and ashes. She is not fit, either by manner, education, or anything else, to be your mother's daughter, and you know it; you know that when the glamour of her beauty is over you will wonder at your own madness and folly. Be warned in time."

"You may as well reason with a madman as a man in love," said the young lordling, "and I am in love."

"And you are mad," said Sir Frank, quietly; "one day you will know how mad."

Lord Chandos laughed.

"There is method in my madness. Come, Frank, we have been such friends I would do anything you asked me."

"I should never ask you to do anything so foolish, Lance; I wish that I had not given my word of honor to keep your secret; I am quite sure that I ought to send word to the earl and countess at once; I cannot, as I have promised not to do so, but I regret it."

"My dear Frank, nothing in the world would stop me; if anything were done to prevent my marriage now, I would simply await another and more favorable opportunity; my mind is made up. I love the girl with all my heart, and she, no other, shall be my wife. If you refuse to act for me, well and good; I shall find some one else."

"If you would but be reasonable, Lance," said his friend.

"I am not reasonable. When did you ever see reason and love go hand in hand together?"

"They should do so always, and do, when the love is worth having."

"Now, Frank, I have listened patiently; I have heard all that you have had to say; I have weighed every argument, and I remain unconvinced. You have but to say whether you will do this to oblige me or not."

"If I do it, remember, it is under protest, Lance."

"Never mind what it is under, if you only promise."

"I promise, to save you from greater risk, but I do it against my will, my reason, my good sense, my conscience, and everything else."

Lord Chandos laughed aloud.

"You will forget everything of that kind," he said, "when you see Leone."

And the two friends parted, mutually dissatisfied.

CHAPTER VIII
THE PROPHECY

"A very impatient young man," said the good old vicar. "No man in his senses would want to be married before ten in the morning. I call it unchristian."

Good old Mr. Barnes had been roused from his early slumbers by the announcement that the young man had come to be married.

Married, while the early morning sun was shining, and the birds singing their morning hymn.

He was almost blind, this good old vicar, who had lived so long at Oheton. He was very deaf, and could hardly hear, but then he did not require very keen sight or hearing at Oheton; there was never more than one marriage in a year, and funerals were very rare; but to be called before nine in the morning to perform the marriage ceremony was something unheard of. He had duly announced the bans, and no one had taken the least notice of them; but to come so early, it was positively cruel.

Others had risen early that morning. Leone had not slept well, for this July morning, which was to bring such mingled joy and sorrow to others, was a day of deepest emotion to her.

Her love-dream was to be realized. She was to marry the ardent young lover who swore that he would not live without her.

She had thought more of her love than of the worldly advantages it would bring her. She had not thought much of those until they stood, on the evening before their wedding-day, once more by the mill-stream. It was bright moonlight, for the smiling summer day was dead. It was their farewell to the beautiful spot they both loved.

"I am so glad," said Lord Chandos, "that we can say good-bye to it by the light of the moon. I wonder, Leone, when we shall see the mill-stream again? I have a fancy that the pretty water has helped me in my wooing."

As they sat there the wind rose and stirred the branches of the alder-trees. In some way the great wavy masses of dark hair became unfastened, and fell like a thick soft veil over Leone's shoulders. Lord Chandos touched it caressingly with his hand.

"What beautiful hair, Leone—how thick and soft; how beautiful those wavy lines are—what makes them?"

"A turn of Dame Nature's fingers," she replied, laughingly.

"I should like to see diamonds shining in these coils of hair," he said. "Leone, one of the first things we must do to-morrow when we reach London, is to buy a very handsome traveling-dress. I have written to-day to my father to ask him to meet us at Dunmore House."

She repeated the words.

"Where is Dunmore House?" she asked.

"I forgot," he said, "that all places so familiar to me are strange to you. One of my father's titles is Baron Dunmore, and his London residence is called Dunmore House. We shall meet him there to-morrow, and then you will be my wife."

For the first time she realized what an immense difference there was in their positions. She glanced at him in sudden fear.

"Lance," she said, "shall I seem very much out of place in your home, and among your friends?"

"My darling, you would grace any home," he replied; "mine has had no fairer mistress in all the generations it has stood."

"I am half frightened," she said, gently.

"You need not be, sweet. Before this time next year all London will know and admire the beautiful Lady Chandos."

"It seems a long leap to take in life," she said, "from being Farmer Noel's niece to bear the name of Lady Chandos."

"You will grace the name, Leone," he replied. "I shall be the proudest man in England—I shall have the most beautiful wife in England. This is our last separation, our last parting; after this, we need never part."

He stooped down and caught some of the running water in his hand.

"A libation," he said, as he poured it back again. "I feel as though I were losing a friend when I leave the mill-stream."

Loving and loved, no thought came to them there of how they should see the mill-stream again.

"Leone, Lady Chandos." More than once that evening she said those words to herself. It was after eight when she came in, and the farmer had long finished his supper; he sat thinking over his pipe.

"You are late, my lady lass," he said; "sit down and talk to me before I go to rest."

Obediently enough, she sat down while he told her the history of his visits to the different markets. She heard, but did not take in the sense of one single word he uttered. She was saying to herself over and over again, that by this time to-morrow she should be Lady Chandos. Her happiness would have been complete if she could have told her uncle. He had been so kind to her. They were opposite as light and darkness, they had not one idea in common, yet he had been good to her and she loved him. She longed to tell him of her coming happiness and grandeur, but she did not dare to break her word.

Robert Noel looked up in wonder. There was his beautiful niece kneeling at his feet, her eyes dim with tears.

"Uncle," she was saying, "look at me, listen to me. I want to thank you. I want you always to remember that on this night I knelt at your feet and thanked you with a grateful heart for all you have ever done for me."

"Why, my lady lass," he replied, "you have always been to me as a child of my own," he replied.

"A tiresome child," she said, half laughing, half crying. "See. I take this dear, brown hand, so hard with work, and I kiss it, uncle, and thank you from my heart."

He could not recover himself, so to speak. He looked at her in blank, wordless amazement.

"In the years to come," she continued, "when you think of me, you must say to yourself, that, no matter what I did, I loved you."

"No matter what you did you loved me," he repeated. "Yes, I shall remember that."

She kissed the toil-worn face, leaving him so entirely bewildered that the only fear was lest he might sit up all night trying to forget it.

Then she went to her room, but not to sleep—her heart beat, every pulse thrilled. This was to be the last night in her old home—the last of her girlish life; to-morrow she would be Lady Chandos—wife of the young lover whom she loved with all her heart and soul.

The birds woke her with their song, it was their wedding-day. She would not see Robert Noel again; he took his breakfast before six and went off to the fields again. She had but to dress herself and go to the station. Oheton was some three miles from the station, but on a summer's morning that was a trifle.

They were all three there at last—Sir Frank looking decidedly vexed and cross, Lord Chandos happy as the day was long, and Leone beautiful as a picture.

"Look," said the young lordling to his friend, "have I no excuse?"

Sir Frank looked long and earnestly at the beautiful southern face.

"Yes," he replied; "so far as beauty and grace can form an excuse, you have one; but, Lance, if I loved that girl a thousand times better than my life, I should not marry her."

"Why?" asked Lord Chandos, with a laugh.

"Because she has a tragedy in her life. She could not be happy. She will neither have a happy life nor a happy death."

"My dear Frank, do not prophesy such evil on our wedding-day."

"I do not mean to prophesy, I say what I think; it is a beautiful face, full of poetry and passion, but it is also full of power and unrest."

"You shall not look at her again if you say such things," cried Lord Chandos.

And then the good vicar, still distressed at being aroused so early, came to the church. Had it been less pitiful and pathetic, it would have been most comical, the number of times the old vicar dropped his book, forgot the names, the appalling mistakes he made, the nervous hesitation of his manner. Sometimes Lord Chandos felt inclined to say hard, hot words; again, he could not repress a smile. But at length, after trembling and hesitating, the vicar gave the final benediction, and pronounced them man and wife.

In the vestry, when the names were signed, some ray of light seemed to dawn on the old vicar.

"Chandos," he said, "that is not a common name about here."

"Is it not?" said the young lord; "it seems common enough to me."

"Chandos," repeated the minister, "where have I heard that name!"

"I have heard it so often that I am tired of it," said the young husband.

And then it was all over.

"Thank God to be out in the sunlight," he cried, as he stood, with his beautiful wife, in the churchyard. "Thank God it is all over, and I can call my love my wife. I thought that service would never end. Frank, have you no good wishes for my wife?"

Sir Frank went to Leone.

"I wish you joy," he said; "I wish you all happiness—but——"

And then he played nervously with the hat he held in his hand.

"But," she said with a bright smile, "you do not think I shall get it?"

Sir Frank made no answer; he did not think she would be happy, but she had chosen her own way; he had said all he could. Perhaps his eyes were clearer than others, for he could read a tragedy in her face. Then Sir Frank left them, having performed his part with a very ill grace.

"Leone, have you said good-bye to your uncle?" asked Lord Chandos.

"I left a little note to be given him when he returns home this evening. How he will miss me."

"And how fortunate I am to have you, my darling; there is no one in the wide world so happy. We will drive over to Rashleigh Station. I do not care who sees me now, no one can part us. Dr. Hervey thinks I went home to London this morning, but I won a wife before starting, did I not, Leone, my beautiful love? You are Lady Chandos now. What are you thinking of, my darling?"

"I was wondering, Lance, if there was anything in our marriage that could possibly invalidate it and make it illegal?"

"No," he replied, "I have been too careful of you, Leone, for that. You are my wife before God and man. Nothing shall take you from me but death."

"But death," she repeated slowly.

And in after years they both remembered the words.

CHAPTER IX
A MYSTERIOUS TELEGRAM

Cawdor took rank among the most stately homes of England: it had been originally one of the grand Saxon strongholds, one, too, which the Normans had found hard to conquer.

As time wore on the round towers and the keep fell into ruins— picturesque and beautiful ruins, round which the green ivy hung in luxuriant profusion; then the ruins were left standing.

Little by little the new place was built, not by any particular design; wing after wing, story after story, until it became one of the most picturesque and most magnificent homes in England. Cawdor it was called; neither court, hall nor park, simply Cawdor; and there were very few people in England who did not know Cawdor. There was no book of engravings that had not a view of Cawdor for its first and greatest attraction; there was no exhibition of pictures in which one did not see ruins of Cawdor. It had in itself every attribute of beauty, the ivy-mantled ruins, the keep, from which one could see into five different counties, the moat, now overgrown with trees; the old-fashioned draw-bridge which contrasted so beautifully with the grand modern entrance, worthy of a Venetian palace; the winding river, the grand chain of hills, and in the far distance the blue waters of the Channel.

There could not have been a more beautiful or picturesque spot on earth than Cawdor. It had belonged to the Lanswell family for many generations. The Lanswells were a wealthy race—they owned not only all the land surrounding the fair domain of Cawdor, but nearly the whole of the town of Dunmore. The Earl of Lanswell was also Baron of Raleigh, and Raleigh Hall, in Staffordshire, was a very grand estate. In one part of it an immense coal mine had been discovered, which made Lord Lanswell one of the wealthiest men of the day.

Cawdor, Raleigh Hall, and Dunmore House, three of the finest residences in England, together with a rent-roll counted by hundreds of thousands, should have made the earl a happy man. He married a wealthy heiress in accordance with the old proverb that "Like seeks like." His wife, Lucia, Countess of Lanswell, was one of the proudest peeresses in England;

she was unimpeachable in every relation of life, and had little pity for those who were not; she had never known sorrow, temptation, doubt, or anything else; she had lived in an atmosphere of perfect content and golden ease; she had the grandest mansion, the finest diamonds, the finest horses in London; she had the most indulgent husband, the handsomest son, and the prettiest daughter; she did not know the word want in any shape, she had not even suffered from the crumpled rose-leaf. The nearest approach to trouble of any kind that she had known was that her son, Lord Chandos, had failed in one of his examinations. He asked that he might go into the country for some months to read, and permission was most cheerfully given to him. With her daughter, Lady Imogene Chandos, the countess had never had and never expected to have any trouble; she was one of the fairest, sweetest, and most gentle of girls; she was docile and obedient; she had never in her life given the least trouble to any one.

Lord Lanswell was walking up and down one of the broad terraces at Cawdor one fine morning in July, when one of the servants brought to him a telegram. He opened it hastily, it was from his son, Lord Chandos:

"Dearest Father,—Will you run up to town, and meet me at Dunmore House this evening? I have something very important to tell you. Not one word to mother yet."

Lord Lanswell stood still to think with the telegram in his hand.

"What can be the matter now?" he said to himself; "that boy will give me trouble. He has done something now that he will not let my lady know."

He had a dull, heavy presentiment that the boy who should have been the pride and delight of his life would be a drawback and a torment.

"I must go," said the earl to himself, "I must make some excuse to satisfy my lady."

It was typical of Lady Lanswell that her husband seldom spoke of her as my wife, the children more seldom still as "my mother;" every one alike called her "my lady." She might have been the only peeress in England, so entirely did every one agree in giving her that title. "My lady" was pleased, meant sunshine at Cawdor; "my lady" was angry, meant gloom. She regulated the moral and mental atmosphere of the house with a smile or a frown.

Lord Lanswell knew that he dare not show the telegram to Lady Lanswell; she would have started off at once for Dunmore House, and there would have been war. He must deceive her. He carefully destroyed the telegram, in some queer fashion which he did not own even to himself he had a kind of sympathy with his son.

He had been wild in his youth and made allowances for the same in others. His worst thought now was that his handsome young heir, with the frank blue eyes and sunny hair, had been gambling or betting.

"A few thousand pounds would set him straight," he thought, "and after all, one must not be too hard on the follies of youth."

No need to tell my lady; she looked on these exploits with a keen, cold eye. He went to the drawing-room, where my lady sat looking regally beautiful in black velvet and point lace.

The countess of Lanswell was considered one of the handsomest women in England. She had married very young, and her beauty was still so well preserved that she took her place with the beauties of the day. Husband and children both felt in awe of the beautiful woman, with her queenly grace and bearing.

"Lucia," said the earl, "I thought of running up to town this afternoon. I shall return to-morrow."

"Indeed," said my lady, slowly. "Why this sudden resolution, Ross?"

"There is some little business that no one can attend to but myself," he said. "I shall not be long absent."

"Business of what nature?" asked my lady, her fine eyes fixed on his face.

"Why, dear, it is surely not needful for me to explain my business to you? I have none of which you would not approve. I want to call on my bankers—I want to sell some shares. I have several little reasons for running up to town."

"You remember, of course, that the Beauvoirs dine here to-day?" said my lady.

"Yes, I have not forgotten, but with your usual tact you can apologize for me, Lucia."

The compliment pleased her.

"Certainly, I can, if your absence is really needful, Ross," said my lady.

"It is needful, I assure you. I can tell you all I have done when I return; just now I must hurry off, or I shall not catch the train."

As the earl quitted Cawdor, he regretted deeply that his son should have complicated the situation by enforcing silence as regarded his mother.

He pondered a great deal on what he should say when he returned—above all, if the boy's trouble was, as he imagined, the loss of money.

"I must not let his mother know," thought the earl. "Boys are boys; she would think he was lost altogether if she knew that he had betting and gambling debts. Whatever he owes, no matter what it is, I will give him a check for it, and make him promise me that it shall be the last time."

He never thought of any other danger; that his son had fallen in love or wanted to marry never occurred to him. He was glad when he reached Dunmore House; the old housekeeper met him in the hall.

"I have dinner ready, my lord," she said. "Lord Chandos told me you were coming."

He looked round expectantly.

"Is not Lord Chandos here?" he asked.

It occurred to him that the housekeeper looked troubled and distressed.

"No," she replied, "he is not staying here—they are staying in the Queen's Hotel, in Piccadilly."

"They," he cried, "whom do you mean by they? Has Lord Chandos friends with him?"

The woman's face grew pale. She shrunk perceptibly from the keen, gray eyes.

"I understood his lordship that he was not alone," she replied. "I may have made a mistake. I understood him also that he should be with you by eight this evening, when you had finished dinner."

"Why could he not dine with me?" he thought. "Sends a telegram for me, and then leaves me to dine alone. It is not like Lance."

But thinking over it would not solve the mystery; the earl went to his room and dressed for dinner. He had ordered a bottle of his favorite Madeira, of which wonderful tales were told.

Then he sat thinking about his son, and his heart softened toward him. He thought of the handsome, curly-headed young boy whose grand spirit no one but my lady could subdue. He laughed aloud as he remembered the struggles between himself and his heir—they had always ended in his defeat; but when my lady came on the scene it was quite another thing, the defeat was on the other side then, and my Lord Chandos was usually carried off defeated and conquered.

He thought of the handsome stripling who used to wander about the grounds at Cawdor, trying to conceal from my lady the fact that he smoked cigars. He did not fear his father and smoked boldly before him, but at the first sound of my lady's rustling silk he flew rather than ran. Lord Lanswell laughed aloud as he thought of it all.

"He is just as frightened at my lady now," he said to himself. "I cannot help feeling touched and flattered that he has sent for me in his trouble. I will help him and my lady shall never know."

His heart warmed to his son and heir—no one knew how dearly he loved him, nor how completely his life was wrapped up in him. Then he heard a cab drive up to the door. Surely that must be Lance.

He listened in impatient suspense—he heard whispering in the outer hall, as though some consultation were being held.

"What in the world is the boy making a mystery over?" he asked himself.

Then he started from his chair in unutterable amazement.

Before him stood Lance, Lord Chandos, holding the hands of the most beautiful girl he had ever seen in his life.

CHAPTER X
A SHOCKED FATHER

"I am quite sure of one thing," Lord Chandos had said, as they drew near London, "and that is, Leone—if my father sees you before my mother has time to interfere, it will be all right. He can resist anything but a pretty face—that always conquers him."

"I wish," said Leone, with a sigh, "that I were less proud. Do you know, Lance, that I cannot endure to hear you speak as though I were to be received as a great favor. I wonder why I am so proud? I am a farmer's niece, and you are the son of a powerful earl, yet I—please do not be offended; I cannot help it—I feel quite as good as you."

He laughed aloud. There was nothing he enjoyed better than this proud frankness of hers, which would never yield to or worship rank or title.

"I am glad to hear it, Leone," he replied. "For my own part, I think you very much better than myself. I have no fear, if my father sees you first, and that is why I have telegraphed to him to meet us at Dunmore House."

"But," she insisted, "suppose that he does not like me—what shall we do then?"

"Why," he replied, "the right and proper thing for me to do then will be to try to love you, if possible, even better than I do now. Leone, the first thing we must do is to drive to one of the court milliners; no matter what follows, your dress must be attended to at once—first impressions are everything. You look royally beautiful in all that you wear, but I would much rather that my father saw you in a proper costume. Suppose we drive to a milliner's first, and choose a handsome dress, and all things suitable, then we can go to the Queen's Hotel; the trunks can be sent after us. We can dine there; and when you have dressed *a la* Lady Chandos, we will go to Dunmore House, and carry everything before us."

He did as he had said. They drove first to Madame Caroline's. Lord Chandos was accustomed to the princely style of doing things. He sent for madame, who looked up in wonder at his fair young face.

"This is my wife," he said, "Lady Chandos. We have been in the country and she wants everything new, in your best style."

It seemed to him hours had passed when madame reappeared. Certainly he hardly knew the superbly beautiful girl with her. Was it possible that after all the poets had said about "beauty unadorned" that dress made such a difference? It had changed his beautiful Leone into a beautiful empress. Madame looked at him for approval.

"I hope your lordship is satisfied," she said; with the usual quickness of her nation, she had detected the fact that this had been a runaway marriage.

"I am more than satisfied," he replied.

Before him stood a tall, slender girl, whose superb figure was seen to advantage in one of Worth's most fashionable dresses — trailing silk and rich velvet, so skillfully intermixed with the most exquisite taste; a lace bonnet that seemed to crown the rippling hair; pearl-gray gloves that might have grown on the white hands. Her dress was simply perfect; it was at once elegant and ladylike, rich and costly.

"I shall not be afraid to face my father now," he said, "I have a talisman."

Yet his fair young face grew paler as they reached Dunmore House. It was a terrible risk, and he knew it — a terrible ordeal. He realized what he had done when the housekeeper told him the earl awaited him in the dining-room. A decided sensation of nervousness came over him, and he looked at the fresh, proud, glowing beauty of his young wife to reassure himself. She was perfect, he felt that, and he was satisfied.

"Give me your hand, Leone," he said, and the touch of that little hand gave him new courage.

He went in leading her, and the earl sprung from his seat in startling amaze. Lord Chandos went boldly up to him.

"Father," he said, "allow me to introduce to you my wife, Leone, Lady Chandos."

The earl gave a terrified glance at the beautiful southern face, but made no answer.

"I have to ask your forgiveness," continued the young lordling, "for having married without your consent; but I knew, under the circumstances, it was useless to ask it, so I married without."

Still the same terrified look and utter silence.

"Father," cried Lord Chandos, "why do you not welcome my young wife home?"

Then Lord Lanswell tried to smile—a dreadful, ghastly smile.

"My dear boy," he said, "you are jesting; I am quite sure you are jesting. It cannot be real; you would not be so cruel!"

"Father," repeated the young lord, in an imperative voice, "will you bid my wife welcome home?"

"No," said the earl stoutly, "I will not. The young lady will excuse me if I decline to bid her welcome to a home that can never be hers."

"Father," cried the young man, reproachfully, "I did not expect this from you."

"I do not understand what else you could expect," cried the earl, angrily. "Do you mean to tell me that it is true that this person is your wife?"

"My dear and honored wife," replied the young man.

"Do you mean to tell me that you have actually married this lady, Lance—really married her?"

"I have, indeed, father, and it is about the best action of my life," said Lord Chandos.

"How do you intend to face my lady?" asked the earl, with the voice and manner of one who proposes a difficulty not to be solved.

"I thought you would help us, father; at least, speak to my wife."

The earl looked at the beautiful, distressed face.

"I am very sorry," he said, "sorry for you, Lance, and the lady, but I cannot receive her as your wife."

"She is my wife, whether you receive her or not," said Lord Chandos. "Leone, how can I apologize to you? I never expected that my father would receive you in this fashion. Father, look at her; think how young, how beautiful she is; you cannot be unkind to her."

"I have no wish to be unkind," said the earl, "but I cannot receive her as your wife."

Then, seeing the color fade from her face, he hastened to find her a chair, and poured out a glass of wine for her; he turned with a stern face to his son.

"What have you been doing?" he cried. "While your mother and I thought you were working hard to make up for lost time, what have you been doing?"

"I have been working very hard," he replied, "and my work will bring forth good fruit; but, father, I have found leisure for love as well."

"So it seems," said the earl, dryly; "perhaps you will tell me who this lady is, and why she comes home with you?"

"My wife; her name was Leone Noel; she is now Lady Chandos."

For the first time Leone spoke.

"I am a farmer's niece, my lord," she said, simply.

Her voice had a ring of music in it so sweet that it struck the earl with wonder.

"A farmer's niece," he replied. "You will forgive me for saying that a farmer's niece can be no fitting wife for my son."

"I love him, my lord, very dearly, and I will try hard to be all that he can wish me to be."

"Bravely spoken; but it is quite in vain; my lady would never hear of such a thing—I dare not—I cannot sanction it, even by a word, my lady would never forgive me. Can you tell me when this rash action was accomplished?"

"This is our wedding-day, father," cried Lord Chandos. "Only think of it, our wedding-day, and you receive us like this. How cruel and cold."

"Nay, I am neither," said the earl; "it is rather you, Lance, who do not seem to realize what you have done. You seem to think you belong to yourself; you are mistaken; a man in your position belongs to his country, his race, to his family, not to himself; that view of the question, probably, did not strike you."

"No," replied Lord Chandos, "it certainly did not; but, father, if I have done wrong, forgive me."

"I do forgive you, my dear boy, freely; young men will be foolish—I forgive you; but do not ask me to sanction your marriage or receive your wife. I cannot do it."

"Then, of what use is your forgiveness? Oh, father, I did not expect this from you; you have always been so kind to me. I had fancied difficulties with my mother, but none with you."

"My dear Lance, we had better send for my lady; she is really, as you know, the dominant spirit of our family. She will decide on what is to be done."

"I insist on my wife being treated with due respect," raged the young lord.

"My dear Lance, you must do as you will; I refuse to recognize this lady in any way. Will you tell me when and where you were married?"

"Certainly: this morning, by the Reverend Mr. Barnes, at the Church of St. Barnabas, in Oheton, a little village twenty miles from Rashleigh. The marriage was all *en regle*; we had the bans published and witnesses present."

"You took great pains to be exact, and the lady, you tell me, is a farmer's niece."

"My uncle is Farmer Robert Noel; he has a farm at Rashleigh," said Leone, "and in his way is an honest, loyal, honorable man."

The earl could not help feeling the sweet, soft music of that voice; it touched his heart.

"I believe you," he said, "but it is a sad thing Farmer Noel did not take more care of his niece. I am sorry it has happened; I can do nothing to help you; my lady must manage it all."

"But, father," pleaded the young man, "it was on you I relied; it was to your efforts I trusted. Be my friend; if you will receive my wife here and acknowledge her, no one else can say a word."

"My dear boy, only yesterday your mother and I were speaking of something on which the whole desire of her heart was fixed; remembering that conversation I tell you quite frankly that I dare not do what you ask me; your mother would never speak to me again."

"Then, Leone, darling, we will go; Heaven forbid that we should remain where we are not welcome. Father," he cried, in sudden emotion, "have you not one kind word, not one blessing for me, on my wedding-day?"

"I refuse to believe that it is your wedding-day, Lance. When that day does come, you shall have both kind words and blessings from me."

CHAPTER XI
THE LAWYER'S STATEMENT

Lady Lanswell stood in the library at Dunmore House, her handsome face flushed with irritation and annoyance, her fine eyes flashing fire. She looked like one born to command; her tall, stately figure bore no signs of age; her traveling dress of rich silk swept the ground in graceful folds. She had not removed her mantle of rich lace; it hung from her shoulders still; she had removed her bonnet and gloves. With one jeweled hand resting on the table, she stood, the picture of indignation and anger.

Lord Lanswell had sent a telegram at once, when his son left him, begging her to come at once, as Lance had something important to tell her.

My lady lost no time; she was far more quick and keen of judgment than the earl. She never thought of gambling or betting, her thoughts all went to love. It was something about a girl, she said to herself; but she should stand no nonsense. Lance must remember what was due to his family. If he had made any such mistake as that of falling in love with one beneath him, then he must rectify the mistake as quickly as possible; there could be no *mesalliance* in a family like theirs. As for any promise of marriage, if he had been so foolish as to make one he must break it. A sum of money would doubtless have to be expended over the matter, then it would be all right.

So thought my lady, and as the express drew near London she promised herself that all would be well. Her spirits rose, her fears abated; no son of hers would ever make a mistake so utterly absurd. There was something of scorn in my lady's face as she entered Dunmore House. The earl met her in the entrance hall.

"I have lost no time, as you see," she said. "What is all this nonsense, Ross?"

He did not answer until they stood together in the library, with the door closed, and then she repeated the words. Something in her husband's face dismayed her.

"Speak, Ross; I dislike suspense. Tell me at once; what has the boy done?"

"He is married," said the earl, solemnly.

"Great Heaven!" cried my lady. "Married! You cannot mean it. Married—how—whom—when?"

"You will be dreadfully distressed," he began, slowly.

My lady stamped her foot.

"I can bear distress better than suspense. Tell me quickly, Ross, has he disgraced himself?"

"I am afraid so," was the brief reply.

"And I loved him so—I trusted him so; it is impossible; tell me, Ross."

"He has married a farmer's niece. The girl is beautiful. I have seen no one so beautiful; she seems to be well educated and refined. Her uncle has a farm at Rashleigh."

"A farmer's niece," cried my lady; "you cannot possibly mean it. There must be some mistake—the boy has been playing a practical joke on you."

"It is no joke; I only wish it were. Lance gave me the details. He was married yesterday morning by the Reverend Mr. Barnes, at the Church of St. Barnabas, at Oheton, a village somewhere near Rashleigh."

"Married—really and actually married," cried my lady. "I will not believe it."

"Unhappily, it is true. He expected, I think, to make his home here; he had no idea of leaving Dunmore House; but I told him that I could not receive him or her."

"Her! You do not mean to say that he had the audacity to bring her here, Ross?"

"Yes, they came together last night; but I would not receive her. I told them plainly that you must settle the matter, as I could not."

"I should think not," said my lady, with emphasis.

"I must own, though," continued the earl, "that I was rather sorry for Lance; he had trusted entirely to my good offices and seemed to think it very cruel of me to refuse to plead for him."

"And the girl," said my lady, "what of her?"

"You will think I am weak and foolish, without doubt," he said, "but the girl distressed me even more than Lance. She is beautiful enough to arouse the admiration of the world; and she spoke so well for him."

"A farmer's niece—an underbred, forward, designing, vulgar country girl—to be Countess of Lanswell," cried my lady, in horror.

"Nay," said the earl, "she is a farmer's niece, it is true, but she is not vulgar."

"It is not possible that she can be presentable," said my lady. "We must move heaven and earth to set the marriage aside."

"I had not thought of that," said the earl, simply.

Then my lady took the lace mantilla from her shoulders, and sat down at the writing-table.

"I will send for Mr. Sewell," she said. "If any one can give us good advice, he can."

Mr. Sewell was known as one of the finest, keenest, and cleverest lawyers in England; he had been for more than twenty years agent for the Lanswells of Cawdor. He knew every detail of their history, every event that happened; and the proud countess liked him, because he was thoroughly conservative in all his opinions. She sent for him now as a last resource; the carriage was sent to his office, so that he might lose no time. In less than an hour the brisk, energetic lawyer stood before the distressed parents, listening gravely to the story of the young heir's marriage.

"Have you seen the girl?" he asked.

"Yes, I have seen her," said the earl.

"Is she presentable?" he inquired. "Would any degree of training enable her to take her rank— —"

Lady Lanswell interrupted him.

"The question need never be asked," she said, proudly. "I refuse ever to see her, or acknowledge her. I insist on the marriage being set aside."

"One has to be careful, my lady," said Mr. Sewell.

"I see no need for any great care," she retorted. "My son has not studied us; we shall not study him. I would rather the entail were destroyed, and the property go to one of Charles Seyton's sons, than my son share it with a low-born wife."

My lady's face was inflexible. The earl and the lawyer saw that she was resolved—that she would never give in, never yield, no matter what appeal was made to her.

They both knew that more words were useless. My lady's mind was made up, and they might as well fight the winds and the waves. Lord Lanswell was more inclined to pity and to temporize. He was sorry for his son, and the beautiful face had made some impression on him; but my lady was inflexible.

"The marriage must be set aside," she repeated.

The earl looked at her gravely.

"Who can set aside a thoroughly legal marriage?" he asked.

"You will find out the way," said my lady, turning to Mr. Sewell.

"I can easily do that, Lady Lanswell; of course it is for you to decide; but there is no doubt but that the marriage can easily be disputed—you must decide. If you think the girl could be trained and taught to behave herself—perhaps the most simple and honorable plan would be to let the matter stand as it is, and do your best for her."

"Never!" cried my lady, proudly. "I would rather that Cawdor were burned to the ground than to have such a person rule over it. It is useless to waste time and words, the marriage must be set aside."

The lawyer looked from one to the other.

"There can be no difficulty whatever in setting the marriage aside," said Mr. Sewell. "In point of fact, I must tell you what I imagined you would have known perfectly well."

My lady looked at him with redoubled interest.

"What is that?" she asked, quickly.

The earl listened with the greatest attention.

"It is simply this, Lady Lanswell, that the marriage is no marriage; Lord Chandos is under age—he cannot marry without your consent; any marriage that he contracts without your consent is illegal and invalid—no marriage at all—the law does not recognize it."

"Is that the English law?" asked Lady Lanswell.

"Yes, the marriage of a minor, like your son, without the consent of his parents, is no marriage; the law utterly ignores it. The remedy lies, therefore, in your own hands."

Husband and wife looked at each other; it was a desperate chance, a desperate remedy. For one moment each thought of the sanctity of the marriage tie, and all that was involved in the breaking of it. Each thought how terribly their only son must suffer if this law was enforced.

Then my lady's face hardened and the earl knew what was to follow.

"It remains for us, then, Mr. Sewell," she said, "to take the needful steps."

"Yes, you must make an appeal to the High Court, and the marriage will be at once set aside," said Mr. Sewell. "It is a terrible thing for the young wife, though."

"She should have had more sense than to have married my son," cried my lady. "I have pity for my son—none for her."

"I think it would be more fair to tell Lord Chandos what you intend doing," said Mr. Sewell. "Not that he could make either resistance or defense—the law is absolute."

"What will the end be?" asked my lady.

"The marriage will be declared null and void; they will be compelled to separate now; but again he has the remedy in his own hand. If he chooses to remain true and constant to her, the very next day after he becomes of age he can remarry her, and then she becomes his lawful wife; if he forgets her the only remedy for her would be money compensation."

"It shall be the business of my life to see that he does forget her," said my lady.

"You can commence proceedings at once," said Mr. Sewell. "You can file your petition to-morrow."

"It will make the whole matter public," hesitated my lady.

"Yes, that is the one drawback. After all it does not matter," said Mr. Sewell, "many young men make simpletons of themselves in the same way. People do not pay much attention."

Lord Lanswell looked at his wife's handsome, inflexible face.

"It is a desperate thing to do, Lucia," he said, "for Lance loves her very dearly."

"It was a desperate action on his part to marry without consulting us," said my lady.

"He will be of age next June," said the earl, "do you think that he will be true to her?"

"No," said the countess, proudly. "I can safely pledge you my word that he will not."

CHAPTER XII
"THEY WILL NOT FORGIVE ME"

"Thank Heaven," said the countess, "that the matter can be set straight. If there had been no remedy I should have lost my reason over it. The boy must have been mad or blinded, or very probably drawn into it in some disgraceful fashion or other."

My lady was triumphant, her handsome face lighted with satisfaction, but the earl looked grave. The lawyer had taken his leave, and they still remained to discuss matters. Lord Lanswell did not seem so well pleased; he went up to my lady where she was standing.

"Lucia," he began, "do you think that if we succeed in parting these two we shall do quite right?"

"Right," cried my lady. "I shall think it one of the most virtuous actions of my life."

"Well," said the earl, "I am sorry that I cannot quite agree with you. No doubt this marriage is vexatious enough, but whether it is well to obliterate all traces of it, or rather to do away with it altogether, is quite another thing."

"I am the best judge of what is right in this case," said my lady, haughtily; "I will have no interference. The business part of it must be attended to at once."

"At least you will write to Lance and tell him what you intend doing?"

"Yes, I have no objection to that," she replied; "it can make no possible difference to him."

"He may try to make some compromise," said Lord Lanswell, whose heart smote him as he thought of the passionate, beautiful face.

"There can be no compromise; he must give her up at once, and marry some one in his own rank," said the countess. "I will write the letter at once, and I must ask you, Ross, not to be weak. A weak man is the most contemptible object in creation."

"I will try not to be weak, my dear," said the earl, submissively; "but I am concerned for Lance."

"Lance must take his chance," said my lady, too angry to be conscious of the rhyme; "he has done wrong, and he must suffer for it. He will thank Heaven in a year's time from now that I have saved him."

Still Lord Lanswell looked at his wife with a grave expression of doubt.

"You think, then, Lucia, that in a year's time he will have forgotten that poor young wife?"

"I am quite sure of it. Long before I had heard of this foolish affair I had decided in my own mind whom he should marry, and I see no reason for changing my plans."

Lord Lanswell thought with regret and sympathy of the young wife. Could it be possible, he thought, that his son would be so disloyal, so unfaithful as to forget in twelve short months the wife he had risked so much to win? He looked at the countess.

"The matter then lies in a nutshell and depends entirely upon whether Lance continues true to his love or not. If he remains true, your scheme for parting them will have but little effect; if he prove false, why then all will be well, according to your way of thinking."

"We will finish with the subject," she said. "You may make your mind quite easy about it. I guarantee all my knowledge of the world that he will not only have forgotten her in twelve months' time, but that he will be ashamed of having ever fancied himself in love with her."

Lord Lanswell went, in obedience to his wife's command, to assist in the commencement of the proceedings, and as soon as my lady was left alone, she sat down to write to her son. She told him, in the plainest possible words, that his marriage was not only unlawful, but invalid, as he, being minor, could not contract a legal marriage without the consent of his parents. My lady had faith enough in herself to add openly:

"You can, of course, please yourself, as soon as you are of age; you can then remarry the young person without our consent if you will; but my opinion is you will not."

The time which had passed so unpleasantly for the earl and countess was bright and light for the young bride and bridegroom. Leone had shed some bitter tears when they left Dunmore House, but Lord Chandos laughed; he was angry and irritated, but it seemed to him that such a state of things could not last. His father and mother had indulged him in everything— surely they would let him have his way in marriage. He kissed the tears from his young wife's face, and laughed away her fears.

"It will be all right in the end," he said. "My father may hold out for a few days, but he will give way; in the meantime, we must be happy, Leone. We will stay at the Queen's Hotel until they invite us to Cawdor. It will not be long; my mother and father cannot get on without me. We will go to the opera to-night, that will distract your thoughts."

The opera had been but hitherto an empty word to Leone. She had a vague idea that it consisted of singing. After all there was some compensation to be found; her young husband was devoted to her, she was magnificently dressed, and was going in a beautiful closed carriage to the opera.

She uttered no word of surprise, but her whole soul was filled with wonder. The highest festivity and the greatest gayety she had ever witnessed was a choir tea-party. She had a most beautiful voice; in fact, neither herself nor any of those around her knew the value of her voice or appreciated it.

On great occasions the choir were entertained by the rector—once during the summer when they made merry out in the green woods, and once in the winter when they were entertained in the school-room. Leone had thought these parties the acme of grandeur and perfection; now she sat in that brilliant circle and wondered into what world she had fallen.

Before the curtain was raised she was engrossed in that brilliant circle. She had never seen such dresses, such diamonds, such jewels, faces so beautiful, toilets so exquisite; it was all quite new to her. The beautiful and poetic side of it appealed to her. Her beautiful face flushed with delight, her dark eyes were lustrous and radiant.

Lord Chandos, looking round the opera-house, where some of the handsomest women in England were, said to himself that among all these fair and noble faces there was not one so beautiful as Leone's.

She herself was quite unconscious of the admiration she excited; she did not see how the opera-glasses were turned to her face; she could not hear people asking: "Who is that with Lord Chandos? What a beautiful face, what a lovely girl! Who is she?" Lord Chandos saw it, and was not only proud, but flattered by it.

"My mother will yield at once when she sees her," he thought; "she will be pleased that the most beautiful woman in England is my wife."

He made no introductions, though many of his friends bowed to him, with a secret hope that he would ask them into his box. But he had arranged his own plans. His mother—the proud, exclusive, haughty Countess of Lanswell—should be the one to introduce his beautiful wife to the world; that of itself would be a passport for her. So that he was careful not to ask any one into his box, or even to exchange a word with any of the people he knew.

From the time the curtain was drawn up until the opera ended, Leone was in a trance. Quite suddenly she had entered this new and beautiful world of music and art—a world so bright and dazzling that it bewildered her.

Lord Chandos watched her with keen delight—her lustrous eyes, the intense face, the parted lips.

The opera was one of the most beautiful—"Norma"—and the part of Norma was taken by the greatest *prima donna* of her time. Leone's eyes filled with tears as those passionate reproaches were sung; she knew nothing of the language, but the music was full of eloquence for her. She turned suddenly to her husband; her whole soul seemed awake and thrilling with dramatic instinct.

"Lance," she said in a low voice, "I could do that; I do not mean that I could sing so well, but I could feel the jealousy she feels. I could utter those reproaches. Something seems to have awoke in my soul that never lived before; it is all new to me, yet I understand it all; my heart is on fire as I listen."

"And you have enjoyed it?" he said, when the curtain fell on the last grand scene.

She answered him with a low sigh of perfect content.

So it was that to her her wedding-day became the most marked day of her life, for on it she awoke to the knowledge of the world of art and music.

There was nothing for it but to remain at the hotel.

Lord Chandos merely laughed at the notion of his parents holding out against him. He was wonderfully sanguine.

"We shall hear the carriage stop some fine morning," he said, "and they will be here to seek a reconciliation."

He laughed when the waiter gave him my lady's letter; he turned triumphantly to his wife.

"This is from my mother," he said; "I knew she would relent, it is probably to ask us to Cawdor."

But as he read it his face changed; the smile and the triumph died from it. He said no word to Leone, but tore the letter into shreds. She looked on with a wistful face.

"Is it from your mother, Lance?" she asked.

He took her in his arms and kissed her.

"My darling, do not trouble about them; you are all the world to me. They will not forgive me; but it does not matter. I am proud of what I have done. I am quite independent. I shall take a pretty little villa at Richmond, and we shall live there until they come to their senses."

"That will be giving up all the world for me," she said.

"The world will be well lost, Leone. We will go to-morrow and find a pretty little house where we shall be quite happy. Remember one thing always—that my mother will love you when she sees you."

"Then let her see me now, Lance, at once," she cried, eagerly, "if you think so. Why wait? I should be more happy than any one else in the world if you would do that."

"It is too soon yet," he replied; "all will be right in time."

She wished that he had offered to show her his mother's letter; but she did not like to ask what the contents were.

Lord Chandos dare not tell her, besides which he laughed in scorn at the idea. They might threaten as they would; but he felt quite certain there was no power on earth which could set aside his marriage, therefore he should not trouble himself about it. He would go to Richmond and look out for a house there.

CHAPTER XIII
A PERFECTLY HAPPY WOMAN

"They would never dare do it," Lord Chandos repeated to himself with a laugh of contempt. Set his marriage aside. They were mad to think of such a thing.

From time to time strange-looking documents came to him; he thrust them aside without even looking at them. He only laughed at the notion. Part him from Leone. It was not in the power of any one on earth to do it. He never mentioned the matter to Leone at all; it was not worth while to disturb her.

They had been to Richmond, and had found there a villa so beautiful it seemed to have been built for them—a quaint, picturesque, old English house, full of pretty nooks and corners, with large latticed windows, over which roses and jasmine hung in abundance; a smooth, green lawn on which stood a superb cedar-tree; beautiful grounds that reached down to the river. The views from the windows were superb. It was worth anything to stand on that green lawn and watch the sunset on the Thames.

Leone was delighted with it; she had never dreamed of a home so beautiful. Lord Chandos furnished it with the utmost luxury, and there the first few happy months of their life was spent. Lord Chandos did not wish exactly that his marriage should be kept secret, but he did not want it known to the world in general until his mother was willing to introduce and receive his wife.

To Leone that life that opened to her was like a heaven on earth; her husband surrounded her with "kind observances;" he purchased for her a wardrobe that was a marvel of beauty and elegance; he found a French lady's-maid, who understood all the duties of the toilet. What was more, he had the best masters in London to instruct her. Her voice was one of the finest ever heard, her taste for music so great that she was soon proficient.

He taught her himself to ride. There was one thing singular, every master who attended her was aware of a great hidden power within her, they said among each other that she was something wonderful—that the world would hear of her some day. There was an innate sense of power, a grand dramatic instinct, a keen sense of everything beautiful, noble and great. There were times when an electric flash of genius made them marvel.

"It is a thousand pities," said the music-master to himself, "that she has married a nobleman. If she had been dependent on her own exertions, I could have made her one of the finest singers in the world."

Again, the drawing-master said:

"If I had the training of Lady Chandos I would make her the finest artist in England."

None of them had discovered the real secret of her genius, or what was the true fire that every now and then seemed to brighten them all as it flashed over them.

A few weeks completely changed her; she had that keen, quick insight into everything, that wondrous tact and intelligence which make some women seem as though they were magicians.

When she went first to River View, she had some traces of her rustic training. Before six weeks had passed over it had all disappeared. Lord Chandos himself had taught her; her intonation and accent were clear and refined, her words well chosen, her expressions always poetical and full of grace; no one meeting her then could have told that she had spent her life in the rural shades of Rashleigh.

New beauty came to her with this development of mind; new, spiritual, poetical loveliness; and Lord Chandos, looking at his peerless young wife, felt always quite confident that when his mother saw her all would be well—she would be proud of her.

While Leone seemed to have gone straight to heaven, she could not realize that this was the same life she rebelled against with such fierce rebellion. Now the days were not long enough to hold in them all the happiness that fell to her share. The birds woke her with their singing; the sun with its shining; another beautiful day had dawned for her—a day that was full of beauty and love. They passed like a dream.

She took breakfast always with her husband; perhaps the happiest hour of the day was that. The windows of the pretty breakfast-room looked over a wilderness of flowers; the windows were always open. The soft, sweet summer air came in, parting the long, white curtains, bringing with it the breath of roses and the odor of a hundred flowers.

She looked as fresh and fair as the morning itself. Lord Chandos wondered more and more at her radiant loveliness. Her soul was awake now, and looked out of her dark eyes into the world she found so beautiful.

Then Lord Chandos went up to town for a few hours, while Leone took her different lessons and studied. They met again at lunch, and they spent the afternoon out-of-doors. An ideal life—an idyl in itself. Leone, while she lived, retained a vivid remembrance of those afternoons, of the shade of the deep woods, of the ripple of the river through the green banks, of the valleys where flowers and ferns grew, of the long alleys where the pleasant shade made a perfect paradise. She remembered them—the golden glow, the fragrance, the music of them, remained with her until she died. All the most pleasant times of our lives are dreams.

Then they dined together; and in the evening Lord Chandos took his beautiful young wife to the opera or the play, to concert or lecture.

"As soon as I am of age," he would say, "I shall take you on the Continent; there is no education we get like that we get by traveling one year on the Continent; and you will be at home on every subject, Leone," he would say; and Leone longed for the time to come.

"When I am of age," was his universal cry.

When Leone expressed any anxiety or sorrow over his separation from his parents, he would laugh and answer:

"Never mind, my darling, it will be all right when I am of age. Never mind, darling, you will have my mother asking for the pleasure of knowing you then—the tables will be turned; let the great world once see you, and you will be worshiped for your beauty, your grace, and your talent."

She looked wistfully at him.

"Do they love beauty so much in your world, Lance?" she asked.

"Yes, as a rule, a beautiful face has a wonderful influence. I have known women without a tithe of your beauty, Leone, rise from quite third-rate society to find a place among the most exclusive and noblest people in the land. Your face would win for you, darling, an entrance anywhere."

"The only thing I want my face to do," she said, "is to please your mother."

"And that, when she sees it, it is quite sure to do," replied the lover-husband.

"Lance," said Lady Chandos, "what shall we do if your parents will neither forgive us nor see us?"

"It will be very uncomfortable," said Lord Chandos; "but we shall have to bear it. It will not much matter so far as worldly matters are concerned;

when I am of age I shall have a separate and very handsome fortune of my own. My mother will soon want to know you when you become the fashion—as you will, Leone."

So she dismissed the future from her mind. She would not think of it. She had blind reliance, blind confidence in her husband; he seemed so carelessly happy and indifferent she could not think there was anything vitally wrong. She was so unutterably happy, so wonderfully, thoroughly happy. Her life was a poem, the sweetest love-story ever written or sung.

"Why am I so happy?" she would ask herself at times; "why has Heaven given me so much? all I ever asked for—love and happiness?"

She did not know how to be grateful enough.

One morning in autumn, a warm, beautiful morning, when the sun shone on the rich red and brown foliage—they were out together on the fair river—the tide was rising and the boat floated lazily on the stream. Lady Chandos wore a beautiful dress of amber and black that suited her dark, brilliant beauty to perfection. She lay back among the velvet cushions, smiling as her eyes lingered on the sky, the trees, the stream.

"You look very happy, Leone," said Lord Chandos.

"I am very happy," she replied. "I wrote to my uncle yesterday, Lance. I should like to send him a box filled with everything he likes best."

"You shall, if it pleases you, my darling," he answered.

She leaned over the side of the boat watching the water, drawing her hand through the clear stream.

"Happy," she repeated, rather to herself than to him; "I can safely say this, that I have had so much happiness since I have been here that if I were wretched all my life afterward I should still have had far more happiness than falls to the lot of many people."

She remembered those words in after years; and she owned to herself that they had been most perfectly true.

The few months passed at River View had been most perfectly happy—no shade of care had come over her, no doubt, no fear—nothing that chilled the warmth of her love, nothing that marred its perfect trust. In some lives there comes a pause of silent, intense bliss just before the storm, even as the wind rests before the hurricane.

"You make me very proud, Leone," said Lord Chandos, "when you tell me of your happiness; I can only say may it be like the light of heaven, eternal."

CHAPTER XIV
"TRUE UNTIL DEATH"

For some long months that case stood on the records. Every paper in England had some mention of it; as a rule people laughed when they read anything about it. They said it was a case of Corydon and Phyllis, a dairy-maid's love, a farce, a piece of romantic nonsense on the part of a young nobleman who ought to know better. It created no sensation; the papers did not make much of it; they simply reported a petition on the part of the Right Honorable the Earl of Lanswell and Lucia, his wife, that the so-called marriage contracted by their son, Lancelot, Lord Chandos, should be set aside as illegal, on account of his being a minor, and having married without their consent.

There was a long hearing, a long consideration, a long lawsuit; and it was, as every one had foreseen it would be, in favor of the earl against his son. The marriage was declared null and void—the contract illegal; there could be no legal marriage on Lord Chandos' side without the full and perfect consent of his parents.

When that decision was given, Lady Lanswell smiled. Mr. Sewell congratulated her on it. My lady smiled again.

"I may thank the law," she said, "which frees my son from the consequences of his own folly."

"Remember," said the lawyer, "that he can marry her, my lady, when he comes of age."

"I know perfectly well that he will not," replied the countess; but Mr. Sewell did not feel so sure.

The earl, the countess, and the solicitor sat together at Dunmore House, in solemn consultation; they were quite uncertain what should be the next step taken. Due legal notice had been given Lord Chandos; he had simply torn the paper into shreds and laughed at it—laughed at the idea that any law, human or divine, could separate him from his young wife; he took no notice of it; he never appeared in answer to any inquiry or summons; he answered no questions; the lawyer into whose hands he had half laughingly placed the whole matter had everything to do for him, and wondered at the recklessness with which the young lord treated the whole affair.

It was all over now; and the decree which had parted them, which severed the tie between them, had gone forth—the marriage was void and worth nothing.

The matrons of Belgravia who read it said it was perfectly right; there was no doubt that he had been inveigled into it; and if such a thing were allowed to go unpunished there would be no more safety for their curled darlings; they would be at the mercy of any designing, underbred girl who chose to angle for them.

Men of the world smiled as they read it, and thought Lord Chandos well out of what might have been a very serious trouble. Young people thought little about it; the Belgravian belles merely said one to another that Lord Chandos had been in some kind of trouble, but that his parents had extricated him. And then all comment ended; even the second day after the judgment was given it had been forgotten.

When the Countess of Lanswell held in her hands the letter which told her the desire of her heart was granted, and her son free, for a few moments she was startled; her handsome face paled, her hands trembled; it had been a desperate step, but she had won. She had the greatest faith in her own resources; she felt a certain conviction that in the end she would win; but for one moment she was half startled at her own success.

"Let us send for Lance here to Cawdor," she said to the earl, "while Mr. Sewell sees the girl and arranges with her. He must have *carte blanche* over money matters; whatever he thinks fit to mention I shall agree to. If a thousand a year contents her, I am willing."

"Yes, yes—it is no question of money," said the earl. "It will be a great trouble to her naturally, and we are bound to make what compensation we can. If you wish me to send for Lance I will do so at once. I will send a telegram from the station at Dunmore; he will be here soon after noon."

There had been little or no communication between the young heir and his parents since the lawsuit began. Once or twice Lord Chandos and the earl had met; but the earl always refused to discuss matters with him.

"You must talk to my lady, my dear boy," he would reply; "you know that she manages everything;" and Lord Chandos, fearing no evil, laughed at what he considered an amiable weakness on his father's part.

"I love my wife," he said to himself, "but no woman should ever be so completely mistress of me. I shall always keep my independence, even though I love my wife perhaps better than any man living; but I will never give up my independence."

He was somewhat startled that morning in September to find a telegram waiting him at River View, from Cawdor, stating that Lord Lanswell wished him to take the first train, as he had news of the utmost importance to him. Lady Lanswell, who was a most complete woman of the world, had warily contrived that a piece of real good fortune should at the same time fall to his lot. She had great influence at court, and she had used it to some purpose. There was a royal wedding on the Continent, and he was one of the two English noblemen chosen as the representatives of English royalty. There could be no refusal of such an honor, Lady Lanswell knew that; and she, knowing that Lord Chandos would be delighted over it, had used all her influence, hoping that it would distract his attention from the decision given and from his wife. She had arranged a little programme in her mind—how it should all be managed; she would send a telegram summoning him to Cawdor; she would first show him the letter of appointment, induce him to answer by accepting it, then when the letter accepting the appointment had gone, and he was committed beyond recall, she would tell him the judicial decision over his marriage.

The telegram reached River View one morning when Lord Chandos and Leone sat at a late breakfast-table, Leone looking like a radiant spring morning, her beautiful face, with its exquisite coloring, and her dainty dress of amber and white.

"A telegram," she said. "Oh, Lance, how I dread the sight of those yellow envelopes; they always fill me with horror; they always seem to be the harbinger of bad news."

He kissed the beautiful face before he opened the telegram.

"There is no very bad news here," he said. "I must go to Cawdor at once; my father has some very important news for me."

Some instinct seemed to warn her of coming danger; she rose from her seat and went over to him; she laid her tender arms round his neck; she laid her beautiful face on his.

"It means harm to us, Lance," she said; "I am sure of it."

"Nonsense, my darling," he cried; "how can it be about us? Most likely there is a general election, or some business of that kind coming on, and he wants to see me about it."

A Mad Love | 73

Still the beautiful face grew paler, and the shadows deepened in the dark eyes.

"Shall you go at once?" she asked.

Lord Chandos looked at his watch.

"The train starts at twelve," he said. "I must go in half an hour's time, Leone."

"Half an hour," she said, and the tender hands clasped him more tightly, "only half an hour, Lance?"

Some prophetic instinct seemed to come over her; the passionate love on her beautiful face deepened into tragedy; yet he had never breathed one word to her of what had taken place. She knew nothing of the lawsuit; and Lord Chandos never intended her to know anything about it; but with the chill of that autumn morning came a chill of doubt and fear such as she had never known before.

"How long shall you be away?" she asked.

"Not one moment longer than I am compelled to stay," he replied. "If my father really wants to see me on election affairs I may be absent two days; trust me, Leone; the first moment I am free I shall return;" and drawing her beautiful face down to his own the young husband kissed it with passionate devotion, little dreaming of what lay before him.

"Only half an hour," said Leone. "Oh, Lance, let me spend it with you. I will order your portmanteau to be packed; my dear, do not let me leave you for one moment."

She drew a little stool and sat down at his feet.

Lord Chandos laughed.

"One would think we were lovers still."

She looked at him with that wonderful expression of face, so earnest, so intent, so lofty.

"So we are," she said; "we will be lovers until we die; shall we not, Lance?"

"I hope so; but we shall be unlike most married people, Leone, if we do that," he replied.

"I will not believe you," she answered. "You laugh, sometimes, Lance, at love; but I am sure if I were your wife for fifty years you would never tire of me or love me less."

"I never wish to do so," he replied.

"You never will," said Leone, "my faith is as strong as my love, and you have it all. I could rather believe now that the heavens would fall over my head than you could ever for one moment forget me."

"I shall never forget you, sweet," he said; "this is the first time we have ever been parted since we have been married; you must not be sad and lonely, Leone."

"I shall spend all my time in thinking of your return," she said. "Lance, it will comfort me all the time you are away; you will say some of those beautiful words I love to hear."

He took both her white hands in his.

"My darling," he said, "I love you with all my heart, and I will be true to you until death."

The sweetness of the words seemed to content her for a time; she laid her face on his hands for some minutes in wistful silence.

"Leone," said the rich, cheerful voice of the young earl, "I have an idea that I will bring you good news from home. My father would not have sent for me unless he wanted me, and I shall make a bargain with him. If he wants me to do anything, I shall consent only on condition that I take you to Cawdor."

They talked of it for some minutes; then Leone rose and busied herself for some time in helping him—her face was pale and her hands trembled. When the moment came for him to say good-bye he held her in his arms.

"Once again," she whispered.

And he answered:

"My darling wife, I love you, and will be true to you until death."

And those were the last words that for some time she heard him speak.

CHAPTER XV
AN EXCITING INTERVIEW

Lady Lanswell looked somewhat startled when her son entered the room. During those few months of his married life he had altered much; he looked taller and stronger; the handsome face was covered with a golden beard and mustache; he looked quite three years older than before his marriage.

He was a handsome stripling when his mother kissed him and sent him, with many injunctions as to study, to Dr. Hervey's, a handsome stripling, with golden down on his lip, and the hue of a ripe peach on his face; now he was a man of the world, assured, confident, easy in his carriage and bearing.

He looked at his mother with half-defiance, half-amusement in his eyes.

The strong, handsome woman, whose brave nature had never known fear, trembled for one moment when she remembered what she had to tell her son.

He bent down to kiss her, and for one moment her heart relented to her son. She steeled herself with the recollection that what she had done was for his benefit.

"I have good news for you, Lance," she said, with her stately grace; "very excellent news."

"I am glad to hear it, mother," replied Lord Chandos, thinking to himself how much more this interview resembled that of a queen and a crown prince than of mother and son.

"You have traveled quickly and would probably like some refreshment—you would like a glass of Madeira?"

The truth was that her ladyship herself, with all her courage, felt that she required some artificial stimulant—the courage and pride of the proudest woman in England ebbed; she feared what she had to say.

"An honor has been bestowed on you," she said, "one which would make any peer in England proud."

His face brightened—he was keenly susceptible to the flattery implied in his mother's words.

"You have been asked, together with Lord Dunferline, to represent our gracious sovereign at the marriage of the Princess Caroline at Hempsburg. Such an invitation, I need not tell you, is equivalent to a royal command."

"I know it, mother, and I am delighted," he said, wondering in his own mind if he should be able to take Leone with him.

"The notice is rather short," continued the countess; "but that is owing to some delay on the part of Lord Dunferline. I hear that you are the envy of every man at the club. You will have to leave England for Germany in three days; to-morrow you must be at the palace. I congratulate you, Lance; it is very seldom that a man so young as you receives so signal a favor."

He knew it, and was proud accordingly; yet he said to himself that Leone must go with him; he could not live without Leone.

Lady Lanswell continued:

"Your father is delighted over it; I cannot tell you how pleased he is."

Then Lord Chandos looked wonderingly around.

"Where is my father?" he said. "I have not seen him yet."

Lady Lanswell knew that he would not see him. The earl had fled ignominiously; he had declined to be present at the grand fracas between his wife and his son; he had left it all in my lady's hands.

"Your father had some business that took him away this morning; he knew that I could say for him all that he had to say."

Lord Chandos smiled, and the smile was not, perhaps, the most respectful in the world. My lady did not observe it.

"I am quite sure," he said, "that you can interpret all my father's ideas."

It was then, with her son's handsome face smiling down on her, that the countess grew pale and laid her hand, with instinctive fear, on the papers spread before her. She nerved herself for the struggle; it would never do to give way.

"I have other news for you, Lance," she said, and he looked with clear, bright, defiant eyes in her face.

She drew herself to her full height, as though the very attitude gave the greatest strength; there was no bend, no yielding in her. Stern, erect, proud, she looked full in her son's face; it was as though they were measuring their strength one against the other.

"I have never said to you, Lance, what I thought of this wretched mistake you call your marriage," she began; "my contempt and indignation were too great that you should dare to give the grand old name you bear to a dairy-maid."

Leone's beautiful Spanish face flashed before him, and he laughed at the word dairy-maid; she was peerless as a queen.

"Dare is not the word to use to a man, mother," he retorted.

"Nor should I use it to a man," said my lady, with a satirical smile. "I am not speaking to a man, but to a hot-headed boy; a man has self-control, self-denial, self-restraint, you have none; a man weighs the honor of his name or his race in his hands; a man hesitates before he degrades a name that kings have delighted to honor, before he ruins hopelessly the prestige of a grand old race for the sake of a dairy-maid. You, a hot-headed, foolish boy, have done all this; therefore, I repeat that I am not speaking to a man."

"You use strong language, mother," he said.

"I feel strongly; my contempt is strong," she said. "I know not why so great a humiliation should have fallen on me as that my son—the son of whom I was proud—should be the first to bring shame on his name."

"I have brought no shame on it, mother," he said, angrily.

"No shame!" said the countess, bitterly. "I can read, fancy, the short annals of the Lanswells—'Hubert, Earl Lanswell, died while fighting loyally for his king and his country; Ross, Earl Lanswell, was famed for political services; Lancelot, Earl Lanswell, married a dairy-maid.' I would rather," she cried, with flashing eyes, "that you had died in your childhood, than lived to bring such bitter shame on a loyal race."

His face grew pale with anger, as the bitter words were hurled at him.

"Will you understand, once for all, mother, that I have *not* married a dairy-maid?" he cried. "My wife is a wonder of beauty; she is dainty and lovely as a princess. Only see her, you would change your opinion at once."

"I hope never to do that. As for seeing her, I shall never so far lose my own self-respect as to allow such a person to speak to me."

Lord Chandos shook his head with a rueful smile.

"If you had ever seen Leone, mother, you would laugh at the idea of calling her a person," he said.

Lady Lanswell moved her hand with a gesture of superb pride.

"Nay, do not continue the subject. If the girl was not actually a dairy-maid, in all probability she was not far removed from it. I have no wish to discuss the question. You have stained the hitherto stainless name of your family by the wretched mistake you call a marriage."

"I do not *call* it a marriage; it *is* one," he said.

And then my lady's face grew even paler.

"It is not one. I thank Heaven that the law of the land is just and good; that it very properly refuses to recognize the so-called marriage of a hot-headed boy. You have ignored our letters on the subject, you have laughed at all threats, treated with disdain all advice; now you will find your level. The judicial decree has been pronounced; the marriage you have talked of with such bravado is no marriage; the woman you have insulted me by mentioning is not your wife."

She neither trembled nor faltered when he turned to her with a white, set face.

"Pardon me; I must speak plainly; that which you have said is a lie!"

"You forget yourself, Lord Chandos," she said, with cold dignity.

"You force me to use words I do not like, mother," he cried "Why do you irritate me—why say those things?"

"They are perfectly true; here on the table lie the papers relative to the suit; the judicial opinion has been pronounced; our petition is granted, and your marriage, as you choose to call it, is set aside, is pronounced illegal, null, void!"

The fierce, white anger of his face startled her.

"It shall not be!" he cried.

"It must be," she repeated; "you cannot prevent it. You must have been singularly devoid of penetration and knowledge not to know from the first that it must be decided against you; that no minor can marry without the consent of his parents. A wise law it is, too; there would soon be an end of the aristocracy of England if every hot-headed, foolish boy of nineteen could marry without the consent of his parents or guardian."

If his antagonist had been a man, there would have been hot, angry words, perhaps blows; as it was, to a lady, and that lady his mother, he could say nothing. He sunk back with a white face and clinched hands; his mother resolutely stifled all pity, and went on, in her clear voice:

"The law has decided for us against you; you know now the truth. If you have any respect for that unfortunate girl, you will not see her again; she is not your wife, she is not married to you. I need not speak more plainly; you know what relationship she will hold to you if you do not leave her at once."

The handsome face had in these five minutes grown quite haggard and worn.

"My God!" he cried; "I refuse to believe it, I refuse to believe one word of it!"

With her clear, pitiless voice, she went on telling him what would happen.

"You have one resource," she said, "and I tell you quite honestly about it; when you are of age you can remarry this person if you wish."

He sprung from his seat with a cry of wounded pain and love.

"Mother, is it really true?" he asked. "I married that young girl before Heaven, and you tell me that if I persist in returning to her she loses her fair name! If it be so, you have done a very cruel thing."

"It is so," said my lady, coldly. "I grant that it seems cruel, but better that than tarnish the name of a whole race."

"I shall remarry Leone, mother, the day after I am twenty-one," he said.

The countess raised her eyebrows.

"The same man does not often make a simpleton of himself in the same fashion, but if you will do it, you will. For the present, if you have any regard for the person who is not your wife, you will let her go home again. I will return and talk over your journey with you."

So saying, the Countess of Lanswell quitted the room, leaving her son overwhelmed with a sense of defeat.

CHAPTER XVI
LEONE'S DETERMINATION

Lucia, Countess of Lanswell, stood alone in the superb drawing-room at Cawdor. It was evening, one of the warmest and brightest in September. Nearly three months had passed since the fatal marriage which had grieved and distressed her, and now she fondly hoped all her distress was ended. The decree had gone forth that the marriage was null and void; was, in fact, no marriage, Lord Chandos being under age when it was contracted. She said to herself all was null now. True, her son was in a most furious rage, and he had gone to consult half the lawyers in London, but she did not care for that; he was sure to rage and rave; he was a spoiled child, who never in his life had been contradicted or thwarted. The more angry he was the better; she knew by experience the hotter the fire the more quickly it burns away. Had he been cool, calm, collected and silent she would have dreaded the after consequences.

"He will exhaust himself with furious words," she said to herself with a slow smile. "When he has done that, all danger will be over."

She had smiled when she heard of his rapid journeys, his fierce denunciations, his violent invectives, his repeated oaths that no power on earth should take him from his young wife.

She had smiled when the earl, whose conscience was more tender than her own, had said over and over again that it was a terrible thing to set aside a marriage, to call a religious ceremony null and void. He would not have done it himself, but my lady had firm nerves, and a will of iron; nothing daunted her. She laughed at his persuasions and arguments. She told him the day would come on which he would thank Heaven that the honor of his name and race had been saved from destruction. My lady was triumphant. Knowing her son was spending his whole time in these journeys, she had requested Mr. Sewell himself to go to the pretty little villa at Richmond, to see the young wife himself, and tell her the truth about the marriage; to speak what she was pleased to call plain English to her; to tell her that in the eyes of the law and of all honest, honorable men she was not his wife; that every hour she called herself by his name, or lived under his roof, added to her disgrace and increased her shame.

"You can tell her," said my lady, with ill-concealed contempt, "that next June he will be twenty-one, and then he can please himself; he can remarry her if he will; no one then will have the least control over him; he will be his own master and can do as he likes. In all probability," she continued, "the girl will please herself with fanciful ideas about his being true to her; do not contradict her if she believes it—she will part from him more easily; but, believe me, my son will never return to her—never!"

Mr. Sewell had tried in vain to escape the interview; he was neither particularly tender of heart nor given to sentiment, but he shrunk from seeing the young girl who called herself Lady Chandos; he shrunk from telling her the truth; but my lady was inexorable; he must do it, and no one else.

He did it, but until the day of his death he never forgot it; he could not bear to think of it, and he never mentioned it. Until the day of his death he was haunted by a beautiful, passionate face, white with terrible despair.

He was compelled to speak in what my lady called plain English, or she would never have understood him. She could not understand in the least why the fact of Lord Chandos being under twenty-one should make her marriage null and void; illegal, because contracted without his parents' consent. She had turned to him with flashing eyes.

"Are the laws of England all framed for the convenience of the rich?" she asked.

And, proud as he was of his legal knowledge, the lawyer had hesitated before the fire of her question.

She understood at last—she saw what Mr. Sewell called the justice of the case—the reasons why such a law was needful, and she knew that she was not the lawful wife of Lancelot, Lord Chandos. She looked into the stern face of her companion with eyes filled with awful despair.

"He did not know it," she said; "only tell me that, and I shall be happier. He did not know it?"

"No," said Mr. Sewell; "I am quite sure that Lord Chandos was ignorant of the fact—it never occurred to him; if it had done so, he would have deferred his marriage until he came of age."

"I shall take some comfort in that," she said, slowly. "If he has erred, it has been done in ignorance and innocence. You say that the wrong can be righted next June; that he can marry me then without the consent of either of his parents."

"Certainly he can," replied the lawyer.

Something of the shock of despair passed from her face as he uttered these words. She folded her arms over her breast with the repressed passion of a tragedy queen.

"Then I have no fear," she said. "Were the time twice as long, the cruelty twice as great, the law twice as strong, he would return to me true and faithful, as he loves me. You can tell his mother that."

"I will," said Mr. Sewell, relieved to see some of the horror fall from her face.

She would not discuss her future arrangements with him. Lady Lanswell was anxious that she should take a large sum of money and return home. She looked at him with the dignity of an outraged queen.

"Before Heaven, and in my own eyes, Lord Chandos is my husband," she said, with calm dignity; "and with him only will I discuss my future. You can tell his mother that also. No other creature living shall interfere with my fate or destiny."

She tried hard—and she was a woman of wonderful resource—she tried hard to keep her dignity, not to fail or falter before him, the cold emissary of that cruel mother; but unutterable woe looked out of her eyes at him, her white face had on it the passion of despair, her voice the ring of anguish, the small white hands on which the wedding-ring shone, trembled like leaves stirred in the summer wind; the very repression of her passionate despair made it seem more terrible. He clearly explained to her her position at last, she must consent to an immediate separation from Lord Chandos; she must give up his name, leave the shelter of his roof, or men and women, too, would brand her with the scarlet letter—would look on her as one lost and dead to all sense of honor.

"You will see for yourself," added the lawyer, "that the wisest and best plan is for you to go away at once—this very day even—then you will stand a better chance when next June comes. Even one more day spent under this roof would be fatal to your character and reputation. You must go at once."

Once more she raised her despairing eyes to him. Her voice trembled as though it were all tears.

"Tell me," she said, gently, "has this been done by Lady Lanswell's desire more than by the earl's?"

"Yes, I believe it is so," he said.

Leone continued:

"If the countess relented now, and gave her consent, could we be legally married at once?"

"If the earl and countess consent you could be remarried to-day. Nothing is wanted but their permission."

"Thank you," she said, gently. Then with pathos and dignity that touched him greatly she held out her hand to him. "I do not blame you for the message you have brought," she said; "the fault lies with Lady Lanswell and the English law, not with you. You have fulfilled your mission as kindly as you could. I forgive you what you have done and what you have said."

The white lips closed firmly, no other sound came from them, but Mr. Sewell looked back as he closed the door, and she lay then with her face on the floor. He did not go to her; he thought it was better to leave her alone. He said to himself, as he quitted the house, that not for all the wealth of the Lanswells would he pass through another such scene.

The hour came in which she raised her face once again to the sunlight, and tried to realize what had happened. She had risen that morning the happiest girl in all England, her only anxiety being to make herself more beautiful than ever in her husband's eyes. The morning itself was not more fresh and fair; everything had been *couleur de rose.*

Her husband, as she believed him, thought so little of the quarrel with his parents that she had imbibed his careless, happy ideas about it. There was no cloud in her sky, no doubt in her heart; now her heart was full of despair. She looked at the blue September sky, and asked herself if it were possible to realize what had happened. She was dazed, stunned, as though some one had struck her a violent blow. She went out of the pretty drawing-room where she had heard what seemed to her her death-warrant. She opened her white lips to breathe the pure, fresh air of heaven.

As she stood there panting for breath, one of the servants came to her, holding a letter in her hand. Leone opened it. The few hastily-written lines were from her husband. They said, simply:

> "My Darling,—I shall not be able to return home to-day. I have some disagreeable business in town, of which I will tell you more anon. I shall be at home for luncheon to-morrow. Believe me, always your loving husband,
>
> "Lance."

She looked at the word "husband" until the letters seemed to burn like fire. He had signed himself her husband. Ah, then, it was quite plain that he neither believed, or, perhaps, had not even heard, of what had been done. As she stood there with the fading boughs of a spreading tree over her head, the words came to her again and again:

"Those vows were all forgotten,
The ring asunder broke."

She seemed once more to hear the falling of the waters. Would the vows made to her ever be broken? Ah, no! a thousand times no!

She would go to his mother and appeal to her. A woman must, of course, be merciful to a woman. She would go herself and appeal to Lucia, Countess of Lanswell.

CHAPTER XVII
"I WOULD RATHER SEE MY SON DEAD"

The countess stood alone in the drawing-room. The sun was setting over the trees in the park, and a warm glow filled the beautiful room with rosy light—a light that fell on costly pictures, on marble statues, on buhl and jasper, on silver and gold, on mirrors and flowers, whose fragrance was delicious even to breathe, but it fell on my lady's proud face and figure as though it liked best to linger there.

The dressing-bell had not rung, and she, waiting for it, had fallen into a reverie. She was sure she had done right, yet, without doubt, the girl would feel it keenly. What matter? "Women must weep," it was part of their lives. Whoever paused or cared for a woman's tears? Women had wept before and would weep again. She looked round on the superb home where she reigned mistress, and laughed with scorn as she tried to picture the farmer's niece queen of these ancient walls.

Right? Most certainly she had done right; let weak minds and weak hearts think as they would. The golden sunset, the rosy clouds, the soft, sweet song of the birds, the fragrance of the thousand blooming flowers, the faint whisper of the odorous wind appealed to her in vain. What was a bleeding heart and weeping eyes to her?

Yet she was but a woman; and these sweet voices of nature could not leave her quite unsoftened. She wondered where Lance was. She remembered him a fair-haired, laughing, defiant boy, playing there under the trees when the red light fell. She started suddenly when one of her well-trained footmen opened the door, and said a lady wished to see her. The countess looked at him in haughty vexation.

"Why do you bring a message so vague? I see no lady who gives neither card nor name."

"I beg pardon, my lady," said the man, humbly. "I did not forget. The lady herself said you did not know her, but that her business was most important."

"You must say that I decline to see any one who gives neither name nor card," said the countess. Then, seeing the man look both anxious and undecided, she added, sharply: "Is it a lady?"

He looked greatly relieved.

"It is, my lady. She is young and beautiful," he would have added, if he had dared.

"You would surely be able to discriminate between a lady and—a person of any other description?" said the countess.

The man bowed.

"The lady wishes me to add that her business was of great importance, and that she had traveled some distance to see you."

"Show her in here," said the countess.

The red light of the setting sun had moved then, and fell over her in great gleams on her dark velvet dress, on her exquisite point lace, and fine, costly gems. She looked regally proud, haughty, and unbending—the type of an English aristocratic matron, true to her class, true to her order, intolerant of any other. As she stood in the heart of the rosy light the door opened, and this time the countess of Lanswell was startled out of her calm. There entered the most beautiful girl she had ever beheld—tall, slender, graceful, exquisitely dressed, moving with the most perfect grace and harmony; her face like some grand, passionate poem—a girl lovely as a houri, who walked up to her with serene and queenly calm, saying:

"Lady Lanswell, I am your son's wife."

The countess, taken so entirely by surprise, looked long and keenly into that beautiful face—looked at the clear, bright eyes, so full of fire and passion—at the lovely, imperial mouth, and the whole face so full of tragedy and beauty; then in a clear, distinct voice, she answered:

"My son has no wife."

Leone drew the glove from her left hand, holding it before my lady's eyes.

"Will you look at my wedding-ring?" she asked.

A scornful smile played round my lady's lips.

"I see a ring," she said, "but not a wedding-ring. There can be no wedding-ring where there is no marriage."

"Do you believe that marriages are known in Heaven?" Leone asked. "Do you believe that if a marriage had been contracted in the presence of Heaven, witnessed by the angels, do you suppose that a mere legal quibble can set it aside?"

"You choose your arguments badly," said the countess. "If you appeal to Heaven, so can I. One of the greatest commandments given from there says, 'Children, obey your parents.' My son is commanded by a divine voice to obey me, and I forbid him to marry until he is of age."

"You have not the power!" cried Leone.

"You are mistaken; not only the power is mine, but I have used it. The foolish ceremony you choose to call your marriage is already set aside."

Leone drew one step nearer to her with flashing eyes.

"You know that in your heart you cannot believe it. You cannot think it," she cried. "You know that I am your son's wife. You have brought the great strong arm of the law upon me. You have taken from me my husband's name. Yet neither you, nor any human power can make me less his wife. He married me," she continued, her eyes flashing, her face flushing, "he married me before God, and I say that you cannot undo that marriage. I defy you."

"True, I could not undo it, but the law both can and has done so. Half-educated young ladies, who wish to make such grand marriages, should have common sense first. No youth under age, like my son, can legally marry without the consent of his parents."

The flush faded from the beautiful face, and gave place to a white horror. Leone looked at the countess.

"You do not surely think that I married your son for any other reason except that I loved him?" she cried.

"Pray, believe that I have never troubled myself in the least to think of your motive," said my lady.

"I loved him, Lady Lanswell, you could never know how much. You are proud and haughty; you love a hundred things. I loved but him. I love him with my whole heart and soul. If he had been a peasant, instead of an earl, being what he is, I should have loved him just the same."

Lady Lanswell's face darkened with scorn.

"I am willing to listen to anything you may wish to say, but I beg of you leave all such nonsense as love out of the discussion. You have probably come to see me because you want money. Let us come to the point at once."

The pride that flushed the beautiful face of the girl startled the haughty patrician who stood before her.

"Money," cried Leone, "I have never thought of money. I do not understand. Why should I want money from you?"

To do her justice, the countess shrunk from the words.

"I should suppose," she said, "that you will require some provision made for you, now that you are leaving my son?"

It was with difficulty that Leone controlled herself. Her whole frame trembled with indignation. Then the color receded from her face and left her white, silent, and motionless.

"I have been too hard," thought the countess, "no one can suffer beyond her strength."

She motioned the girl to take a chair, sitting down herself for the first time since the interview began. There was no feeling of pity in her heart, but she felt there were certain things to be said, and the best way would be to say them and have it all over.

Leone did not obey. She stood silent for a few minutes. Then she said, simply:

"I would never take money from you, Lady Lanswell, not even if I were dying of hunger. You do not like me; you are cruel to me."

Lady Lanswell interrupted her with a superb gesture of scorn.

"I could not possibly like or dislike you," she said; "you are less than nothing to me. It was natural that I should think you came to me for money. If that be not your object, may I ask what it is?"

"Yes; I will tell you. I thought, as you were a woman, I might appeal to you."

My lady smiled haughtily.

"You are the first that has ever ventured to address me as a woman. What appeal do you want to make to me?"

The passion of despair seemed to die away from her. A great calm came over her. She went up to Lady Lanswell, and knelt at her feet. The countess would have given much for the power of moving away, but there was that in the beautiful, colorless face raised to hers which compelled her to listen.

"I humble myself to you," pleaded the sweet voice. "I pray of you, who are so great, so powerful, so mighty, to have pity upon your son and upon me. One word from you will go so far; you can undo all that has been done. If you will give your consent all will be well."

Lady Lanswell looked at her in silent wonder. Leone went on:

"I plead to you. I pray to you, because I love him so. In my heart I am as proud as you, may be prouder; but I lay my pride under my feet, I humble myself. I pray of you to take pity upon your son, and on myself. I love him so well, he loves me too. Life would hold nothing for either of us if we are parted. For the sake of all the love you have ever felt for husband, father, brother, son—for God's sake, I pray you to take pity on us, and do not separate us."

The passionate torrent of words stopped for one minute; tears streamed down the beautiful upraised face; then she went on:

"I would do all that you wished me; I would try hard to improve myself; I would work so hard and work so well that no one would even guess, ever so faintly, that I belonged to a different class. I would be the most devoted of daughters to you; I would live only to please you, I——"

The countess held up her hand with a warning gesture.

"Hush!" she said; "you are talking the most arrant nonsense."

But Leone this time would not be controlled. All the passion and love within her seemed to find vent in the next few words. They might have burned the lips which uttered them, but they fell unheeded on the ears of the proudest woman in England.

"Hush," she said again. "Neither pleading nor prayers will avail with me. I speak the simple truth when I say that I would rather see my son dead than see you his wife."

CHAPTER XVIII
A WRONGED WOMAN'S THREAT

For some five minutes there was silence, and the two who were to be mortal enemies looked at each other. Leone knew then that all prayers, all pleadings were in vain; that they were worse than useless; but in the heart of the foe there was no relenting, no pity, nothing but scorn and hate. She had poured out the whole of her soul in that supplication for pity, and now she knew that she had humbled herself in vain; the mother's cruel words smote her with a pain like that of a sharp sword. She was silent until the first smart of that pain was over, then she said, gently:

"Why do you say anything so cruel?—why do you hate me?"

"Hate you?" replied my lady, "how can you be so mistaken? It is not you I hate, but your class—the class to which you belong—although the word hate is much too strong. I simply hold them in sovereign contempt."

"I cannot help my class," she said, briefly.

"Certainly not; but it is my place to see that my son takes no wife from it. To you, yourself, I can have no dislike; personally I rather like you; you have a pleasant face, and I should take you to be clever. But you have not even one of the qualifications needful—absolutely necessary for the lady whom my son calls wife."

"Yet he chose me," she said, simply.

"You have a nice face, and my son has fancied it," said the countess contemptuously. "You ought to be grateful to me for separating you from my son now. I am doing for him the kindest thing that any one could do. I know Lord Chandos better than any one else, and I know that he tires of everything in a short time. He would have wearied of you by Christmas, and would have loathed the chains he had forged for himself. When he was a child he tired of a new toy in half an hour—his disposition has not changed."

"I cannot believe it," cried Leone. "I will not believe it, great lady as you are. You are wicked to malign your own son."

"I do not malign him," said the countess, indifferently. "Many gentlemen think it quite complimentary to be called changeable. My son has always been known as one of the most variable of men; nothing pleases him long; it is seldom that anything pleases him twice. You think he will always love you; let me ask you why? You have a pretty face, granted; but there is nothing under the sun of which a man tires sooner. You have nothing else; you have no education, no accomplishments, no good birth; I should say no good breeding, no position, rank, or influence. If I may speak my mind plainly, I should say that it was a most impertinent presumption for you, a farmer's niece, even to dream of being Lady Chandos—a presumption that should be punished, and must be checked. You would, without doubt, make an excellent dairy-maid, even a tolerable housekeeper, but a countess never. The bare idea is intolerable."

She grew more angry as she spoke; for the girl's grace and beauty, the wonderful sweetness of her voice, the passion, the power, the loveliness of her face, began to tell upon her; she could not help owning to herself that she had seen nothing so marvelous as this wonderful girl.

"Then," said Leone, calmly, "I have appealed to you in vain?"

"Quite in vain," replied my lady. "Remember that against you personally I have nothing to say, neither have I any dislike; but if you have common sense, you will see that it is utterly impossible for my son to take the future Countess of Lanswell from a farmhouse. Now try and act rationally—go away at once, leave my son, and I will see that you have plenty to live upon."

"Whatever may be said of the class from which I spring," cried Leone, "I believe in the sanctity of marriage, and I would scorn to barter my love for anything on earth."

"Yes, that is all very pretty and very high-flown," said the countess, with a contemptuous laugh; "but you will find a few thousand pounds a very comfortable matter in a few years' time."

"You said you would rather see your son dead than married to me, Lady Lanswell; I repeat that I would rather die of hunger than touch money of yours. I did not know or believe that on the face of God's earth there was ever a creature so utterly hard, cold and cruel as you."

The light of the setting sun had somewhat faded then, and it moved from the proud figure of the countess to the lovely young face of Leone, but even as the light warmed it, new pride, new energy, new passion seemed to fill it. The prayer and the pleading died—the softened light, the sweet tenderness left it; it was no longer the face of a loving, tender-hearted girl, pleading with hot tears that she might not be taken from her husband—it was the face of a tragedy queen, full of fire and passion. She stood, with one hand upraised, like a sibyl inspired.

"I have done, Lady Lanswell," she said; "you tell me that Lord Chandos is free to marry as he will when he is twenty-one."

"If you can find any comfort in that statement, I can verify it," she replied; "but surely you are not mad enough to think that, when my son is of age, he will return to you."

"I am sure of it," said Leone. "I believe in my husband's love, and my husband's constancy, as I believe in Heaven."

"I hope your faith in Heaven will be more useful to you," sneered the countess. "I have womanly pity enough to warn you not to let your hopes rest on this. I prophesy that Lord Chandos will have utterly forgotten you by next June, and that he does not see you again."

"I will not believe it, Lady Lanswell. You are my superior by birth and fortune, but I would neither exchange mind nor heart with you. You have sordid and mean ideas. My husband will be true, and seek me when the time comes."

My lady laughed.

"You are very happy to have such faith in him; I have not half so much in any creature living. You hold that one card in your hand—you seem to think it a winning one; it may or may not be. I tell you one thing frankly: that I have already settled in my own mind who shall be my son's wife, and I seldom fail in a purpose."

"You are a wicked woman," cried Leone. "I have no fear of you. You may try all that you will. I do not believe that you will take my husband from me. You are a wicked woman, and God will punish you, Lady Lanswell. You have parted husband and wife who loved each other."

"I am not very frightened," laughed my lady. "I consider that I have been a kind of providence to my son. I have saved him from the effect of his own folly. Will you allow me to say now that, having exhausted a very disagreeable subject, this interview must be considered closed! If you would like any refreshments my housekeeper will be pleased to— —"

But the girl drew back with an imperial gesture of scorn.

"I want nothing," she said. "I have a few words to say to you in parting. I repeat that you are a wicked woman, Lady Lanswell, and that God will punish you for the wicked deed you have done. I say more, whether Heaven punishes you or not, *I will*. You have trampled me under your feet; you have insulted, outraged, tortured me. Listen to the word—you have tortured me;

you have received me with scorn and contumely; you have laughed at my tears; enjoyed my prayers and humiliation. I swear that I will be revenged, even should I lose all on earth to win that revenge. I swear that you shall come and plead to me on your knees, and I will laugh at you. You shall plead to me with tears, and I will remind you how I have pleaded in vain. You have wrung my heart, I will wring yours. My revenge shall be greater than your cruelty; think, then, how great it will be."

"I repeat that I am not frightened," said the countess, but she shrunk from the fire of those splendid eyes.

"I was mad to think I should find a woman's heart in you. When the hour of my revenge comes, my great grief will be that I have a heart of marble to deal with!" cried Leone.

"You cannot have such great affection for your husband, if you speak to his mother in this fashion," said the countess, mockingly.

The girl stretched out her white arms with a despairing cry.

"Give me back my husband, and I recall my threats."

Then, seeing that mocking smile on that proud face, her arms fell with a low sigh.

"I am mad," she said, in a low voice, "to plead to you—quite mad!"

"Most decidedly," said the countess. "It appears to me there is more truth in that one observation than in any other you have made this evening. As I am not particularly inclined to the society of mad men or mad women, you will excuse me if I withdraw."

Without another word, my lady touched the bell. To the servant who entered she said:

"Will you show this person out as far as the park gates, please?"

And, without another look at Leone, she quitted the room.

Leone followed in silence. She did not even look around the sumptuous home one day she believed to be hers; she went to the great gates which the man-servant held open as she passed through. The sun had set, and the gray, sweet gloaming lay over the land. There was a sound of falling water, and Leone made her way to it. It was a cascade that fell from a small, but steep rock. The sound of the rippling water was to her like the voice of an old friend, the sight of it like the face of some one whom she loved. She sat down by it, and it sung to her the same sweet old song:

"A ring in pledge he gave her,
And vows of love we spoke;
Those vows are all forgotten,
The ring asunder broke."

It would not be so with her, ah no! If ever the needle was true to the pole, the flowers to the sun, the tides to the moon, the stars to the heavens, Lord Chandos would be true to her.

So she believed, and, despite her sorrow, her heart found rest in the belief.

CHAPTER XIX
LEONE'S PROPHECY

No words could do justice to the state of mind in which Lord Chandos found himself after that interview at Cawdor. He rushed back to London. Of the three previous days remaining he spent one in hunting after the shrewdest lawyers in town. Each and all laughed at him—there was the law, plain enough, so plain that a child could read and understand it. They smiled at his words, and said, half-contemptuously, they could not have imagined any one so ignorant of the law. They sympathized with him when he spoke of his young wife, but as for help, there was none.

The only bright side to it was this, he could remarry her on the day he came of age. Of that there was and could be no doubt, he said, but he was bent on finding some loop-hole, and marrying her at once, if it were really needful for the ceremony to be performed again. It could not be, and there was nothing for it but to resign himself to the inevitable. He did not know that Leone had heard the terrible sentence, and he dreaded having to tell her. He was worn out with sorrow and emotion. In what words was he to tell her that she was not his wife in the eyes of the law, and that if they wished to preserve her character unspotted and unstained she must leave him at once?

He understood his mother's character too well to dare any delay. He was sure that if Leone remained even one day under his roof, when the time came that he should introduce her to the world as his wife, his mother would bring the fact against her, and so prevent her from even knowing people.

There was no help for it—he must tell her. He wrote a letter telling her he would be at River View for luncheon on the following day; he knew that he must leave that same evening for the Continent.

He would have given the world to have been able to renounce the royal favor, of which he had felt so proud, but he could not. To have done so would have been to have deprived him not only of all position, but to have incurred disgrace. To have refused a favor so royally bestowed would have been an act of ingratitude which would have deprived him of court favor for life.

He must go; and when the first pain was over, he said to himself it was, perhaps, the best thing that could have happened. He could not have borne to know that Leone was near him, yet not see or speak to her.

It was all for the best, painful as it was. If for these long months they must be parted, it was better for him to be abroad—he dare not have trusted himself at home. He loved Leone so well that he knew his love would have broken down the barriers which the law had placed between them. He would go to River View, and, let it pain him as it would, he would tell her all, he would leave her as happy as was possible under the circumstances. He would stay away until the time was over; then, the very day he came of age, he would return and remarry her. He laughed to scorn his mother's prophecy. He prove untrue to his darling! The heavens must fall first. Not for him the mill-wheel story—not for him the broken ring.

How happy they would be, then, when the time had passed, and he could introduce Leone as his beloved wife to the whole world. He would try and think of that time without dwelling more than he could help on the wretched present. He went home to River View, but the first glance at Leone's face told him that she knew all.

It was not so much that the beauty had gone from it, that the beautiful eyes were dim with long, passionate weeping, or that the lips trembled as she tried to smile. Her whole face had changed so completely; its tragic intensity, the power of its despair, overmastered him.

Lord Chandos clasped her in his arms, and covered the sad young face with kisses and tears.

"My darling," he said, "you know all; I can see you know all."

The ring of happy music had quite died from her voice—he hardly recognized it.

"Yes," she answered him, "I know all."

"My darling," he cried, "it is not my fault. You will think I ought to have known it; but I swear to Heaven that I never even thought or suspected it. I would rather have been dead than have put you in a false position, Leone—you know that."

She laid her fair arms on his neck, and hid her white face on his breast.

"I am sure of it," she said, gently; "I have never thought of that: I know that you intended to make me your wife."

"So you are my wife, let who will say to the contrary—you are my beloved, revered, honored wife, Leone. Why, my darling, all the strength has left you! Look up, Leone. They have done the worst they can do, and what is it? They have parted us for a few months. When the parting is ended we shall be together for life."

She tightened the clasp of her fair arms around his neck.

"I know; I have faith in you, but it is so hard to bear, Lance. We were so happy, and you were all the world to me. How shall I live through the long months to come? Lance, perhaps you will be angry with me—I have done something that perhaps you will not like."

"That would not be possible, Leone. I must always like everything you do. Why, my darling, how you tremble! Sit down, there is nothing in all the world to fear."

"No; let me tell you what I have to say with my head here on your breast. You must not be angry with me, Lance. When I had seen Mr. Sewell, I felt that I could not bear it. I went down to Cawdor and saw Lady Lanswell."

He started with surprise. She raised her face to his, longing to see if he were angry, yet half afraid.

"You went to Cawdor to see my mother," he repeated. "My darling, it was a strong measure. What did she say or do?"

"You are not angry with me for it, Lance?" she asked, gently.

"I angry, my darling? No, a thousand times no. I could not be angry with you. Why did you go—for what purpose?"

"I went to ask her to have pity on us; not to enforce this cruel sentence; to be pitiful to me, because I love you so dearly."

"And her answer?" asked Lord Chandos, eagerly.

"Her answer was everything that was cruel and wicked. Ah, forgive me, Lance, she is your mother, I know, but she has taken in her cruel hands a divine power. She has parted us and I prayed her to be merciful. I told her how dearly we loved each other, but she had no pity—no mercy—no woman's kindness, no sympathy. She was cold, cruel, proud, haughty. She insulted, humiliated and outraged me. She refused to hear one word, and when I left her, I swore to be revenged on her."

The slender form trembled with passion. He drew her even more closely to his breast.

"My darling, you need not think of vengeance," he said. "I am grieved that my mother was unkind to you. Had you consulted me, I should most certainly have said do not go. Mind, I am not angry or annoyed, only so far as this, that I would not have you irritated for the world. I must say that I had always felt that if my mother could see you our cause was won. I did not believe that any creature living could resist that face."

She looked up at him with unutterable love.

"Do you really care so much for it, Lance? Have you never seen a face you like as well?"

"No, and never shall see one, my darling; when we are parted it will live in my heart bright and fair until we meet again."

Then the tender arms clung more tightly to him.

"Must we be parted, Lance?" she whispered. "We were married in the sight of Heaven—must we leave each other? Oh, Lance, it cannot be true; no one can say that I am not your wife."

Quietly and calmly trying to command himself, he told her then how inevitable it was that they must submit to the voice of the law during the next few months, so as to insure their future happiness and fair name. And then he told her of the favor conferred upon him, and how he was compelled to accept it or never to hope for court favor again.

She listened with a face that seemed turned to stone. Slowly the tender arms unwound themselves and fell by her side; slowly the beautiful eyes left his and filled with despair. He tried to console her.

"You see, my darling," he said, "that in any case we must have parted. Though this appointment is a mark of royal regard, still it is quite imperative. I could not have refused it without ruin to my future career, and I could not have taken you with me, so that for a time we must have parted."

"I see," she said, gently, but her hands fell, and a shudder that she could not control passed over her.

"Leone," said Lord Chandos, "we have not long to be together, and we have much to arrange. Tell me, first, what you thought of my mother?"

"She is very beautiful, very proud, very haughty, cold and cruel—if not wicked," said the young girl, slowly.

"That is not very flattering," said Lord Chandos.

"I could have loved and worshiped her if she had been kind to me," said Leone; "but she was cruel, and some time or other I shall have my revenge."

He looked gravely at her.

"I do not like to hear that, my darling. How can you be revenged?"

A light came over her face.

"I do not know. I have a prophetic insight at times into the future. As I stand here, I know that a time will come when your mother will weep to me as bitterly as I wept to her, and just as much in vain."

"I hope not," he answered. "All will be well for us, Leone. But revenge, my darling, is a horrible word, and does not suit those sweet lips at all. Let me kiss away the sound of it."

He bent his handsome head and kissed her lips with love that seemed stronger than death and true as eternity.

CHAPTER XX
THE PARTING

They had been talking for more than an hour. He had given her the whole history of the royal wedding, of what his embassy consisted of, of the length of time he would be absent, how he should think of her continually, how he implored her to write to him every day, and she had given him every detail of her interview with Mr. Sewell and Lady Lanswell. Then he said to himself that it was time they made some arrangement over the future.

"So we are to live apart until next June, Leone," he said, gently. "It is a terrible sentence; but the time will soon pass. Tell me, my darling, where you would like to live until June comes?"

She looked at him with startled eyes.

"Need I leave home, Lance? Let me live here; I could not fancy any other place was home. I feel as though if I once left here I should never see you again."

"My darling, that is all fancy—nothing but fancy. No matter where you are, my birthday comes on the thirtieth day of June, and on that day I shall return to you to make you what I have always believed you to be—my wife."

"I am your wife, Lance; let others say what they will, you will not deny it."

"Not I, Leone. You are my wife; and the very first day the law permits you shall bear my name, just as you now share my heart and life."

"On the thirtieth day of June," she sighed. "I shall count every hour, every minute until then. I wish, Lance, I could sleep a long sleep from the hour of parting until the hour of meeting—if I could but turn my face from the light of day and not open my eyes until they rest on you again. I shall have to live through every hour and every minute, and they will be torture."

"The time will soon pass, Leone, my darling; it will be full of hope, not despair. When the green leaves spring and the sunshine warms the land, you will say to yourself, 'June is coming, and June brings back my love;' when the lark sings and the wood-pigeons make their nests, when the hawthorn blooms on the hedges and the lilac rears its tall plumes, you will say 'June is near.' When the roses laugh and the lilies bloom, when the brook sings in the wood, when the corn grows ripe in the meadows, you will say 'June is come, and it brings my love.'"

"My love—oh, my love," sighed the girl, and her voice had the passionate sweetness of a siren.

"I shall come back to you, Leone, with everything bright, smiling, and beautiful; every rose that blooms, every bird that sings, every green leaf that springs will be a message from me to you to say that I am coming; when the wind whispers, and the trees murmur, it will be the same story, that I am coming back to my darling. Let us picture the thirtieth of June, and your mind shall rest on that picture. It will be a bright day, I know, the sky all blue and clear, not a cloud in it; but with the half-golden light one sees in June skies. You can see that picture, Leone?"

"Yes," she replied, drawing nearer him, and resting her head again on his breast.

"The sun will be low on the hills, and every living thing will be laughing in its light. The great trees will have grown strong in it, the flowers will have brightened, and the river there, Leone, will be running so deep and clear, kissing the green banks and the osier beds, carrying with it the leaves and flowers that will fall on its bosom, and the garden will be filled with the flowers we love the best. You see that picture, too, my love?"

"Yes, I see it," she whispers.

"Wherever I may be," he continued, "I shall so arrange my journey that I may be with you on the morning of my birthday. You see the pretty white gate yonder where the tall white roses climb in summer? My darling, rise early on the thirtieth of June and watch that gate. Even should such an impossible thing be as that you should never have one word of or from me, get up and watch that gate on the thirtieth of June. You will see me enter. I will part the clustering roses; I shall gather the sweetest, together with the fairest lily that blooms, and bring them to you as emblems of your own dearest self. You will see me walk down the broad path there, and you will meet me at the door."

"Oh, my love, my love!" sighed the girl, "would that it were June now."

He bent down to kiss the loving lips.

"It will come," he said; "let me finish the picture. I shall have a special license with me so that we can be remarried that day; and then the world shall know who is Lady Chandos. Then my lady mother shall seek you who have sought her; then she shall ask to know you, my darling, and this hideous past shall be to us a dream and nothing more. Leone, when sad thoughts come to you promise me that you will dwell on this side of the picture and forget the other."

"I promise, Lance," she said, gently.

"You see, my love—whom I shall so soon call again by the beautiful name of wife—you see that your life does not lie in ruins round you; the only difference is that I shall be away."

"And that makes the difference of the whole world to me," said Leone.

"And to me," said Lord Chandos; "but it will soon be over, Leone. You can go on living here—it is no unusual thing for a lady to live alone while her husband is abroad. You can keep the same servants; you need not make the least alteration in your life in any way. Only remain here in silence and patience until I return. Now do you see, my darling, it is not so dreadful?"

"It is hard enough," she replied; "but you have taken away the sting. Oh, my darling, you will be true to me? I am only a simple village girl, with nothing, your mother says, to recommend me; but I love you—I love you. You will be true to me?"

"My dearest Leone, you may as well ask if the stars will be true to heaven, or heaven to itself, as ask me if I will be true to you. You are my life—a man is not false to his own life. You are soul of my soul—no man betrays his soul! It would be easier for me to die than be false to you, my love."

The passionate words reassured her—something of hope came over the beautiful face.

"Lance," she said, "do you remember the mill-wheel and how the water used to sing the words of the song?"

"Yes, I remember it; but those will never come true over us, Leone, never. I shall never break my vows or you yours."

"No; yet how the water sung it over and over again:

"'Those vows were all forgotten,
The ring asunder broke.'

I can hear it now, Lance. It seems to me the wind is repeating it."

"It is only your fancy, my darling," he said.

But she went on:

"'I would the grave would hide me,
For there alone is peace.'

Ah, Lance, my love—Lance, will it happen to either of us to find peace in the grave?"

"No, we shall find peace in life first," he said.

She laid her hand on his arm.

"Lance," she said, "I had a terrible dream last night. I could not sleep for many hours. When at last my eyes closed I found myself by the old mill stream. I thought that I had been driven there by some pain too great for words, and I flung myself into the stream. Oh, Lance, my love—Lance, I felt myself drowning. I felt my body floating, then sinking. My hair caught in the bending branches of a tree. The water filled my eyes and my ears. I died. In my sleep I went through all the pain of death. My last thought was of you. 'Lance,' I cried, in death as in life, 'Lance, come back to me in death!' It was a horrible dream, was it not? Do you think it will ever come true?"

"No," he replied; but his handsome face had grown paler, and the shadows of deep trouble lay in his eyes.

She raised her face to his again.

"Lance," she asked gently, "do you think that any creature—any one has ever loved another as well as I love you? I often wonder about it. I see wives happy and contented, and I wonder if their husbands' smiles make heaven to them as yours do to me."

"I do not think there are many people capable of loving as you do, Leone," he replied, "and now, my darling, I must leave you. Leone, spend all your time in study. A few months more of work as hard as the last three months, and my beautiful wife will be as accomplished as she is graceful. Study will help you to pass away the time."

"I will do anything you tell me, Lance. You will let me write to you every day, and you must write often to me."

"I will, sweet; but you will not be uneasy if my letters are not so frequent as yours; the foreign post is not so regular as ours; and if we travel in Germany I may not always be able to write."

"I will trust you," said the loving voice. "I am sure you will never fail me."

She was proud as an empress, she had the high spirit of a queen; but now that the moments of parting had come, both failed her. She clung to him, weeping passionate tears—it was so cruelly hard, for she loved him so well. Her tears rained on his face, her trembling lips could utter no words for the bitter sobs. Never was sorrow so great, or despair so pitiful. She kissed his face with all the passion of her love.

"Good-bye, my love," she sighed. "Oh, Lance, be true to me—my life lies in yours."

"If ever I prove untrue to you, my darling, let Heaven be false to me," he said. "Leone, give me one smile; I cannot go until I have seen one."

She tried. He kissed the white lips and the weeping eyes.

"Good-bye, my beloved," he said. "Think of the thirteenth of June, and the roses I shall bring back with me."

And then he was gone.

CHAPTER XXI
WAITING FOR THE DAY

How the days of that dreary summer passed Leone never knew; the keenest smart of the pain came afterward. At first she was too utterly stunned and bewildered by the suddenness of the blow to realize all that happened. It was impossible to believe that her marriage had been set aside, and that her husband, as she called him, had gone away; but, as the days rolled on, she slowly but surely realized it. There was no break in the terrible monotony. The voice that made such music in her ears was silent, the footsteps that had made her heart beat and her pulse thrill were heard no more; the handsome face, always brightened with such tender love for her, no longer brought sunshine and warmth; it was as though the very light had gone out of her life, and left it all bleak, dark and cold.

For some days the proud heart, the proud, unyielding spirit gave way, and she longed for death; life without Lance seemed so utterly unbearable. Then youth and a naturally strong constitution triumphed. She began to think how much she could learn so as to surprise him on his return. Her soul was fired with ambition; in a few months she would achieve wonders. She set herself so much; she would become proficient on the piano and the harp; she would improve her singing; she would practice drawing; she would take lessons in French and Italian.

"I can learn if I will," she said to herself; "I feel power without limit in myself. If I fix my own will on attaining a certain object I shall not fail. Lance shall find an accomplished wife when he returns."

She resolved to give her whole time and attention to it. Thanks to the old books in Farmer Noel's house, she was better read than the generality of ladies. No toil, no trouble daunted her. She rose in the morning long hours before the rest of the household were awake, and she read for hours after they were asleep. The masters who attended her, not knowing her motive, wondered at her marvelous industry. They wondered, too, at the great gifts nature had bestowed upon her—at the grand voice, capable of such magnificent cultivation; at the superb dramatic instinct which raised her so completely above the commonplace; at the natural grace, the beauty of face and attitude, the love of the beautiful and picturesque. They wondered why so many great gifts, such remarkable beauty and talent should have been lavished on one creature. They strove with her—the more she learned the more they tried to teach her; the harder she worked the harder they worked with her.

As the weeks passed on her progress was wonderful. She was often amazed at herself. It was so sweet to study for his sake, to rise in the early morning and work for him.

She watched with the keenness of love the last leaves fall from the trees—she watched with the keen avidity of love for the white snow and the wail of wintery winds, for the long, dark nights and gray, cold dawn. Each one brought her nearer and nearer; every day was a pain past and a nearer joy. Welcome to the nipping frost and the northern winds; welcome the hail, the rain, the sleet—it brought him nearer. How she prayed for him with the loving simplicity of a child. If Heaven would but spare him, would save him from all dangers, would send him sunny skies and favorable winds, would work miracles in his behalf, would avert all accident by rail and road, would bring him back to her longing, loving arms—ah, if the kind, dear Heaven would do this. When she went out for her daily walks she met the poor, the wretched—she would give liberal alms; and when they said:

"God bless your bonny face, my lady," she would say:

"No, not mine; ask him to bless some one else; some one whom I love and who is far away."

It seemed to her like the turning point of a life-time when Christmas Day was passed. Now for the glad New Year which was to bring him back to her.

The first days of the year were months to her. This year was to bring her love, her husband, her marriage—all—blessed new year. When the bells chimed on the first day she went to church, and kneeling with those true of heart and simple of faith as herself she prayed the new year might bring him home.

It was pitiful to see how the one precious hour of the day was the hour in which she wrote to him those long, loving letters that were poems in themselves. He wrote, but not so often; and she saw from the newspaper reports of all that he did and where he went.

She will never forget the day on which she saw the first snow-drop. It was like a message from a lovely modest flower, raising its white head as though it would say to her, "No more tears; he is coming."

She went into a very ecstasy of delight then. Golden primroses and pale cowslips came; the sweet violets bloomed, the green leaves budded, the birds began to sing; it was spring, delicate, beautiful spring, and in June he would come.

She was almost ready for him. It was April now, and she had worked without intermission. She loved to think of his pleasure when he found her so improved. She delighted in picturing what he would say, and how he would reward her with kisses and caresses; how he would praise her for her efforts; how proud even he would be of her.

"I want you to tell me the exact truth," she said to one of the masters.

"I will tell you any truth you wish to hear," he said.

"I want you to tell me this. If you met me anywhere, and did not know that in my youth I had received no training, should you, from anything in my manner, find it out?"

"No," he replied, frankly. "I would defy any one to know that you have not been born the daughter of a duke. Permit me to say, and believe me I am sincere, your manner and conversation are perfection."

She was happy after that; people would not be able to laugh at him and say he had married a low-born wife. She would be equal to any lady in the land when she was Lady Chandos.

The spring was giving place to the laughing, golden-hued summer. He had gone to Italy; his parents were there; they had been spending the spring in Rome and he had joined them.

Nothing, Leone thought, could be more natural. His letters from Rome were not so frequent or so long; but that was no matter; he had less time, perhaps; and being with his parents not so much opportunity.

Her faith in him never lessened, never faltered, never wavered.

True, she wondered at times why he had gone to his parents, why he had joined them after the cruel way in which they had behaved. She could not quite understand.

It seemed to her at times almost disrespect to her that he should associate with them until they had apologized to her, and made amends for the wrong done; but then, she said to herself, he knew best; all he did was well done, and there was nothing to fear.

Then May came—so short the time was growing. Everything he had spoken of was here—the green leaves, the singing birds, the soaring lark, the cooing wood-pigeon. Only a few more weeks now, and the girl grew more beautiful every day as her hope grew nearer its fulfillment.

She was much struck by a conversation she had one day with Signor Corli, her singing-master. She had sung, to his intense delight and satisfaction, one of the most difficult and beautiful cavatinas from "Der Freischutz," and he marveled at her wonderful voice and execution.

"It is ten thousand pities," he said, "that you have a position which forbids you to think of the stage."

She laughed at the time.

"The stage?" she repeated. "Why, signor?"

"Because you have the genius which would make you the finest dramatic singer in the world," he replied; "you would be the very queen of song. I repeat it—it is ten thousand pities you have been placed in such a position the stage could never attract you."

"No, it certainly will not," she said. "But do you think I have really talent for it, signor?"

"No, not talent," he replied, "but genius. Once in every hundred years such a one is given to the world. If you went on the stage I venture to prophesy you would drive the world mad."

She laughed.

"It is just as well, then, that the world is saved from madness," she said.

"It is not well for the world of art," said Signor Corli.

She smiled after he was gone, half flattered by his words, yet half amazed. Could what he said be true? Was this dramatic power, as he called it, the power she had felt within herself which made her different to others? Then she laughed again. What did it matter to her—her life would be spent under the shelter of her husband's love—the husband who was to claim her in June.

CHAPTER XXII
THE RECONCILIATION

Those few months had been filled with excitement for Lord Chandos. The pain he had felt at leaving his wife had been great and hard to bear, but life differs so greatly for men and women. Women must sit at home and weep. For them comes no great field of action, no stir of battle, no rush of fight; their sorrow weighs them down because they have nothing to shake it off. With men it is so different; they rush into action and forget it.

Leone was for some days prostrate with the pains of her sorrow. Lord Chandos suffered acutely for a couple of hours; then came the excitement of his journey, the whirl of travel and adventure, the thousand sources of interest and pleasure.

He was compelled to take his thoughts from Leone. He had a hundred other interests; not that he loved or cared for her less, but that he was compelled to give his attention to the duties intrusted to him. He was compelled to set his sorrow aside.

"I must work now," he said to himself, "I shall have time to think afterward."

He would have time to look his sorrow in the face—now it must stand aside.

When he really brought himself face to face with the world, it was impossible to help feeling flattered by the position he held. Every one congratulated him.

"You start to-morrow," one would say. "Glad to hear you have been chosen," said another. One prophesied continual court favor. Another that he would receive great honors. Every one seemed to consider him quite a favorite of fortune. No one even ever so faintly alluded to his marriage, to the lawsuit, or to the decision.

He was divided between gratitude for the relief and irritation that what had been of such moment to him had been nothing to others. Yet it was a relief to find his darling's name held sacred. He had dreaded to hear about it—to have the matter discussed in any word or shape; but it seemed as though the world had formed one grand conspiracy not to mention it.

Then came the excitement of traveling. His companion, Lord Dunferline, one of the most famous statesmen and noblest peers of England, was many years older than himself. He was a keen, shrewd, clever man, full of practical knowledge and common sense; he was the best friend who could have been chosen for the young lord; and Lady Lanswell congratulated herself on that as a magnificent piece of business. Lord Dunferline had not an iota of sentiment in his whole composition; his idea was that people came into this world to make the very best use they can of it—to increase in wealth, prosperity, and fortune; he believed in buying well, selling well, doing everything well, making the best use of life while it is ours to enjoy; he believed in always being comfortable, bright, cheery; he knew nothing of trouble; sickness, poverty, loss of friends, were all unknown evils to him; he had a prosperous, busy, happy life.

He was one on whom no honor was ever wasted, lost, or thrown away. He made the most of everything; he was rigid in the observation of etiquette, and exacted the utmost deference in his turn. He talked so long and so grandly of the honor conferred on them both that at last Lord Chandos began to find the importance of it too.

The marriage was to take place at Berlin; and they were received with something like royal honors. Society opened its arms to them; the *elite* of Berlin vied with each other in giving *fetes* of all kinds to the English noblemen who represented the English queen.

Still Lord Chandos made time for his letters; he would rather have gone without food than have missed that daily letter from Leone. He wrote to her as often as possible; and his letters would have satisfied even the most loving and sensitive heart. He told her how he loved her, how he missed her, how empty the world seemed, in spite of all its grandeur, because she was not near him—words that comforted her when she read them. Were they true or false? Who shall tell?

Then when the wedding festivities were held, it was not possible for him to write often, his time was so fully occupied. He wrote one sentence that consoled her and it was this—that, although he was surrounded by some of the loveliest women in Europe, there was not a face or a figure that could compare with hers. How she kissed the words as she read them, as women do the written words of the men they love!

It was such a different world, this he lived in now. It was all a blaze of color and brightness, a blaze of jewels, a scene of festivity and mirth, a scene of regal splendor and ever-changing gayety. There was no time for thought or reflection. Lord Chandos was always either being feted or feting others.

The few hasty words dashed off home said but little—it was a different world. If ever at night he found himself under the light of the stars, if he heard the ripple of water, if he stood for a moment watching the swaying of green boughs, his thoughts at once flew to her—the happy, simple home-life at Richmond was like some quiet, beautiful dream, the very memory of which gives rest. He found himself at times wondering how he liked it so well, it was such a contrast to the feted courtier's life he led now. He thought of its calm as he thought of a far-off summer lake.

There had been no flash of jewels, no sheen of cloth of gold there, no grand uniforms, no thrones there, no crowns, no kings or queens—Leone and himself; yet how happy they had been. How he loved her; and his young heart warmed with his love.

What would the world say when she came forth in her imperial loveliness? He liked to think about it. There were many handsome women and beautiful girls, but none to compare to her—not one.

He had intended to love her always with the same warmth and truth; he meant to be constant to her as the needle to the pole. He believed himself to be so; but insensibly the new life changed him—the gay, bright, glistening world influenced him.

After a time—even though he loved her just the same—after a time his thoughts ceased to dwell with such fervent interest on the pretty, simple home. After a time he began to feel his old keen sense of pleasure in all that the world had of the beautiful and bright; he began to feel an interest in its honors and titles.

"I have been lotus-eating," he said to himself; "there is nothing for it but to rouse myself."

In a short time he became very popular in Berlin. The young English noble, Lord Chandos, was as popular as any young sovereign, and there was little need to hurry home.

He went one evening to a very select ball given by the wife of the English embassador, Lady Baden. She smiled when she saw him.

"I have a surprise for you," she said, warmly. "I have what I know to be a most charming surprise. Will you go to the little *salon*, the third on the left? The door is closed, open it, and you will see what you will see."

Lord Chandos bowed and went in the direction she indicated. He did not expect to see anything particular, but he respected the caprices of *les grandes dames*. He opened the door carelessly enough and started back in amaze. There stood his father and mother, his mother's handsome face pale with anxiety, her jeweled arms outstretched, her fine eyes full of love.

"Lance," she said, "my dear son, how good it is to see you again!"

With the cautious avoidance of anything like a scene that distinguishes Englishmen, Lord Chandos turned first and carefully closed the door. Then the earl spoke:

"My dear boy," he said, "I am so pleased to see you!"

But there was no response for either on the face of their son. He bowed coldly, and his mother's jeweled arms fell by her side.

"This is a surprise, indeed," he said. "I should have considered some little notice more agreeable."

"Lance, you may say what you will to me," said the earl, "but remember, not one word to your mother."

"My mother was very cruel to me," he said, coldly, turning from her.

But my lady had recovered herself. She held out her hands with charming grace; she looked at her son with a charming smile.

"My dearest Lance," she said, "children call the physician who cuts off a diseased limb cruel, yet he is most merciful. I am even more merciful than he. I did what I did in the spirit of truest kindness to you, my son."

"Let there be no mention of the word kindness between us," he said. "You nearly broke the heart, and certainly ruined the life of the girl whom I loved. Mother, if that be what you call kindness, then I do not understand the English tongue."

"I did it for your sake, my dearest Lance," said my lady, caressingly.

"One would have thought that, loving the girl with my whole heart, for my sake you would have loved her also."

"Love plays but a poor part in life, Lance," said the Countess of Lanswell. "You have too much sense to mar one of the brightest futures a man has before him for the sake of sentimental nonsense called love."

"Mother," said the young lord, "I shall marry her on my twenty-first birthday. I shall not delay one hour. You understand that clearly?"

The Countess of Lanswell shrugged her graceful shoulders.

"You will certainly be able to do as you like then," she said; "but we need not quarrel over it in prospective; we can wait until the event happens; then it will be quite time enough to discuss what we shall do."

"I am quite resolved," said Lord Chandos. "No persuasion, no argument shall induce me to change."

"I have no arguments to use," said my lady, with a proud laugh. "When you are of age you shall do as you like, marry whom you will—no interference of mine will avail; but let us wait until the time comes. My object in coming here is to seek a reconciliation with you. You are our only son, and though you think me proud and cold, I still love and do not care to be at variance with you. Let us be friends, Lance, at least until you are of age."

She held out her hands again with a smile he could not resist.

"I tell you frankly," continued my lady, "that the young person has been to see me. We had quite a melodramatic interview. I do not wish to vex you, Lance, but she would make a capital fifth-rate actress for a tragedy in a barn."

"Come, my lady, that is too bad," said the earl.

The countess laughed.

"It was really sensational," she said. "The conclusion of the interview was a very solemn threat on her part that she would be revenged upon me, so that I must be prepared for war. But, Lance, let it be as it may, we must be friends. You will not refuse your mother when she asks a favor, and it is the first favor, mind."

"I cannot refuse," he replied. "I will be friends, as you phrase it, mother, but you must change your opinion about Leone."

"Another time," said my lady, with a wave of the hand. "Kiss me now, Lance, and be friends. Shake hands with your father. We are staying at the Hotel France. When the ball is over, join us at supper."

And in that way the solemn reconciliation was effected.

CHAPTER XXIII
A SHREWD SCHEME

There had been nothing very sentimental in the reconciliation scene between parents and son. The earl and Lord Chandos walked home through the quiet streets of Berlin, while my lady drove. They smoked the cigar of peace, while Lord Chandos reported his social triumphs to his father. No more passed between them on the most important of all subjects—his love, his marriage, and the lawsuit; they spoke of anything and everything else. The only words which went from the heart of the father to the heart of the son, were these:

"I am glad you have made friends with my lady, Lance. She has pined after you, and she is so proud. She says nothing, but I know that she has felt the separation from you most keenly. I am glad it is all right; you must not vex her again, Lance."

"I will not, if I can help it," replied the young lord; and so the conversation ended.

Lord Chandos was a clever man, but he was in the hands of a far more clever woman. When a woman has the gift of strategy, she excels in it, and the countess added this to her other accomplishments. She was a magnificent strategist. Her maneuvers were of the finest; quite beyond the power of one less gifted to detect. A man in her skillful hands was a toy, to be played with as she would. The strongest, the wisest, the most honest, the best, were but wax in her hands. She did just as she would with them, and it was so cleverly done, so skillfully managed, that they never had the faintest idea my lady was twining them around her little fingers. She had two modes of strategy. One was by grand moves, one alone of which was enough to carry a nation. The other means was by a series of finest possible details of intrigue.

She said to herself that her son's marriage with this person should be set aside in some fashion or other, and in the end she prevailed. That was by one grand move.

She was equally resolved that her son should marry Lady Marion Erskine, the beauty, the belle, the wealthiest heiress of the season, and by a series of fine, well-directed maneuvers, she was determined to accomplish that.

The fates were propitious to her. Lady Marion Erskine was the niece and ward of Lady Cambrey, and Lady Cambrey, though guardian of one of the wealthiest heiresses in Europe, was herself poor and almost needy. She was a distant relative of Lady Marion's mother, who had asked her to undertake the charge of her child, and Lady Cambrey had been only too pleased to undertake it. It was arranged that she should remain with Lady Marion Erskine until her marriage, and Lady Cambrey was wise enough to know that she must find her future fortune from the marriage. She must use all her influence in favor of the lover who offered the greatest advantages, and Lady Lanswell was the only woman in England who had the wit to find it out.

That was the darling wish of her life, that her son should marry Lady Marion Erskine, the belle, beauty and heiress; and she saw the beginning of her tactics from this fact, that Lady Cambrey's influence would go with the most munificent lover.

They had one interview in London. The countess had invited Lady Cambrey to a five-o'clock tea.

"We have hardly met this year," said the countess. "We are staying in London for a week or two, though it is quite out of season, and I am so pleased to see you. Is Lady Erskine in town?"

"No; I merely came up to give orders for the redecoration of Erskine House; Lady Marion is tired of it as it is."

"I call it a special providence that you should be in town just now," said Lady Lanswell; "I was quite delighted when I heard it. There is nothing I enjoy more than a cup of tea and a chat with a congenial friend."

This from the countess, to whom champagne and politics were baby play, was refreshing. Lady Cambrey was delighted, and before long the two ladies had opened their hearts to each other. The countess, in the most ingenuous manner possible, told her friend the sad history of her dear boy's entanglement and infatuation; how, in his simplicity, he had positively married the girl, and how, fortunately, the law had freed him.

"You know, my dear Lady Cambrey," she said, "it might have been his ruin, but now, thank Heaven," she added, piously, "it is all over, and my boy is free. I have looked all round England to find a suitable wife for him, and there is no one I should like him to marry half so well as Lady Marion Erskine. You see that I show you the cards in my hands very freely."

"It would be a very good match," said Lady Cambrey, thoughtfully.

"If you use your influence, you will not find me ungrateful," continued the countess; "indeed, I should consider myself bound to assist you in every way—my home, carriages, purse, would always be at your services."

"You are very kind," said Lady Cambrey, and in those few words they perfectly understood each other.

The mother knew that she had virtually sold the honor and loyalty of her son, as Lady Cambrey had sold the free will of her niece.

Then they enjoyed a cup of tea, after which my lady became more confidential.

"Promise," she said, "to persuade Lady Marion to spend the winter in Rome and I shall be quite content."

"She will do it if I advise it," said Lady Cambrey. "She is very docile."

"We can decide on our plans of action when we meet there," said the countess. "The chief thing is to keep all idea of 'our ideas' from my son. Instead of drawing his attention to Lady Marion, we must seem to avoid bringing them together. I understand men. The first result of that will be an intense anxiety on his part to see her. Do you understand?"

"Quite," said Lady Cambrey. "It is really a pleasure to meet some one who understands human nature as you do, Lady Lanswell."

The countess smiled graciously at the compliment, feeling as though it were well deserved.

So it was arranged, and Lady Cambrey's part of the plot was very easy. She had but to suggest to her niece that she should spend the winter in Rome and she would at once fall in with her wish.

Lady Lanswell had settled in her own mind the plan of the whole campaign. She intended to go to Berlin, there to seek a reconciliation with her son, and persuade him to go to Rome with them. She managed it all so well, saying nothing at first of their intended journey, but making herself very agreeable to her son. She brought to him all the flattering things said of them. She studied every little whim, wish, or caprice. She put him on a pedestal and made an idol of him. She was all that was gay, amiable, pleasant and kind. She made herself not only his friend and companion, but everything else in the world to him. She was gay, amiable, gracious, witty.

With her still beautiful face and fine figure, she made herself so attractive and charming that Lord Chandos was soon entirely under her influence.

How many mothers might have taken a hint for the management of their sons from her. She found no fault with cigars or latch-keys. She was the essence of all that was kind, yet, at the same time, she was so animated, so bright, so witty, that the time spent with her passed quickly as a dream. Lord Chandos did not even like to think of parting from her; and then, when she was most kind and most attentive to him, she mentioned Rome.

"We are going to Rome, Lance, for the winter," said the countess to her son.

He looked up from the paper he was reading in blank amazement.

"To Rome, mother? Why, what is taking you there?"

"I find there will be some very nice English people there," she said; "I am tired of Paris; it is one eternal glare; I long for the mysterious quiet and dreamy silence of Rome. It will be a pleasant change. I really like a nice circle of English people out of England."

That was the beginning. She was too wise and diplomatic to ask him to go with them. She contented herself by speaking before him of the gayeties they expected, the pleasures they anticipated; then, one day, as they were discussing their plans, she turned to him and said:

"Lance, what do you intend doing this winter? Are you going back to England to think over the fogs?"

"I am not quite sure," he said; and then he wondered why she said nothing about going to Rome with them. At last, when she saw the time had come, she said, carelessly:

"Lance, if you do not care about returning to England, come with us to Rome."

"I shall be delighted."

He looked up with an air of relief. After all, he could not see Leone until summer: why return to England and melancholy? He might just as well enjoy himself in Rome. He knew what select and brilliant circles his mother drew around her. Better for him to be the center of one of those than alone and solitary in England.

"Of course," said the countess, diplomatically, "I will not urge you, I leave it entirely to you. If you think what the fashion of the day calls your duties demand that you should return, do not let me detain you, even for one day."

"I have no particular duties," he said, half gloomily.

He would have liked his mother to have insisted on his going, to have been more imperative, but as she left it entirely to him, he thought her indifferent over the matter.

He was a true man. If she had pressed him to go, urged him, tried to persuade him, he would have gone back to England, and the tragedy of after years would never have happened. As it occurred to him that his mother simply gave the invitation out of politeness, and did not care whether he accepted or not, he decided on going. So when the festivities of Berlin were all ended, he wrote to Leone, saying that he was going to spend the winter with his parents in Rome; that if he could not spend it with her, it mattered little enough to him where is was; but that he was longing with all his heart for the thirtieth of June.

CHAPTER XXIV
IN THE HANDS OF A CLEVER WOMAN

"In Rome," said Lady Marion Erskine, to her cousin; "how strange it seems to be really here! Do you know that when I was a little girl and learned Roman history I always thought it a grand fable. I never believed such a place really existed. Rome is a link between the old world and the new."

"Yes," replied Lady Cambrey, "it is quite true, my dear."

She had no notion, even ever so vague, of what her beautiful young kinswoman meant.

Lady Cambrey was not given to the cultivation of ideas, but she was always most amiably disposed to please Lady Marion. It was something very delightful to be the chaperon of a beautiful young heiress like Lady Erskine, and she was always delighted to agree with Lady Marion's words, opinions, and ideas.

Lady Marion was submissive and gentle by nature. She was one of the class of women born to be ruled and not to rule. She could never govern, but she could obey. She could not command, but she could carry out the wishes of others to the last letter.

Lady Cambrey, from motives of her own, wanted her to go to Rome. She had managed it without the least trouble.

"Marion," she said, "have you decided where to spend the winter?"

"No," was the quiet reply, "I have not thought much about it, Aunt Jane; have you?"

The words were so sweetly and placidly spoken.

"Yes, I have thought a great deal about it. I hear that a great many very nice English people have gone to Rome. They say that there will be one of the nicest circles in Europe there."

"In Rome," said Lady Marion, musingly. "Do I know many of those who are going?"

"Yes, some of our own set. One of the great Roman princes, Dorio, has just married a beautiful English girl, so that for this year at least the English will be all the rage in Rome. I should like to go there. I knew some of the Dorio family, but not the one just married."

"Then, if you would like it, we will go there," said Lady Marion; "I shall be pleased if you are."

So without any more difficulty the first part of the programme was carried out, and Lady Marion Erskine, with her chaperon, Lady Jane Cambrey, settled in Rome for the winter. They took a beautifully furnished villa, called the Villa Borgazi, near to some famous gardens. Lady Cambrey took care that, while she reveled in Italian luxuries, no English comfort should be wanting—the Villa Borgazi soon had in it all the comforts of an English home.

She came home one morning, after many hours of shopping, with a look of some importance on her face.

"Marion," she said, "I have heard that the Lanswells are here. I am very pleased. I thought of calling this afternoon; if you are tired, I will go alone."

And from the tone of her voice, rather than her words, Lady Marion fancied that she would prefer to pay her visit alone.

"You remember the Countess of Lanswell; she was la grande dame par excellence in London last summer. She admired you very much, if you recollect."

"I remember her," said Lady Marion; then, with some interest, she added, "It was her son, Lord Chandos, who got himself into such difficulties, was it not?"

Lady Cambrey was slightly taken by surprise; her ward had always shown such a decided distaste for gossip of all kinds that she trusted she had never even heard of this little escapade. However, Lady Marion's question must be answered.

She shook her head gravely.

"It was not his fault, poor boy!" she said; "his mother has told me all about it. I am very sorry for him."

"Why does he deserve so much pity?" she asked.

And Lady Cambrey answered:

"He was but a boy at the time, and she, this person, a dairy-maid, I believe, took advantage of his generosity, and either persuaded him to marry her, or wrung from him some promise of marriage when he should be of age."

"I thought," said straightforward Lady Marion, "that he was married, and his parents had petitioned that the marriage be considered null and void as he was under age."

"I think, my dear," said the diplomatic aunt, "that it would be as well not to mention this. Two things are certain, if Lord Chandos had been properly married, his marriage could never have been set aside; the other is, that the countess can never endure the mention of her son's misfortune."

"Do you know Lord Chandos?" asked Lady Marion, after a time.

"Yes, I know him, and I consider him one of the most charming men I have ever met, a perfect cavalier and chivalrous gentleman."

"That is high praise," said Lady Marion, thoughtfully.

"I know of none higher," said her aunt, and then with her usual tact changed the subject; but more than once that day Lady Marion thought of the man who was a cavalier and a gentleman.

Meanwhile the time passed pleasantly for the countess and her son. They were staying at the grand palace of the Falconis—once the home of princes, but now let by the year to the highest bidder. Lady Lanswell took good care that her son should be well amused; every morning a delicious little sketch of the day's amusement was placed before him; the countess laid herself out to please him as man had never been pleased before.

The countess saw that he received letters from England continually. She was above all vulgar intrigue, or she might have destroyed more than one-half which came, without his seeing them. She would not do that; the war she carried into the enemy's camp was of the most refined and thorough-going kind. She would set aside a marriage on a mere quibble, but she would not destroy a letter. She had said, openly and defiantly to her son's face, that she felt sure he would not remarry Leone in June, but she would stoop to no vulgar way to prevent it.

It often happened that the countess herself opened the letter-bag. When she did so, and there was a letter from Leone, she always gave it to her son with a smile, in which there was just a shade of contempt.

"Another letter," she would say; "my dear Lance, you contribute quite your share to the inland revenue."

She never alluded to Leone, but she did permit herself, at rare intervals, to relate some ludicrous anecdotes of people who had suffered from a severe attack of love.

Lord Chandos found the time pass very pleasantly; he said to himself he might as well remain in Rome and enjoy himself, as go back to England and be miserable. Wherever he went, he could not see Leone. He would not trust himself; he loved her too much, if he were in the same land, not to be near her.

Being in Rome, he did as the Romans did; he amused himself to the very utmost of his power; he seized every golden hour that passed, and though he loved Leone as much as ever, he ceased to feel the keen pain which their separation had caused him at first. One morning, from the Countess of Lanswell to Lady Jane Cambrey, there passed a little note. It said, simply:

"Shall we take the first step to-night? Bring Lady Marion to the Princess Galza's concert, and leave the rest to me."

Lady Cambrey lost no time. She sought her ward and said so much to her about the concert, for which they both had invitations, that Lady Marion was eager to go.

"I must superintend your toilet, Marion; as it is your first appearance in Roman society, you must make a favorable impression."

She selected one of the loveliest toilets that could have been chosen — a white brocade, embroidered with flowers of the palest blue.

"You must wear pearls and pale-blue flowers," she said, "and you will find that to-morrow every one will be talking of the new beauty that has risen over Rome."

Lady Marion looked perfectly beautiful; she was perfect in her style, the very queen of blondes, with her soft, shining hair, and eyes blue as the summer skies. Her face was the purest mixture of rose and white, with the dainty, delicate color described in that one line:

"Crimson shell, with white sea foam."

She had a beautiful, fresh mouth, a dimpled chin, a neck and shoulders white as ivory, arms so rounded and white it was a treat to see them. She was of the queenly type — tall, with the promise of a grand womanhood; her white throat was firm, her arms rounded and strong; she was the ideal of an English gentlewoman; her pure, proud face, clear eyes, and sweet lips were beautiful beyond words. When she was dressed that evening for the princess' concert she looked most charming. Lady Cambrey had said truly that among the dark-eyed daughters of Italy she would shine white and fair as a white dove among colored ones.

Her dress was the perfection of taste—it was trimmed with pale-blue forget-me-nots and white heath; a string of pearls was twisted in her fair hair, and another round her white throat.

"If he does not fall in love with her," said Lady Cambrey to herself, "it will be because he has no admiration left in him for any one except his dairy-maid."

Lady Lanswell had been very successful in her diplomacy. She had spoken of the concert before her son, who had received an invitation, but said nothing about his going. He listened in silence, wondering if she would ask him to go with her, saying to himself that he should decline, for he did not like concert-going. Then, as she did not ask him, he began to feel piqued over it and wonder why.

After a short time he volunteered to go, and my lady took it very coolly, reminding him of how often he had grown tired of a hot concert-room. Then he resolved to go and made arrangements accordingly, his mother smiling sweetly all the time. When all was settled, and he had quitted the room, my lady laughed quietly. It was wonderful with what bland sweetness and fine tact she managed men. She could lead her son as though he were deaf, blind, and dumb, yet of all men he believed himself most firm and secure in his opinion.

Heaven help the man who falls helplessly into the hands of a clever woman!

CHAPTER XXV
THE INTRODUCTION

If Lady Lanswell had purposely designed the meeting between her son and the beautiful blonde to have taken place in the most picturesque spot in Europe, she could not have chosen better. The great *salon* of the Palazzo Golza had, in former days, been used as a royal audience-room; the noblest princes in Rome had met there, and had given audience to the grandest nobles. It was a superb apartment; there was a background of purple tapestry from which the blonde loveliness of the English girl shone resplendent as a snow-drop on a black ground. There were many beautiful women present; the Princess Ainla, whose dark beauty was the wonder of all who saw it; the famous American belle, Miss Sedmon, whose auburn hair resembled that given by the old masters to the Madonna; but there was not one in that vast assembly who could vie with Lady Marion.

The Countess of Lanswell, with her son, was one of the last to enter the *salon*; with one keen, comprehensive glance the countess took in, as it were, the whole situation; she saw the pure, proud face of Lady Erskine, saw that she was seated in the very place where her beauty was seen to the best advantage, then she took her seat, never even looking in that direction, and saying nothing to her son.

It was just like laying a trap for a bird—he fell into it with the same helplessness.

Lady Lanswell neither looked at Lady Erskine nor her son, yet she knew exactly the moment when his eyes first fell on her. She saw him start; then she sat quite still, waiting for the question she knew must follow.

It came at last.

"Mother," he said, "who is that beautiful girl?"

My lady looked at him with languid eyes.

"What beautiful girl, Lance? There are so many."

"An English girl, I am sure. She has a string of pearls in her hair. Who can she be?"

Still Lady Lanswell feigned ignorance. She looked on the wrong side of the room, and she affected not to understand where he meant, and when she could affect no longer, she said:

"Do you mean Lady Marion Erskine, the young lady near Princess Golza?"

"Yes, it must be Lady Erskine," he replied. "How beautiful she is, mother. She shines like a fair pearl with that background of dark tapestry. I heard some one say yesterday that she was in Rome. What a perfect face."

My lady looked at it coldly.

"Do you think so, Lance?" she said. "I thought that you gave the preference to dark beauties."

His heart went back for one moment to the beautiful, passionate face he had seen by the mill stream. The gorgeous *salon*, the beautiful women, the peerless face of Lady Marion, the exquisite music, all floated away from him, and he was once more by the mill-stream, with Leone's face before him. So strong, so vivid was the memory, that it was with difficulty he refrained from calling the name aloud.

My lady guessed by the sudden expression of pain on his face where his thoughts had gone. She recalled them.

"Tastes differ so greatly," she said. "Do you really consider Lady Marion beautiful, Lance?"

"Yes, I have seen no one more lovely," he answered.

Then the countess dismissed the subject—too much must not be said at once. She did not mention Lady Marion's name again that evening, but she saw that her son looked often at her, and she smiled to think the bait had taken.

Again they were walking through the vast gardens of one of the Roman palaces, when the whole party met. Lady Cambrey was with her niece; Lord Chandos was near the countess, but not close by her side. The ladies met, exchanged a few words, then parted, the countess not having made the least effort to introduce her son; he spoke of it afterward.

"Mother," he said, "you did not introduce me to Lady Erskine."

Lady Lanswell smiled calmly.

"It was out of pure consideration for her; they tell me she has so many admirers in Rome. From what I know of her, you would not be quite in her style."

The words piqued him.

"Why not?" he asked.

His mother laughed again.

"She is very proud, Lance, and very exclusive. I need say no more."

My lady always knew exactly when to leave off. She turned away now, leaving her son with the impression that Lady Erskine would not care to know him, on account of his unfortunate love affair.

They were destined to meet again that evening. A ball was given by an English lady, Mrs. Chester, who had one of the best houses in Rome. Lady Erskine looked very beautiful; her dress was of pale blue velvet, superbly trimmed with white lace; she wore diamonds in her hair, and carried a bouquet of white lilies in her hand. She was the belle of the ball, and it was Mrs. Chester who introduced Lord Chandos to her. She was quite innocent of any intrigue, but had she been the chosen confidante of Lady Lanswell, she could not have done more to further her views. She had been dancing with Lord Chandos herself, and began to speak to him of the beautiful blonde.

"Lady Marion Erskine realizes my idea of a fair woman," said Mrs. Chester. "I have read the words in prose and poetry, now I understand them."

"I do not know Lady Erskine," said the young earl.

"Not know her. Why, I should have thought that all the Englishmen in Rome knew their beautiful country-woman."

"I have never been introduced to her," said Lord Chandos.

"Then this is the last hour in which you shall lay any such complaint against fate," said Mrs. Chester. "Come with me, my lord."

Like all other English ladies in Rome, Mrs. Chester had a great admiration for the heir of the Lanswells. It was impossible to withhold it. He was so handsome, so brave and gallant, with the bearing of a prince, the chivalry of a knight, and in his temper the sweet, sunny grace of a woman. They all liked him; he seemed to have the geniality, the generosity, the true nobility of an Englishman, without the accompanying reserve and gloom. At that time there was no one more popular in Rome than the young lord, about whom so many romantic stories were told. He followed Mrs. Chester to where Lady Marion stood, the brilliant center of a brilliant group. It pleased him to see what deference was paid to him—how Italian princes and French dukes made way when Mrs. Chester presented him to the beautiful heiress.

The first moment the proud clear eyes smiled in his face he liked her. She was most charming in her manner; she had not the fire and passion of Leone; she was not brilliant, original or sparkling, but she was sweet, candid, amiable, and gentle.

One found rest in her—rest in the blue eyes, in the sweet, smiling lips, in the soft, low voice, in the graceful, gentle movements—rest and content.

She never irritated, never roused any one to any great animation; she received rather than gave ideas; she was one of those quiet, gentle, amiable women whose life resembles the rippling of a brook rather than the rush of a stream. She looked with a smile into the handsome face of the young lord, and she, too, liked him.

They stood together for a few minutes while Lord Chandos begged for a dance, and even during the brief time more than one present thought what a handsome pair they were. Lord Chandos was much pleased with her—the low voice, the exquisitely-refined accent, the gentle grace, all delighted him.

She lacked passion, power, fire, originality, the chief things which went for the making up of Leone's character; no two people could be more dissimilar, more unlike; yet both had a charm for Lord Chandos; with the one he found the stimulant of wit and genius, with the other sweetest rest.

They had several dances together; in her quiet, gentle way Lady Marion confided to him that she preferred Englishmen to Italians, whom she thought wanting in frankness and ease.

"Why did you come to Rome?" asked Lord Chandos; and the beautiful blonde was almost at a loss how to answer the question. The only answer that she could give was that Lady Cambrey had first mentioned it.

"It was not from any great wish, then, to see the antiquities or the art treasures of Rome?" asked Lord Chandos, thinking as he spoke with what rapture Leone would have thought of a visit to Italy.

"No, it was not that, although I would not have missed seeing Rome on any account. What brought you here, Lord Chandos?"

He also hesitated for a moment, then he answered:

"I really do not know. I came, so far as I know my own mind, because my mother came," and then their eyes met with a curious, half-laughing gaze.

It was strange that they should have both come there without having any clear or distinct notion why.

"It seems to me," said Lord Chandos, "that we are both under guidance."

"I am glad, for my own part," said Lady Erskine. "It is much easier to be guided than to guide. I find it easier to obey than to command."

"Do you?" he asked, laughingly. "You will find it very easy then some day 'to love, honor and obey.'"

"I do not doubt it," said the beautiful heiress, calmly. "I should not care to go through life alone; I want a stronger soul than my own to lean on."

And again Lord Chandos went back in thought to the noble, self-reliant girl who would hold her own against the world if need should be.

And yet he liked Lady Marion; her graceful, languid helplessness had a great charm for him. When he bade her good-evening, it was with the hope that they would soon meet again.

CHAPTER XXVI
MAN'S FICKLENESS

They did meet again and again, always with pleasure on his part, and very soon with something else on hers. Wherever she was she looked out above the dark Italian heads for the tall, erect figure and brave English face of Lord Chandos. She did not talk much to him, but there was a light in her eyes and a smile on her face most pleasant to see when he was near. She never sought him, she never, either directly or indirectly, gave him any idea of where she was going. She never contrived to meet him, but there were very few days during which they did not spend some hours together.

Lady Lanswell paid not the least attention when Lady Erskine joined their party. She was kind and cordial, but she never made the least effort either to entertain her or to induce her to stay. If ever by chance Lord Chandos named her, his mother received the remark in total silence—in fact, she completely ignored her—in which she showed her tact. Had she ever made the least attempt to bring them together, he would have seen through the little plot, and would have taken fright; as it was, the net was so skillfully woven, that he was caught in it before he knew there was a net at all. If the countess arranged a party for any place, she never included the young heiress among her guests.

So that their frequent interviews were so completely accidental, neither of them thought anything of it; they drifted unawares into an intimacy at which every one smiled but themselves. It flattered Lord Chandos to see dukes and princes drawback when he came near the beautiful heiress, as though it were quite understood that he had the right to claim her attention—to see a proud Roman prince, with a long pedigree, make way with a bow—to see a courtly French duke resign the seat he had waited half the night for—to see the eyes of envy that followed him—it flattered him, and he never asked where it would end.

Lady Lanswell saw it all with well-pleased eyes, but said nothing; she was biding her time.

One evening they met at Mrs. Chester's. There was neither ball nor party, but a quiet at home; and their friendship made greater strides than it hitherto had done.

Some one asked Lady Erskine to sing. Lord Chandos looked at her.

"Do you sing?" he asked.

And she answered with a quiet smile:

"Yes, it is one of the few things I do well enough to content myself. I have a good voice and I sing well."

"Are you what people call fond of music?" he asked.

And she answered:

"Yes, I often put my own thoughts to music, and if I meet any words that seem to me very good or very sweet I never rest until I have found a melody that fits them. I came across some the other day. Shall I sing them to you?"

There was a slight commotion in the room when people saw the beautiful English girl led to the piano. She turned with a smile to Lord Chandos.

"My song is English," she said, "and will not be understood by every one."

"I shall understand it," he said; "you must sing it to me."

When he heard the words he understood the blush that covered her face.

"I should change my song," she said, "if another came into my mind. These words are by a poetess I read and admire much. It is called 'Somewhere or Other.'"

She sung in a sweet, pure voice; there was neither fire, power, nor passion in it; but the words were clear and distinct.

> "'Somewhere or other there must surely be
> The face not seen, the voice not heard,
> The heart that never yet—never yet—ah, me,
> Made answer to my word.
>
> "'Somewhere or other, may be near or far,
> Past land and sea, clear out of sight,
> Beyond the wandering moon, the star,
> That tracks her night by night.
>
> "'Somewhere or other, may be far or near,
> With just a wall, a hedge between,
> With just the last leaves of the dying year
> Fallen on a turf so green.'"

He stood by her side while she sung, his eyes fixed on her face, thinking how pure and fair she was. When the sweet strain of music ended, he said:

"Somewhere or other—you will find it soon, Lady Marion."

"Find what?" she asked.

"'The heart that has never yet answered a word,'" he replied, quoting the words of her song. "People do often meet their fate without knowing it."

When he saw the fair face grow crimson he knew at once that she thought she was speaking of himself and her. After that there seemed to be a kind of understanding between them. When others were speaking he would quote the words: "Somewhere or other," and then Lady Marion would blush until her face burned. So a kind of secret understanding grew between them without either of them quite understanding how it was.

Lady Lanswell was quite happy; the bait was taking; there was no need for her to interfere, all was going well.

"Mother," said Lord Chandos, "I cannot understand it; you invite all the old dowagers and spinsters in Rome to your afternoon teas and *soirees*, but you never invite any young ladies, and there are some very pretty ones."

"My dear Lance, I know it, and deeply regret it; but you see I have no one to entertain young ladies."

He raised his head with an injured air.

"You have me," he replied.

The countess laughed.

"True, I have you, but I mean some one free and eligible."

"Am I not free and eligible?" he asked, quickly; and then his brave young face grew fiery red under his mother's slow, sneering smile. "I do not mean that; of course I am not free or eligible in that sense of the word, yet I think I am quite as well able to entertain young and pretty girls as old dowagers."

Lady Lanswell looked keenly at him.

"My dear Lance, I will do anything to please you," she said, "but if you persist in considering yourself an engaged man, you must forego the society of charming girls. I have no desire for another visit from that tempestuous young person."

Lance, Lord Chandos, shuddered at the words—"a tempestuous young person"—this was the heroine of his romance, his beautiful Leone, whose voice always came to him with the whisper of the wind, and the sweet ripple of falling water. "A tempestuous young person," his beautiful Leone, whose passionate kisses were still warm on his lips, whose bitter tears seemed wet on his face—Leone, who was a queen by right divine. He turned angrily away, and Lady Lanswell, seeing that she had gone far enough, affected not to see his anger, but spoke next in a laughing tone of voice.

"You see, Lance, in my eyes you are very eligible, indeed, and it seems to me almost cruel to bring you into a circle of young girls, one of whom might admire you, while I know that you can never admire them. Is it not so?"

"I am not free, mother, you know as well as all the world knows; still, I repeat it that it is no reason why you should fill the house with dowagers and never bring the bloom of a young face near it."

"I will do as you wish, Lance," said my lady, and her son smiled.

"Though I consider myself, and am, in all solemn truth, engaged, still that does not make me a slave, mother. I am free to do as I like."

"Certainly," said my lady, and for some minutes there was silence between them.

Lord Chandos broke in.

"Why do you never ask Lady Erskine to visit you, mother? She is a charming girl, and you like her."

The countess looked at him straight in the face.

"I think it more prudent not to do so," she said. "Lady Marion is one of the most perfect women I know; I know, too, that she admires you, and as you are not free to admire her, you are better apart."

He flung himself down on the carpet, and laid his handsome head on his mother's knee, looking up to her with coaxing eyes, as he had done when he was a boy.

"Does she really admire me, mother? This beautiful girl, who has all the grandees in Rome at her feet—does she really admire me?"

"I have said it," laughed my lady.

"Who told you, mother? How do you know?"

"I shall not tell you, Lance; sufficient for you to know that it is quite true, and that I consider I am simply acting as prudence dictates. I should admire you, Lance, if I were a young girl myself."

"I am very much flattered," he said, slowly. "Even if it be true, mother, I do not quite see why you should think so much prudence needful. I admire Lady Marion; why should we not be friends?"

"Would the tempestuous young person like it, Lance?" asked my lady.

And it is very painful to state that an exceedingly strong and highly improper word came from between Lord Chandos' closed lips.

"Do not tease me, mother. I see no harm in it; if I did, be quite sure I would not do it. Lady Marion and I can always be friends. I like her and admire her; there is a certain kind of repose about her that I enjoy. Why should we not be friends?"

"Be friends if you like," said Lady Lanswell; "but if, in the course of a few weeks, you find that mutual admiration does not answer, do not blame me."

From that day Lady Lanswell laid aside all pretense at scruple, and allowed matters to go as they would; she visited the young heiress constantly, and smiled when she saw that her son was becoming, day by day, more attracted to her. She noticed another thing, too, with keen pleasure, and it was that, although the same number of letters came from England, not half so many went there.

"A step in the right, direction," thought my lady; "I shall succeed after all."

To do Lord Chandos justice, he was quite blind to the danger that surrounded him. He intended to be true to Leone—he had no other desire, no other wish—he had never contemplated for one moment the act of deserting her; he would have denounced any one who even hinted at such a thing.

But he was young, she was beautiful, they were in sunny Italy. And he never dreamed of loving her.

They were friends, that was all; they were to be exceptions to the general rule—they were to be friends, without any of the elements of love or flirtation marring their intercourse.

Only friends. Yet in the beginning of May when Lady Cambrey and her ward declined to return to England for the summer, but resolved to spend it in Naples, Lord Chandos went there also, without feeling at all sure that he would be back in London by June.

CHAPTER XXVII
"TELL ME YOUR SECRET"

The sunny summer days at Nice—who can tell of their beauty, the glory of the sunny blue sky, the glory of the foliage, the sweet, balmy breath of the wind, which seemed daily to bring with it the perfume from a hundred new flowers? How did the time pass? No one knew; it was a long roll of pleasure and gayety. There was pleasure enough in being out-of-doors; a picnic there was a very simple matter. They heard of a very beautiful spot, drove there, remained there so long as it suited them, then went back again. There were, as there always are, some very nice English people at Nice, but none like fair, sweet Lady Marion.

As the charm of her sweet character grew upon him, Lord Chandos liked her more and more. He enjoyed her society. She was not witty, she could not amuse a whole room full of people, she could not create laughter, she was not the cause of wit in others, nor did talking to her awake the imagination and arouse all the faculties of one's mind.

Talking to her was rest, grateful as the shade of green trees after the glare of the summer's sun. The sweet voice, the clear, refined accent, the gracious and gentle thoughts, the apt quotations, all were something to remember. She was by no means a genius, but she was well read, and had the power of remembering what she read, had the gift of making most of her knowledge. If you wished for an hour's interesting conversation, there was no one like Lady Marion. She had such curious odds and ends of information; her reading had been universal. She had some knowledge on every point. She had her own ideas, too, clearly defined and straightforward, not liable to vary with every paper she read, and in these days one learns to be thankful for consistency. On those warm, lovely, life-giving days, when the sun and sky, earth and air, flower and tree did their best, it was Lord Chandos who liked to linger under the vines talking to this fair girl whose very face was a haven of rest.

He never thought of love at all in connection with her, he felt so sure of the one great fact that he loved his wife; he forgot that there could be such a thing as danger or temptation. Lady Marion had grown to love him; it was impossible to help it; he had great and grave faults, as all men have, but he was so brave and fearless, so gallant and generous, so kind and chivalrous, no one could help loving him; his faults were lovable, a fact that was much to be regretted; since, if they had been disagreeable, he might have been cured of them.

Lady Marion, in her quiet, gentle fashion, had learned to love him. She appealed to him continually; the reading of a book, the singing of a song, the arrangement of a day's plans, the choosing of acquaintances, on each and all of these points she made him her confidant and guide; it was so gently and so naturally done that he insensibly guided her whole life without knowing it. What Lord Chandos said or thought was her rule. It was such a pleasure to guide and advise her, she was so yielding, so gentle, she took such a pride in obeying him; she would apologize to him at times and say:

"I told you, Lord Chandos, that I must always have a stronger mind than my own to lean upon."

He listened to the words with a smile, but it did just occur to him that she would not have his mind to lean upon much longer, for he must go home to England to Leone. Once or twice lately he had been much struck with Lady Marion's manner. She was so gracious, so charming with him. When he had suddenly entered the room where she was sitting he had seen the crimson blush that rose over her white neck and brow. He noticed too, that she had rarely, if ever, raised her eyes to his face until that blush had passed away, lest they should tell their own secret. And one day he said to her:

"Why do you never give me a frank, open look, Lady Marion—such as you gave me always when I knew you first? now you turn your face away, and your eyes droop. Have I displeased you?"

"No," she replied, gently; "it is not that; you could not displease me."

"Then you are keeping some secret from me," he said, and she smiled a slow, sweet, half-sad smile that stirred his heart with curious power.

"I have no secret," she said; "or if I have it matters little to any one but myself."

"Tell me your secret, Lady Marion," he said, with a sigh.

"I will answer you in the words of my favorite poet," she said; "listen, Lord Chandos."

They were standing under the shade of a clustering vine, the wind that kissed both fair young faces was full of perfume, the flowers that bloomed around them were full of sweetest odors, the whisper of the odorous wind was no sweeter than the voice in which she quoted the words:

"'Perhaps some languid summer day,
When drowsy birds sing less and less,
And golden fruit is ripening to excess;
If there's not too much wind or too much cloud,
And the warm wind is neither still nor loud,
Perhaps my secret I may say,
Or—you may guess.'"

"What beautiful words," he cried. "It seems to me, Lady Marion, that you have a whole storehouse full of the most apt and beautiful quotations. You ought to have been a poet yourself."

"No," she replied, "I can appreciate, but I cannot invent. I can make the words and the thoughts of a poet my own, but I cannot invent or create; I have no originality."

"You have what is rarer, still," he cried; "a graceful humility that raises you higher than any other gift could do."

He spoke so warmly that she looked up in wonder, but Lord Chandos turned abruptly away; there might be danger if he said more.

So the lovely, leafy month of May ended, and June began. Then Lord Chandos began to think of home—his birthday was on the thirtieth of June, and he knew what he had promised for that day. He could see the pretty, flower-covered window—the roses which must be thrust aside—the gate he had promised to open; he remembered every detail. Well, it was all very pretty and very pleasant; but, he could not tell why, the bloom of the romance was gone, that was quite certain. He had learned to associate poetry with the pale moonlight and golden hair, with a very fair face and a soft ripple of sweet speech. Still he intended most honorably to keep his promise; he took great delight, too, in thinking of Leone's passionate happiness, of her beautiful face, of the ecstasy of welcome she would give him. Then, of course, he must marry her; the very day after that would be the first of July, and, for the first time, he thought of his coming marriage with a sigh—it would separate him so entirely from his mother, and from Lady Marion; in all probability he would never see much of her again. He thought more of her loss than of his own.

"How she will miss me," he said to himself; "she will have no one to consult, no one to advise her. I wish we could always be the same good friends as now."

Then it occurred to him that perhaps, after all, his wife would not care to know that he was on such confidential terms with any one but herself.

He would have felt far less sure of either his return or his marriage if he had overheard a slight conversation that took place between his mother and Lady Marion. The Countess of Lanswell called one day and took the young heiress out for a drive with her; when they were seated, driving through scenery so beautiful one could hardly believe it to be a fallen world, the countess in her sweetest manner, which she knew how to make quite irresistible, said:

"Lady Marion, I want you to help me to do something, if you will."

"You know I will do anything I can for you, Lady Lanswell," said the girl, gently; "I could have no greater pleasure."

She did not add, because I love your son, but this was in her mind, and the countess quite understood it.

She continued:

"You know how I love my dear and only son, how anxious I am for his welfare, how devoted to his interests."

"I can imagine it all," said Lady Marion, warmly.

The countess went on:

"He has an idea, a quixotic, foolish and most unhappy one, one that if carried out will mar his life and ruin his prospects, and in the end break his heart. Now, I want you to help me break off this idea; he thinks of returning to England in June, and if he does, all hope is over. He never allows himself to be coerced or persuaded; as to the word 'marriage' it would be a fatal one, but we might, I am sure, influence him—that is, if you will help me."

"I will do all I can," said Lady Marion, earnestly; her sweet face had grown very pale.

"He must not go back to England," said the countess: "we must keep him here until August—how can we do it?"

"Ask him to stay," said the young girl, simply; "that seems the most straightforward plan."

"Yes, but it would not be of the least use; he must be influenced. Now I think that he prefers your society to any other; suppose you plan a tour through Spain, and ask him to go with us."

The pale face flushed.

"I will if you think he would agree," she replied.

"I believe he would; if he seems inclined to refuse, and you are in the least degree disturbed over it, I believe firmly that he will go. I do not think that he knows the strength of his own feelings for you. Let us try it. You can speak to me about it before him, then I will leave you with him and you can finish your good work."

"He is not likely to be vexed, is he?" asked Lady Marion, timidly.

"Vexed, my dear child, no; he will consider himself highly favored. You see it is in this way. I cannot show any eagerness for it, and you can. My son would suspect my motive; he knows yours must be a good one, and will feel sure that it is liking for his society—you do like it, do you not, Lady Marion?"

"Yes, I cannot deny it," replied the young girl, "and I will help you all I can. You do not wish him to return to England in June. I will do my best to keep him away."

And the question was—would she succeed?

CHAPTER XXVIII
HOW IT HAPPENED

"Mother," said Lord Chandos, "I never knew a month pass as this has done—the days have wings. It is the sixteenth to-day, and it does not seem to be twenty-four hours since it was the first."

"That shows, at least, that life has been pleasant to you," said the countess.

"Yes, it has been very pleasant," he replied, and then he sighed deeply.

"Why do you sigh, Lance? The future can be as pleasant as the past, can it not?"

He looked up half impatiently.

"I sigh to think that my share in it is all ended. I must be in England by the end of June."

"Make the most of the time left," said my lady; "there's another week, at least. Let us go everywhere and see everything. In all probability, we shall not meet at Nice again."

He had expected contradiction, he had expected his mother to oppose his desire of returning home, and he was slightly piqued to find that so far from opposing him, she seemed to fall into the idea as though it were the most natural one.

"I think," he pursued, "that if I leave here on the twenty-seventh that will be soon enough."

"Yes," said the countess, quietly. "It is not such a long journey, after all."

So she would not oppose him, she would not argue with him, but left him to take his own way. The handsome face grew shadowed, the frank eyes troubled. It is very hard when a man cannot force any one to contradict him. He rose from his chair, he walked uneasily up and down the room; he spoke almost nervously on one or two points and then he said:

"Mother, I suppose you know what I intend doing."

She looked up at him with the blandest smile and the sweetest air.

"Doing, Lance—about the boat to-night, do you mean?"

She purposely affected to misunderstand him.

"The boat?" he repeated. "No, I mean about—my—my—future—my marriage."

"I cannot say that I know what you intend doing, Lance, but I am quite sure you will never again have the bad taste to offend your father and me. I can trust you so far."

He looked still more uncomfortable; he could always manage the countess better when she was angry than when she was amiable. He stopped abruptly before her, and looking at her said:

"I must marry Leone, mother, I must."

"Very well, Lance. When you are twenty-one, you can do as you like."

"Oh, mother," cried the young lord, "be more humane, do not be so frigid and cold; speak to me about it. I am your only son, surely my marriage is a matter of some importance to you."

There was a passion of entreaty in his voice, and Lady Lanswell looked kindly at him.

"Certainly your marriage is of more importance than anything else on earth; but you cannot expect me to look with favor on that tempestuous young person who ranted at me like a third-rate actress from a traveling theater; you must excuse me, Lance, but there are limits to human endurance, and she is beyond mine."

"Mother, let me be happy, let me go and marry her, let me bring her back here and we shall all be happy together."

"My dear Lance, I should not consider a person of her position a fit companion for my maid; for myself, I quite declare I shall not oppose your marriage with the girl—it is quite useless, since you are of age, to do as you like; but I shall never see you or speak to you again; when you leave me here for that purpose our good-bye will last beyond death. Still you understand I do not seek to win you from your purpose, you are free to do as you will."

The misery on his handsome young face touched her a little, and she had to remind herself that she was doing all she did for his own good.

"We will not talk any more about it, Lance," she said, kindly; "words will not alter facts. Did your father tell you what we proposed about the boat to-night?"

His lips trembled as he tried to answer her.

"I cannot throw off sorrow as you can, mother; I am talking to you about that which will make the misery or the happiness of my life, and you think of nothing but a boat."

"Words are so useless, Lance," repeated my lady; "they are but empty sounds. I am going out to look for some cameos; I think I should like a set, they are very elegant and *recherche*."

So saying, my lady left the room as though no serious thought occupied her mind.

Then, for the first time, something like impatience with his fate came over the young lord, something like impatience with Leone, for whose love he had so much to suffer. He loved his proud, beautiful mother, who had, unknown to him, such great influence over him. He could not endure the thought of life-long separation from her. The glamour of a boy's first mad love had fallen from him, and he saw things as they were; he could estimate better than he had done before, what it meant to give up father, mother and friends all for one love.

He did not recover his spirits all day, but the temptation never once came near him to break his word or forget Leone. That night, one of the loveliest that ever dawned on earth, they were all going to a *fete* given by the Countess Spizia, and one part of the entertainment was that the beautiful grounds were to be illuminated.

Lord Chandos had never seen his mother look so proud, so brilliant or so handsome as on that night. She wore a superb dress of green velvet, with a suit of diamonds worth a king's ransom. Lady Marion wore a dress of rich lace, with cream color roses and green leaves. The *fete* was well attended; a great number of French people and English were there. The earl had declined. Moonlit gardens and illuminated grounds had not much attraction for him.

Lord Chandos sat for some little time by his mother's side; he was enjoying an ice, and as he watched her he felt a sensation of pride in her beauty—a keen sense of regret that they should ever be parted.

An involuntary cry of admiration came from the countess, and Lord Chandos looking in the direction where her eyes were fixed, saw Lady Erskine. Never had the great queen of blondes looked so lovely; the fine, fairy-like web of costly lace fell in graceful folds around a figure that stood alone for grace and symmetry. She wore nothing but green leaves in her golden hair; her arms, bare to the shoulders, were white, firm, and statuesque. Over her face, when she saw Lord Chandos, came a beautiful, brilliant flush.

The countess and her son were sitting in one of the pretty *salons*, where some of the most famous works of art were collected. There was an exquisite bust of Clytie which attracted much attention; they had been commenting on it, and Lady Lanswell was saying how much she would like a copy of it.

"Here comes something more beautiful than Clytie," she said, as Lady Marion advanced to meet them.

She made room for the young heiress by her side. Lady Marion had schooled herself well, but her task was no easy one—she was so candid, so loyal, so true in all her dealings, that the least attempt at anything savoring of deception was unpleasant to her; still, she would, of course, do anything to help Lady Lanswell. So she sat down by her side and talked with her usual gentle grace.

She said, after a time:

"Lady Lanswell, I have a great favor to ask of you. If you do not wish to go back to England just yet, will you join me? I am trying to persuade Lady Cambrey to make a tour through Spain."

She drew a long breath of relief when the words were spoken, she was so thankful to have them said and done with. She mentally resolved that never would she promise to do anything of this kind again. Lady Lanswell's calm restored hers.

"To Spain?" repeated the countess. "What a traveler you are, Lady Marion. What has put Spain into your mind?"

"I have always longed to see the Alhambra," said Lady Marion, with perfect truth. "As we are so near, it would be a pity to go back without seeing it."

"I quite agree with you. It may be some years before you come on the Continent again—you are quite right to go to Spain. And you really wish us to join your party?"

"Certainly, I should be delighted; it would increase my pleasure a hundred-fold," replied the young heiress, promptly.

"You are very kind to say so. I will go if you can persuade Lord Chandos to go with us."

"How can I do that?" she asked, with a smile. "Teach me how to 'persuade,' Lady Lanswell. I have never been able to 'persuade' any one."

The countess rose from her seat with a light laugh.

"I am afraid that in this case, persuasion, argument, and reason would be in vain. Lance, take Lady Marion to see the lamps in the almond trees — they are really very fine."

He took the soft, silken wrapper from her and wrapped it round her shoulders.

"Let us go and see the lamps," he said, and they went.

Ah, well. The sky above was filled with pale, pure stars; the almond-trees filled the air with delicate perfume; the nightingales were singing in the distant trees; great floods of silver moonlight fell over the grounds, in which the lilies gleamed palely white, and the roses hung their heavy heads.

They went together to the grove where the lamps shone bright as huge pearls. The path was a narrow one and he drew the white hand through his arm. How did it come about? Ah, who shall tell? Perhaps the wind whispered it, perhaps the nightingales sung about it, perhaps something in the great white lily leaves suggested it, perhaps the pale, pure stars looked disapproval; but it happened that the white hand felt the arm, and was clasped in a warm, strong hand — a clasp such as only love gives.

Who shall say how it happened? She raised her fair face to his in the soft, pure moonlight, and said to him:

"Must you really go back to England, Lord Chandos?"

The voice was sweet as music — the face, so fair, so pure, so proud.

"Must you," she added, "really go?"

"Yes, I am compelled to return," he answered slowly.

"Need it be yet?" she said. "I know you must go, but the journey through Spain will be so pleasant, and we might make a compromise. I will shorten the journey if you will delay your return."

And before he left the almond grove Lord Chandos had promised to do so, and as he made the promise he bent down and kissed the white hand lying in his.

CHAPTER XXIX
WAITING FOR HIM

Never had June seen such roses, never had lilies opened such white chalices, never had the trees looked so green, or the grass so long and thick, never had the birds sung as they sung this June, never had the light of the sun been so golden bright. The smile of the beautiful summer lay over the land, but in no place was it so fair as in River View. It was a scene like fairyland.

So Leone thought it as she watched day by day the beauty of blossom and leaf. It was in the month of May she first began to watch the signs of coming summer; with the first breath of the hawthorn, her heart grew light and a new beauty of hope came in her face. It was May and he was coming in June. She worked harder than ever. She rose early and retired late; these months of hard study and hard reading had changed her more than she knew herself. One year ago she had risen a beautiful, strong, healthy girl, full of fire, and life, and power. Now she was a refined, intellectual woman, full of genius and talent, full of poetry and eloquence, full of originality and wit; then she was a girl to be admired, now she was a woman who could rule a kingdom, whose power was unlimited.

She had acquired more in these few months of study than some people learn in years. She knew how great his delight would be, and she smiled to think how entirely at her ease she should be, even with his stately lady mother; she should feel no great awe of her in the future, for if Heaven had not given her the position of a lady by birth, she had made herself one by study and refinement.

So he was coming, and their real married life was to begin. She thought with a shudder of the pain she had passed through, of the horror of that terrible discovery. It was all over now, thank Heaven. It had never been any brand or stigma to her; she had never felt any false shame over it; she had never bowed her bright head as though a blight had passed over her. She said to herself it was not her fault, she was not in the least to blame. She had believed herself in all honor to be the wife of Lord Chandos, and she could not feel that the least shadow of blame rested on her.

He was coming home. Through the long hours of the summer day, she thought of nothing else. True, since the month of June, his letters had been very few and much cooler. True, it had been a severe shock to her, to hear that he had gone to Nice; but, as his letter said nothing of Lady Marion, and she knew nothing even of the existence of such a person, that did not matter. Why had he gone to Nice when June was so near? She wrote to him to ask the question, but his answer was: Because his parents had gone there. Then she said no more; that seemed quite natural. The only thing that occurred to her was, he would have a longer journey in June; he would come to her as he had promised, but he would take a longer time in traveling.

Lose faith in him! She flung back her head, with a bright, proud laugh. No, nothing could shake her faith in him; his proud lady mother had managed to get him under her influence—what did that matter? He loved her and her alone. She remembered the words spoken on her wedding-day; when she had asked him if he was quite sure their marriage was legal, his answer was, "Yes, and that nothing could part them except death."

How well she remembered those words, "except death"! He had taken her in his arms and kissed her, as though even death itself should not claim her. No shadow of fear entered her mind. She knew that he would come, as surely as she knew that the sun would rise and the day would dawn.

The thirtieth of June. No gift of second sight came to her, to tell her that on the twenty-seventh of June Lord Chandos had sat down and wrote her a very long letter, telling her that it was impossible for him to be at home on the thirtieth of June, as he had promised to go with his parents to Spain. A large party were going, and he must join them; but his heart would be with her on that day. He should think of her from morning dawn until sunset, and he would be with her soon. He was vexed that he had to take the journey; it was quite against his will, yet he had been over-persuaded. He should soon see her now; and, whatever he did, she must not feel in the least degree distressed, or put about. Their happiness was only delayed for a short time.

A long letter. She had no gift of second sight; she could not see that his face burned with a shameful flush as he wrote it; that for himself he had no pity; that his heart went out to her with a warmer love than ever, but that the fear of his mother's taunts and the pain on Lady Marion's face kept him where he was.

Then, when the long letter was written, he directed it and sent it by his valet to post; nor could she see how that same valet intended going to post it at once, but was prevented, and then laid it aside for an hour, as he thought, and forgot it for two whole days; then, fearing his master's anger, said nothing about it, trusting that the delay might be attributed to something wrong in the post; and so, on the very day it should have been given to her, it was put into the post-office, three days too late. She could not know all this, and she longed for the thirtieth of June as the dying long for cold water, as the thirsty hart for the clear spring.

It came. She had longed for it, waited for it, prayed for it, and now it was here. She awoke early in the morning; it was to her as though a bridegroom were coming; the song of the birds woke her, and they seemed to know that he was coming—they were up and awake in the earliest dawn. Then a great flood of golden sunlight came to welcome her; she hastened to the window to see what the day was like, and whether the sky was blue. It seemed to her that every little bird sung, "He is coming."

Here were the roses laughing in at the window, nodding as though they would say, "This is the thirtieth of June." There flashed the deep, clear river, hurrying on to the great sea over which he must have crossed; the wind whispered among the leaves, and every leaf had a voice. "He is coming to-day," they all said—"coming to-day."

There was a great stir even at that early hour in the morning between the white and purple butterflies; there was a swift, soft cooing from the wood-pigeons; the world seemed to laugh in the warm embrace of the rising sun. She laughed too—a sweet, happy laugh that stirred the rose leaf and jasmine.

"Oh, happy day!" she cried—"oh, kindly sun and kindly time, that brings my love back to me."

She looked at the gate through which he would pass—at the rose tree from which he would gather the rose; and she stretched out her hands with a great, longing cry.

"Send him quickly—oh, kind Heaven!" she cried. "I have waited so long, my eyes ache to look at him. I thirst for his presence as flowers thirst for dew."

She looked at her watch, it was but just six—the laborers were going to the field, the maids to the dairy, the herdsmen to their flocks. She could see the hay-makers in the meadow, and the barges dropped lazily down the stream. The time would soon pass and he would be here before noon. Could it be possible that she should see him so soon?

"In six hours," she repeated, "she should see him in six hours."

Ah, well, she had plenty to do. She went round the pretty villa to see if everything was as he liked best to see it, then she occupied herself in ordering for his enjoyment every dish that she knew he liked; and then she dressed herself to sit and wait for him at the window. She looked as though she had been bathed in dew and warmed by the golden sun, so bright, so sparkling, so fresh and brilliant, her eyes radiant with hope and love, the long, silken lashes like fringe, the white lids half-drooping, her face, with its passionate beauty heightened by the love that filled her heart and soul. She wore a dress of amber muslin with white lace, and in the rich masses of her dark hair lay a creamy rose. Fair and bright as the morning itself she took her place at the window to watch the coming of him who was so many miles away. It is thus women believe men, it is thus that men keep the most solemn vows that they can make.

The maid who brought her tea wondered why her young mistress chose to sit at the window to drink it; indeed, she started with wonder at the brilliant beauty of the face turned to her.

It struck her now that she might in very truth begin to expect him; the sun was growing warmer, the flowers were wide awake, the brown bees were busy among the carnations, the birds had done half their day's work; some of the tall-plumed lilacs were beginning to droop, and the white acacia blossoms had fallen on the long grass. Her whole soul in her eyes, and those eyes fixed longingly on the white gate, she sat there until noon.

Great city bells rang out the hour; in the villages it was told by sweet old chimes. The hay-makers sat down to rest, the butterflies rested in the great hearts of the red roses, the bees settled in the carnations, the languid, odorous wind was still while the strokes rang out one after another— fragrant, sunny, golden noon.

He had not come; but every moment was bringing him nearer. Some one brought her a glass of wine, some fruit and biscuits. She would not touch them because she would not take her eyes from the white gate through which he had to pass.

CHAPTER XXX
THE THIRTIETH OF JUNE

She did not grow impatient; the love which sustained her, the hope that inspired her was too sweet; her soul seemed to be in a blissful, happy trance; no doubt, no fear, no presentiment of coming disappointment dimmed the radiance of those sunny brows. He was coming fast as steam could bring him; it did not matter if he would not come yet, if more of the sunny hours passed—even if he delayed until even-tide, he would come so sure as the sun shone in the blue sky.

Noon passed. One—two—three—still she had never moved or stirred. Four and five struck, still the light had not died from her eyes nor the smile from her face; he would come; the stars might fall from the heaven, the great earth upheave, the rivers rise, the hills fall, night become day, darkness light, but he would come. Who so faithful, so fond, so true? And at five her maid came again; this time she had a cup of strong, fragrant coffee, and Leone drank it eagerly. She would wait for dinner; she expected some one, and she would wait. Quickly enough she replaced the cup and returned to her watch; he might have come while she had the cup to her lips; but, ah, no, no one had trodden on the white acacia blossoms—they were uncrushed.

Perhaps the long watching had wearied her, or the warm glow of the June afternoon fatigued her, or the strong odor of the flowers reached her brain. She looked at her watch; it was after five. He would come, most certainly; she knew that; but she was tired, and a great tearless sob rose to her lips. The heat of the June sun was growing less; she leaned her head against the casement of the window, and the white eyelids fell over the dark, passionate, tender eyes. She was dreaming, then; she heard the ripple of running water that sung as it ran, and the words were:

> "A ring in pledge I gave her,
> And vows of love we spoke—
> Those vows were all forgotten,
> The ring asunder broke."

Over and over again the sweet, sad words were repeated. She was standing on the brink of the mill-stream again, her lover's kisses warm on her lips, her lover's hands clasping hers. Ah, Heaven, that the dream could have lasted or she never woke! A bird woke her by perching on her hand; perhaps he thought it was a lily, and she started in affright. The bells were ringing six; she had lost one whole hour, yet Heaven had sent that sleep in mercy; one hour of forgetfulness strengthened her for what she had to suffer. She woke with a start; for one moment her brain was confused between the dream and the reality. Was it the ripple of the mill-stream, or was it the sighing of the wind among the roses? She had slept for an hour. Had he come? Had she slept while he entered the garden? Was he hiding in jest?

She rang the bell quickly as the trembling hands would allow: and when the pretty, coquettish maid answered it she asked had any one come, had any one called; and the answer was, "No." Still she could not rest; she looked through the rooms, through the garden; ah, no, there were no traces of any arrival—none.

Once more to her watch at the window; but the scene began to change. There was no longer the golden glow over land and water, no longer the golden glare of a summer's day, no longer the sweet summer's noise, and the loud, jubilant songs of the birds. A gray tint was stealing over earth and sky; the lilies were closing their white cups; the birds singing their vesper hymn; longer shadows fell on the grass; cooler winds stirred the roses. He would come. The sky might pale, the earth darken, the sun set, the flowers sleep; but he would come. She would let no doubt of him enter her faithful heart. Let the night shadow fall, the sun of her love and her hope should still keep light.

And then from sky and earth, from clear river and green wood the light of day faded—eight, nine, and ten struck—the world grew dark and still—she kept her watch unbroken. It might be night when he returned; but she would hear the click of the gate and be there to welcome.

Ah, me, the sorrow that gathered like a storm-cloud over the beautiful face—the light, brightness and hope died from it as the light died from the heavens. Still she would not yield. Even after the shadows of evening had fallen over the land she kept her place. He would come. The servants of the household grew alarmed at last; and one by one they ventured in to try to persuade their young mistress to eat, to sleep, or to rest.

To one and all she said the same thing:

"Hush, do not speak; I am listening!"

It had grown too late to see; there was no moon, and the pale light of the stars revealed nothing; it had grown colder, too. There was a faint sound in the wind that told of coming rain. Her own maid—more at liberty to speak than the others—prayed her to come in; but all advice, reason, remonstrance received the same answer:

"I must not leave this spot until the twenty-four hours are ended."

She would not have suffered half the torture had the letter arrived; she would have known then at once that she was not to expect him; and the ordeal of waiting would have been over at once; but she clung to the hope he would come, he must come. She recalled his promises given solemnly—she said to herself with a little shudder:

"If he does not come to-day he will never come."

And then she hated herself for the half-implied doubt of him. No matter if the sun had fallen and the nightingale was singing; no matter if the solemn hush of night had fallen, and soft, deep shadows lay around, he would come. The sighs of the wind grew deeper; the roses drooped. She leaned forward, for it seemed to her there was a stir among the trees; it was only some night bird in quest of its prey. Again she bent her head; surely, at last, there was the click of the gate. But no; it was only the swaying of the branches in the wind.

Then clear and full and distinct, cleaving the air, rang out the hour of twelve; it was midnight, and he had not come. The thirtieth of June was over, and he had failed.

One by one she counted those strokes as they fell, in the vain hope that she must be mistaken, that it was only eleven. When she realized it she rose from her solitary watch with a long, low sigh. He had failed; he had not come. She would not judge him; but he had not kept that promise which was more solemn to her than any oath. There were many perils, both by sea and land; the steamer might have run ashore, the train may have been delayed; but if the appointment had been for her to keep she would have kept it in spite of all obstacles and all cost.

She rose from her long dull watch; she tried to cross the room and ring the bell, but the strength of her limbs failed her. She did not fall, she sunk into a senseless, almost helpless heap on the floor; and there, long after midnight, her servants found her, and for some time believed her dead. That was the thirtieth of June—for which she had hoped, worked, and prayed as woman never did before.

They raised her from the ground and took her to her room. One kinder than the others sat by her until the dawn, when the dark eyes opened with a look in them which was never to die away again.

"This is the first of July," she said, faintly.

And the maid, seeing that the morning had dawned, said:

"Yes, it is July."

She never attempted to rise that day, but lay with her face turned to the wall, turned from the sunlight and the birds' song, the bloom of flowers, the ripple of leaves, the warmth and light of the summer, thinking only of the mill-stream and the words that for her had so terrible a prophecy:

"A ring in pledge I gave her,
And vows of love we spoke—
Those vows are all forgotten,
The ring asunder broke."

Over and over again they rang through her brain and her heart, while she fought against them, while she lay trying to deaden her senses, to stifle her reason, doing deadly battle with the fears that assailed her. She would not give in; she would not doubt him; there would come to her in time some knowledge; she should know why he had failed.

Failed, oh, God! how hard the word was to say—failed. Why, if every star in the sky had fallen at her feet it would not have seemed so wonderful.

Perhaps his mother—that proud, haughty woman, who seemed to trample the world under her feet—perhaps she had prevented his coming; but he would come, no matter what the mill-stream said, no matter what his mother wished. The day passed and the morrow came—the second of July. She rose on that day and went down-stairs the shadow of her former self—pale, cold, and silent. She did not say to herself "He will come to-day," hope was dying within her. Then at noon came the letter—her maid brought it in. She gave a low cry of delight when she saw the beloved handwriting, that was followed by a cry of pain. He would not have written if he had been coming; that he had written proved that he had no intention of coming. She took the letter, but she dared not trust herself to open it in the presence of her maid; but when the girl was gone, as there was no human eye to rest on the tortured face she could not control, she opened it.

Deadly cold seemed to seize her; a deadly shudder made the letter fall from her hands.

No, he was not coming.

He *must* go to Spain—to Spain, with his parents and a party of tourists—but he loved her just the same, and he should return to her.

"He is weak of purpose," she said to herself when she had read the last word; "he loves me still; he will come back to me; he will make me his wife in the eyes of the law as he has done in the sight of Heaven. But he is weak of purpose. The Countess of Lanswell has put difficulties in his way, and he has let them conquer him."

Then came to her mind those strong words:

"Unstable as water, thou shalt not excel."

For the second time her servants found her cold and senseless on the ground; but this time she had an open letter in her hand.

The pity was that the whole world could not see how women trust the promises of men, and how men keep theirs.

CHAPTER XXXI
A MAN OF WAX

It is not pleasant to tell how the foundations of a noble building are sapped: to tell how the grand, strong trunk of a noble tree is hacked and hewn until it falls; how the constant rippling of water wears away a stone; how the association with baser minds takes away the bloom from the pure ones; how the constant friction with the world takes the dainty innocence of youth away. It is never pleasant to tell of untruth, or infidelity, or sin. It is not pleasant to write here, little by little, inch by inch, how Lord Chandos was persuaded, influenced, and overcome.

The story of man's perfidy is always hateful—the story of man's weakness is always contemptible. Yet the strongest of men, Samson, fell through the blandishments of a woman. Lord Chandos was neither as strong as Samson nor as wise as Solomon; and that a clever woman should get the upper hand of him was not to be wondered at.

He was a brave, gallant, generous gentleman, gay and genial; he could not endure feeling unhappy, nor could he bear the thought of any other person's unhappiness; he had no tragedy about him; he was kind of heart and simple of mind; he was clever and gifted, but he was like wax in the hands of a clever woman like Lady Lanswell.

He was singularly unsuspicious, believed in most things and most persons; he never misjudged or gave any one credit for bad qualities. He had no more intention of deserting Leone when he left England than he had of seizing the crown of Turkey. His honest, honorable intention was to return to her and marry her on the first hour that such a marriage could be legal. He would have laughed to scorn any one who would have hinted at such a thing. His love then was his life, and he had nothing beside it.

Gradually, slowly but surely, other interests occupied him. A great writer says: "Love is the life of a woman, but only an episode in the life of a man." That was the difference—it was Leone's life; to him it had been an episode—and now that the episode was somewhat passed, other interests opened to him. He meant to be faithful to her and to marry her; nothing should ever shake that determination; but he had ceased to think it need be so hurriedly done; he need not certainly forego the pleasure of the tour and hurry home for his birthday; that was quixotic nonsense; any time that year would do. After his marriage he should lose his mother and Lady Marion; he would enjoy their company as long as he could; Leone was right, she had a luxurious home, the assurance of his love and fidelity, the certainty of being his wife—a few weeks or months would make but little difference to her. He did not think he had done any great harm in going to Spain. One might call it a broken promise; but then most promises are made with a proviso that they shall be kept if possible; and this was not possible; he would have been very foolish—so he said to himself—if he had made matters worse by refusing to go with his mother to Spain. It would have increased her irritation and annoyance all to no purpose.

He tried to convince himself that it was right; and he ended by believing it.

He felt rather anxious as to what Leone would say—and the tone of her letter rather surprised him. She had thought, long before she answered him, reproaches were of no avail—they never are with men; if he had not cared to keep his promise no sharply written words of hers could avail to make him keep it. She made no complaint, no reproaches; she never mentioned her pain or her sorrow; she said nothing of her long watch or its unhappy ending; she did not even tell him of the delayed letter—and he wondered. He was more uncomfortable than if her letter had been one stinging reproach from beginning to end. He answered it—he wrote to her often, but there was a change in the tone of her letters, and he was half conscious of it.

He meant to be true to her—that was his only comfort in the after years; he could not tell—nor did he know—how it first entered his mind to be anything else. Perhaps my lady knew—for she had completely changed her tactics—instead of ignoring Leone she talked of her continually—never unkindly, but with a pitying contempt that insensibly influenced Lord Chandos. She spoke of his future with deepest compassion, as though he would be completely cut off from everything that could make life worth living; she treated him as though he were an unwilling victim to an unfortunate promise. It took some time to impress the idea upon him—he had never thought of himself in that light at all. A victim who was giving up the best mother, the kindest friend, everything in life, to keep an unfortunate promise. My lady spoke of him so continually in that light at last he began to believe it.

He was like wax in her hands; despite his warm and true love for his wife that idea became firmly engraved on his mind—he was a victim.

When once she had carefully impressed that upon him my lady went further; she began to question whether really, after all, his promise bound him or not.

In her eyes it did not—certainly not. The whole thing was a most unfortunate mistake; but that he should consider himself bound by such a piece of boyish folly was madness.

So that the second stage of his progress toward falsehood was that, besides looking on himself as a kind of victim, he began to think that he was not bound by his promise. If it had been an error at first it was an error now; and the countess repeated for him very often the story of the Marquis of Atherton, who married the daughter of a lodge-keeper in his nineteenth year. His parents interfered; the marriage was set aside. What was the consequence? Two years after the girl married the butler, and they bought the Atherton Arms. The marquis, in his twenty-fifth year, married a peeress in her own right, and was now one of the first men in England. My lady often repeated that anecdote; it had made a great impression on her, and it certainly produced an effect on Lord Chandos.

My lady had certainly other influences to bring to bear. The uncle of Lady Erskine, the Duke of Lester, was one of the most powerful nobles in England—the head of the Cabinet, the most influential peer in the House of Lords, the grandest orator and the most respected of men. My lady enjoyed talking about him—she brought forward his name continually, and was often heard to say that whoever had the good fortune to marry Lady Erskine was almost sure to succeed the duke in his numerous honors. Lord Chandos, hearing her one day, said:

"I will win honors, mother—win them for myself—and that will be better than succeeding another man."

She looked at him with a half-sad, half-mocking smile.

"I have no ambition, no hope for you, Lance. You have taken your wife from a dairy—the most I can hope is that you may learn to be a good judge of milk."

He turned from her with a hot flush of anger on his face. Yet the sharp, satirical shaft found its way to his heart. He thought of the words and brooded over them—they made more impression on him than any others had done. In his mother's mind he had evidently lost his place in the world's race, never to regain it.

The duke—who knew nothing of the conspiracy, and knew nothing of the young lord's story, except that he had involved himself in some tiresome dilemma from which his parents had rescued him—the Duke of Lester, who heard Lord Chandos spoken of as one likely to marry his niece, took a great fancy to him; he had no children of his own; he was warmly attached to his beautiful niece; it seemed very probable that if Lord Chandos married Lady Erskine, he would have before him one of the most brilliant futures that could fall to any man's lot. Many people hinted at it, and constant dropping wears away a stone.

The last and perhaps the greatest hold that the countess had over her son was the evident liking of Lady Marion for him. In this, as in everything else, she was most diplomatic; she never expressed any wish that he should marry her; but she had a most sympathetic manner of speaking about her.

"I doubt, Lance," she said one day, "whether we have done wisely—at least whether I have done wisely—in allowing Lady Marion to see so much of you; she is so sweet and so gentle—I am quite distressed about it."

"Why, mother? I see no cause for distress," he said, abruptly.

"No, my dear; men all possess the happy faculty of never seeing that which lies straight before their eyes. It is one of their special gifts—you have it to perfection."

"Do speak out what you mean, mother; that satire of yours puzzles me. What do I not see that I ought to see?"

"Nothing very particular. What I mean is this, Lance, that I am almost afraid Lady Marion has been too much with us for her peace of mind. I think, when you go back to England on this wild-goose chase of yours, that she will feel it deeply."

He looked anxiously at her.

"Do you, mother, really think that?" he asked.

"I do, indeed. Of course I know, Lance, no words of mine will ever avail; but it seems to me you are in this position—if you leave Lady Marion and return to your pretty dairy-maid that Lady Marion will never be happy again. If you marry Lady Marion and dower that young person with a good fortune she will marry some one in her own rank of life and be much happier than she could be with you."

"Ah, mother," he said, sadly, "you do not know Leone."

"No, and never shall; but I know one thing—if I stood in your place and was compelled to make one or the other unhappy, I know which it would be. In marrying Lady Marion you make yourself at once and you delight me, you gratify every one who knows and loves you. In marrying that tempestuous young person you cut yourself adrift from fame, friends, and parents."

"But honor, mother, what about my honor?"

"You lose it in marrying a dairy-maid. You preserve it in marrying Lady Marion."

And with this Parthian shot my lady left him.

CHAPTER XXXII
AN ACT OF PERFIDY

So—inch by inch, little by little, step by step—Lord Chandos was influenced to give up his faith, his promise, his loyalty. I, who write the story, offer no excuse for him—there is none for the falseness and perfidy of men—yet it is of so common occurrence the world only jests about it—the world makes poetry of it and sings, cheerfully:

"One foot on land and one on shore,
Men were deceivers ever."

A promise more or less, a vow more or less, a broken heart, a ruined life, a lost soul, a crime that calls to Heaven for vengeance—what is it? The world laughs at "Love's perfidies;" the world says that it serves one right. The girl is slain in her youth by a worse fate than early death, and the man goes on his way blithely enough.

Lord Chandos could not quite trample his conscience under foot; under the influence of his mother he began to see that his love for Leone had been very unfortunate and very fatal; he had begun to think that if one of two women must be miserable it had better be Leone. That which was present influenced him most. He loved his mother, he was flattered by Lady Marion's love for him. So many influences were brought to bear upon him, the earl and countess were so devoted to him, Lady Marion charmed him so much with her grace and kindness of manner, her sweetness of disposition, her wonderful repose, that his faith grew weak and his loyalty failed.

There came an evening when they two—Lord Chandos and Lady Marion—stood alone in one of the most beautiful courts of the Alhambra. The whole party had been visiting that marvelous palace, and, more by accident than design, they found themselves alone. The sun was setting—a hundred colors flamed in the western sky; the sun seemed loath to leave the lovely, laughing earth; all the flowers were sending her a farewell message; the air was laden with richest odors; the ripple of green leaves made music, and they stood in the midst of the glories of the past and the smile of the present.

"I can people the place," said Lady Marion, in her quiet way. "I can see the cavaliers in their gay dresses and plumes, the dark-eyed senoras with veil and fan. How many hearts have loved and broken within these walls, Lord Chandos!"

"Hearts love and break everywhere," he said, gloomily.

She went on:

"I wonder if many dreams of this grand Alhambra came to Queen Catharine of Arragon, when she lay down to rest—that is, if much rest came to her?"

"Why should not rest come to her?" asked Lord Chandos, and the fair face, raised to answer him, grew pale.

"Why? What a question to ask me. Was she not jealous and with good cause? How can a jealous woman know rest? I am quite sure that she must have thought often with longing and regret, of her home in sunny Granada."

"I have never been jealous in my life," said Lord Chandos.

"Then you have never loved," said Lady Marion. "I do not believe that love ever exists without some tinge of jealousy. I must say that if I loved any one very much, I should be jealous if I saw that person pay much attention to any one else."

He looked at her carelessly, he spoke carelessly; if he had known what was to follow, he would not have spoken so.

"But do you love any one very much?" he said.

The next moment he deeply repented the thoughtless words. Her whole face seemed on fire with a burning blush. She turned proudly away from him.

"You have no right to ask me such a question," she said. "You are cruel to me, Lord Chandos."

The red blush died away, and the sweet eyes filled with tears.

That was the *coup de grace*; perhaps if that little incident had never happened, this story had never been written; but the tears in those sweet eyes, and the quiver of pain in that beautiful face, was more than he could bear. The next moment he was by her side, and had taken her white hands in his.

"Cruel! how could I be cruel to you. Lady Marion? Nothing could be further from my thoughts. How am I cruel?"

"Never mind," she said, gently.

"But I do mind very much indeed. What did I say that could make you think me cruel? Will you not tell me?"

"No," she replied, with drooping eyes, "I will not tell you."

"But I must know. Was it because I asked you, 'if you ever loved any one very much?' Was that cruel?"

"I cannot deny, but I will not affirm it," she said. "We are very foolish to talk about such things as love and jealousy; they are much better left alone."

There was the witchery of the hour and the scene to excuse him; there was the fair loveliness of her face, the love in her eyes that lured him, the trembling lips that seemed made to be kissed; there was the glamour that a young and beautiful woman always throws over a man; there was the music that came from the throats of a thousand birds, the fragrance that came from a thousand flowers to excuse him. He lost his head, as many a wiser man has done; his brain reeled, his heart beat; the warm white hand lay so trustingly in his own, and he read on her fair, pure face the story of her love. He never knew what madness possessed him; he who had called himself the husband of another; but he drew her face to his and kissed her lips, while he whispered to her how fair and how sweet she was. The next moment he remembered himself, and wished the deed undone. It was too late—to one like Lady Marion a kiss meant a betrothal, and he knew it. He saw tears fall from her eyes; he kissed them away, and then she whispered to him in a low, sweet voice:

"How did you guess my secret?"

"Your secret," he repeated, and kissed her again, because he did not know what to say.

"Yes; how did you find out that I loved you?" she asked, simply. "I am sure I have always tried to hide it."

"Your beautiful eyes told it," he said; and then a sudden shock of horror came to him. Great Heaven! what was he doing? where was Leone? She did not perceive it, but raised her blushing face to his.

"Ah, well," she said, sweetly, "it is no secret since you have found it out. It is true, I do love you, and my eyes have not told you falsely."

Perhaps she wondered that he listened so calmly, that he did not draw her with passionate words and caresses to his heart, that he did not speak with the raptures lovers used. He looked pale and troubled, yet he clasped her hand more closely.

"You are very good to me," he said. "I do not deserve it, I do not merit it. You—you—shame me, Marion."

She looked at him with a warm glow of happiness on her face.

"It would not be possible to be too good to you; but I must not tell you of all I think of you, or you will grow vain. I think," she continued, with a smile that made her look like an angel, "I think now that I know how much you love me I shall be the happiest woman on the face of the earth."

He did not remember to have said how much he loved her, or to have spoken of his love at all, but evidently she thought he had, and it came to the same thing.

"How pleased Lady Lanswell will be!" said the young heiress, after a time. "You will think me very vain to say so, but I believe she loves me."

"I am sure of it; who could help it?" he said, absently.

He knew that he had done wrong, he repented it, and made one desperate effort to save himself.

"Lady Marion," he said, hurriedly, "let me ask you one question. You have heard, of course, the story of my early love?"

He felt the trembling of her whole figure as she answered, in a low voice:

"Yes; I know it, and that makes me understand jealousy. I am very weak, I know, but if you had gone to England, I should have died of pain."

He kissed her again, wondering whether for his perfidy a bolt from Heaven would strike him dead.

"You know it," he said; "then tell me—I leave it with you. Do you consider that a barrier between us, between you and me? You shall decide?"

She knew so little about it that she hastily answered:

"No; how can it be? That was folly. Lady Lanswell says you have forgotten it. Shall a mere folly be a barrier between us? No; love levels all barriers, you know."

He kissed her hands, saying to himself that he was the greatest coward and the greatest villain that ever stood on earth. Words he had none. Then they heard Lady Cambrey calling for her niece.

"Let me tell her," whispered the beautiful girl; "she will be so pleased, she likes you so much." Then, as they passed out of the court, she looked at the grand old walls. "I shall always love this place," she said, "because it is here that you have first said that you loved me."

And the pity is that every girl and every woman disposed to give her whole chance of happiness in a man's hand was not there to see how women believe men, and how men keep the promises they make.

He told his mother that same night.

"I have done it," he said; "circumstances have forced me into it, but I have forsworn myself. I have lost my self-respect, and I shall never be happy again while I live."

But she embraced him with eager delight.

"You have done well," she said; "you have risen above the shackles of a miserable promise, and have proved yourself a noble man by daring to undo the mad act of folly which might have blighted your life. I approve of what you have done, and so will any other sensible person."

And that was his consolation, his reward for the greatest act of perfidy that man ever committed, or a woman sanctioned.

CHAPTER XXXIII
"I HAVE PERJURED MYSELF"

Lady Lanswell was triumphant; she lost no time; before noon of the day following she had sent to the Duke of Lester saying that they were staying at Granada, and that important family business awaited him there. She knew that he would lose no time in going there. In the days that intervened she managed her son most cleverly; she said little or nothing to him of Lady Marion. If he broached the subject, she changed it at once, saying: "Let the matter rest for awhile;" she was so sorely afraid he would draw back. She was kind to him in her way; if she saw his handsome face looking distressed, pained, or anxious, she would cheer him up with bright words, with laughter, or anything that would take the weight of thought or care from him.

The Duke of Lester was soon there. Anything in which his niece was interested was of vital consequence to him; he had no particular liking for Lady Cambrey, and always regretted that the young heiress had been given into her charge rather than in that of his amiable wife. He went to Granada, delighted with the news; he had heard so much of the talents of Lord Chandos that he was charmed with the idea of his belonging to the family. It had been a sore and heavy trial to the duke that he had no son, that so many honors and such great offices should die with him. It was from that motive that he had always felt an especial interest in the marriage of his beautiful young niece.

"If she marries well," he had said to himself more than once, "her husband must stand to me in the place of a son."

If he had to choose from the wide world, he would prefer Lord Chandos from his singular talent, activity, and capability for political life. He knew, as every one else did, that there had been some little drawback in the young lord's life, some mysterious love-affair, and he had not interested himself in it; he never did take any interest in matters of that kind. Evidently if, at any time, there had been a little *faux pas*, it was remedied, or so worldly-wise a woman as Lady Lanswell would never have introduced him to his niece.

So the Duke of Lester, all amiability and interest, gave the finishing touch to Lord Chandos' fate. When he had once spoken of the matter, there was no receding from it without a scandal that would have horrified all England. The duke's first words settled the whole matter; he held out his hand in frankest, kindliest greeting to Lord Chandos.

"I hear very pleasant intelligence," he said; "and while I congratulate you, I congratulate myself that I am to have the good fortune of an alliance with you."

Lady Lanswell stood by, and there was a moment's pause; perhaps she never suffered such intensity of suspense as she did during that moment, for her son's face grew colorless, and he looked as if he were going to draw back. The next minute he had recovered himself, and returned the duke's greeting: then, and only then, did the countess give a great sigh of relief; there could be no mistake, no drawing back from anything which the duke sanctioned.

That same day there was a family meeting; the earl and countess, Lord Chandos, the Duke of Lester, Lady Marion Erskine, and Lady Cambrey; they all dined together, and the duke discussed with the countess the time of the marriage.

There was little said, but that little was binding; there could be no retreat. In the autumn, about September, the countess thought; and she suggested that they should not return to England for the marriage; it could take place at the Embassy at Paris. There would be plenty of time for discussing these details; the thing now was to settle the engagement. It gave great delight; the earl, it is true, had some little scruple, which he ventured to express to his wife.

"I ought to add my congratulation," he said; "but I am in doubt over it. This seems a very suitable marriage, and Lady Marion is a most charming girl. But what about that other girl, my lady?"

"That has nothing to do with us," she replied, haughtily. "I am prepared to be very liberal; I shall not mind a thousand a year; she shall have nothing to complain of."

Lord Lanswell did not feel quite so sure, but as he never had had any management of his own affairs, it was too late to begin now. My lady would probably bring a hornet's nest about her ears—that was her own business; if he were any judge, either of looks or character, that young girl, Leone, would not be so lightly set aside.

However, he said nothing. Lord Lanswell had learned one lesson in his life; he had learned that "Silence was golden."

The matter was settled now; the duke had given his sanction, expressed his delight; several of the highly connected and important families belonging to the Lanswells and the Lesters had sent in their congratulations; everything was in trim.

There was no need for the duke to remain; he would join them in Paris for the wedding. No word was spoken on the subject between Lady Lanswell and himself, but there was a certain tacit understanding that the wedding must not take place in England, lest it should be disturbed.

The duke returned to England, taking back with him a sincere liking and a warm admiration for Lord Chandos; he was impatient for the time to come when he should be able to claim him as a relation of his own. The remainder of the party stayed at Granada; there was plenty to interest them in and about that charming city.

Some few days after his departure, Lord Chandos sought his mother. She had felt anxious over him of late. He looked like anything but a happy lover; he was thin, worn, and the face that had been so bright had grown shadowed and careworn. My lady did not like it. Any man who had won such a prize as Lady Erskine ought to feel delighted and show his pleasure.

So argued my lady, but her son did not seem to share her sentiments. She sat on this morning, looking very stately and beautiful, in a dress of moire antique, with a morning-cap of point lace—a woman to whom every one involuntarily did homage.

Lord Chandos looked at her with wonder and admiration; then he sighed deeply as he remembered why he had sought her. He sat down near her, the very picture of dejection and misery.

"Mother," he said, abruptly, "I have behaved like a villain and a coward. In what words am I to excuse myself?"

My lady's face darkened.

"I have not the pleasure of understanding you," she said. "Will you explain yourself?"

"I have perjured myself. I have broken the most solemn vows that a man could make. I have forsworn myself. Tell me in what words am I to tell my guilt, or excuse it?"

A contemptuous smile stole over the face of my lady.

"Are you troubling yourself about that tempestuous young person, Leone? Shame on you, when you have won the sweetest woman and the wealthiest heiress in England for your wife!"

His voice was broken with emotion as he answered her:

"I cannot forget that I believed her to be my wife once, and I loved her."

My lady interrupted him.

"My dear Lance, we all know what a boy's first love is. Ah, do believe me, it is not worth thinking of; every one laughs at a boy's love. They take it just as they take to whooping-cough or fever; it does not last much longer either. In another year's time you will laugh at the very mention of what you have called love. Believe me," continued her ladyship, proudly, "that Lady Marion is the wife Heaven ordained for you, and no other."

The handsome young head was bent low, and it seemed to my lady as though a great tearless sob came from his lips. She laid her hand on his dark, crisp waves of hair.

"I do sympathize with you, Lance," she said, in a kind voice; and when Lady Lanswell chose to be kind no one could rival her. "You have, perhaps, made some little sacrifice of inclination, but, believe me, you have done right, and I am proud of you."

He raised his haggard young face to hers.

"I feel myself a coward and a villain, mother," he said, in a broken voice. "I ought to have gone back to that poor girl; I ought not to have dallied with temptation. I love Leone with the one love of my heart and mind, and I am a weak, miserable coward that I have not been true to her. I have lost my own self-respect, and I shall *never* regain it."

My lady was patient; she had always expected a climax, and, now it had arrived, she was ready for it. The scorn and satire gave place to tenderness; she who was the most undemonstrative of women, caressed him as though he had been a child again on her knees. She praised him, she spoke of his perfidy as though it were heroism; she pointed out to him that he had made a noble sacrifice of an ignoble love.

"But, mother," he said, "I have broken my faith, my honor, my plighted word," and her answer was:

"That for a great folly there could only be a great reparation; that if he had broken his faith with this unfortunate girl he had kept it, and his loyalty also, to the name and race of which he was so proud, to herself and to Lady Marion."

Like all other clever women, she could argue a question until she convinced the listener, even against his own will, and she could argue so speciously that she made wrong seem right.

He listened until he was unable to make any reply. In his heart he hated and loathed himself; he called himself a coward and a traitor; but in his mother's eyes he was a great hero.

"There is one thing I cannot do," he said; "I cannot write and tell her; it seems to me more cruel than if I plunged a dagger in her heart."

Lady Lanswell laughed.

"That is all morbid sentiment, my dear Lance. Leave the matter with me, I will be very kind and very generous; I will arrange everything with her in such a manner that you will be pleased. Now promise me to try and forget her, and be happy with the sweet girl who loves you so dearly."

"I will try," he said, but his young face was so haggard and worn that my lady's heart misgave her as she looked at him.

"I have done all for the best," she murmured to herself. "He may suffer now, but he will thank me for it in the years to come."

CHAPTER XXXIV
A PALE BRIDEGROOM

The writing of that letter was a labor of love to Lady Lanswell. She did not wish to be cruel; on the contrary, now that she had gained her wish, she felt something like pity for the girl she had so entirely crushed. Lord Chandos would have been quite true to his first love but for his mother's influence and maneuvers. She knew that. She knew that with her own hand she had crushed the life and love from this girl's heart. Writing to her would be the last disagreeable feature in the case. She would be finished with them, and there would be nothing to mar the brightness of the future.

My lady took up a jeweled pen; she had paper, white and soft, with her crest at the head; every little detail belonging to her grandeur would help to crush this girl for whom she had so much contempt and so little pity. She thought over every word of her letter; it might at some future day, perhaps, be brought against her, and she resolved that it should be a model of moderation and fairness. She had learned Leone's name, and she began:

"My dear Miss Noel,—My son has commissioned me to write to you, thinking, as I think, that the business to be arranged will be better settled between you and myself. I am glad to tell you that at last, after many months of infatuation, my son has returned to his senses, and has now but one idea, which is at once and forever to put an end to all acquaintance between you and himself. My son owns that it was a great mistake; he blames himself entirely, and quite exculpates you; he holds you blameless. Permit me to say that I do the same.

"My son, having recovered his senses, sees that a marriage between you and himself would be quite impossible. He regrets having promised it, and begs that you will forgive what seems to be a breach of that promise; but it is really the best and wisest plan of his life. Neither your birth, training, education, manners, nor appearance fit you to hold the position that my son's wife must hold. You must, therefore, consider the whole affair at an end; it was, at its worst, a piece of boyish folly and indiscretion, while you are blameless. It is my son's wish that ample compensation should be made to you, and I have placed the matter in the hands of Mr. Sewell, my lawyer, whom I have instructed to settle a thousand per annum on you. Let me add, further, that if ever you are in any pecuniary difficulty, I shall find a pleasure in helping you.

"One thing more: Lord Chandos is engaged to be married to one of the wealthiest women in England—a marriage which makes his father and myself extremely happy, which opens to him one of the finest careers ever opened to any man, and will make him one of the happiest of men. Let me add an earnest hope that your own good sense will prevent any vulgar intrusion on your part, either on my son or the lady to whom he is passionately attached. You will not need to answer this letter. Lord Chandos does not wish to be annoyed by any useless appeals; in short, no letter that you write will reach him, as we are traveling from place to place, and shall be so until the wedding-day.

"In conclusion, I can but say I hope you will look at the matter in a sensible light. You, a farmer's niece, have no right to aspire to the position of an earl's wife, and you have every reason to think yourself fortunate that worse has not happened.

"Lucia, Countess of Lanswell."

"There," said my lady, as she folded up the letter, "to most people that would be a quietus. If she has half as much spirit as I give her credit for, that little touch about the 'vulgar intrusion' will prevent her from writing to him. I think this will effectually put an end to all further proceedings."

She sealed the letter and sent it, at the same time sending one to her solicitor, Mr. Sewell, telling him of the happy event pending, and begging of him to arrange with the girl at once.

"If one thousand a year does not satisfy her, offer her two; offer her anything, so that we are completely rid of her. From motives of prudence it would be better for her to leave that place at once; advise her to go abroad, or emigrate, or anything, so that she may not annoy us again, and do not write to me about her; I do not wish to be annoyed. Settle the business yourself, and remember that I have no wish to know anything about it."

That letter was sent with the other, and my lady sunk back with an air of great relief.

"Thank Heaven!" she said to herself, "that is over. Ah, me! what mothers have to suffer with their sons, and yet few have been so docile as mine."

A few days afterward the countess sought her son. She had no grounds for what she said, but she imagined herself speaking the truth.

"Lance," she said, "I have good news for you. That tiresome little affair of yours is all settled, and there will be no need for us ever to mention the subject again. The girl has consented to take the thousand a year, and she— she is happy and content."

He looked at her with haggard eyes.

"Happy and content, mother?" he said. "Are you quite sure of that?"

"Sure as I am that you, Lance, are one of the most fortunate men in this world. Now take my advice, and let us have no more mention of the matter. I am tired of it, and I am sure that you must be the same. Try from this time to be happy with Lady Marion, and forget the past."

Did he forget it? No one ever knew. He never had the same light in his eyes, the same frank, free look on his face, the same ring in his laugh; from that day he was a changed man. Did he think of the fair young girl, whose passionate heart and soul he had woke into such keen life? Did he think of the mill-stream and the ripple of the water, and the lines so full of foreboding:

"The vows are all forgotten,
The ring asunder broke."

Ah, how true Leone's presentiment had been! The vow was forgotten, the ring broken, the pretty love-story all ended. He never dared to ask any questions from his mother about her; he turned coward whenever the English letters were delivered; he never dared to think about her, to wonder how she had taken this letter, what she had thought, said, or done. He was not happy. Proud, ambitious, mercenary, haughty as was the Countess of Lanswell, there were times when she felt grieved for her son. It was such a young face, but there was a line on the broad, fair brow; there was a shadow in the sunny eyes; the music had gone out from his voice.

"Marion will soon make it all right," said the proud, anxious, unhappy mother; "there will be nothing to fear when once they are married."

Lady Marion was the most gentle and least exacting of all human beings, but even she fancied Lord Chandos was but a poor wooer. He was always polite, deferential, attentive, and kind; yet he seldom spoke of love.

After that evening in the Alhambra he never kissed her; he never sought any *tete-a-tete* with her. She had had many lovers, as was only natural for a beauty and a great heiress. None of them had been so cool, so self-contained as Lord Chandos.

Lady Lanswell managed well; she ought to have been empress of some great nation; her powers of administration were so great. She persuaded them to have the wedding in the month of September, and to travel until that came.

"It will be a change from the common custom," she said; "most people are married in England, and go to the Continent for their honey-moon; you will be married in the Continent, and go to England for the honey-moon."

It was some little disappointment to Lady Marion; like all girls she had thought a great deal of her marriage. She had always fancied it in the grand old church at Erskine, where the noble men and women of her race slept their last sleep, where the Erskines for many generations had been married. She had fancied a long train of fair, young bridemaids, a troop of fair, fond children strewing flowers; and now it would be quite different. Still she was content; she was marrying the man whom she loved more than any one, or anything else in the world.

She had wondered so much why the countess desired the wedding to take place in Paris. She had even one day ventured to ask her, and Lady Lanswell answered first by kissing her, then by telling her that it was best for Lord Chandos. That was quite enough to content the loving heart, if it were better for him in any way. She did not inquire why. She would sacrifice any wish or desire of her own.

So the day of the wedding came, and a grand ceremonial it was. The noblest and most exclusive English in Paris attended it, and everything was after the wish of Lady Lanswell's heart. There had never been a fairer or more graceful bride. There had never been a handsomer or more gallant bridegroom. One thing struck the Countess of Lanswell and made her remember the day with a keen sense of pain, and it was this: when the bride retired to change her superb bridal dress for a traveling costume she had time to notice how white and ill her son looked. He was one of the most temperate of men; she did not remember that he had ever in his life been in the least degree the worse for wine, but she saw him go to the buffet and fill a small glass with strong brandy and drink it—even that, strong as it was, did not put any color into his face. Then he came to speak to her. She looked anxiously at him.

"Lance," she said, "I do not like asking you the question—but—have you really been drinking brandy?"

She never forgot the bitter laugh that came from his lips.

"Yes, I have indeed, mother. It is just as well a glass of poison did not stand there; I should have drunk it."

She shuddered at the words, and it must be owned they were not cheerful ones for a wedding-day.

The bride and bridegroom drove away; slippers and rice were thrown after them. And the pity is that every woman inclined to put faith in the vows and promises of a man was not there to see how they were kept.

CHAPTER XXXV
"I LEAVE THEM MY HATRED AND MY CURSE"

Leone was alone when the letter of the Countess of Lanswell was delivered to her: she had been wondering for some days why no news came from Lord Chandos—why he did not write. She had written most urgent and affectionate letters to him, praying for news of him, telling him how bravely and happily she was bearing the separation from him, only longing to know something of him.

The warm, sultry month of August had set in, and she was working hard as ever; there was but one comfort to her in this long absence—the longer he was away from her, the more fit she should be to take her place as his wife when he did return. She felt now that she could be as stately as the Countess of Lanswell herself, with much more grace.

She had been thinking over her future when that letter came; it found her in the same pretty room where he had bidden her good-bye. When the maid entered with the letter on a salver, she had looked up with a quick, passionate sense of pleasure. Perhaps this was to tell her when he would come. She seized the dainty envelope with a low cry of intense rapture.

"At last," she said to herself, "at last. Oh, my love, how could you be silent so long?"

Then she saw that it was not Lance's writing, but a hand that was quite strange to her. Her face paled even as she opened it; she turned to the signature before she read the letter; it was "Lucia, Countess of Lanswell." Then she knew that it was from her mortal enemy, the one on whom she had sworn revenge.

She read it through. What happened while she read it? The reapers were reaping in the cornfields, the wind had sunk to the lightest whisper, some of the great red roses fell dead, the leaves of the white lilies died in the heat of the sun, the birds were tired of singing; even the butterflies had sunk, tired out, on the breasts of the flowers they loved; there was a golden glow over everything; wave after wave of perfume rose on the warm summer air; afar off one heard the song of the reaper, and the cry of the sailors as the ships sailed down the stream; there was life, light, lightness all around, and she stood in the middle of it, stricken as one dead, holding her death warrant in her hand. She might have been a marble statue as she stood there, so white, so silent, so motionless.

She read and reread it; at first she thought it must be a sorry jest; it could not be true, it was impossible. If she took up the Bible there, and the printed words turned blood-red before her eyes, it would be far less wonderful than that this should be true. A sorry, miserable jest some one had played her, but who—how? No, it was no jest.

She must be dreaming—horrible dreams come to people in their sleep; she should wake presently and find it all a black, blank dream. Yet, no— no dream, the laughing August sunlight lay all round her, the birds were singing, there was the flash of the deep river, with the pleasure-boats slowly drifting down the stream. It was no dream, it was a horrible reality; Lord Chandos, the lover whom she had loved with her whole heart, who ought, under the peculiar circumstances, to have given her even double the faith and double the love a husband gives his wife; he, who was bound to her even by the weakness of the tie that should have been stronger, had deserted her.

She did not cry out, she did not faint or swoon; she did not sink as she had done before, a senseless heap on the ground; she stood still, as a soldier stands sometimes when he knows that he has to meet his death blow.

Every vestige of color had faded from her face and lips; if the angel of death had touched her with his fingers, she could not have looked more white and still. Over and over again she read the words that took from her life its brightness and its hope, that slew her more cruelly than poison or steel, that made their way like winged arrows to her heart, and changed her from a tender, loving, passionate girl to a vengeful woman.

Slowly she realized it, slowly the letter fell from her hands, slowly she fell on her knees.

"He has forsaken me!" she cried. "Oh, my God! he has forsaken me, and I cannot die!"

No one cares to stand by the wheel or the rack while some poor body is tortured to death; who can stand by while a human heart is breaking with the extremity of anguish? When such a grief comes to any one as to Leone, one stands by in silence; it is as though a funeral is passing, and one is breathless from respect to the dead.

The best part of her died as she knelt there; the blue of the sky, the gold of the shining sun, the song of the birds, the sweet smell of flowers were never the same to her again. Almost all that was good and noble, brave and bright, died as she knelt there. When that letter reached her, she was, if anything, better than the generality of women. She had noble instincts, grand ideas, great generosity, and self-sacrifice; it was as though a flame of fire came to her, and burned away every idea save one, and that was revenge.

"He loved me," she cried; "he loved me truly and well; but he was weak of purpose and my enemy has taken him from me."

Hours passed—all the August sunlight died; the reapers went home, the cries of the sailors were stilled, the birds were silent and still. She sat there trying to realize that for her that letter had blotted the sun from the heavens and the light from her life; trying to understand that her brave, handsome, gallant young love was false to her, that he was going to marry another while she lived.

It was too horrible. She was his wife before God. They had only been parted for a short time by a legal quibble. How could he marry any one else?

She would not believe it. It was a falsehood that the proud mother had invented to part her from him. She would not believe it unless she heard it from others. She knew Mr. Sewell's private address; he would know if it were true; she would go and ask him.

Mr. Sewell was accustomed to tragedies, but even he felt in some degree daunted when that young girl with her colorless face and flashing eyes stood before him. She held out a letter.

"Will you read this?" she said, abruptly. "I received it to-day from Lucia, Countess of Lanswell, and I refuse to believe it."

He took the letter from her hands and read it, then looked at the still white face before him.

"Is it true?" she asked.

"Yes," he replied, "perfectly true."

"Will you tell me who it is that is going to marry my husband?" she asked.

"If you mean will I tell you whom Lord Chandos is to marry, I am sorry to say my answer must be 'No.' I am not commissioned to do so. You may see it for yourself in the newspapers."

"Then it is true," she said slowly; "there is no jest, no doubt, no mistake about it?"

"No, none. And as you have shown me your letter," said Mr. Sewell, "I may as well show you the one I have received, and you may see for yourself what Lady Lanswell's intentions about you are. Take a chair," added the lawyer, "I did not notice that you were standing all this time; you took me by surprise. Pray be seated."

She took the chair which he had placed for her, and read the letter through. She laid it down on the table, her face calm, white, the fire in her eyes giving place to utter scorn.

"I thank you," she said. "The letter written you is cruel and unjust as the one written to me. I decline the thousand per annum now and for all time. My husband loved me and would have been quite true to me, but that his mother has intrigued to make him false. I refuse her help, her assistance in any way; but I will have my revenge. If I had money and influence I would sue for my rights—ah, and might win then. As it is, and for the present, I am powerless; but I will have my revenge. Tell Lucia, Countess of Lanswell, so from me."

The passion, the dramatic force, the eager interest, the power of her beautiful face, struck him. In his heart he felt sorry for this girl, who he knew had been cruelly treated.

"I would not think about revenge," he said; "that is a kind of thing one reads about in novels and plays, but it is all out of date."

"Is it?" she asked, with a slow, strange smile.

"Yes. Take the advice of a sensible man who wishes to see you do well. Yours is a false position, a cruel position; but make the best of it—take the thousand per annum, and enjoy your life."

He never forgot the scorn those wonderful eyes flashed at him.

"No," she said, "I thank you; I believe when you give me that advice you mean well, but I cannot follow it. If I were dying of hunger I would not touch even a crumb of bread that came from Lady Lanswell. I will never even return to the house which has been my own. I will take no one single thing belonging to them. I will leave them my hatred and my curse. And you tell Countess Lucia, from me, that my hatred shall find her out, and my vengeance avenge me."

She rose from her chair and took the letter she had brought with her.

"I will never part with this," she said; "I will keep it near me always, and the reading of it may stimulate me when my energy tires. I have no message for Lord Chandos; to you I say farewell."

"She is going to kill herself," he thought; "and then, if it gets into the papers, my lady will wax wroth."

She seemed to divine his thoughts, for she smiled, and the smile was more sad than tears.

"I shall not harm myself," she said: "death is sweeter than life, but life holds 'vengeance.' Good-bye."

CHAPTER XXXVI
AFTER THREE YEARS

"The question is," said Lord Chandos, "shall we go or not? Please yourself, Marion, and then," he added, with an air of weariness, "you will be sure to please me."

"I should like to go, certainly, if you really have no other engagement, Lance," said Lady Chandos.

"My engagements always give place to your pleasure," replied the young husband. "If you really desire to see this new star we will go. I will see about it at once."

Still Lady Chandos seemed irresolute.

"It is quite true," she said, "that all London has gone mad about her, just as Paris, Vienna, and St. Petersburg did."

"London is always going mad about something or other, but the madness never lasts long."

"I have read many things," continued his wife calmly, "but I have never read anything like the description of the scene at the opera-house last evening; it really made me long to see her."

"Then let the longing be gratified, by all means," said Lord Chandos. "We will go this evening. Consider it settled, Marion, and do not think of changing your plans."

It was breakfast-time, and the husband and wife were discussing the advent of a new actress and singer—one who was setting the world on fire—Madame Vanira. Lord and Lady Chandos always took breakfast together; it was one of the established rules, never broken; it was the only time in the day when they were quite sure of seeing each other.

It was three years since they were married, and time had not worked any great change in either. Lady Chandos was even more beautiful than in her maiden days. She had the same sweet repose of manner, the same high-bred elegance and grace, the same soft, low voice, but the beauty of her face had grown deeper.

There was more light in the blue eyes, a deeper sheen on the golden hair, a richer tint on the fair face; there was more of life, animation, and interest, than she had displayed in those days when she seemed to glide through life like a spirit, rather than battle through it like a human being. Perhaps for her the battle had to come. In figure she had developed, she looked taller and more stately, but the same beautiful lines and gracious curves were there. As she sits in her morning-dress, the palest blue, trimmed with the most delicate cream color, a pretty, coquettish cap on her golden head, the bloom and freshness of early youth on her face, she looks the loveliest picture of lovely and blooming womanhood, the perfection of elegance, the type of a patrician. Her white hands are covered with shining gems—Lady Chandos has a taste for rings. She is altogether a proper wife for a man to have to trust, to place his life and honor in her, a wife to be esteemed, appreciated and revered, but not worshiped with a mad passion. In the serene, pure atmosphere in which she lived no passion could come, no madness; she did not understand them, she never went out of the common grooves of life, but she was most amiable and sweet in them.

Nor had Lord Chandos altered much in these three years; he had grown handsomer, more manly; the strong, graceful figure, the erect, easy carriage, were just the same; his face had bronzed with travel, and the mustache that shaded his beautiful lips was darker in hue.

Had they been happy, these three years of married life? Ask Lady Chandos, and she will say, "Happy as a dream." She has not known a shadow of care or fear, she has been unutterably happy; she is the queen of blondes, one of the most popular queens of society, the chosen and intimate friend of more than one royal princess, one of the most powerful ladies at court; no royal ball, or concert, or garden-party is ever given without her name being on the list; she is at the head of half the charities in London; she lays foundation stones; she opens the new wings of hospitals; she interests herself in convalescent homes; she influences, and in a great many instances leads the fashions. "Hats *a la* Chandos," "the Marion costume," are tributes to her influence. To know her, to be known to be on her visiting list, is a passport everywhere. She has the finest diamonds and the finest rubies in London; her horses are the envy and admiration of all who see them; her mansion in Belgravia is the wonder of all who see it—every corner of the earth has been racked to add to its luxury and comfort. She has more money—just as pin-money—than many a peer has for the keeping up of title and estate. She has a husband who is all kindness and indulgence to her; who has never denied her the gratification of a single wish; who has never spoken one cross word to her; who is always devoted to her service. What could any one wish for more? She would tell you, with a charming, placid smile on her sweet face, that she is perfectly happy. If there be higher bliss than hers she does not know it yet; if there is a love, as there is genius, akin to madness, she has never felt it. Passion does not enter her life, it is all serene and calm.

In those three years Lord Chandos had made for himself a wonderful name. The Duke of Lester had done all that he could for him, but his own talents and energy had done more. He had proved himself to be what the leading journals said of him, "a man of the times." Just the man wanted— full of life, activity, energy, talent, and power. He had made himself famous as an orator; when Lord Chandos rose to speak, the house listened and the nation applauded; his speeches were eagerly read. He was the rising man of the day, and people predicted for him that he would be prime minister before he was thirty. His mother's heart rejoiced in him—all her most sanguine hopes were fulfilled. Ask him if he is happy. He would laugh carelessly, and answer, "I am as happy as other men, I imagine." Ask him if his ambition and pride are gratified, and he will tell you "Yes." Ask him if ambition and pride can fill his life to the exclusion of all else; he will tell you "No." Ask him again if he has a thousand vague, passionate desires unfulfilled, and his handsome face will cloud and his eyes droop.

They are very popular. Lord Chandos gives grand dinners, which are considered among the best in London, Lady Chandos gives balls, and people intrigue in every possible way for invitations. She gives quiet dances and *soirees*, which are welcomed. She is "at home" every Wednesday, and no royal drawing-room is better attended than her "at home." She has select little teas at five o'clock, when some of the most exclusive people in London drink orange pekoe out of the finest Rose du Barri china. They are essentially popular; no ball is considered complete unless it is graced by the presence of the queen of blondes. As the Belgravian matrons all say, "Dear Lady Chandos is so happy in her marriage." Her husband was always in attendance on her. Other husbands had various ways; some went to their clubs, some smoked, some drank, some gambled, others flirted. Lord Chandos was irreproachable; he did none of these things.

There had never been the least cloud between them. If this perfect wife of his had any little weakness, it was a tendency to slight jealousies, so slight as to be nameless, yet she allowed them at times to ruffle her calm, serene repose. Her husband was very handsome—there was a picturesque, manly beauty about his dark head and face, a grandeur in his grand, easy figure that was irresistible. Women followed him wherever he went with admiring eyes. As he walked along the streets they said to each other, with smiling eyes, what a handsome man he was. If they went to strange hotels all the maids courtesied with blushing faces to the handsome young lord. At

A Mad Love | 181

Naples one of the flower-girls had disturbed Lady Marion's peace—a girl with a face darkly beautiful as one of Raphael's women, with eyes that were like liquid fire, and this girl always stood waiting for them with a basket of flowers. Lord Chandos, in his generous, princely fashion, flung her pieces of gold or silver; once my lady saw the girl lift the money he threw to her from the ground, kiss it with a passionate kiss, and put it in the bodice of her dress. In vain after that did Carina offer Parma violets and lilies from Sorrento, Lady Chandos would have no more, and Carina was requested soon afterward by the master of the hotel to take her stand with her flowers elsewhere.

Lord Chandos never made any remark upon it—every lady has some foible, some little peculiarity. She was a perfect wife, and this little feeling of small jealousies was not worth mentioning. If they went to a ball and he danced three times with the same lady, he knew he would hear something in faint dispraise. If he admired any one as a good rider or a good dancer, out would come some little criticism; he smiled as he heard, but said nothing— it was not worth while. Like a kind-hearted man he bore this little failing in mind, and, if ever he praised one woman, he took care to add something complimentary to his wife. So the three years had passed and this was the spring-tide of the fourth, the showery, sparkling month of April; violets and primroses were growing, the birds beginning to sing, the leaves springing, the chestnuts budding, the fair earth reviving after its long swoon in the arms of winter. The London season of this year was one of the best known, no cloud of either sorrow or adversity hung over the throne or the country; trade was good, everything seemed bright and prosperous; but the great event of the season was most certainly the first appearance in England of the new singer, Madame Vanira, whose marvelous beauty and wonderful voice were said to drive people mad with excitement and delight.

It was to see her that Lord and Lady Chandos went to the Royal Italian Opera on that night in April on which our story is continued.

CHAPTER XXXVII
A MEETING OF EYES

The newspapers had already given many details of Madame Vanira. For many long years there had been nothing seen like her. They said her passion and power, her dramatic instinct, her intensity were so great, that she was like electric fire. One critic quoted of her what was so prettily said of another great actress:

"She has a soul of fire in a body of gauze."

No one who saw her ever forgot her; even if they only saw her once, her face lived clear, distinct, and vivid in their memory forever afterward. No one knew which to admire most, her face or her voice. Her face was the most wondrously beautiful ever seen on the stage, and her voice was the most marvelous ever heard—it thrilled you, it made you tremble; its grand pathos, its unutterable sadness, its marvelous sweetness; those clear, passionate tones reached every heart, no matter how cold, how hardened it might be—one felt that in listening to it that it was the voice of a grand, passionate soul. It was full, too, of a kind of electricity; when Madame Vanira sung she could sway the minds and hearts of her hearers as the winter winds sway the strong boughs. She drew all hearts to herself and opened them. When she sung, it was as though she sung the secret of each heart to its owner.

They said that her soul was of fire and that the fire caught her listeners; she had power, genius, dramatic force enough in her to electrify a whole theater full of people, to lift them out of the commonplace, to take them with her into the fairyland of romance and genius, to make them forget everything and anything except herself.

Such a woman comes once in a century, not oftener. They called her a siren, a Circe. She was a woman with a passionate soul full of poetry; a genius with a soul full of power; a woman made to attract souls as the magnet attracts the needle.

She made her *debut* in the theater of San Carlo, in Naples, and the people had gone wild over her; they serenaded her through the long starlit night;

they cried out her name with every epithet of praise that could be lavished on her; they raved about her beautiful eyes, her glorious face, her voice, her acting, her attitudes.

Then a royal request took her to Russia; a still warmer welcome met her there; royal hands crowned her with diamonds, royal voices swelled her triumph; there was no one like La Vanira. She was invited to court and all honors were lavished on her.

From there she went to Vienna, where her success was as great; to Paris, where it was greater, and now she was to make her *debut* before the most critical, calm, appreciative audience in Europe. The papers for weeks had been full of her; they could describe her grand, queenly beauty, her wonderful acting, her genius, which was alone in the world, her jewels, her dresses, her attitudes; but there was nothing to say about her life.

Even the society journals, usually so well informed, had nothing to say about Madame Vanira. Whether she were single, or married, or a widow, none of them knew; of what town, of what nation, even of what family, none of them knew.

She seemed to be quite alone in the world, and against her even the faintest rumor had never been heard; she was of irreproachable propriety, nay, more, she was of angelic goodness—generous, truthful, charitable and high-minded. There was not a whisper against her good name—not one. She had a legion of admirers, none of whom could boast of a favor; she answered no letters; she gave no interviews; she accepted no invitations; she visited among some of the most exclusive circles, where she was received as an equal; she had had offers of marriage that would have made any other woman vain; she refused them all; she seemed to live for her art, and nothing else. Such a description naturally excited the curiosity of people, and the result was a house so crowded that it was almost impossible to find room.

"We may think ourselves fortunate," said Lady Chandos. "I have never seen the house so crowded, and, do not laugh, Lance, I do not see a prettier toilet than my own."

Lady Chandos was always well pleased when her husband complimented her on her dress; if he forgot it, she generally reminded him of it. She looked very beautiful this evening; her dress was of white satin, effectively trimmed with dead gold, and she wore diamonds with rubies— no one there looked better than the queen of blondes.

"I am quite impatient to see La Vanira," she said to her husband. "I wonder why she has chosen this opera, 'L'Etoile du Nord;' it is not the usual thing for a *debutante*."

Then the words died on her lips and for some minutes she said no more. The curtain was drawn up and Madame Vanira appeared. There was a dead silence for some few minutes, then there was a storm of applause; her beautiful face won it, her grand figure, her eyes, with their fire of passion, seemed to demand it.

Of all characters, perhaps that of the loving, impassionate Star of the North suited her best. In it she found expression for love, her passion and despair. She stood before what was perhaps the most critical audience in the world, and she thrilled them with her power. It was no more a woman; she seemed more like an inspired sibyl; her audience hung on every note, on every word from those wonderful lips; while she charmed all ears she charmed all eyes; the beauty of her magnificent face, the beauty of her superb figure, the grandeur of her attitudes, the inimitable grace of her actions were something new and wonderful. From the first moment the curtain rose until it fell the whole audience was breathless.

Lady Chandos laid down her jeweled opera-glass while she drew a breath of relief, it was so wonderful to her, this woman all fire, and genius and power.

"Lance," she said to her husband, "what a wonderful face it is. Have you looked well at it?"

She glanced carelessly at her husband as she spoke, then started at the change in him; his whole face had altered, the expression of careless interest had died, the color and light had died, his dark eyes had a strained, bewildered look; they were shadowed as though by some great doubt or fear.

"Lance," said his wife, "are you not well? You look so strange—quite unlike yourself."

He turned away lest she should see his face more plainly, and then she continued:

"If you are not well, we will go home, dear; nothing will interest me without you."

He made a great effort and spoke to her; but the very tone of his voice was altered, all the sweetness and music had gone out of it.

"I am well," he said, "pray do not feel anxious over me; the house is very full and very warm."

"What do you think of La Vanira?" continued Lady Chandos; "how very different she is to any one else."

He laughed, and the sound was forced and unnatural.

A Mad Love | 185

"I think she is very wonderful," he replied.

"And beautiful?" asked Lady Marion, with a look of eager anxiety.

He was too wise and too wary to reply with anything like enthusiasm.

"Beautiful for those who like brunettes," he answered coldly, and his wife's heart was at rest. If he had gone into raptures she would have been disgusted.

"If she would but leave me in peace," thought Lord Chandos to himself.

He was bewildered and confused. Before him stood the great and gifted singer whom kings and emperors had delighted to honor, the most beautiful and brilliant of women; yet surely those dark, lustrous eyes had looked in his own; surely he had kissed the quivering lips, over which such rich strains of music rolled; surely he knew that beautiful face. He had seen it under the starlight, under the shade of green trees by the mill-stream; it must be the girl he had loved with such mad love, and had married more than four years ago. Yet, how could it be? Of Leone he had never heard one syllable.

Mr. Sewell had written to Lady Lanswell to tell her of her indignant rejection of all help, of her disappearance, how she never even returned to River View for anything belonging to her, and after some time the countess had told her son. He went to River View and he found the house closed and the servants gone; he made some inquiries about Leone, but never heard anything about her. He deplored the fact—it added to his misery over her. If he could have known that he left her well provided for he would not have suffered half so much.

All these years he had never heard one word of her. He had thought of her continually, more than any one would have imagined; he never knew what it was to forget her for one minute. His heart was always sad, his soul sorrowful, his mind ill at ease. The more he thought of it, the more despicable his own conduct seemed. He hated the thought of it, he loathed the very memory.

And here was the face he had seen by the mill-stream, the face which had haunted him, the face he loved so well—here it was alight with power, passion and genius. Could this brilliant, gifted singer be Leone, or was he misled by a wonderful likeness? He could not understand it, he was bewildered.

He had wondered a thousand times a day what had become of Leone; he remembered her wonderful talent, how she read those grand old tragedies of Shakespeare until she knew them by heart; but could it be possible that Leone had become the finest singer and the grandest actress in the world?

It was in the last grandly pathetic scene that their eyes met, and for one half moment the gifted woman, on whose lightest breath that vast crowd hung, swayed to and fro as though she would have fallen; the next minute she was pouring out the richest streams of melody, and Lady Chandos said:

"Is it my fancy, Lance, or was La Vanira looking at you?"

"I should say it was your fancy, Marion—La Vanira sees nothing lower than the skies, I think."

And then the opera ended.

CHAPTER XXXVIII
LANCE'S DETERMINATION

"You have not much to say to me to-night, Lance," said Lady Marion, in a tone of gentle expostulation. "I wonder if that beautiful singer was really looking at you. It seemed to me that the moment her eyes caught yours she faltered and almost failed."

Lord Chandos roused himself.

"Give me a woman's fancy," he said; "it is boundless as the deep sea."

"I think a beautiful singer is like a siren," continued Lady Chandos, "she wins all hearts."

He laughed again, a tired, indifferent, reckless laugh.

"I thought we had agreed that you had won mine, Marion," he said, "and, if that be true, it cannot be won again."

She was silent for a few minutes, then she continued:

"Which do you really admire most, Lance, blonde or brunette, tell me?"

"A strange question to ask a man who was fortunate enough to win the queen of blondes for his wife," he replied.

He would have paid her any compliment—said anything to please her—if she would only have given him time to think.

They were driving home together, but he felt it was impossible to remain under any roof until he had learned whether Leone and La Vanira were the same. If his dear, good, amiable wife would but give him time to think. He could hear the sound of the mill-wheel, he could hear the ripple of the waters, the words of the song:

"In sheltered vale a mill-wheel
Still sings its busy lay.
My darling once did dwell there,
But now she's gone away."

The stars were shining as they shone when he sat by the mill-stream, with that beautiful head on his heart. He shuddered as he remembered her forebodings. Lady Chandos took his hand anxiously in hers.

"My dearest Lance, I am quite sure you are not well, I saw you shudder as though you were cold, and yet your hands are burning hot. What is it you say about going to your club? Nothing of the kind, my darling. You must have some white wine whey; you have taken cold. No; pray do not laugh, Lance, prevention is better than cure."

She had exactly her own way, as those very quiet, amiable wives generally have. He did not go to his club, but he sat by his dressing-room fire, and drank white wine whey. He had the satisfaction of hearing his wife say that he was the best husband in the world; then he fell asleep, to dream of the mill-stream and the song.

It grew upon him—he must know if that was Leone. Of course, he said to himself, he did not wish to renew his acquaintance with her—he would never dare, after his cruel treatment of her, even to address one word to her; but he should be quite content if he could know whether this was Leone or not. If he could know that he would be happy, his sorrow and remorse would be lessened.

He knew that the best place for hearing such details was his club— the Royal Junior—every one and everything were discussed there, no one escaped, and what was never known elsewhere was always known at the Royal Junior. He would take luncheon there and by patient listening would be sure to know. He went, although Lady Chandos said plaintively that she could not eat her luncheon alone.

"I am compelled to go," he said. "I have business, Marion, that is imperative."

"I think husbands have a reserve fund of business," said Lady Chandos. "What a mysterious word it is, and how much it covers, Lance. Lord Seafield is never at home, but whenever his wife asks him where he is going, he always says 'on business.' Now, in your case what does business mean?"

He laughed at the question.

"Parliamentary interests, my dear," he replied, as he hastened away. Such close questions were very difficult to answer.

He found the dining-rooms well filled, and, just as he had foreseen, the one subject was La Vanira. Then, indeed, did he listen to some wonderful stories. The Marquis of Exham declared that she was the daughter of an illustrious Sicilian nobleman, who had so great a love for the stage nothing could keep her from it. The Earl of Haleston said he knew for a fact she was the widow of an Austrian Jew, who had taken to the stage as the means of gaining her livelihood. Lord Bowden said she was the wife of an Austrian officer who was possessed of ample means. There were at least twenty different stories about her, and not one agreed with another.

"I wonder," said Lord Chandos, at last, "what is the real truth?"

"About what?" said a white-haired major, who sat next to him.

"About La Vanira," he replied; "every one here has a different story to tell."

"I can tell you as much truth as any one else about her," said the major, "I was with the manager last evening. La Vanira is English. I grant that she looks like a Spaniard—I never saw such dark eyes in my life; but she is English; accomplished, clever, good as gold, and has no one belonging to her in the wide world. That much the manager told me himself."

"But where does she come from?" he asked, impatiently. "Everybody comes from somewhere."

"The manager's idea is that she was brought up in the midland counties; he thinks so from a few words she said one day."

"Is she married or single?" asked Lord Chandos.

"Single," was the reply; "and in no hurry to be married. She has refused some of the best offers that could be made; and yet she wears a ring on the third finger of her left hand—perhaps it is not a wedding-ring."

"I should like to see her," said Lord Chandos.

The white-haired major laughed.

"So would half the men in London, but no one visits her—she allows no introductions. I know a dozen and more who have tried to see her in vain."

He was not much wiser after this conversation than before; but he was more determined to know. That same evening he made another excuse, and left his wife at Lady Blanchard's ball while he drove to the opera-house. The opera was almost over, but he saw the manager, to whom he briefly stated his errand.

"I believe," he said, "that in Madame Vanira I recognize an old friend. Will you introduce me to her?"

"I am sorry to say that I cannot," was the courteous reply. "I promised madame not to make any introductions to her."

"Will you take my card to her? If she is the lady I take her to be she will send word whether she wishes to see me or not."

The manager complied with his request. He soon returned.

"Madame Vanira wishes me to say that she has not the pleasure of your lordship's acquaintance, and that she is compelled to decline any introduction."

"Then it is not Leone," he said to himself, and a chill of disappointment came over him.

His heart had been beating quickly and warmly, yet he persuaded himself it was only that he was so pleased to know she was all right and safe from the frowns of the world. It was not Leone, but she was so much like Leone that he felt he must go to see her again.

"The opera to-night?" said Lady Marion, in her sweetest tones. "Why, my dear Lance, you were there three nights since."

"Yes, I know, but I thought it pleased you, Marion. We will ask my mother to go with us. It is the 'Crown Diamonds,' a very favorite opera of hers."

"Will Madame Vanira sing?" asked Lady Chandos, and her husband quietly answered:

"Yes."

He was anxious for Lady Lanswell to go, to see if she would recognize Leone, or if any likeness would strike her. As his chief wish seemed to be to give pleasure to his mother, and he expressed no desire to see the beautiful singer again, Lady Chandos was very amiable. She sent a kind little note to the countess, saying what pleasure it would give them if she would go to the opera with them, and Lady Lanswell was only too pleased. The earl had grown tired of such things and never cared to go out in the evening.

How anxiously Lord Chandos watched his mother's face. He saw delight, surprise and wonder, but no recognition—except once, and then the magnificent arms of the actress were raised in denunciation. Then something of bewilderment came over Lady Lanswell's face, and she turned to her son.

"Lance," she said, "Madame Vanira reminds me of some one, and I cannot think who it is."

"Have you seen her before, mother, do you think?" he asked.

"No, I think not; but she reminds me of some one, I cannot think whom. Her gestures are more familiar to me than her face."

Evidently the thought of Leone never entered her mind; and Lord Chandos was more puzzled than ever. The countess was charmed.

"What fire, what genius, what power! That is really acting," she said. "In all my life I have seen nothing better. There is truth in her tenderness, reality in her sorrow. I shall often come to see Vanira, Lance."

So she did, and was often puzzled over the resemblance of some one she knew; but she never once dreamed of Leone, while, by dint of earnest watching and study, Lord Chandos became more and more convinced that it was she.

He was determined to find out. He was foolish enough to think that if he could once be sure of it, his heart and mind would be at rest, but until then there was no rest for him.

What could he do—how could he know? Then the idea came, to follow her carriage home. By dint of perseverance he found, at last, that Madame Vanira had a very pretty house in Hampstead called the Cedars, and he determined to call and see her there. If he had really been mistaken, and it were not Leone, he could but apologize; if it were— —

Ah, well, if it were, he would ask her forgiveness, and she would give it to him, on account of the love she bore him years ago.

CHAPTER XXXIX
NEITHER WIFE NOR WIDOW

It was with some trepidation that Lord Chandos presented himself at the gates of the Cedars, yet surely she who had loved him so well would never refuse him admission into her house? that is, if it were Leone. As he walked through the pretty garden and saw all the pretty flowers blooming, he said to himself, that it was like her. She had always so dearly loved the spring flowers, the flame of the yellow crocus, the faint, sweet odor of the violets, the pure heads of the white snow-drops. He had heard her say so often that she loved these modest, sweet flowers that come in the spring more than the dainty ones that bloom in summer-time.

It was like her, this garden, and yet, he could not tell why. Great clusters of lilac-trees were budding, the laburnums were thinking of flowering; but there was no song of running brook, and no ripple of fountains, no sound of falling water; the birds were busy wooing and they had so much to sing about.

There was a profusion of flowers, all the windows seemed full of them; there was a picturesque look about the place that reminded him of Leone. On the lawn stood two large cedars, from which the place derived its name. He went to the hall door. What if she should meet him suddenly and turn from him in indignant anger? What if it should not be Leone, but a stranger?

A pretty housemaid, Parisian, he knew from the type, answered the door, from whom he inquired, in his most polite fashion, if Madame Vanira was at home.

There is no denying the fact that all women are more or less susceptible to the charms of a handsome face, and Lord Chandos was handsome— exceedingly. The girl looked up into the dark face and the dark eyes that always looked admiringly when a woman was near.

"Madame Vanira sees no one," she replied.

Something passed rapidly from his hand to hers.

"You look kind," he said, "be my friend. I think that, years ago, I knew Madame Vanira. If she be the lady whom I believe her to be, she will be pleased to see me, and no possible blame can be attached to you. Tell me where she is that I may find her."

"Madame is in the morning-room," said the girl, with some hesitation, "but I shall lose my place if I admit you."

"I promise you no," said Lord Chandos; "on the contrary, your lady will be pleased that you are able to discriminate between those whom she would like to see, and those whom she would not."

"At least, let me announce you," pleaded the pretty housemaid, in broken English.

"No, it would serve no purpose; that is, of course, you can go before me and open the door—I will follow you immediately. You need only say, 'A gentleman to see you, madame.' Will you do this?"

"Yes," said the girl, reluctantly.

As he followed her through the passage, it did occur to him that if it were not Leone, he should be in a terrible dilemma. It occurred to him also, that if it were Leone, what right had he there, with that fair, sweet wife of his at home—what right had he there?

He followed the pretty maid through the hall and through a suit of rooms, furnished with quiet elegance. They came to the door of a room before which the maid stopped, and Lord Chandos saw that her face had grown pale.

She opened it.

"A gentleman to see you, madame," she said, hastily.

And then the maid disappeared, and he entered the room.

Leone was standing with her face to the window when he entered, and he had one moment in which to look round the room—one moment in which to control the rapid beating of his heart; then she turned suddenly, and once more they were face to face.

Ah, to see the heaven of delight and rapture that came over hers—the light that came into her eyes; it was as though her face was suddenly transfigured; all the past in that one moment of rapture was forgotten, all the treachery, the perfidy, the falsity.

She uttered one word, "Lance," but it was a cry of unutterable delight. "Lance," she repeated, and then, with all the light of heaven still shining in her face, she hid her face on his breast. She did not remember, she only knew that it was the face of her lost lover, the same strong, tender arms were clasped round her, the same warm kisses were on her face, the same passionate, loving heart was beating near her own. Ah, Heaven, how sweet that one moment was. To die while it lasted, never to leave the shelter of those dear arms again. She had waited for him for years, and he had come at last.

There were a few minutes of silent, rapturous greeting, and then, suddenly, she remembered, and sprung from him with a low cry.

"How dare you?" she cried, "I had forgotten. How dare you?"

Then the sight of the beloved face, the dear eyes, the well-remembered figure, took all the hot anger from her.

"Oh, Lance, Lance, I ought not to speak to you or look at you, and yet I cannot help it. God help me, I cannot help it."

He was down on his knees by her side, clasping her hands, the folds of her dress, crying out to her to pardon him; that he had no excuse to offer her; he had been guilty beyond all guilt; that neither in heaven nor on earth could there be any pardon for him; that he would have died a hundred deaths rather than have lost her.

For some five minutes it was a mad whirl of passion, love and regret. She was the first to recollect herself, to say to him:

"Lord Chandos, you must not kneel there; remember you have a wife at home."

The words struck him like a sharp sword. He arose and, drawing a chair for her, stood by her side.

"I am beside myself," he said, "with the pleasure of seeing you again. Forgive me, Leone; I will not offend. Oh, what can I say to you? How can I look upon your face and live?"

"You were very cruel to me and very treacherous," she said; "your treachery has spoiled my life. Oh, Lance, how could you be so cruel to me when I loved you so—how could you?"

Tears that she had repressed for years rained down her face; all the bitter grief that she had held in as with an iron hand, all the pride so long triumphant, all the pain and anguish, and the desolation, that had been in check, rushed over her, as the tempestuous waves of the sea rush over the rocks and sands.

"How could you, Lance?" she cried, wringing her hands; "how could you? You were cruel and treacherous to me, though I trusted you so. Ah, my love, my love, how could you?"

The beautiful head fell forward in the very abandonment of sorrow; great sobs shook the beautiful figure.

"Oh, Lance, I loved you so, I believed in you as I believed in Heaven. I loved you and trusted you, you forsook me and deceived me. Oh, my love, my love!"

His face grew white and his strong figure trembled under the pain of her reproaches.

"Leone," he said, gently, "every word of yours is a sword in my heart. Why did I do it? Ah me, why? I have no word of excuse for myself, not one. I might say that I was under woman's influence, but that would not excuse me. I take the whole blame, the whole sin upon myself. Can you ever forgive me?"

She raised her face to his, all wet with tears.

"I ought not to forgive you," she said; "I ought to drive you from my presence; I ought to curse you with my ruined life, but I cannot. Oh, Lance, if I only lay under the waters of the mill-stream, dead."

The passion of her grief was terrible to see. He forgot all and everything but her—the wife at home, the plighted vows, honor, truth, loyalty—all and everything except the girl whom he had loved with a mad love, and her grief. He drew her to his breast, he kissed away the shining tears; he kissed the trembling lips.

"Leone, you will drive me mad. Great God, what have I done? I realize it now; I had better have died," and then the strength of the strong man gave way, and he wept like a child. "It is no excuse," he said, "to plead that I was young, foolish, and easily led. Oh, Leone, my only love, what was I doing when I gave you up—when I left you?"

The violence of his grief somewhat restrained hers; she was half frightened at it.

"We are making matters worse," she said. "Lance, we must not forget that you are married now in earnest."

"Will you ever forgive me?" he asked. "I have no excuse to offer. I own that my sin was the most disloyal and the most traitorous a man could commit, but forgive me, Leone. I have repented of it in sackcloth and ashes. Say you forgive me."

The beautiful, colorless face did not soften at the words.

"I cannot," she said; "I cannot forgive that treachery, Lance; it has wounded me even unto death. How can I forgive it?"

"My darling—Leone—say you will pardon me. I will do anything to atone for it."

She laid one white hand on his arm.

"You see, Lance," she said, earnestly, "it is one of those things for which you can never atone—one that can never be undone—but one which will brand me forever. What am I? Did you stop to think of that when your new love tempted you? What am I? not your wife—not your widow. Oh God, what am I?"

He drew her to him again, but this time she resisted his warm kisses.

"Leone," he said sadly, "I deserve to be shot. I hate myself—I loathe myself. I cannot imagine how I failed in my duty and loyalty to you. I can only say that I was young and thoughtless—easily led. Heaven help me, I had no mind of my own, but I have suffered so cruelly and so have you, my darling—so have you."

"I?" she replied. "When you can count the leaves in the forest, or the sands on the seashore, you will know what I have suffered, not until then."

Her voice died away in a melancholy cadence that to him was like the last wailing breath of the summer wind in the trees.

CHAPTER XL
"FORGIVE ME, LEONE"

"Lance," she said, suddenly, "or, as I ought to say, Lord Chandos—how can I forgive you? What you ask is more than any woman could grant. I cannot pardon the treachery which has ruined my life, which has stricken me, without blame or fault of mine, from the roll of honorable women—which has made me a by-word, a mark for the scorn and contempt of others, a woman to be contemned and despised. Of what use are all the gifts of Heaven to me, with the scarlet brand you have marked on my brow?"

He grew white, even to the lips, as the passionate words reached his ears.

"Leone," he cried, "for God's sake spare me. I have no defense—no excuse; spare me; your words kill me. They are not true, my darling; none of what happened was your fault—you were innocent and blameless as a child; you are the same now. Would to Heaven all women were pure and honorable as you. Say what you will to me, no punishment would be too great for me—but say nothing yourself; never one word, Leone. Could you forgive me? I have done you the most cruel wrong, and I have no excuse to offer—nothing but my foolish youth, my mad folly, my unmanly weakness. I have known it ever since I married. You are my only love; I have never had another. Ah, my darling, forgive me. If I have ruined your life, I have doubly ruined my own."

She raised her beautiful, colorless face to his.

"Lance," she said, gently, "what a prophecy that song held for us. And the running water—how true a foreboding it always murmured:

"'The vows are all forgotten,
The ring asunder broken.'

How true and how cruel. I hear the song and I hear the murmur of the water in my dreams."

"So do I," he replied, sadly. "My darling, I wish we never left the mill-stream. I would to Heaven we had died under the running water together."

"So do I," she said, "but we are living, not dead, and life holds duties just as death holds relief. We must remember much harm has been done—we need not do more."

"Say that you will forgive me, Leone, and then I do not care what happens. I will do anything you tell me. I will humble myself in every way. I will do anything you can desire if you will only forgive me. Do, for Heaven's sake. I am so utterly wretched that I believe if you refuse to say one word of pardon to me I shall go mad or kill myself."

There was a long struggle in her mind. Could she forgive the injury which seemed greater than man had ever inflicted on woman? She was very proud, and her pride was all in arms. How could she pardon a traitor? She had loved him better than her life, and with the first sight of his handsome, beloved face all the glamour of her love was over her again.

How could she forgive him? Yet the proud figure was bent so humbly before her, the proud head so low.

"What am I to say?" she cried. "I was a good and innocent girl—now it seems to me that the evil spirits of passion and unrest have taken possession of me. What am I to say or to do? Heaven help and teach me."

"Forgive me," he repeated. "Your refusal will send me away a madman, ready for any reckless action. Your consent will humble me, but it will make me happier. Oh, my darling, forgive me."

"Suppose that harm follows my forgiveness—we are better enemies than friends, Lord Chandos."

"We will never be enemies, and no harm can come except that I shall be happier for it. Say you will forgive me, Leone. See, I ask your pardon on my knees. For Heaven's sake, for my great love's sake, say you forgive me!"

He knelt before her humbly as a child, he bowed his handsome head until his face rested on her knees; he sobbed aloud in his sorrow and his deep regret. She stood for a few minutes quite uncertain; her clear reason and common sense told her that it would be better if she would refuse him pardon, and that they should part for all time; but love and pity pleaded, and of course love and pity won. She laid her hand on the dark head of the man whom she had once believed her husband; her beautiful face quivered with emotion.

"I forgive you," she said, "freely, frankly, fully, as I hope Heaven will forgive me all my sins. Nay, you must not kiss me, not even my hand. Your kisses belong to some one else now—not to me. I forgive you, but we must part again. Come what may—we must part, we must not meet again."

"I can never part with you," he said, in a hoarse voice. "You have been life of my life, heart of my heart too long for that."

She held up her hand with a superb gesture of warning and silence.

"Hush, Lord Chandos," she said; "if you speak to me in that strain, I shall never see you again. Remember you have a wife; you must not be false to two women—keep true to one. Neither your kisses nor your loving words belong to me now."

"I will not offend you," he said, sadly.

She leaned her beautiful arms on the table, her white hands under her chin, looking steadily at him.

"I have forgiven you," she said, musingly, "I, who have sworn such terrible oaths, such bitter revenge, I have ended by forgiving you, after the fashion of the most milk-and-water type of women. I have forgiven you, and Heaven knows how I tried to hate you, and have tried to take pleasure in the thoughts of my vengeance."

"You have had your vengeance on me, Leone, in the shape of the love that has never left me, and the memories which have haunted me. You swore vengeance against my mother, but you will forego that."

A slow smile came over her face and died away again.

"Lord Chandos," she said, "you will not be my debtor in generosity. You have asked me to pardon you; I have done so. Grant me one favor in return—tell me who influenced you to forsake me?"

He looked puzzled.

"I hardly know, Leone, I can hardly tell you."

"It was not the lady whom you have married," she continued, "of that I am sure. Who was it?"

"I think if any one influenced me it must have been my mother," he said, gently; "she was always violently opposed to it."

The beautiful lips paled and trembled.

"I thought it was your mother," she said, gravely, "No, I shall not forego my vengeance against her, although I know not when I may gain it."

"You will forget all that," he said. "You are too noble to care for vengeance."

"I am not too noble," she replied. "All that was best and noble in me died on the day you forsook me. And now, Lord Chandos, listen to me. Words of peace and pardon have passed between us. It has raised a heavy funeral pall from my life; it has, perhaps, raised a black cloud from yours. Lord Chandos, we must not meet again."

"You cannot be so cruel, Leone. Having found you, how can I lose you again?"

"You must, it is imperative," she said slowly.

"But, Leone, why should we not be friends?" he said, gently.

She laughed a hard, scornful laugh that struck him in the face like the sting of a sharp blade.

"Friends?" she repeated. "Could we who have been wedded lovers ever be friends? You do not know what words mean if you think that."

He stood before her with a stern, white face.

"Leone," he cried, "are you really going to be cruel enough to send me away out of your life again, I who have been mad with joy at finding you?"

"If I were cruel," she said, slowly, "now I would take my vengeance. I should say as you once left me so now I leave you, but I am not cruel, and that is my reason. My reason is a good and pure one; we could never remain friends, we love each other too much for that; we must live as strangers now; and remember, it is your fault, not mine."

"I cannot submit to it," he cried.

But she looked at him with a face stern, resolute, fixed as his own.

"Remember, Lord Chandos," she said, "that I am my own mistress. I can choose my friends and associates. I refuse to admit you among the number."

"You cannot prevent me from coming to see you, Leone."

"No; but I can, and shall, refuse to see you when you come," she replied; "and I shall do so."

"Oh, my love, my cruel, beautiful love," he cried.

The girl's face flushed with hot anger and indignation.

"Will you be silent?" she cried. "Shame on you, Lord Chandos, to use such words. You have a beautiful and beloved wife at home to whom all your love and fidelity belong. If you say one more such word to me I will never see you again."

"But, Leone, it seems so very hard; you might let me call at times and see you."

"No, I cannot, I cannot trust myself, even if I could trust you. I have had no other husband, no other love; you have married. I would not trust myself; my love is as great now as ever it was, but it shall not run away with me; it shall not be my master. I will master it. You must not come near me."

"But, surely, if I meet you in the street, you will not ask me to pass you by?" he said.

"No; if we meet quite by chance, quite by accident, I will always speak to you. Ah, Lance," she added, with a smile, "I know you so well, I know every look in your eyes; you are thinking to yourself you will often see me by accident. You must not; such honor as you have left me let me keep."

"If this is to be our last interview, for some time, at least," he continued, "tell me, Leone, how is it that you have become so famous?"

"Yes, I will tell you all about that; I am rather proud of my power. It is not a long story, and it dates from the day on which your mother sent me that letter."

She told him all her studies, her struggles, her perseverance, her success, finally her crowning by fame.

"It is like a romance," he said.

"Yes, only it is true," she replied.

He tried to prolong the interview, but she would close it; and he was compelled to leave her, when he would have given years of his life to have remained one hour longer.

CHAPTER XLI
"LET US BE FRIENDS"

"Lance," said the sweet voice of Lady Marion, plaintively, "I am beginning to have a faint suspicion about you."

"Indeed. Your suspicions are not faint as a rule. What is this?"

"I am afraid that you are growing just a little tired of me," said the beautiful queen of blondes.

"What makes you think so?" he asked, trying to laugh, as he would have done a few weeks since at such an accusation.

"Several reasons. You are not so attentive to me as you used to be; you do not seem to listen when I speak; you have grown so absent-minded; and then you say such strange things in your sleep."

He looked grave for half a minute, then laughed carelessly.

"Do I? Then I ought to be ashamed of myself. Men talk enough in their waking hours without talking in their sleep. What do I say, Marion?"

He asked the question carelessly enough, but there was an anxious look in his dark eyes.

"I cannot tell; I hardly remember," said Lady Chandos; "but you are always asking some one to forgive you and see you. Have you ever offended any one very much, Lance?"

"I hope not," he replied. "Dreams are so strange, and I do not think they are often true reflections of our lives. Have you any further reason for saying I am growing tired of you? It is a vexed question, and we may as well settle it now as renew the argument."

"No, I have no other reason. Lance, you are not cross with me, dear?"

"No, I am not cross; but, at the same time, I must say frankly I do not like the idea of a jealous wife; it is very distasteful to me."

Lady Marion raised her eyes in wonder.

"Jealous, Lance?" she repeated. "I am not jealous. Of whom could I be jealous? I never see you pay the least attention to any one."

"Jealous wives, as a rule, begin by accusing their husbands of cooling love, want of attention, and all that kind of thing."

"But, Lance," continued the beautiful woman, "are you quite sure that there is no truth in what I say?"

He looked at her with a dreamy gaze in his dark eyes.

"I am quite sure," he replied. "I love you, Marion, as much as ever I did, and I have not noticed in the least that I have failed in any attention toward you; if I have I will amend my ways."

He kissed the fair face bent so lovingly over him; and his wife laid her fair arms round his neck.

"I should not like to be jealous," she said; "but I must have your whole heart, Lance; I could not be content with a share of it."

"Who could share it with you?" he asked, evasively.

"I do not know, I only know that it must be all or none for me," she answered. "It is all—is it not, Lance?"

He kissed her and would fain have said yes, but it came home to him with a sharp conviction that his heart had been given to one woman, and one only—no other could ever possess it.

A few days afterward, when Lord Chandos expressed a wish to go to the opera again, his wife looked at him in wonder.

"Again?" she said. "Why, Lance, it is only two nights since you were there, and it is the same opera; you will grow tired of it."

"The only amusement I really care for is the opera," he said. "I am growing too lazy for balls, but I never tire of music."

He said to himself, that if for the future he wished to go to the opera he would not mention the fact, but would go without her.

They went out that evening: the opera was "Norma." Lord Chandos heard nothing and saw nothing but the wondrous face of Norma; every note of that music went home to his heart—the love, the trust, the reproaches. When she sang them in her grandly pathetic voice, it was as though each one were addressed to himself. Three times did Lady Chandos address him without any response, a thing which in her eyes was little less than a crime.

"How you watch La Vanira," she said. "I am sure you admire her very much."

He looked at her with eyes that were dazed—that saw nothing; the eyes of a man more than half mad.

"And now look," she said. "Why, Lance, La Vanira is looking at me. What eyes she has. They stir my very heart and trouble me. They are saying something to me."

"Marion, hush! What are you talking about?" he cried.

"La Vanira's eyes—she is looking at me, Lance."

"Nonsense!" he said, and the one word was so abruptly pronounced that Lady Chandos felt sure it was nonsense and said no more.

But after that evening he said no more about going to the opera. If he felt any wish to go, he would go; it would be quite easy for him to make some excuse to her.

And those evenings grew more and more frequent. He did not dare to disobey Leone; he did not dare to go to her house, or to offer to see her in the opera house. He tried hard to meet her accidentally, but that happy accident never occurred; yet he could not rest, he must see her; something that was stronger than himself drew him near her.

He was weak of purpose; he never resolutely took himself in hand and said:

"I am married now. I have a wife at home. Leone's beauty, Leone's talents, are all less than nothing to me. I will be true to my wife."

He never said that; he never braced his will, or his energies to the task of forgetting her; he dallied with the temptation as he had done before; he allowed himself to be tempted as he had done before; the result was that he fell as he had fallen before.

Every day his first thought was how he could possibly get away that evening without drawing particular attention to his movements; and he went so often that people began to laugh and to tease him and to wonder why he was always there.

Leone always saw him. If any one had been shrewd and quick enough to follow her, they would have seen that she played to one person; that her eyes turned to him continually; that the gestures of her white arms seemed to woo him. She never smiled at him, but there were times, when she was singing some lingering, pathetic notes, it seemed as though she were almost waiting for him to answer her.

He did not dare to go behind the scenes, to linger near the door, to wait for her carriage, but his life was consumed with the one eager desire to see her. He went night after night to the box; he sat in the same place; he leaned his arms on the same spot, watching her with eyes that seemed to flash fire as they rested on her.

People remarked it at last, and began to wonder if it could be possible that Lord Chandos, with that beautiful wife, the queen of blondes, was beginning to care for La Vanira; he never missed one night of her acting, and he saw nothing but her when she was on the stage.

Again one evening Lady Chandos said to him:

"Lance, have you noticed how seldom you spend an evening—that is, the whole of an evening—with me? If you go to a ball with me, it seems to me that you are always absent for an hour or two."

"You have a vivid imagination, my dear wife," he replied.

And yet he knew it was on the night Leone played; he could no more have kept from going to see her than he could have flown; it was stronger than himself, the impulse that led him there.

Then his nights became all fever; his days all unrest; his whole heart and soul craved with passionate longing for one half hour with her, and yet he dared not seek it. Even then, had he striven to conquer his love, and have resolutely thought of his duty, his good faith and his loyalty, he would have conquered, as any strong man can conquer when he likes; he never tried. When the impulse led him, he went; when the temptation came to him to think of her, he thought of her, when the temptation came to him to love her, he gave way to it and never once set his will against it.

Then, when the fever of his longing consumed him, and his life had grown intolerable to him, he wrote a note to her; it said simply:

"Dear Leone,—Life is very sad. Do let us be friends—why should we not? Life is so short. Let us be friends. I am very miserable; seeing you sometimes would make me happy. Let us be friends, Leone. Why refuse me? I will never speak of love—the word shall never be mentioned. You shall be to me like my dearest, best-beloved sister. I will be your brother, your servant, and your friend; only give me, for God's dear sake, the comfort of seeing you. Leone, be friends."

It was one evening when she was tired that this letter was brought to her. She read it with weeping eyes; life was hard; she found it so. She loved her art, she lived in it, but she was only a woman, and she wanted the comfort of a human love and friendship.

Wearily enough she repeated the words to herself:

"Let us be friends. As he says, 'life is short.' The comfort will be small enough, Heaven knows, but it will be better than nothing. Yes, we will be friends."

So she answered the letter in a few words, telling him if he really wished what he said, she would discuss the prudence of such a friendship with him.

This letter of hers fell into the hands of Lady Marion. She looked at the fine, beautiful, clear handwriting.

"Lance, this is from a lady," she said.

When he took it from her his face flushed, for he knew the hand.

"It is from a lady," she repeated.

"It is on business," he replied, coldly, putting the envelope aside; and, to his intense delight, Lady Marion forgot it.

He was to go and see her. It was wrong to be so pleased, he knew, but he did not even try to hide his delight over it.

When should he go? He should count the hours—he could not wait longer than to-morrow. Would she be willing; or would she not? How long the hours seemed, yet they passed, and once more he was at the Cedars.

CHAPTER XLII
BECOMING SUSPICIOUS

So they made the second great mistake of their lives. These two, who had been married lovers, fancied they could be friends. If it had not been so sad and so pitiful, it would have been amusing to have heard the conditions of that friendship—they were as numerous as the preliminaries of an article of peace. They made all arrangements; their friendship was to be of the purest and most platonic nature; there was to be nothing said which would remind them of the past; he was to shake hands with her when he came and when he went; he might pay her a visit twice or three times a week; if they met, they were to be on friendly terms; they would discuss art, literature, and music—anything and everything except their own story; they were to take an interest in each other's lives and fortunes.

"I shall take such a pride in your career, Leone," said Lord Chandos, in all good faith; "it will be the dearest part of my life."

She held up one white finger with a smile; that was trespassing on forbidden ground. He must not break the new code of friendship by saying such things.

"We are friends, not lovers, Lord Chandos," she said, gently; "you will annoy me if you forget that. The dearer part of your life is at home."

He apologized for the words.

"I mean," he said, "that I shall take the keenest interest in your career, and watch it with pride."

"That is right, as I shall yours, Lord Chandos. I am proud of you, I am proud when I read your speeches; it seems to me no other man ever spoke so well. I am proud when I read that the rising man of the day is Lord Chandos, that England looks to Lord Chandos as a great power and a promising statesman. Ah, yes, I am proud of you when I read those things. Your face, your eager, hopeful eyes rise before me, and I say to myself, 'Ah, yes, he is a genius, and the world knows it.' It is pleasant to have true friends, such as we shall be to each other."

"Yes," he had answered her, with a sigh; "we should have been foolish indeed, Leone, to have deprived ourselves of this, the only consolation left in life for either of us. We shall be more happy as friends, Leone; it would have been too horrible to have been always apart."

They hedged themselves round with precautions; they were to be so prudent; they were not to address each other as Lance and Leone; they were never to sing old songs together; he was not to go behind the scenes in the theater, he was not to wait for her in the evening. She said to him laughingly, that they ought to have these conditions of friendship written down as they write down the articles of war or the preliminaries of peace.

"We ought to have parchment strong as parchment can be; but, Lord Chandos, we must keep to our rules, no matter what happens."

So they intended, and neither of them had the faintest idea of ever deviating from the rules laid down. It was better than nothing, spending a few hours with her each week was refreshing as an oasis in a desert; he eagerly looked forward to those days on which he was permitted to call, and before long these visits became chiefly the event of his life—he thought of little else.

So it gradually came about that the stronger nature gained the ascendency, the stronger soul gained the upper hand in his life. The love of Leone had always been by far the strongest element in his life; it had been set aside by a series of clever maneuvers, but now it resumed its sway. He did not intend it; he was weak enough and foolish enough to think that the prudent friendship could replace mad love, and he was not very long before he found out his mistake. But at first all went well—her praise stimulated him, he gave loose to the fiery eloquence that was natural to him. Knowing that she would read and criticise every word, he took more pride and pleasure in his public life than he had ever done before; he liked to hear her criticisms on his opinions and actions; he was delighted with the interest she took in his works.

At times the visits he paid were all occupied with the discussion of these details. He would tell her of some great oration or speech that he intended to make on some important measure, she would talk it over to him, and her marvelous intelligence, her bright wit and originality always threw some new light on the matter, some more picturesque view. In this she differed from Lady Marion, who was more timid and retiring, who looked upon everything connected with public life as a dreadful ordeal, who, fond as she was of literature, could not read a newspaper, who, dearly as she loved her husband, could not interest herself in his career.

So gradually and slowly the old love threw its glamour over them, slowly the master passion took its place again in Lord Chandos' life, but just at that time it was unknown to himself. It came at last that the only real life for him was the time spent with her—the morning hours when he discussed all the topics of the day with her, and the evening when he leaned over his opera box, his eyes drinking in the marvelous beauty of her face.

Then, as a matter of course, Lady Marion began to wonder where he went. He had been accustomed, when he had finished his breakfast, always to consult her about the day's plans—whether she liked to walk, ride, or drive, and he had always been her companion; but now it often happened that he would say to her:

"Marion, drive with my mother this morning, she likes to have you with her; my father goes out so little, you know."

She always smiled with the most amiable air of compliance with his wishes, but she looked up at him on this particular morning.

"Where are you going, Lance?" she asked. Her eyes took in, in their quiet fashion, every detail of his appearance, even to the dainty exotic in his button-hole.

Lord Chandos had a habit of blushing—his dark face would flush like a girl's when any sudden emotion stirred him—it did so now, and she, with wondering eyes, noticed the flush.

"Why, Lance," she said, "you are blushing; blushing just like a girl, because I just asked you where you were going."

And though the fiery red burned the dark skin, he managed to look calmly at his wife and say:

"You are always fanciful over me, Marion, and your fancies are not always correct."

She was one of the sweetest and most amiable of women, no one ever saw her ruffled or impatient. She went up to him now with the loveliest smile, and laid her fair arms round his neck; the very heaven of repose was in the eyes she raised to his.

"My darling Lance," she said, "I can never have any fancy over you; my thoughts about you are always true." She laid one slim, white hand on his face. "Why, your face burns now," she said, and he made some little gesture of impatience, and then his heart smote him. She was so fair, so gentle, and loved him so dearly.

"Have I vexed you, Lance?" she said. "I did not mean to do so. If you do not like me to ask you where you are going, I will not, but it seems to me such a simple thing."

"How can I object, or, rather, why should I object to tell you where I go, Marion? Here is my note-book; open it and read."

But when he said the words he knew that on his note-book there was no mention of Leone's name, and again his heart smote him. It was so very easy to deceive this fair, trusting woman. Lady Chandos put the note-book back in his pocket.

"I do not want to see it, Lance. I merely asked you the question because you looked so very nice, and you have chosen such a beautiful flower. I thought you were going to pay some particular visit."

He kissed the sweet, wistful face raised to his, and changed the subject.

"Do I not always look what you ladies call 'nice'?" he asked, laughingly; and she looked admiringly at him.

"You are always nice to me, Lance; there is no one like you. I often wonder if other wives are as proud of their husbands as I am of you? Now I shall try to remember that you do not like me to ask you where you are going. The greatest pleasure I have on earth is complying with every little wish of yours."

He could not help kissing her again, she was so sweet, so gentle, so kind, yet his heart smote him. Ah, Heaven! if life had been different to him; if he had been but firmer of purpose, stronger of will! He left her with an uneasy mind and a sore heart.

Lady Marion was more than usually thoughtful after he had gone. She could not quite understand.

The time had been when he had never left the house without saying something about where he was going; now his absences were long, and she did not know where his time was spent.

Lady Lanswell noticed the unusual shadow on the girl's sweet face, and in her quick, impetuous way asked her about it.

"Marion, you are anxious or thoughtful—which is it?" she asked.

"Thoughtful," said Lady Chandos. "I am not anxious, not in the least."

"Of what are you thinking, that it brings a shadow on that dear face of yours?" said Lady Lanswell, kindly.

Lady Chandos turned to her, and in a low tone of voice said:

"Has Lance any very old or intimate friends in London?"

"No; none that I know of. He knows a great many people, of course, and some very intimately, but I am not aware of any especial friendship. Why do you ask me?"

"I fancied he had; he is so much more from home than he used to be, and does not say where he goes."

"My dear Marion," said the countess, kindly, "Lance has many occupations and many cares; he cannot possibly tell you every detail of how and where he passes the time. Let me give you a little warning; never give way to any little suspicions of your husband; that is always the beginning of domestic misery; trust him all in all. Lance is loyal and true to you; do not tease him with suspicions and little jealousies."

"I am not jealous," said Lady Chandos, "but it seems to me only natural that I should like to know where my husband passes his time."

The older and wiser woman thought to herself, with a sigh, that it might be quite as well that she should not know.

CHAPTER XLIII
"DEATH ENDS EVERYTHING"

Madame Vanira became one of the greatest features of the day. Her beauty and her singing made her the wonder of the world. Royalty delighted to honor her. One evening after she had entranced a whole audience, keeping them hanging, as it were, on every silvery note that came from her lovely lips—people were almost wild over her—they had called her until they were tired. Popular enthusiasm had never been so aroused. And then the greatest honor ever paid to any singer was paid to her. Royal lips praised her and the highest personage in the land presented her with a diamond bracelet, worthy of the donor and the recipient. Her triumph was at its height; that night the opera in which she played was the "Crown Diamonds." Her singing had been perfection, her acting magnificent; she bad electrified the audience as no other *artiste* living could have done; her passion, her power, her genius had carried them with her. When she quitted the stage it was as though they woke from a long trance of delight.

That evening crowned her "Queen of Song." No one who saw her ever forgot her. The next morning the papers raved about her; they prophesied a new era for music and for the stage; it was, perhaps, the most triumphant night of her great career. She had the gift which makes an actress or a singer; she could impress her individuality on people; she made a mark on the hearts and minds of those who saw her that was never effaced; her gestures, her face, her figure, her magnificent attitudes stood out vivid and clear, while they lived distinct from any others.

"Where royalty smiles, other people laugh," says the old proverb. No sooner was it known that the warmest praise kindly and royal lips could give had been given to Madame Vanira than she became at once the darling of the world of fashion.

Invitations poured in upon her, the most princely mansions in London were thrown open to her; the *creme de la creme* of the *elite* sought her eagerly; there was nothing like her; her beauty and her genius inthralled every one. The time came when she was the most popular and the most eagerly sought after woman in London, yet she cared little for society; her art was the one thing she lived for, and her friendship with Lord Chandos. One day she said to him:

"I have never seen Lady Marion. What is she like?"

He noticed then and afterward that she never spoke of the queen of blondes as Lady Chandos, or as "your wife," but always as Lady Marion.

This was a beautiful morning in May, and there, sitting under the great cedar-tree on the lawn, all the sweet-smelling wind wafting luscious odors from jasmine and honeysuckle, the brilliant sun shining down on them, he had been reading to her the notes of a speech by which he hoped to do wonders; she had suggested some alterations, and, as he found, improvements; then she sat silently musing. After some time she startled him with the question:

"What is Lady Marion like?"

"Did you not see her," he replied, "on the first evening we were at the opera? She was by my side, and you saw me. Nay, I remember that she told me you were looking at her, and that your eyes magnetized hers."

"I remember the evening," said Leone sadly, "but I do not remember seeing my lady. I—I saw nothing but you. Tell me what she is like. Is she very beautiful?" she asked, and the tone of her voice was very wistful.

"Yes; she is very fine and queenly," he replied; "she is very quiet, gentle, and amiable. Would you like to see her, Leone?"

A sudden flame of passion flashed in those dark eyes, and then died away.

"Yes, I should like just once to see her. She is very clever, is she not?"

"Yes, in a quiet way. She plays beautifully, and she composes pretty airs to pretty words."

Leone looked up, with vivid interest in her face.

"Does she? Ah, that is greater art than being able to sing the music another has written."

"I do not think so," he replied. "If you are thinking of Lady Marion in comparison with yourself, there is no comparison; it is like moonlight and sunlight, water and wine. She has the grace and calm of repose. You have the fire of genius, before which everything grows pale. She quiets a man's heart. You stir every pulse in it. She soothes one into forgetfulness of life. You brace and animate and brighten. You cannot compare the two characters, because they are quite different. You are smiling. What amuses you?"

"Nothing. I was not amused, Lord Chandos. I was thinking, and the thought I smiled over was not amusing."

"What was it?"

"I was thinking of how it would be the same, the end of all; all grace, gifts, and talents; all beauty and genius. I read some lines yesterday that have haunted me ever since. Shall I repeat them to you?"

"It is always a great treat to hear you recite poetry," he replied. "I shall be only too delighted."

Her beautiful face grew more beautiful and more earnest, as it always did under the influence of noble words. Her voice was sweeter than that of a singing-bird, and stirred every pulse in the heart of the listener as she recited this little poem:

"While roses are so red,
While lilies are so white,
Shall a woman exalt her face
Because it gives delight?
She's not so sweet as a rose,
A lily is straighter than she,
And if she were as red or white,
She'd be but one of three.

"Whether she flush in love's summer,
Or in its winter grow pale,
Whether she flaunt her beauty,
Or hide it in a veil;
Be she red or white,
And stand she erect or bowed,
Time will win the race he runs with her,
And hide her away in a shroud."

"Those words took my fancy, Lord Chandos," continued Leone; "they are so true, so terribly true. All grace and beauty will be hidden away some day in a shroud."

"There will be no shroud for the soul," he said.

She rose from her seat and looked round with a weary sigh.

"That is true. After all, nothing matters, death ends everything; nothing matters except being good and going to heaven."

He smiled half sadly at her.

"Those are grave thoughts for the most brilliant beauty, the most gifted singer, the most popular queen of the day," he said.

"The brilliant beauty will be a mere handful of dust and ashes some day," she said.

Then Lord Chandos rose from his seat with a shudder.

"Let us go out into the sunlight," he said; "the shade under the old cedar makes you dull. How you have changed! I can remember when you never had a dull thought."

"I can remember when I had no cause for dull thoughts," she answered. Then, fancying that the words implied some little reproach to him, she continued, hastily: "My soul has grown larger, and the larger one's soul the more one suffers. I have understood more of human nature since I have tried to represent the woes of others."

He glanced at her with sudden interest.

"Which, of all the characters you represent, do you prefer?" he asked.

"I can hardly tell you. I like Norma very much—the stately, proud, loving woman, who has struggled so much with her pride, with her sense of duty, with her sacred character, who fought human love inch by inch, who yielded at last; who made the greatest sacrifice a woman could make, who risked her life and dearer than her life for her love. All the passion and power in my nature rises to that character."

"That is easily seen," he replied. "There have been many Normas, but none like you."

Her face brightened; it was so sweet to be praised by him!

"And then," she continued, "the grand tragedy of passion and despair, the noble, queenly woman who has sacrificed everything to the man she loves finds that she has a rival—a young, beautiful, beloved rival." She clasped her hands with the manner of a queen. "My whole soul rises to that," she continued; "I understand it—the passion, the anguish, the despair!"

His dark eyes, full of admiration, were riveted on her.

"Who would have thought," he said, gravely, "that you had such a marvel of genius in you?"

"You are very good to call it genius," she said. "I always knew I had something in me that was not to be described or understood—something that made me different from other people; but I never knew what it was. Do you know those two lines:

"'The poets learn in suffering
What they tell in song.'

"I think the passion of anguish and pain taught me to interpret the pains and joys of others. There is another opera I love—'L'Etoile du Nord.' The grave, tender, grand character of Catherine, with her passionate love, her despair, and her madness, holds me in thrall. There is no love without madness."

A deep sigh from her companion aroused her, and she remembered that she was on dangerous ground; still the subject had a great charm for her.

"If I ever wrote an opera," she said, "I should have jealousy for my ground-work."

"Why?" he asked, briefly.

"Because," she replied, "it is the strongest of all passions."

"Stronger than love?" he asked.

"I shall always think they go together," said Leone. "I know that philosophers call jealousy the passion of ignoble minds; I am not so sure of it. It goes, I think, with all great love, but not with calm, well-controlled affection. I should make it the subject of my opera, because it is so strong, so deep, so bitter; it transforms one, it changes angels into demons. We will not talk about it." She drew a little jeweled watch from her pocket. "Lord Chandos," she said, "we have been talking two hours, and you must not stay any longer."

When he was gone she said to herself that she would not ask him any more questions about Lady Marion.

CHAPTER XLIV
THE RIVALS FACE TO FACE

Madame de Chandalle gave a grand soiree, and she said to herself that it should be one of the greatest successes of the season. Three women were especially popular and sought after: Madame Vanira, whose beauty and genius made her queen of society; Lady Chandos, whose fair, tranquil loveliness was to men like the light of the fair moon, and Miss Bygrave, the most brilliant of brunettes—the most proud and exclusive of ladies.

Madame de Chandalle thought if she could but insure the presence of all three at once, her *soiree* would be the success of the season. She went in person to invite the great singer herself, a compliment she seldom paid to any one, and Leone at first refused. Madame de Chandalle looked imploringly at her.

"What can I offer as an inducement? The loveliest woman in London, Lady Chandos, will be there. That will not tempt you, I am afraid."

She little knew how much.

As Leone heard the words, her heart beat wildly. Lady Chandos, the fair woman who was her rival. She had longed to see her, and here was a chance. She dreaded, yet desired to look at her, to see what the woman was like whom Lance had forsaken her for. The longing tempted her.

"Your desire to welcome me," she said, gracefully, "is the greatest inducement you can offer me."

And Madame de Chandalle smiled at her victory.

Madame de Chandalle was the widow of an eminent French general. She preferred London to Paris. She was mistress of a large fortune, and gave the best entertainments of the season.

She knew that the beautiful singer accepted but few of the many invitations sent to her. Last week she had declined the invitations of a duchess and the wife of an American millionaire. She was doubly delighted that her own was accepted. The same was for Tuesday evening. On that evening Leone was free, and she had some idea that madame had chosen it purposely.

At last she was to see Lance's wife, the woman whom the laws of man, of society, and the world had placed in her place, given her position, her name, her love—the woman whom a mere legal quibble had put in her place.

The hours seemed long until Tuesday evening came. It struck her that if Lady Chandos were there Lord Chandos would be there too; he would see her at last in the regal position her own genius had won for herself; a position that seemed to her a thousand times grander than the one derived from the mere accident of birth. He would see then the world's estimation of the woman he had forsaken. She was pleased, yet half frightened, to know that at last she and her rival would meet face to face.

She had so noble a soul that vanity was not among her faults, but on this evening she was more than usually particular. Never had the matchless beauty of the great actress shown to greater advantage. She wore a dress of faint cream-colored brocade, half hidden in fine, costly lace, in the beautiful waves of her hair a large, cream-colored rose nestled, and with that she wore a set of diamonds a princess might have envied. The superb beauty, the half stately, half-languid grace, the southern eyes, the full, sweet lips, the wondrous beauty of her white neck and arms, the inexpressible charm of her attitudes, the play of her superb features—all made her marvelous to look upon. A dainty, delicate perfume came from the folds of her dress. She had a richly jeweled fan, made from the delicate amber plumage of some rare tropical bird; the radiance and light of her beauty would have made a whole room bright. She reached Madame de Chandalle's rather late. She gave one hasty glance round the superb reception-room as she passed to where madame was receiving her guests, but the dark, handsome head and face of Lord Chandos were nowhere to be seen.

Madame overwhelmed her with civilities, and Leone soon found herself the center of an admiring crowd. The assembly was a most brilliant one; there were princes of the blood, royal dukes, marshals of France, peers of England, men of highest note in the land; to each and all the radiant, beautiful artist was the center of all attraction.

A royal duke was bending over her chair, one of the noblest marshals of France, with the young Marquis of Tyrol to assist him, was trying to entertain her. They were lavishing compliments upon her.

Suddenly she saw some slight stir in the groups, the French marshal murmured: "*Comme elle est belle!*" and, looking up, she saw a fair, regal woman bowing to Madame de Chandalle—a woman whose fair, tranquil loveliness was like moonlight on a summer's lake. Leone was charmed by her. The graceful figure was shown to the best advantage by the dress of rich white silk; she wore a superb suit of opals, whose hundred tints gleamed and glistened as she moved.

"The very queen of blondes," she overheard one gentleman say to another, her eyes riveted by the fair, tranquil loveliness of this beautiful woman, whose dress was trimmed with white water-lilies, who wore a water-lily in her hair and one on her white breast.

Leone watched her intently. Watching her was like reading a sweet, half-sad poem, or listening to sweet, half-sad music—every movement was full of sweet harmony. Leone watched this beautiful woman for some time; every one appeared to know her; she was evidently a leader of fashion; still she had no idea who she was. She expected, she did not know why, to see Lord and Lady Chandos enter together.

The French marshal was the first to speak.

"You admire La Reine des Blondes, madame?" he said. "Ah, Heaven, how we should rave in Paris over so fair a lady. Do you know who she is?"

"No," answered Leone, "but I should like to know very much. She is very beautiful."

"It is the beauty of an angel," cried the marshal. "She is the wife of one of the most famous men in England—she is Lady Chandos."

"Ah," said Leone, with a long, low cry.

The very mention of the name had stabbed her through the heart.

The marshal looked up in wonder.

"I beg pardon," she said, quickly, "what name did you say? A sudden faintness seized me; the room is warm. What is the lady's name?"

She would not for the whole world that he should have known what caused either the pain or the cry.

The marshal repeated:

"That is Lady Chandos, the wife of Lord Chandos, who is the rising light of this generation."

"There are so many rising lights," she said, carelessly; but her heart was beating fast the while.

Ah, me! so fair, so graceful, so high-bred! Was it any wonder that he had loved her? Yet to this gorgeous woman, with her soul of fire, it seemed that those perfect features were almost too gentle, and lacked the fire of life.

She saw several gentlemen gather round the chair on which Lady Chandos sat, like a queen on a throne; and then the golden head was hidden from her sight.

So at last she was face to face with her rival—at last she could see and hear her—this fair woman who had taken her lover from her. It was with difficulty that she was herself, that she maintained her brilliant repartees; her fire of wit, her *bon mots* that were repeated from one to the other. Her powers of conversation were of the highest order. She could enchain twenty people at once, and keep all their intellects in active exercise. It was with difficulty she did that now; she was thinking so entirely of the golden head, with its opal stars. Then came another stir among the brilliant groups— the *entree* of a prince, beloved and revered by all who knew him. Leone, with her quick, artistic eye, thought she had never seen a more brilliant picture than this—the magnificent apartment, with its superb pictures, its background of flowers, its flood of light; the splendid dresses and jewels of the women, the blending of rich colors, the flashing of light made it a picture never to be forgotten.

Suddenly she saw Madame de Chandalle smiling in her face, and by her side was the beautiful rival who supplanted her.

"Madame Vanira," said their hostess, "permit me to make known to you Lady Chandos, who greatly desires the pleasure of your acquaintance."

Then the two who had crossed each other's lives so strangely looked at each other face to face. Leone's heart almost stood still with a great throb of pain as she glanced steadily at the fair, lovely face of her rival. How often had he sunned himself in those blue eyes? how often had he kissed those sweet lips and held those white hands in his own? She recovered herself with a violent effort and listened. Lady Chandos was speaking to her.

"I am charmed to see you, Madame Vanira," she said; "I am one of your greatest admirers."

"You are very kind, Lady Chandos," said Leone.

Then Lady Marion turned to her hostess.

"I should like to remain with Madame Vanira," she said; "that is, if you will, madame?"

Leone drew aside her rich cream-colored draperies and lace. Lady Chandos sat down by her side.

"I am so pleased to meet you," she continued, with what was unusual animation with her. "I have longed to see you off the stage."

Leone smiled in the fair face.

"I can only hope," she said, "that you will like me as well off the stage as you do on."

"I am sure of that," said Lady Chandos, with charming frankness.

She admired the beautiful and gifted singer more than she cared to say. She added, timidly:

"Now that I have met you here, madame, I shall hope for the pleasure and honor of receiving you at my own house."

She wondered why Madame Vanira drew back with a slight start: it seemed so strange to be asked into the house that she believed to be her own.

"I shall be delighted," continued Lady Chandos. "I give a ball on Wednesday week; promise me that you will come."

"I will promise you to think of it," she replied, and Lady Chandos laughed blithely.

"That means you will come," she said, and the next moment Lord Chandos entered the room.

CHAPTER XLV
AN INVITATION

They both saw him at the same moment. Leone, with a sudden paling of her beautiful face, with a keen sense of sharp pain, and Lady Chandos with a bright, happy flush.

"Here is my husband," she said, proudly; little dreaming that the beautiful singer had called him husband, too.

He came toward them slowly; it seemed to him so wonderful that these two should be sitting side by side—the woman he loved with a passionate love, and the woman he married under his mother's influence.

There were so many people present that it was some time before he could get up to them, and by that time he had recovered himself.

"Lance," cried Lady Chandos, in a low voice, "see how fortunate I am; I have been introduced to Madame Vanira."

Yes, his heart smote him again; it seemed so cruel to deceive her when she was so kind, so gentle; she trusted in him so implicitly that it seemed cruel to deceive her. She turned with a radiant face to Leone.

"Let me introduce my husband, Lord Chandos, to you, Madame Vanira," she said, and they looked at each other for one moment as though they were paralyzed.

Then the simple, innate truth of Leone's disposition came uppermost. With the most dignified manner she returned the bow that Lord Chandos made.

"I have had the pleasure of meeting Lord Chandos before," she said.

And Lady Marion looked at her husband in reproachful wonder.

"And you never told me," she said. "Knowing my great admiration for Madame Vanira, you did not tell me."

"Where was it, madame?" he asked, looking at her with an air of helpless, hopeless entreaty.

Then she bethought herself that perhaps those few words might cause unpleasantness between husband and wife, and she tried to make little of them.

"I was at the French Embassy here in London, Lord Chandos, at the same time you were," she said.

And Lady Marion was quite satisfied with the explanation, which was perfectly true.

Then they talked for a few minutes, at the end of which Lady Chandos was claimed by her hostess for a series of introductions.

Lord Chandos and Leone were left alone.

She spoke to him quickly and in an undertone of voice.

"Lord Chandos," she said, "I wish to speak to you; take me into the conservatory where we shall not be interrupted."

He obeyed in silence; they walked through the brilliant throng of guests, through the crowded, brilliant room, until they reached the quiet conservatory at the end.

The lamps were lighted and shone like huge pearls among the blossoms. There were few people and those few desired no attention from the newcomers. He led her to a pretty chair, placed among the hyacinths; the fragrance was very strong.

"I am afraid you will find this odor too much, beautiful as it is," he said.

"I do not notice," she said; "my heart and soul are full of one thing. Oh, Lord Chandos, your wife likes me, likes me," she repeated, eagerly.

"I am not surprised at it; indeed, I should have been surprised if she had not liked you," he said.

The dark, beautiful eyes had a wistful look in them as they were raised to his face.

"How beautiful she is, how fair and stately!" she said.

"Yes, beautiful; but compared to you, Leone, as I said before, she is like moonlight to sunlight, like water to wine."

"I have done no wrong," continued Leone, with a thrill of subdued passion in her voice; "on the contrary, a cruel wrong was done to me. But when I am with her, I feel in some vague way that I are guilty. Does she know anything of your story and mine?"

His dark face burned.

"No," he replied; "she knows nothing of that except that in my youth—ah, Leone, that I must say this to you—in my youth I made some mistake; so my lady mother Was pleased to call it," he added, bitterly. "She does not know exactly what it was, nor could she ever dream for one moment that it was you."

She looked at him with a serious, questioning gaze.

"Surely you did not marry her without telling her that you had gone through that service already, did you? If so, I think you acted disloyally and dishonorably."

He bent his head in lowly humility before her.

"Leone," he said—"ah, forgive me for calling you Leone, but the name is so sweet and so dear to me—Leone, I am a miserable sinner. When I think of my weakness and cowardice, I loathe myself; I could kill myself; yet I can never undo the wrong I have done to either. She knows little, and I believe implicitly she has forgotten that little. Why do you ask me?"

"It seems so strange," said Leone, musingly, "I asked you to come here to speak to me that I might ask your advice. She, Lady Marion, has asked me to her house—has pressed me, urged me to go; and I have said that I will think of it. I want you to advise me and tell me what I should do."

"My dear Leone, I—I cannot. I should love above all things to see you at my house, but it would be painful for you and painful to me."

She continued, in a low voice:

"Lady Marion has asked me to be her friend; she is good enough to say she admires me. What shall I do?"

He was silent for some minutes, then he said:

"There is one thing, Leone, if you become a friend, or even a visitor of Lady Marion's, I should see a great deal of you, and that would be very pleasant; it is all there is left in life. I should like it, Leone—would you?"

Looking up, she met the loving light of the dark eyes full upon her. Her face flushed.

"Yes," she whispered, "I, too, should like it."

There was silence between them for some little time, then Leone said:

"Would it be quite safe for me to visit you? Do you think that Lady Lanswell would recognize me?"

"No," he answered, "if the eyes of love failed to recognize you at one glance, the eyes of indifference will fail altogether. My mother is here to-night; risk an introduction to her, and you will see. It would give fresh zest and pleasure to my life if you could visit us."

"It would be pleasant," said Leone, musingly; "and yet to my mind, I cannot tell why, there is something that savors of wrong about it. Lord Chandos," she added, "I like your wife, she was kindness itself to me. We must mind one thing if I enter your house; I must be to you no more than any other person in it—I must be a stranger—and you must never even by one word allude to the past; you promise that, do you not?"

"I will promise everything and anything," he replied. "I will ask Madame de Chandalle to introduce you to my mother—I should not have the nerve for it."

"If she should recognize me there will be a scene," said Leone, with a faint smile; "it seems to me that the eyes of hate are keener than the eyes of love."

"She will not know you. I believe that she has forgotten even your name; who would think of finding Leone in the brilliant actress for whose friendship all men sigh? Why, Leone, forgive me for using the word—life will be quite different to me if we are to be friends, if I may see your face sometimes in the home that should have been yours. It will make all the difference in the world, and I am absurdly happy at the bare thought of it."

"I think our conference has lasted long enough," she said, rising. "You think, then, that I should accept Lady Marion's invitation?"

"Yes, it will give us more opportunities of meeting, and will bring about between Lady Marion and yourself a great intimacy," he said.

"Heaven send it may end well," she said, half sadly.

"Thank Heaven for its kindness," he replied, and then they left the quiet conservatory, where the soft ripple of the scented fountain made sweetest music.

Lord Chandos quitted her, much to his regret, and Leone sought out Madame de Chandalle.

"I should like to ask you, madame, for one more introduction," she said. "I should much like to know the Countess of Lanswell."

Nothing could exceed madame's delight and courtesy. She took Leone to the blue saloon, as it was called, where the Countess of Lanswell sat in state. She looked up in gratified surprise as the name of the great singer was pronounced. If Leone felt any nervousness she did not show it; there must be no hesitation or all would be lost. She raised her eyes bravely to the handsome, haughty face of the woman who had spurned her. In the one moment during which their eyes met, Leone's heart almost stood still, the next it beat freely, for not even the faintest gleam of recognition came into my lady's eyes.

But when they had been talking for some minutes, and the countess had excelled herself in the grace of her compliments, she gazed with keen, bright eyes in that beautiful face.

"Do you know, Madame Vanira, that the first time I saw you there was something quite familiar in your face."

There was something startling in the crimson blush that mounts even to the locks of her dark hair.

"Is it so?" she asked.

And the countess did not relax the questioning gaze.

"I think now," she added, "that I am wrong. I cannot think of any one who is like you. I shall be glad to see you at Dunmore House, Madame Vanira. We have a dinner-party next week, and I hope you will be inclined to favor us. Do you know Lady Chandos?"

"Yes," was the half sad reply, "I was introduced to her this evening."

They talked on indifferent subjects. The countess was most charming to the gifted singer, and Leone could not help contrasting this interview with the last that she had with Lady Lanswell. One thing was quite certain. The countess did not recognize her, and her visits to Dunmore House would be quite safe.

She talked to Lady Lanswell for some time, and went away that night quite pleased with the new prospects opening before her.

CHAPTER XLVI
AT THE BALL

"I like Madame Vanira," said the Countess of Lanswell, a few days after the introduction. "She is not only the most gifted singer of the present day, but she is an uncommon type of woman. Who or what was she?"

My lady was seated in her own drawing-room in the midst of a circle of morning callers. Lord Chandos was there, and he listened with some amusement to the conversation that followed. The countess was speaking to Major Hautbois, who was supposed to know the pedigree of everybody. She looked at him now for the information he generally gave readily, but the major's face wore a troubled expression.

"To tell the truth," he replied, "I have heard so many conflicting stories as to the lady's origin that I am quite at a loss which to repeat."

Lady Lanswell smiled at the naive confession.

"Truth does wear a strange aspect at times," she said. "When Major Hautbois has to choose between many reports, I should say that none of them were true. Myself," she continued, "I should say that Madame Vanira was well-born—she has a patrician face."

Lord Chandos thought of the "dairy-maid," and sighed while he smiled. Ah, if his mother could but have seen Leone with the same eyes with which she saw Madame Vanira all would have been well.

It was quite evident that my lady did not in the least recognize her—there could be no doubt of it. She continued to praise her.

"I have always," she said, "been far above what I consider the littleness of those people who think to show their superiority by abusing the stage, or rather by treating with supercilious contempt those who ornament the stage. Something," she added, with an air of patronage, "is due to queens."

And again Lord Chandos smiled bitterly to himself. If his mother had but owned these opinions a short time before, how different life might have been. Lady Lanswell turned to her son.

"Madame Vanira will be at Lady Marion's ball on Tuesday," she said: "I am sorry that I shall not meet her."

"Are you not coming, mother?" he asked, with a certain secret hope that she was not.

"No; the earl has made an engagement for me, which I am compelled to keep," she said, "much to my regret."

And she spoke truthfully. The proud and haughty countess found herself much impressed by the grace, genius, and beauty of Madame Vanira.

Leone had looked forward to the evening of the ball as to an ordeal that must be passed through. She dreaded it, yet longed for it. She could not rest for thinking of it. She was to enter as a guest the house where she should have reigned mistress. She was to be the visitor of the woman who had taken her place. How should she bear it? how would it pass? For the first time some of the terrible pain of jealousy found its way into her heart—a pain that blanched her face, and made her tremble; a new pain to her in the fire of its burning.

When the night of the ball came it found her with a pale face; her usual radiant coloring faded, and she looked all the lovelier for it. She dressed herself with unusual care and magnificence.

"I must look my best to-night," she said to herself, with a bitter smile. "I am going to see the home that should have been my own. I am going to visit Lady Chandos, and I believed myself to be Lady Chandos and no other. I must look my best."

She chose a brocade of pale amber that looked like woven sunbeams; it was half covered with point lace and trimmed with great creamy roses. She wore a *parure* of rubies, presented by an empress, who delighted in her glorious voice; on her beautiful neck, white and firm as a pillar, she wore a necklace of rubies; on her white breast gleamed a cross of rubies, in which the fire flashed like gleams of light.

She had never looked so magnificently beautiful. The low dress showed the white shining arms and shoulders like white satin. The different emotions that surged through her whole heart and soul gave a softened tenderness to the beautiful, passionate face.

She was a woman at whose feet a man could kneel and worship; who could sway the heart and soul of a man as the wind sways the great branches of strong trees.

On the morning of the day of the ball, a bouquet arrived for her, and she knew that it held her favorite flowers, white lilies-of-the-valley, with sweet hanging bells and gardenias that filled the whole room with perfume. She had nerve enough to face the most critical audience in the world.

She sung while kings and queens looked on in wonder; the applause of great multitudes had never made her heart beat or her pulses thrill; but as she drove to Stoneland House a faint, languid sensation almost overcame her; how should she bear it? What should she do? More than once the impulse almost mastered her to return, and never see Lord Chandos again; but the pain, the fever and the longing urged her on.

It was like a dream to her, the brilliantly-lighted mansion, the rows of liveried servants, the spacious entrance-hall lined with flowers, the broad white staircase with the crimson carpet, the white statues holding crimson lamps.

She walked slowly up that gorgeous staircase, every eye riveted by her queenly beauty. She said to herself:

"All this should have been mine."

Yet, it was not envy of the wealth and magnificence surrounding her, it was the keen pain of the outrageous wrong done to her which stung her to the quick. Brilliantly dressed ladies passed her, and she saw that more deference was paid to her than would have been paid to a duchess.

Then, in the drawing-room that led to the ballroom, she saw Lady Marion in her usual calm, regal attitude, receiving her guests. The queen of blondes looked more than lovely; her dress was of rich white lace over pale blue silk, with blue forget-me-nots in her hair. Leone had one moment's hard fight with herself as she gazed at this beautiful woman.

"She stands in my place, she bears my name; on her finger shines the ring that ought to shine on mine; she has taken the love I believed to be mine for life," said Leone to herself; "how shall I bear it?"

As she stood among the brilliant crowd, a strong impulse came over her to go up to Lady Marion and say:

"Stand aside; this is my place. Men cannot undo the laws of God. Stand aside, give me my place."

Words were still burning from her heart to her lips when she saw Lady Marion holding out her hand in kindliest greeting to her; all the bitter thoughts melted at once in the sunshine of that fair presence; her own hand sought Lady Marion's, and the two women, whose lives had crossed each other's so strangely, stood for one moment hand locked in hand, their eyes fixed on each other.

Lady Marion spoke first, and she seemed to draw her breath with a deep sigh as she did so.

"I am so pleased to see you, Madame Vanira," she said, eagerly. "We must find time for a long talk this evening."

With a bow Leone passed on to the ballroom, where the first person to meet her was Lord Chandos; he looked at the bouquet she carried.

"You have honored my flowers, madame," he said. "I remember your love for lilies-of-the-valley. You will put my name down for the first waltz?"

There was a world of reproach in the dark eyes she raised to his.

"No, I will not waltz with you," she replied, gently.

"Why not?" he asked, bending his handsome head over her.

"I might make false excuses, but I prefer telling you the truth," she answered; "I will not trust myself."

And when Leone took that tone Lord Chandos knew that further words were useless.

"You will dance a quadrille, at least?" he asked, and she consented.

Then he offered her his arm and they walked through the room together.

The ballroom at Stoneland House was a large and magnificent apartment; many people thought it the finest ballroom in London; the immense dome was brilliantly lighted, the walls were superbly painted, and tier after tier of superb blossoms filled the room with exquisite color and exquisite perfume.

The ballroom opened into a large conservatory, which led to a fernery, and from the fernery one passed to the grounds. Leone felt embarrassed; she longed to praise the beautiful place, yet it seemed to her if she did so it would be like reminding him that it ought to have been hers; while he, on the contrary, did not dare to draw her attention to picture, flower, or statue, lest she should remember that they had been taken from her by a great and grievous wrong.

"We are not very cheerful friends," he said, trying to arouse himself.

"I begin to think we have done wrong in ever thinking of friendship at all," she replied.

Lord Chandos turned to her suddenly.

"Leone," he said, "you have quite made a conquest of my mother—you do not know how she admires you!"

A bitter smile curled the beautiful lips.

"It is too late," she said sadly. "It does not seem very long since she refused even to tolerate me."

Lord Chandos continued:

"She was speaking about you yesterday, and she was quite animated about you; she praised you more than I have ever heard her praise any one."

"I ought to feel flattered," said Leone; "but it strikes me as being something wonderful that Lady Lanswell did not find out any good qualities in me before."

"My mother saw you through a haze of hatred," said Lord Chandos; "now she will learn to appreciate you."

A sudden glow of fire flashed in those superb eyes.

"I wonder," she said, "if I shall ever be able to pay my debt to Lady Lanswell, and in what shape I shall pay it?"

He shuddered as he gazed in the beautiful face.

"Try to forget that, Leone," he said; "I never like to remember that you threatened my mother."

"We will not discuss it," she said, coldly; "we shall never agree."

Then the band began to play the quadrilles. Lord Chandos led Leone to her place. He thought to himself what cruel wrong it was on the part of fate, that the woman whom he had believed to be his wedded wife should be standing there, a visitor in the house which ought to have been her home.

CHAPTER XLVII
THE COMPACT OF FRIENDSHIP

The one set of quadrilles had been danced, and Leone said to herself that there was more pain than pleasure in it, when Lady Marion, with an unusual glow of animation on her face, came to Leone, who was sitting alone.

"Madame Vanira," she said, "it seems cruel to deprive others of the pleasure of your society, but I should like to talk to you. I have some pretty things which I have brought from Spain, which I should like to show you. Will it please you to leave the ballroom and come with me, or do you care for dancing?"

Leone smiled sadly; tragedy and comedy are always side by side, and it seemed to her, who had had so terrible a tragedy in her life, who stood face to face with so terrible a tragedy now, it seemed to her absurd that she should think of dancing.

"I would rather talk to you," she replied, "than do anything else." The two beautiful, graceful women left the ballroom together. Leone made some remark on the magnificence of the rooms as they passed, and Lady Chandos smiled.

"I am a very home-loving being myself. I prefer the pretty little morning-room where we take breakfast, and my own boudoir, to any other place in the house; they seem to be really one's own because no one else enters them. Come to my boudoir now, Madame Vanira, and I will show you a whole lot of pretty treasures that I brought from Spain."

"From Spain." She little knew how those words jarred even on Leone's heart. It was in Spain they had intrigued to take her husband from her, and while Lady Marion was collecting art treasures the peace and happiness of her life had been wrecked, her fair name blighted, her love slain. She wondered to herself at the strange turn of fate which had brought her into contact with the one woman in all the world that she felt she ought to have avoided. But there was no resisting Lady Marion when she chose to make herself irresistible. There was something childlike and graceful in the way in which she looked up to Madame Vanira, with an absolute worship of her genius, her voice, and her beauty. She laid her white hand on Leone's.

"You will think me a very gushing young lady, I fear, Madame Vanira, if I say how fervently I hope we shall always be friends; not in the common meaning of the words, but real, true, warm friends until we die. Have you ever made such a compact of friendship with any one?"

Leone's heart smote her, her face flushed.

"Yes," she replied; "I have once."

Lady Chandos looked up at her quickly.

"With a lady, I mean?"

"No," said Leone; "I have no lady friends; indeed, I have few friends of any kind, though I have many acquaintances."

Lady Marion's hand lingered caressingly on the white shoulder of Leone.

"Something draws me to you," she said; "and I cannot tell quite what it is. You are very beautiful, but it is not that; the beauty of a woman would never win me. It cannot be altogether your genius, though it is without peer. It is a strange feeling, one I can hardly explain—as though there was something sympathetic between us. You are not laughing at me, Madame Vanira?"

"No, I am not laughing," said Leone, with wondering eyes. How strange it was that Lance's wife, above all other women, should feel this curious, sympathetic friendship for her!

They entered the beautiful boudoir together, and Lady Marion, with pardonable pride, turned to her companion.

"Lord Chandos arranged this room for me himself. Have you heard the flattering, foolish name for me that the London people have invented? They call me the Queen of Blondes."

"That is a very pretty title," said Leone, "they call me a queen, the Queen of Song."

And the two women who were, each in her way, a "queen," smiled at each other.

"You see," continued Lady Chandos, "that my husband used to think there was nothing in the world but blondes. I have often told him if I bring a brunette here she is quite at a disadvantage; everything is blue, white, or silver."

Leone looked round the sumptuous room; the ceiling was painted by a master hand; all the story of Endymion was told there; the walls were superbly painted; the hangings were of blue velvet and blue silk, relieved by white lace; the carpet, of rich velvet pile, had a white ground with blue corn-flowers, so artistically grouped they looked as though they had fallen on the ground in picturesque confusion. The chairs and pretty couch were covered with velvet; a hundred little trifles that lay scattered over the place told that it was occupied by a lady of taste; books in beautiful bindings, exquisite drawings and photographs, a jeweled fan, a superb bouquet holder, flowers costly, beautiful, and fragrant; a room that was a fitting shrine for a goddess of beauty.

"My own room," said Lady Chandos, with a smile, as she closed the door; "and what a luxury it is, Madame Vanira—a room quite your own! Even when the house is full of visitors no one comes here but Lord Chandos; he always takes that chair near those flowers while he talks to me, and that is, I think, the happiest hour in the day. Sit down there yourself."

Leone took the chair, and Lady Chandos sat down on a footstool by her side. It was one of the most brilliant and picturesque pictures ever beheld; the gorgeous room, with its rich hangings, the beautiful, dark-eyed woman, with the Spanish face, her dress like softened sunbeams, the fire of her rubies like points of flame, her whole self lovely as a picture, and the fair Queen of Blondes, with the golden hair and white roses—a picture that would have made an artist's fortune.

"How pleasant this is," said Lady Chandos, "a few minutes' respite from the music and dancing! Do you love the quiet moments of your life, Madame Vanira?"

Leone looked down on the fair, lovely face with a deep sigh.

"No, I think not," she replied; "I like my stage life best."

Lady Chandos asked, in a half pitying tone:

"Why did you go on the stage? Did you always like it?"

And Leone answered, gravely:

"A great sorrow drove me there."

"A great sorrow? How strange! What sorrow could come to one so beautiful, so gifted as you?"

"A sorrow that crushed all the natural life in me," said Leone; "but we will not speak of it. I live more in my life on the stage than in my home life; that is desolate always."

She spoke unconsciously, and the heart of the fair woman who believed herself so entirely beloved warmed with pity and kindness to the one whose heart was so desolate.

"A great sorrow taught you to find comfort in an artificial life," she said, gently; "it would not do that to me."

And her white hand, on which the wedding-ring shone, caressed the beautiful white arm of Madame Vanira.

"What would it do to you?" asked Leone, slightly startled.

"A really great trouble," replied Lady Chandos, musingly, "what would it do for me? Kill me. I have known so little of it; I cannot indeed remember what could be called trouble."

"You have been singularly fortunate," said Leone, half enviously.

And the fair face of the Queen of Blondes grew troubled.

"Perhaps," she said, "all my troubles are to come. I should not like to believe that."

She was quite silent for some few minutes, then, with a sigh, she said:

"You have made me feel nervous, and I cannot tell why. What trouble could come to me? So far as I see, humanly speakingly, none. No money troubles could reach me; sickness would hardly be a trouble if those I loved were round me. Ah, well, that is common to every one." A look of startled intelligence came over her face. "I know one, and only one source of trouble," she said; "that would be if anything happened to Lord Chandos, to—to my husband; if he did not love me, or I lost him."

She sighed as she uttered the last words, and the heart of the gifted singer was touched by the noblest, kindest pity; she looked into the fair, flower-like face.

"You love your husband then?" she said, with a gentle, caressing voice.

"Love him," replied Lady Chandos, her whole soul flashing in her eyes—"love him? Ah, that seems to me a weak word! My husband is all the world, all life to me. It is strange that I should speak to you, a stranger, in this manner; but, as I told you before, my heart warms to you in some fashion that I do not myself understand. I am not like most people. I have so few to love. No father, no mother, no sisters, or brothers. I have no one in the wide world but my husband; he is more to me than most husbands are to most wives—he is everything."

Leone looked down on that fair, sweet face with loving eyes; the very depths of her soul were touched by those simple words; she prayed God that she might always remember them. There was infinite pathos in her voice and in her face when she said:

"You are very happy, then, with your husband, Lady Marion?"

"Yes, I am very happy," said the young wife, simply. "My husband loves me, I have no rivals, no jealousies, no annoyances; I may say I am perfectly happy."

"I pray God that you may always be so!" said Leone, gently.

And with an impulse she could not resist she bent down and kissed the sweet face.

Then Lady Chandos looked up.

"I am afraid," she said, "that our pleasant five minutes' chat is ended. We must go back to the ballroom. I am afraid all your admirers will be very angry with me, Madame Vanira."

"That is a matter of perfect indifference?" she replied. "I know you better, Lady Marion, for those five minutes spent here than I should have done during a century in ballrooms."

"And you promise that we shall always be friends," said the fair woman who called herself Lady Chandos.

"I promise, and I will keep my word," said the beautiful singer, who had believed herself to be his wife.

And with those words they parted.

CHAPTER XLVIII
THE HUSBAND'S KISS

Lady Marion never did anything by halves. It was seldom that her calm, quiet nature was stirred, but when that happened she felt more deeply, perhaps, than people who express their feelings with great ease and rapidity. She was amused herself at her own great liking for Madame Vanira; it was the second great love of her life; the first had been for her husband, this was the next. She talked of her incessantly, until even Lord Chandos wondered and asked how it was.

"I cannot tell," she replied; "I think I am infatuated. I am quite sure, Lance, that if I had been a gentleman, I should have followed Madame Vanira to the other side of the world. I think her, without exception, the most charming woman in the world."

She raised her eyes with innocent tenderness to his face.

"Are you jealous because I love her so much?" she asked.

He shuddered as he heard the playful, innocent words, so different from the reality.

"I should never be jealous of you, Marion," he replied, and then turned the conversation.

Nothing less than a visit to Madame Vanira would please Lady Chandos. She asked her husband if he would go to the Cedars with her, and wondered when he declined. The truth was that he feared some chance recognition, some accidental temptation; he dared not go, and Lady Marion looked very disappointed.

"I thought you liked Madame Vanira," she said. "I am quite sure, Lance, that you looked as if you did."

"My dear Marion, between liking persons and giving up a busy morning to go to see them there is an immense difference. If you really wish me to go, Marion, you know that I will break all my appointments."

"I would not ask you to do that," she replied, gently, and the result of the conversation was that Lady Chandos went alone.

She spent two hours with Leone, and the result was a great increase of liking and affection for her. Leone sang for her, and her grand voice thrilled through every fiber of that gentle heart; Leone read to her, and Lady Chandos said to herself that she never quite understood what words meant before. When it was time to go, Lady Chandos looked at her watch in wonder.

"I have been here two hours," she said, "and they have passed like two minutes. Madame Vanira, I have no engagement to-morrow evening, come and see me. Lord Chandos has a speech to prepare, and he asked me to forego all engagements this evening."

"Perhaps I should be in the way," said Leone; but Lady Marion laughed at the notion. She pleaded so prettily and so gracefully that Leone consented, and it was arranged that she should spend the evening of the day following at Stoneland House.

She went—more than once. She had asked herself if this intimacy were wise? She could not help liking the fair, sweet woman who had taken her place, and yet she felt a great undercurrent of jealous indignation and righteous anger—it might blaze out some day, and she knew that if it ever did so it would be out of her control. It was something like playing with fire, yet how many people play with fire all their lives and never get burned!

She went, looking more beautiful and regal than ever, in a most becoming dress of black velvet, her white arms and white shoulders looking whiter than ever through the fine white lace.

She wore no jewels; a pomegranate blossom lay in the thick coils of her hair; a red rose nestled in her white breast.

She was shown into the boudoir she had admired so much, and there Lady Chandos joined her.

Lord Chandos had been busily engaged during the day in looking up facts and information for his speech. He had joined his wife for dinner, but she saw him so completely engrossed that she did not talk to him, and it had not occurred to her to tell him that Madame Vanira was coming, so that he was quite ignorant of that fact.

The two ladies enjoyed themselves very much—they had a cup of orange Pekoe from cups of priceless china, they talked of music, art, and books.

The pretty little clock chimed ten. Lady Chandos looked at her companion.

"You have not tried my piano yet," she said. "It was a wedding present from Lord Chandos to me; the tone of it is very sweet and clear."

"I will try it," said Madame Vanira. "May I look through the pile of music that lies behind it?"

Lady Chandos laughed at the eagerness with which Leone went on her knees and examined the music.

Just at that moment, when she was completely hidden from view, the door suddenly opened, and Lord Chandos hastily entered. Seeing his wife near, without looking around the room, in his usual caressing manner, he threw one arm round her, drew her to him, and kissed her.

It was that kiss which woke all the love, and passion, and jealousy in Leone's heart; it came home to her in that minute, and for the first time, that the husband she had lost belonged to another—that his kisses and caresses were never more to be hers, but would be given always to this other.

There was one moment—only one moment of silence; but while it lasted a sharp sword pierced her heart; the next, Lady Chandos, with a laughing, blushing face, had turned to her husband, holding up one white hand in warning.

"Lance," she cried, "do you not see Madame Vanira?"

She wondered why the words seemed to transfix him—why his face paled and his eyes flashed fire.

"Madame Vanira!" he cried, "I did not see that she was here."

Then Leone rose slowly from the pile of music.

"I should ask pardon," she said; "I did not know that I had hidden myself so completely."

It was like a scene from a play; a fair wife, with her sweet face, its expression of quiet happiness in her husband's love; the husband, with the startled look of passion repressed; Leone, with her grand Spanish beauty all aglow with emotion. She could not recover her presence of mind so as to laugh away the awkward situation. Lady Chandos was the first to do that.

"How melodramatic we all look!" she said. "What is the matter?"

Then Lord Chandos recovered himself. He knew that the kiss he had given to one fair woman must have stabbed the heart of the other, and he would rather have done anything than that it should have happened. There came to him like a flash of lightning the remembrance of that first home at River View, and the white arms that were clasped round his neck when he entered there; and he knew that the same memory rankled in the heart of the beautiful woman whose face had suddenly grown pale as his own.

The air had grown like living flame to Leone; the pain which stung her was so sharp she could have cried aloud with the anguish of it. It was well nigh intolerable to see his arm round her, to see him draw her fair face and head to him, to see his lips seek hers and rest on them. The air grew like living flames; her heart beat fast and loud; her hands burned. All that she had lost by woman's intrigue and man's injustice this fair, gentle woman had gained. A red mist came before her eyes; a rush, as of many waters, filled her ears. She bit her lips to prevent the loud and bitter cry that seemed as though it must escape her.

Then Lord Chandos hastened to place a chair for her, and tried to drive from her mind all recollection of the little incident.

"You are looking for some music, madame," he said, "from which I may augur the happy fact that you intended to sing. Let me pray that you will not change your intention."

"Lady Chandos asked me to try her piano," she said shyly.

"I told Madame Vanira how sweet and silvery the tone of it is, Lance," said Lady Chandos.

And again Leone shrunk from hearing on another woman's lip the word she had once used. It was awkward, it was intolerable; it struck her all at once with a sense of shame that she had done wrong in ever allowing Lord Chandos to speak to her again. But then he had pleaded so, he had seemed so utterly miserable, so forlorn, so hopeless, she could not help it. She had done wrong in allowing Lady Marion to make friends with her; Lady Marion was her enemy by force of circumstances, and there ought not to have been even one word between them. Yet she pleaded so eagerly, it had seemed quite impossible to resist her.

She was roused from her reverie by the laughing voice of Lady Marion, over whose fair head so dark a cloud hung.

"Madame Vanira," she was saying, "ask my husband to sing with you. He has a beautiful voice, not a deep, rolling bass, as one would imagine from the dark face and tall, stalwart figure, but a rich, clear tenor, sweet and silvery as the chime of bells."

Leone remembered every tone, every note of it; they had spent long hours in singing together, and the memory of those hours shone now in the eyes that met so sadly. A sudden, keen, passionate desire to sing with him once more came over Leone. It might be rash—it was imprudent.

"Mine was always a mad love," she said to herself, with a most bitter smile. "It might be dangerous—but once more."

Just once more she would like to hear her voice float away with his. She bent over the music again—the first and foremost lay Mendelssohn's beautiful duet. "Oh, would that my love." They sang it in the summer gloamings when she had been pleased and proud to hear her wonderful voice float away over the trees and die in sweetest silence. She raised it now and looked at him.

"Will you sing this?" she asked; but her eyes did not meet his, and her face was very pale.

She did not wait for an answer, but placed the music on a stand, and then—ah, then—the two beautiful voices floated away, and the very air seemed to vibrate with the passionate, thrilling sound; the drawing-room, the magnificence of Stoneland House, the graceful presence of the fair wife, faded from them. They were together once more at the garden at River View, the green trees making shade, the deep river in the distance.

But when they had finished, Lady Chandos was standing by, her face wet with tears.

"Your music breaks my heart," she said; but she did not know the reason why.

CHAPTER XLIX
THE WOUND IN HER HEART

If Leone had been wiser after that one evening, she would have avoided Lord Chandos as she would have shunned the flames of fire; that one evening showed her that she stood on the edge of a precipice. Looking in her own heart, she knew by its passionate anguish and passionate pain that the love in her had never been conquered. She said to herself, when the evening was over and she drove away, leaving them together, that she would never expose herself to that pain again.

It was so strange, so unnatural for her—she who believed herself his wife, who had spent so many evenings with him—to go away and leave him with this beautiful woman who was really his wife. She looked up at the silent stars as she drove home; surely their pale, golden eyes must shine down in dearest pity on her. She clinched her white, soft hands until the rings made great red dents; she exhausted herself with great tearless sobs; yet no tears came from her burning eyes.

Was ever woman so foully, so cruelly wronged? had ever woman been so cruelly tortured?

"I will not see him again," she cried to herself; "I cannot bear it."

Long after the stars had set, and the crimson flush of dawn stirred the pearly tints of the sky, she lay, sobbing, with passionate tears, feeling that she could not bear it—she must die.

It would have been well if that had frightened her, but when morning dawned she said to herself that hers had always been a mad love, and would be so until the end. She made one desperate resolve, one desperate effort; she wrote to Lord Chandos, and sent the letter to his club—a little, pathetic note, with a heart-break in every line of it—to say that they who had been wedded lovers were foolish to think of being friends; that it was not possible, and that she thought they had better part; the pain was too great for her, she could not bear it.

The letter was blotted with tears, and as he read it for whom it was written, other tears fell on it. Before two hours had passed, he was standing before her, with outstretched hands, the ring of passion in his voice, the fire of passion in his face.

"Leone," he said, "do you mean this—must we part?"

They forgot in that moment all the restraints by which they had surrounded themselves; once more they were Lance and Leone, as in the old days.

"Must we part?" he repeated, and her face paled as she raised it to his.

"I cannot bear the pain, Lance," she said, wearily. "It would be better for us never to meet than for me to suffer as I did last evening."

He drew nearer to her.

"Did you suffer so much, Leone?" he asked, gently.

"Yes, more almost than I can bear. It is not many years since I believed that I was your wife, and now I have to see another woman in my place. I—I saw you kiss her—I had to go away and leave you together. No, I cannot bear it, Lance!"

The beautiful head drooped wearily, the beautiful voice trembled and died away in a wail that was pitiful to hear; all her beauty, her genius, her talent—what did it avail her?

Lord Chandos had suffered much, but his pain had never been so keen as now at this moment, when this beautiful queenly woman wailed out her sorrow to him.

"What shall I do, Leone? I would give my life to undo what I have done; but it is useless—I cannot. Do you mean that we must part?"

The eyes she raised to his face were haggard and weary with pain.

"There is nothing for it but parting, Lance," she said. "I thought we could be friends, but it is not possible; we have loved each other too well."

"We need not part now," he said; "let us think it over; life is very long; it will be hard to live without the sunlight of your presence, Leone, now that I have lived in it so long. Let us think it over. Do you know what I wanted to ask you last evening?"

"No," she replied, "what was it?"

"A good that you may still grant me," he said. "We may part, if you wish it, Leone. Leone, let us have one happy day before the time comes. Leone, you see how fair the summer is, I want you to spend one day with me on the river. The chestnuts are all in flower—the whole world is full of beauty, and song, and fragrance; the great boughs are dipping into the stream, and the water-lilies lie on the river's breast. My dear love and lost love, come with me for one day. We may be parted all the rest of our lives, come with me for one day."

Her face brightened with the thought. Surely for one day they might be happy; long years would have to pass, and they would never meet. Oh, for one day, away on the river, in the world of clear waters, green boughs and violet banks—one day away from the world which had trammeled them and fettered them.

"You tempt me," she said, slowly. "A day with you on the river. Ah, for such a pleasure as that I would give twenty years of my life."

He did not answer her, because he dared not. He waited until his heart was calm and at rest again, then he said:

"Let us go to-morrow, Leone, no one knows what twenty-four hours may bring forth. Let us go to-morrow, Leone. Rise early. How often we have gone out together while the dew lay upon the flowers and grass. Shall it be so?"

The angel of prudence faded from her presence as she answered, "Yes." Knowing how she loved him, hearing the old love story in his voice, reading it in his face, she would have done better had she died there in the splendor of her beauty and the pain of her love than have said, "Yes." So it was arranged.

"It will be a beautiful day," said Lord Chandos. "I am a capital rower, Leone, as you will remember. I will take you as far as Medmersham Abbey: we will land there and spend an hour in the ruins; but you will have to rise early and drive down to the river side. You will not mind that."

"I shall mind nothing that brings me to you," she said, with a vivid blush, and so it was settled.

They forgot the dictates of honor; he forgot his duty to his wife at home, and she forgot prudence and justice.

The morning dawned. She had eagerly watched for it through the long hours of the night; it wakes her with the song of the birds and the shine of the sun; it wakes her with a mingled sense of pain and happiness, of pleasure and regret. She was to spend a whole day with him, but the background to that happiness was that he was leaving a wife at home who had all claims to his time and attention.

"One happy day before I die," she said to herself.

But will it be happy? The sun will shine brightly, yet there will be a background; yet it shall be happy because it will be with him.

It was yet early in the morning when she drove to the appointed place at the river side. The sun shone in the skies, the birds sang in the trees, the beautiful river flashed and glowed in the light, the waters seemed to dance and the green leaves to thrill.

Ah, if she were but back by the mill-stream, if she were but Leone Noel once again, with her life all unspoiled before her; if she were anything on earth except a woman possessed by a mad love. If she could but exchange these burning ashes of a burning love for the light, bright heart of her girlhood, when the world had been full of beauty which spoke to her in an unknown tongue.

God had been so good to her; he had given to her the beauty of a queen, genius that was immortal, wit, everything life holds most fair, and they were all lost to her because of her mad love. Ah, well, never mind, the sun was shining, the river dancing far away in the sun, and she was to spend the day with him. She had dressed herself to perfection in a close-fitting dress of dark-gray velvet, relieved by ribbons of rose pink; she wore a hat with a dark-gray plume, under the shade of which her beautiful face looked doubly bewitching; the little hands, which by their royal gestures swayed multitudes, were cased in dark gray. Lord Chandos looked at her in undisguised admiration.

"The day seems to have been made on purpose for us," he said, as he helped her in the boat.

Leone laughed, but there was just the least tinge of bitterness in that laugh.

"A day made for us would have gray skies, cold rains, and bleak, bitter winds," she said.

And then the pretty pleasure boat floated away on the broad, beautiful stream.

It was a day on which to dream of heaven; there was hardly a ripple on the beautiful Thames; the air was balmy, sweet, filled with the scent of hay from the meadows; of flowers from the banks; it was as though they had floated away into Paradise.

Lord Chandos bent forward to see that the rugs were properly disposed; he opened her sunshade, but she would not use it.

"Let me see the beautiful river, the banks and the yews, while I may," she said, "the sun will not hurt me."

There was no sound save that of the oars cleaving the bright waters. Leone watched the river with loving eyes; since she had left River View — and she had loved it with something like passion — it seemed like part of that married life which had ended so abruptly. They passed by a thicket, where the birds were singing after a mad fashion of their own.

"Stop and listen," she said, holding up her hand.

He stopped and the boat floated gently with the noiseless tide.

"I wonder," said Leone, "if in that green bird kingdom there are tragedies such as take place in ours?"

Lord Chandos laughed.

"You are full of fanciful ideas, Leone," he said. "Yes, I imagine, the birds have their tragedies because they have their loves."

"I suppose there are pretty birds and plain birds, loving birds, and hard-hearted ones; some who live a happy life, filled with sunlight and song — some who die while the leaves are green, shot through the heart. In the kingdom of birds and the kingdom of men it is all just the same."

"Which fate is yours, Leone?" asked Lord Chandos.

"Mine?" she said, looking away over the dancing waters, "mine? I was shot while the sun shone, and the best part of me died of the wound in my heart."

CHAPTER L
"AS DEAD AS MY HOPES"

The broad, beautiful river widened, and the magnificent scenery of the Thames spread out on either side, a picture without parallel in English landscapes. The silvery water, the lights and shades ever changing, the overhanging woods, the distant hill, the pretty islets, the pleasure-boats, the lawns, the great nests of water-lilies, the green banks studded with flowers, the rushes and reeds that grew even on the water's edge. On they went, through Richmond, Kew, past Hampton Court, past the picturesque old Hampton windmill, on to one of the prettiest spots on the river—the "Bells" at Ousely, and there Lord Chandos fastened the boat to a tree while they went ashore.

Ah, but it was like a faint, far-off dream of heaven—the lovely, laughing river, the rippling foliage, the gorgeous trees, the quaint old hostelry, the hundreds of blooming flowers—the golden sunlight pouring over all. Sorrow, care and death might come to-morrow, when the sky was gray and the water dull; but not to-day. Oh, lovely, happy to-day. Beautiful sun and balmy wind, blooming flowers and singing birds. Lord Chandos made a comfortable seat for Leone on the river bank, and sat down by her side. They did not remember that they had been wedded lovers, or that a tragedy lay between them; they did not talk of love or of sorrow, but they gave themselves up to the happiness of the hour, to the warm, golden sunshine, to the thousand beauties that lay around them. They watched a pretty pleasure-boat drifting slowly along the river. It was well filled with what Lord Chandos surmised to be a picnic party, and somewhat to his dismay the whole party landed near the spot where he, with Leone, was sitting. "I hope," he thought to himself, "that there is no one among them who knows me—I should not like it, for Leone's sake."

The thought had hardly shaped itself in his mind, when some one touched him on the arm. Turning hastily he saw Captain Harry Blake, one of his friends, who cried out in astonishment at seeing him there, and then looked in still greater astonishment at the beautiful face of Madame Vanira.

"Lady Evelyn is on board the Water Witch," he said. "Will you come and speak to her?"

The handsome face of Lord Lanswell's son darkened.

"No," he replied, "pray excuse me. And—Harry, say nothing of my being here. I rowed down this morning. There is no need for every one in London to hear of it before night."

Captain Harry Blake laughed; at the sound of that laugh Lord Chandos felt the greatest impulse to knock him down. His face flushed hotly, and his eyes flashed fire. Leone had not heard one word, and had persistently turned her face from the intruder, quite forgetting that in doing so she was visible to every one on the boat. Lady Evelyn Blake was the first to see her, and she knew just enough of life to make no comment. When her husband returned she said to him carelessly:

"That was Madame Vanira with Lord Chandos, I am sure."

"You had better bring stronger glasses or clearer eyes with you the next time you come," he replied, laughingly, and then Lady Evelyn knew that she was quite right in her suspicions. It was only a jest to her and she thought nothing of it. That same evening when Lady Ilfield, who was one of Lady Marion's dearest friends, spoke of Stoneland House, Lady Evelyn told the incident as a grand jest. Lady Ilfield looked earnestly at her.

"Do you really mean that you saw Lord Chandos with Madame Vanira at Ousely?" she asked. "Alone, without his wife?"

"Yes," laughed Lady Evelyn, "a stolen expedition, evidently. He looked horrified when Captain Blake spoke to him."

"I do not like it," said Lady Ilfield, who was one of the old school, and did not understand the science of modern flirtation. "I have heard already more of Lord Chandos than has pleased me, and I like his wife."

This simple conversation was the beginning of the end—the beginning of one of the saddest tragedies on which the sun ever shone.

"I am sorry that he saw me," said Lord Chandos, as the captain waved his final adieu; "but he did not see your face, Leone, did he?"

"No," she replied, "I think not."

"It does not matter about me," he said, "but I should not like to have any one recognize you."

He forgot the incident soon after. When the boat was again on the bright, dancing river, then they forgot the world and everything else except that they were together.

"Lance," said Leone, "row close to those water-lilies. I should like to gather one."

Obediently enough he went quite close to the white water-lilies, and placed the oars at the bottom of the boat, while he gathered the lilies for her. It was more like a poem than a reality; a golden sun, a blue, shining river, the boat among the water-lilies, the beautiful regal woman, her glorious face bent over the water, her white hands throwing the drops of spray over the green leaves.

It was the prettiest picture ever seen. Lord Chandos filled the boat with flowers; he heaped the pretty white water-lilies at the feet of Leone, until she looked as though she had grown out of them. Then, while the water ran lazily on, and the sun shone in golden splendor, he asked her if she would sing for him.

"One song, Leone," he said, "and that in the faintest voice. It will be clear and distinct as the voice of an angel to me."

There must have been an instinct of pride or defiance in her heart, for she raised her head and looked at him.

"Yes, I will sing for you, Lance," she replied. "Those water-lilies take me home. I will sing a song of which not one word has passed my lips since I saw you. Listen, see if you know the words:

"'In sheltered vale a mill-wheel
Still sings its tuneful lay.
My darling once did dwell there,
But now she's far away.
A ring in pledge I gave her,
And vows of love we spoke—
Those vows are all forgotten,
The ring asunder broke.'"

The rich, beautiful voice, low and plaintive, now seemed to float over the water: it died away among the water-lilies; it seemed to hang like a veil over the low boughs; it startled the birds, and hushed even the summer winds to silence. So sweet, so soft, so low, as he listened, it stole into his heart and worked sweet and fatal mischief. He buried his face in his hands and wept aloud.

On went the sweet voice, with its sad story: he held up his hand with a gesture of entreaty.

"Hush, Leone," he said, "for God's sake, hush. I cannot bear it."

On went the sweet voice:

"'But while I hear that mill-wheel
My pains will never cease;

I would the grave would hide me,
For there alone is peace,
For there alone is peace.'"

"I will sing that verse again," she said, "it is prophetic."

"'I would the grave would hide me,
For there alone is peace.'"

She bent her head as she sung the last few words, and there was silence between them—silence unbroken save for the ripple of the waters as it washed past the boat, and the song of a lark that soared high in the sky.

"Leone," said Lord Chandos, "you have killed me. I thought I had a stronger, braver heart, I thought I had a stronger nature—you have killed me."

He looked quite exhausted, and she saw great lines of pain round his mouth, great shadows in his eyes.

"Have I been cruel to you?" she asked, and there was a ring of tenderness in her voice.

"More cruel than you know," he answered. "Once, Leone, soon after I came home we went to a concert, and among other things I heard 'In Sheltered Vale.' At the first sound of the first notes my heart stood still. I thought, Leone, it would never beat again; I thought my blood was frozen in my veins; I felt the color die from my face. Lady Marion asked me what was the matter, and the countess thought that I was going to swoon. I staggered out of the room like a man who had drunk too much wine, and it was many hours before I recovered myself; and now, Leone, you sing the same words to me; they are like a death knell."

"They hold a prophecy," said Leone, sadly, "the only place where any one can find rest is the grave."

"My beautiful Leone," he cried, "you must not talk about the grave. There should be no death and no grave for one like you."

"There will be none to my love," she said, but rather to herself than to him. Then she roused herself and laughed, but the laugh was forced and bitter. "Why should I speak of my love?" she said. "Mine was a 'Mad Love.'"

The day drifted on to a golden, sunlight afternoon, and the wind died on the waters while the lilies slept. And then they went slowly home.

"Has it been a happy day, Leone?" asked Lord Chandos, as they drew near home.

"It will have no morrow," she answered, sadly. "I shall keep those water-lilies until every leaf is withered and dead; yet they will never be so dead as my hopes—as dead as my life, though art fills it and praises crown it."

"And I," he said, "shall remember this day until I die. I have often wondered, Leone, if people take memory with them to heaven. If they do, I shall think of it there."

"And I," she said, "shall know no heaven, if memory goes with me."

They parted without another word, without a touch of the hands, or one adieu; but there had been no mention of parting, and that was the last thing thought of.

CHAPTER LI
THE CONFESSION

"I do not believe it," said Lady Marion; "it is some absurd mistake. If Lord Chandos had been out alone, or on a party of pleasure where you say, he would have told me."

"I assure you, Lady Chandos, that it is true. Captain Blake spoke to him there, and Lady Evelyn saw him. Madame Vanira was with him."

The speakers were Lady Chandos and Lady Ilfield; the place was the drawing-room at Stoneland House; the time was half past three in the afternoon; and Lady Ilfield had called on her friend because the news which she had heard preyed upon her mind and she felt that she must reveal it. Like all mischief-makers Lady Ilfield persuaded herself that she was acting upon conscientious motives; she herself had no nonsensical ideas about singers and actresses; they were quite out of her sphere, quite beneath her notice, and no good, she was in the habit of saying, ever came from associating with them. She had met Madame Vanira several times at Stoneland House, and had always felt annoyed over it, but her idea was that a singer, an actress, let her be beautiful as a goddess and talented above all other women, had no right to stand on terms of any particular friendship with Lord Chandos. Lady Ilfield persuaded herself it was her duty, her absolute Christian duty, to let Lady Chandos know what was going on. She was quite sure of the truth of what she had to tell, and she chose a beautiful, sunshiny afternoon for telling it. She wore a look of the greatest importance—she seated herself quite close to Lady Marion.

"My dear Lady Chandos," she said, "I have called on the most unpleasant business. There is something which I am quite sure I ought to tell you, and I really do not know how. People are saying such things—you ought to know them."

The fair, sweet face lost none of its tranquillity, none of its calm. How could she surmise that her heart was to be stabbed by this woman's words?

"The sayings of people trouble me but little, Lady Ilfield," she replied, with a calm smile.

"What I have to say concerns you," she said, "concerns you very much. I would not tell you but that I consider it my duty to do so. I told Lady Evelyn that she, who had actually witnessed the scene, ought to be the one to describe it, but she absolutely refused; unpleasant as the duty is, it has fallen on me."

"What duty? what scene?" asked Lady Chandos, beginning to feel something like alarm. "If you have anything to say, Lady Ilfield, anything to tell me, pray speak out; I am anxious now to hear it."

Then indeed was Lady Ilfield in her glory. She hastened to tell the story. How Captain and Lady Evelyn Blake had gone with a few friends for a river-party, and at Ousely had seen Lord Chandos with Madame Vanira, the great queen of song.

Lady Marion's sweet face colored with indignation. She denied it emphatically; it was not true. She was surprised that Lady Ilfield should repeat such a calumny.

"But, my dear Lady Chandos, it is true. I should not have repeated it if there had been a single chance of its being a falsehood. Lady Evelyn saw the boat fastened to a tree, your husband and Madame Vanira sat on the river bank, and when the captain spoke to Lord Chandos he seemed quite annoyed at being seen."

Lady Marion's fair face grew paler as she listened; the story seemed so improbable to her.

"My husband—Lord Chandos—does not know Madame Vanira half so well as I do," she said; "it is I who like her, nay, even love her. It is by my invitation that madame has been to my house. Lord Chandos was introduced to her by accident. I sought her acquaintance. If people had said she had been out for a day on the river with me there would have been some sense in it."

Lady Ilfield smiled with the air of a person possessed of superior knowledge.

"My dear Lady Chandos," she said, "it is time your eyes were opened; you are about the only person in London who does not know that Lord Chandos is Madame Vanira's shadow."

"I do not believe it," was the indignant reply. "I would not believe it, Lady Ilfield, if all London swore it."

Lady Ilfield laughed, and the tinge of contempt in that laugh made the gentle heart beat with indignation. She rose from her seat.

"I do not doubt," she said, "that you came to tell me this with a good-natured intention. I will give you credit for that always, Lady Ilfield, when I remember this painful scene, but I have faith in my husband. Nothing can shake it. And if the story you tell be true, I am quite sure Lord Chandos can give a good explanation of it. Permit me to say good-morning, Lady Ilfield, and to decline any further conversation on the matter."

"For all that," said Lady Ilfield to herself, "you will have to suffer, my lady; you refuse to believe it, but the time will come when you will have to believe it and deplore it."

Yet Lady Ilfield was not quite satisfied when she went away.

While to Lady Chandos had come the first burst of an intolerable pain, her first anguish of jealousy, her only emotion at the commencement of the conversation was one of extreme indignation. It was a calumny, she told herself, and she had vehemently espoused her husband's cause; but when she was alone and began to think over what had been said her faith was somewhat shaken.

It was a straightforward story. Captain and Lady Evelyn Blake were quite incapable of inventing such a thing. Then she tried to remember how Tuesday had passed. It came back to her with a keen sense of pain that on Tuesday she had not seen him all day. He had risen early and had gone out, leaving word that he should not return for luncheon. She had been to a morning concert, and had stayed until nearly dinner-time with the countess. When she returned to Stoneland House he was there; they had a dinner-party, and neither husband nor wife had asked each other how the day was spent. She remembered it now. Certainly so far his absence tallied with the story; but her faith in her husband was not to be destroyed by the gossip of people who had nothing to do but talk.

What was it Lady Ilfield had said? That she was the only person in London who did not know that her husband was Madame Vanira's shadow. Could that be true? She remembered all at once his long absences, his abstraction; how she wondered if he had any friends whom he visited long and intimately.

Madame Vanira's beautiful face rose before her with its noble eloquence, its grandeur and truth. No, that was not the woman who would try to rob a woman of her husband's love. Madame Vanira, the queen of song, the grand and noble woman who swayed men's hearts with her glorious voice; Madame Vanira, who had kissed her face and called herself her friend. It was impossible. She could sooner have believed that the sun and the moon had fallen from the skies than that her husband had connived with her friend to deceive her. The best plan would be to ask her husband. He never spoke falsely; he would tell her at once whether it were true or not. She waited until dinner was over and then said to him:

"Lance, can you spare me a few minutes? I want to speak to you."

They were in the library, where Lord Chandos had gone to write a letter. Lady Marion looked very beautiful in her pale-blue dinner dress and a suit of costly pearls. She went up to her husband, and kneeling down by his side, she laid her fair arms round his neck.

"Lance," she said, "before I say what I have to say I want to make an act of faith in you."

He smiled at the expression.

"An act of faith in me, Marion?" he said. "I hope you have all faith."

Then, remembering, he stopped, and his face flushed.

"I have need of faith," she said, "for I have heard a strange story about you. I denied it, I deny it now, but I should be better pleased with your denial also."

"What is the story?" he asked, anxiously, and her quick ear detected the anxiety of his voice.

"Lady Ilfield has been here this afternoon, and tells me that last Tuesday you were with Madame Vanira at Ousely, that you rowed her on the river, and that Captain Blake spoke to you there. Is it true?"

"Lady Ilfield is a mischief-making old——" began Lord Chandos, but his wife's sweet, pale face startled him.

"Lance," she cried, suddenly, "oh, my God, it is not true?"

The ring of pain and passion in her voice frightened him; she looked at him with eyes full of woe.

"It is not true?" she repeated.

"Who said it was true?" he asked, angrily.

Then there was a few minutes of silence between them; and Lady Marion looked at him again.

"Lance," she said, "is it true?"

Their eyes met, hers full of one eager question. His lips parted; her whole life seemed to hang on the word that was coming from his lips.

"Is it true?" she repeated.

He tried to speak falsely, he would have given much for the power to say "No." He knew that one word would content her—that she would believe it implicitly, and that she would never renew the question. Still with that fair, pure face before him—with those clear eyes fixed on him—he could not speak falsely, he could not tell a lie. He could have cried aloud with anguish, yet he answered, proudly:

"It is true, Marion."

"True?" she repeated, vacantly, "true, Lance?"

"Yes, the gossips have reported correctly; it is quite true."

But he was not prepared for the effect of the words on her. Her fair face grew pale, her tender arms released their hold and fell.

"True?" she repeated, in a low, faint voice, "true that you took Madame Vanira out for a day, and that you were seen by these people with her?"

"Yes, it is true," he replied.

And the poor child flung her arms in the air, as she cried out:

"Oh, Lance, it is a sword in my heart, and it has wounded me sorely."

CHAPTER LII
A GATHERING CLOUD

It was strange that she should use the same words which Leone had used.

"I cannot bear it, Lance," she said. "Why have you done this?"

He was quite at a loss what to say to her; he was grieved for her, vexed with those who told her, and the mental emotions caused him to turn angrily round to her.

"Why did you take her? What is Madame Vanira to you?" she asked.

"My dear Marion, can you see any harm in my giving madame a day's holiday and rest, whether on water or on land?"

She was silent for a minute before she answered him.

"No," she replied, "the harm lay in concealing it from me; if you had told me about it I would have gone with you."

Poor, simple, innocent Lady Marion! The words touched him deeply; he thought of the boat among the water-lilies, the beautiful, passionate voice floating over the water, the beautiful, passionate face, with its defiance as the words of the sweet, sad song fell from her lips.

"Lance, why did you not tell me? Why did you not ask me to go with you? I cannot understand."

When a man has no proper excuse to make, no sensible reason to give, he takes refuge in anger. Lord Chandos did that now; he was quite at a loss what to say; he knew that he had done wrong; that he could say nothing which could set matters straight; obviously the best thing to do was to grow angry with his wife.

"I cannot see much harm in it," he said. "I should not suppose that I am the first gentleman in England who has taken a lady out for a holiday and felt himself highly honored in so doing."

"But, Lance," repeated his fair wife, sorrowfully, "why did you not take me or tell me?"

"My dear Marion, I did not think that I was compelled to tell you every action of my life, everywhere I went, everything I did, every one I see; I would never submit to such a thing. Of all things in the world, I abhor the idea of a jealous wife."

She rose from her knees, her fair face growing paler, and stood looking at him with a strangely perplexed, wondering gaze.

"I cannot argue with you, Lance," she said, gently; "I cannot dispute what you say. You are your own master; you have a perfect right to go where you will, and with whom you will, but my instinct and my heart tell me that you are wrong. You have no right to take any lady out without telling me. You belong to me, and to no one else."

"My dear Marion, you are talking nonsense," he said, abruptly; "you know nothing of the world. Pray cease."

She looked at him with more of anger on her fair face than he had ever seen before.

"Lord Chandos," she said, "is this all you have to say to me? I am told that you have spent a whole day in the society of the most beautiful actress in the world, perhaps, and when I ask for an explanation you have none to give me."

"No," he replied, "I have none."

"Lance, I do not like it," she said, slowly; "and I do not understand. I thought Madame Vanira was so good and true?"

"So she is," he replied. "You must not say one word against her."

"I have no wish; but if she is so good why should she try to take my husband from me?"

"She has not done so," he replied, angrily. "Marion, I will not be annoyed by a jealous wife."

"I am not jealous, Lance," she replied; "but when I am told such a story, and it proves to be true, what am I to do?"

"Say nothing, Marion, which is always the wisest thing a woman can do," he replied.

His wife gazed at him with proud indignation.

"I do not like the tone in which you speak of this; tell me frankly, is it with Madame Vanira you spend all the time which you pass away from home?"

"I shall say nothing of Madame Vanira," he replied.

She drew nearer to him; she laid one white hand on his shoulder and looked wistfully into his face.

"Lance," she said, "are we to quarrel—over a woman, too? I will not believe it. You have always been honest with me; tell me what Madame Vanira is to you?"

"She is nothing to me," he replied.

Then the remembrance of what she had been to him came over him and froze the words on his lips. His wife was quick to notice it.

"You cannot say it with truth. Oh, Lance, how you pain me."

There was such absolute, physical pain in her face that he was grieved for her.

"Say no more about it, Marion," he cried. "I did ask madame to let me row her on the river; I know she loves the river; I ought to have asked you to go with us, or to have told you about it," he said; "I know that; but people often do imprudent things. Kiss me and say no more about it."

But for the first time that sweet girl looked coldly on him. Instead of bending down to kiss him, she looked straight into his face.

"Lance," she said, "do you like Madame Vanira?"

His answer was prompt.

"Most decidedly I do," he answered; "every one must like her."

"Lady Ilfield says that you are her shadow. Is that true?"

"Lady Ilfield is a gossip, and the wife who listens to scandal about her husband lowers herself."

She did not shrink now from his words.

"I have not gossiped about you, Lance," she said; "but I wish you yourself to tell me why people talk about you and Madame Vanira."

"How can I tell? Why do people talk? Because they have nothing better to do."

But that did not satisfy her; her heart ached; this was not the manner in which she had expected him to meet the charge—so differently—either to deny it indignantly, or to give her some sensible explanation. As it was, he seemed to avoid the subject, even while he owned that it was true.

"I am not satisfied, Lance," she said; "you have made me very unhappy; if there is anything to tell me tell it now."

"What should I have to tell you?" he asked, impatiently.

"I do not know; but if there is any particular friendship or acquaintance between Madame Vanira and yourself, tell me now."

It would have been better if he had told her, if he had made an open confession of his fault, and have listened to her gentle counsel, but he did not; on the contrary, he looked angrily at her.

"If you wish to please me, you will not continue this conversation, Marion; in fact, I decline to say another word on the subject. I have said all that was needful, let it end now."

"You say this, knowing that I am dissatisfied, Lance," said Lady Marion.

"I say it, hoping that you intend to obey me," he replied.

Without another word, and in perfect silence, Lady Chandos quitted the room, her heart beating with indignation.

"He will not explain to me," she said; "I will find out for myself."

She resolved from that moment to watch him, and to find out for herself that which he refused to tell her. She could not bring herself to believe that there was really anything between her husband and Madame Vanira; he had always been so good, so devoted to herself.

But the result of her watching was bad; it showed that her husband had other interests; much of his time was spent from home; a cloud came between them; when she saw him leaving home she was too proud to ask him where he was going, and if even by chance she did ask, his reply was never a conciliatory one.

It was quite by accident she learned he went often to Highgate. In the stables were a fine pair of grays; she liked using them better than any other horses they had, and one morning the carriage came to the door with a pair of chestnuts she particularly disliked.

"Where are the grays?" she asked of the coachman.

"One of them fell yesterday, my lady," said the man, touching his hat.

"Fell—where?" asked Lady Chandos.

"Coming down Highgate Hill, my lady. It is a terrible hill—so steep and awkward," replied the man.

Then she would have thought nothing of it but for a sudden look of warning she saw flash from the groom to the coachman, from which she shrewdly guessed that they had been told to be silent about the visits to Highgate. Then she remembered that Madame Vanira lived there. She remembered how she had spoken of the hills, of the fresh air, and the distance from town; she watched again and found out that her husband went to Highgate nearly every day of his life, and then Lady Chandos drew her own conclusions and very miserable ones they were.

The cloud between them deepened—deepened daily; all her loving amiability, her gentle, caressing manner vanished; she became silent, watchful, suspicious; no passion deteriorates the human mind or the human heart more quickly than jealousy. If, during those watchful days, Lord Chandos had once told his wife the plain truth, she would have forgiven him, have taken him from the scene of his danger, and all might have gone well; as it was, all went wrong.

One day a sense of regret for her lost happiness came over her, and she determined to speak to him about it. She would destroy this shadow that lay between them; she would dispel the cloud. Surely he would do anything for her sake—she would have given up the world for him. He was alone in his study, in the gloaming of a bright day, when she went in to him and stood once more by his side.

"Lance," she said, bending her fair, sweet face over his, "Lance, I want to speak to you again. I am not happy, dear—there is a cloud between us, and it is killing me. You love me, Lance, do you not?"

"You know that I do," he said, but there was no heartiness in his voice.

"I want to tell you, dear, that I have been jealous. I am very unhappy, but I will conquer myself. I will be to you the most loving wife in all the world if you will give up Madame Vanira."

He pushed the outstretched hand away.

"You do not know what you are asking," he said, hoarsely, and his manner so alarmed her that she said no more.

CHAPTER LIII
A QUARREL

From that hour all pretense of peace was at an end between them. Lady Chandos was justly indignant and wounded. If her husband had trusted her all might, even then, have been well, but he did not; he said to himself that she would forget the story of her annoyance in time, and all would be well; he did not give his wife credit for the depth of feeling that she really possessed. Fiercest, most cruel jealousy had taken hold of the gentle lady, it racked and tortured her; the color faded from her face, the light from her eyes; she grew thin and pale; at night she could not sleep, by day she could not rest; all her sweetness, grace and amiability, seemed to have given way to a grave sadness; the sound of her laughter, her bright words, died away; nothing interested her. She who had never known a trouble or a care, now wore the expression of one who was heart-broken; she shrunk from all gayety, all pleasures, all parties; she was like the ghost of her former self; yet after those words of her husband's she never spoke again of Madame Vanira. The sword was sheathed in her heart and she kept it there.

There is no pain so cruel as jealousy; none that so quickly deteriorates a character; it brings so many evils in its train—suspicion, envy, hatred of life, distrust in every one and in everything; it is the most fatal passion that ever takes hold of a human heart, and turns the kindest nature to gall. There was no moment during the day in which Lady Chandos did not picture her husband with her rival; she drove herself almost mad with the pictures she made in her own mind. All the cruel pain, the sullen brooding, the hot anguish, the desolation, the jealousy seemed to surge over her heart and soul like the waves of a deadly sea. If she saw her husband silent and abstracted, she said he was thinking of Madame Vanira; if she saw him laugh and light of heart she said he was pleased because he was going to see Madame Vanira. She had sensible and reasonable grounds for jealousy, but she was unreasonably jealous.

> "Trifles light as air
> Are to the jealous confirmation strong
> As proofs of holy writ."

It was so with Lady Marion, and her life at last grew too bitter to be borne. There was excuse for Lord Chandos, the mistake was in renewing the acquaintance; a mistake that can never be remedied.

People were beginning to talk; when Lord Chandos was mentioned, they gave significant smiles. Against Madame Vanira there had never been even the faintest rumor of scandal; but a certain idea was current in society—that Lord Chandos admired the queen of song. No one insinuated the least wrong, but significant smiles followed the mention of either name.

"Madame Vanira was at Lady Martyn's last night," one would say.

And the laughing answer was always:

"Then Lord Chandos was not very far away."

"La Vanira sung to perfection in 'Fidelio,'" would remark one.

Another would answer:

"Lord Chandos would know how to applaud."

Madame Vanira was more eagerly sought after than other women in London. She reigned queen, not only over the stage, but over the world of fashion also.

The Countess of Easton gave a grand ball—it was the most exclusive of the season. After much praying Madame Vanira had promised to go, and Lady Chandos was the belle of the ball. They had not met since the evening madame had sung for her, and Lord Chandos had many an anxious thought as to what their next meeting would be like. He knew that Leone would bear much for his sake, yet he did not know what his wife would be tempted to say.

They met on the night of Lady Easton's ball; neither knew that the other was coming. If Lady Chandos had dreamed of meeting Leone there she would not have gone. As it was, they met face to face in the beautiful ante-room that led to the ballroom.

Face to face. Leone wore a superb dress of pale amber brocade, and Lady Chandos a beautiful costume of pale-blue velvet, the long train of which was fastened with white, shining pearls.

It was like the meeting of rival queens. Leone's face flushed, Lady Marion's grew deadly pale. Leone held out her hand; Lady Marion declined to see it. They looked at each other for a brief space of time, then Leone spoke.

"Lady Marion," she said, in a low, pained voice, "have I displeased you?"

"Yes, you have," was the brief reply.

"You will not touch my hand?" said Leone.

"No, I decline to touch your hand," said Lady Marion; "I decline to speak to you after this."

"Will you tell me why?" asked Leone.

Lady Marion's face flushed crimson.

"Since you ask me, I will tell you. You have been seeking my husband, and I do not approve of it. You spent a day with him on the river—he never told me about it. I am not a jealous wife, but I despise any woman who would seek to take the love of a husband from his wife."

Conscience, which makes cowards of us all, kept Leone silent.

Lady Chandos continued:

"What is there between my husband and you?"

"True friendship," answered Leone, trying to speak bravely.

"I do not believe it," said Lady Chandos; "true friendship does not hide itself, or make mystery of its actions. Madame Vanira, I loved you when I first saw you; I take my love and my liking both from you. Now that I find that you have acted treacherously I believe in you no more."

"Those are strong words, Lady Chandos," said Leone.

"They are true; henceforth we are strangers. My friends are honorable women, who would seek to steal my jewels rather than seek to steal from me my husband's love."

Leone could have retaliated; the temptation was strong; she could have said:

"He was my husband, as I believed, before he was yours; you stole him from me, not I from you."

The temptation was strong, the words leaped in a burning torrent from her heart to her lips; she repressed them for his sake and bore the crushing words without reply.

"I have always heard," she said, "that there was ample reason that singers, even though they be queens of song, should not be admitted into the heart of one's home; now I see the justice of it; they are not satisfied with legitimate triumphs. You, Madame Vanira, have not been contented with my liking and friendship, with the hospitality of my home, but you must seek to take my husband's interest, time, affection."

"Are you not judging me harshly, Lady Chandos?" asked the singer. "You bring all these accusations against me and give me no opportunity of clearing myself of them."

"You cannot," said Lady Chandos; "I have no wish to hear your defense, you can neither deny nor explain the fact that you spent a day with my husband on the river; all the sophistry in the world cannot deny that fact, and that fact condemns you."

"Would you say the same thing to any of your former friends?" asked Leone—"to Lady Caldwell or Lady Blake?"

"Neither of them would do such a thing," cried Lady Chandos. "Ladies of the class to which I belong do not spend whole days on the river with gentlemen unknown to their wives. Madame Vanira—you and I are strangers from this time."

"You are very hard on me," said Leone; "the day may come when you will admit that."

"The day will never come in which I will mistake good for evil, or right for wrong," said Lady Chandos. "Others may applaud you, you may continue your sway over the minds and hearts of men, but I shall protest against you, and all those like you, who would come between husbands and wives to separate them."

It was such a satire of fate, such a satire of her own life, that Leone's beautiful lips curled with a bitter smile. It was she who had been parted from her husband by a quibble of the law, and this fair, angry woman had taken him for herself.

Lady Chandos saw the smile and misunderstood it. She bowed, and would have passed, but Leone tried to stop her.

"Will you not say one kind word to me before you go, Lady Chandos?" she asked.

"I have not one kind word to say," was the brief reply.

She would have passed on, but fate again intervened in the person of Lord Chandos, who was walking with his hostess, the Countess of Easton. They stopped before the two ladies, and Lord Chandos saw at once that something was wrong. Madame Vanira, after exchanging a few words with the countess, went away, and as soon as he could, Lord Chandos rejoined his wife.

"Marion," he said, curtly, "you have had some disagreeable words with Madame Vanira. I know it by the expression of your face."

"You are right," she said; "I have told her that henceforth she and I shall be strangers."

"You have dared!" he cried, forgetting himself at the thought of Leone's face.

She turned her fair face proudly to him.

"I have dared," she replied; "I refuse to speak or see Madame Vanira again—she must not cross the threshold of my door again."

Lord Chandos grew deadly pale as he heard the words.

"And I say that you wrong a good and blameless woman, Marion, when you say such words."

"My lord, am I or am I not at liberty to choose my friends?" she asked, haughtily.

"Certainly you are at liberty to do just as you please in that respect," he replied.

"Then among them I decline to receive Madame Vanira," she said.

"As you refuse to see my friends, I must go to meet them," said Lord Chandos.

And then between husband and wife began one of those scenes which leave a mark on both their lives—cruel, hard, unjust and bitter words—hard and cruel thoughts.

Then Lady Chandos had her carriage called and went home.

CHAPTER LIV
A MOTHER'S APPEAL

"She would not bear it—she could not bear it," this was Lady Marion's conclusion in the morning, when the sunbeams peeping in her room told her it was time to rise. She turned her face to the wall and said it would be easier to die—her life was spoiled, nothing could give her back her faith and trust in her husband or her love for him.

Life held nothing for her now. It was noon before she rose, and then she went to her boudoir. Lord Chandos had gone out, leaving no message for her. She sat there thinking, brooding over her sorrow, wondering what she was to do, when the Countess of Lanswell was announced.

Lady Marion looked up. It was as though an inspiration from Heaven had come to her; she would tell Lady Lanswell, and hear what she had to say.

"You have been crying," said the countess, as she bent over her daughter-in-law. "Crying, and how ill you look—what is the matter?"

"There is something very wrong the matter," said Lady Marion. "Something that I cannot bear—something that will kill me if it is not stopped."

"My dearest Marion," said the countess, "what is wrong? I have never seen you so distressed before. Where is Lance?"

"I never know where he is now," she said. "Oh, Lady Lanswell, I am so miserable, so unhappy that I wish I were dead."

This outbreak from Lady Marion, who was always so calm, so high-bred, so reticent in expressing her feelings, alarmed Lady Lanswell. She took the cold, trembling hands in her own.

"Marion," she said, "you must calm yourself; you must tell me what is the matter and let me help you."

Lady Chandos told her all, and the countess listened in wondering amaze.

"Are you quite sure?" she said. "Lady Ilfield exaggerates sometimes when she repeats those gossiping stories."

"It must be true, since my husband acknowledged it himself, and yet refused to give me any explanation of it. Some time since, I found that he passed so much of his time away from home I asked you if he had any friends with whom he was especially intimate, and you thought not. Now I know that it was Madame Vanira he went to see. She lives at Highgate, and he goes there every day."

"I should not think much of it, my dear, if I were you," said the countess. "Madame Vanira is very beautiful and very accomplished—all gentlemen like to be amused."

"I cannot argue," said Lady Chandos; "I can only say that my own instinct and my own heart tell me there is something wrong, that there is some tie between them. I know nothing of it—I cannot tell why I feel this certain conviction, but I do feel it."

"It is not true, I am sure, Marion," said the countess, gravely. "I know Lance better than any one else; I know his strength, his weakness, his virtues, his failings. Love of intrigue is not one, neither is lightness of love."

"Then if he cares nothing for Madame Vanira, and sees me unhappy over her, why will he not give her up?"

"He will if you ask him," said Lady Lanswell.

"He will *not*. I have asked him. I have told him that the pain of it is wearing my life away; but he will not. I am very unhappy, for I love my husband."

"And he loves you," said the countess.

"I do not think so. I believe—my instinct tells me—that he loves Madame Vanira."

"Marion, it is wicked to say such things," said the countess, severely. "Because your husband, like every other man of the world, pays some attention to the most gifted woman of her day, you suspect him of infidelity, want of love and want of truth. I wonder at you."

Lady Marion raised her fair, tear-stained face.

"I cannot make you understand," she said slowly, "nor do I understand myself. I only know what I feel, what my instinct tells me, and that is that between my husband and Madame Vanira there is something more than I know. I feel that there is a tie between them. He looks at her with different eyes; he speaks to her with a different voice; when he sung with her it was as though their souls floated away together."

"Marion," interrupted the countess, "my dear child, I begin to see what is the matter with you—you are jealous."

"Yes, I am jealous," said the unhappy wife, "and not without cause—you must own that. Ah, Lady Lanswell, you would be sorry for me if you knew all. See, it is wearing me away; my heart beats, my hands tremble, and they burn like fire. Oh, my God, how I suffer!"

The Countess of Lanswell, in her superb dress of black velvet, sat by in silence; for the first time in her life she was baffled; for the first time in her life she was face to face with a human passion. Hitherto, in her cold, proud presence all passion had veiled itself; this unhappy wife laid hers bare, and my lady was at a loss what to say. In her calm, proud life there had been no room for jealousy; she had never known it, she did not even understand the pain.

If her husband had gone out for a day with the most beautiful woman on earth, she would either have completely ignored the fact, or, with a smiling satire, have passed it by. She did not love the earl well enough to be jealous of him; she did not understand love or jealousy in others. She sat now quite helpless before the unhappy wife, whose grief annoyed her.

"This will not do, Marion," she said, "you will make yourself quite ill."

"Ill," repeated Lady Marion, "I have been ill in heart and soul for many days, and now I am sick unto death. I wish I could die; life has nothing left for me."

"Die, my dear, it seems such a trifle, such a trifle; one day spent together on a river. Is that anything for you to die about?"

The sweet blue eyes raised wistfully to hers were full of pain.

"You do not see, you do not understand. Only think how much intimacy there must have been between them before he would ask her to go, or she consent to go. If they are but strangers, or even every-day friends, what could they find to talk about for a whole day?"

The countess shrugged her shoulders.

"I am surprised," she said, "for I thought Madame Vanira so far above all coquetry. If I were you, Marion, I would forget it."

"I cannot forget it," she cried. "Would to God that I could. It is eating my heart away."

"Then," said my lady, "I will speak to Lance at once, and I am quite sure that at one word from me he will give up the acquaintance, for the simple reason that you do not like it."

And with this promise the countess left her daughter-in-law. Once before, not by her bidding, but by her intrigues, she had persuaded him to give up one whom he loved; surely a few words from her now would induce him to give up her whom he could not surely love. It never occurred to her to dream that they were the same.

She saw him as she was driving home, and, stopping the carriage, asked him to drive with her.

"Lance, I have something very serious to say to you. There is no use beating about the bush, Marion is very ill and very unhappy."

"I am sorry for it, mother, but add also she is very jealous and very foolish."

"My dear Lance, your wife loves you—you know it, she loves you with all her heart and soul. If your friendship with Madame Vanira annoys her, why not give it up?"

"I choose to keep my independence as a man; I will not allow any one to dictate to me what friends I shall have, whom I shall give up or retain."

"In some measure you are right, Lance," said the countess, "and so far as gentleman friends are concerned, I should always choose my own; but as this is a lady, of whom Lady Marion has certain suspicions, I should most certainly give her up."

"My wife has no right to be jealous," he said angrily; "it does not add to my love for her."

"Let me speak seriously to you, Lance," said the countess. "Marion is so unhappy that I should not wonder if she were really ill over it; now why not do as she wishes? Madame Vanira can be nothing to you—Marion is everything. Why not give her up?"

A certain look of settled determination that came to her son's face made the countess pause and wonder. She had seen it there for the first and last time when she had asked her son to renounce his young wife, and now she saw it again. Strange that his next words should seem like an answer to her thoughts.

"Mother," he said, "do not ask me; you persuaded me to give up all the happiness of my life, years ago—do not try me a second time. I refuse, absolutely refuse, to gratify my wife's foolish, jealous wish. I say, emphatically, that I will not give up my friendship for Madame Vanira."

Then my lady looked fixedly at him.

"Lance," she said, "what is Madame Vanira to you?"

He could not help the flush that burned his handsome, angry face, and that flush aroused his mother's curiosity. "Have you known her long? Did you know her before your marriage, Lance? I remember now that I was rather struck by her manner. She reminds me forcibly of some one. Poor Marion declares there is some tie between you. What can it be?"

She mused for some minutes, then looked into her son's face.

"Great Heaven, Lance, it can never be!" she cried. "A horrible idea has occurred to me, and yet it is not possible."

He made no answer, but a look of more dogged defiance came into his face.

"It can never be, and yet I think it is so. Can it be possible that Madame Vanira is the—the dairy-maid to whom you gave your young affections?"

"Madame Vanira is the girl I loved, mother, and whom I believed to be my wife—until you parted us."

And my lady fell back in her carriage with a low cry of "Heaven have mercy on us!"

CHAPTER LV
"WAR TO THE KNIFE"

Lucia, Countess of Lanswell, was in terrible trouble, and it was the first real trouble of her life. Her son's marriage had been rather a difficulty than a trouble—a difficulty that the law had helped her over. Now no law could intervene, and no justice. Nothing could exceed her surprise in finding Madame Vanira, the Queen of Song, the most beautiful, the most gifted woman in England, positively the "dairy-maid," "the tempestuous young person," the artful, designing girl from whom by an appeal to the strong arm of the law she had saved her son. She paused in wonder to think to herself what would have happened if the marriage had not been declared null and void. In that case, she said to herself, with a shrug of the shoulders, in all probability the girl would not have taken to the stage at all. She wondered that she had not sooner recognized her. She remembered the strong, dramatic passion with which Leone had threatened her. "She was born an actress," said my lady to herself, with a sneer. She determined within herself that the secret should be kept, that to no one living would she reveal the fact that the great actress was the girl whom the law had parted from her son.

Lord Chandos, the Duke of Lester, the world in general, must never know this. Lord Chandos must never tell it, neither would she. What was she to do? A terrible incident had happened—terrible to her on whose life no shadow rested. Madame Vanira had accepted an engagement at Berlin, the fashionable journals had already announced the time of her departure, and bemoaned the loss of so much beauty and genius. Lord Chandos had announced his intention of spending a few months in Berlin, and his wife would not agree to it.

"You know very well," she said, "that you have but one motive in going to Berlin, and that is to be near Madame Vanira."

"You have no right to pry into my motives," he replied, angrily; and she retorted that when a husband's motives lowered his wife, she had every reason to inquire into them.

Hot, bitter, angry words passed between them. Lord Chandos declared that if it pleased him to go to Berlin he should go; it mattered little whether his wife went or not; and Lady Chandos, on her side, declared that nothing should ever induce her to go to Berlin. The result was just what one might have anticipated—a violent quarrel. Lady Chandos threatened to appeal to the duke. Her husband laughed at the notion.

"The duke is a great statesman and a clever man," he replied; "but he has no power over me. If he interfered with my arrangements, in all probability we should not meet again."

"I will appeal to him," cried Lady Marion; "he is the only friend I have in the world."

The ring of passionate pain in her voice startled him; a sense of pity came over him. After all, this fair, angry woman was his wife, whom he was bound to protect.

"Marion, be reasonable," he said. "You go the wrong way to work; even supposing I did care for some one else, you do not go the way to make me care for you; but you are mistaken. Cease all these disagreeable recriminations, and I will be the kindest of husbands and the best of friends to you. I have no wish, believe me, Marion, to be anything else."

Even then she might have become reconciled to him, and the sad after consequences have been averted, but she was too angry, too excited with jealousy and despair.

"Will you give up Madame Vanira for me?" she said, and husband and wife looked fixedly at each other. "You say you will be a loving husband and a true friend: prove it by doing this—prove it by giving up Madame Vanira."

Lord Chandos was silent for a few minutes; then he said:

"I cannot, for this reason: Madame Vanira, as I happen to know, has had great troubles in her life, but she is thoroughly good. I repeat it, Marion, thoroughly good. Now, if I, as you phrase it, 'give her up,' it would be confessing that I had done wrong. My friendship is some little comfort to her, and she likes me. What harm is there in it? Above all, what wrong does it inflict on you? Answer me. Has my friendship for Madame Vanira made me less kind, less thoughtful for you?"

No answer came from the white lips of the trembling wife.

He went on:

"Why should you be foolish or narrow-minded? Why seek to end a friendship pure and innocent? Why not be your noble self, Marion—noble, as I have always thought you? I will tell you frankly, Madame Vanira is going to Berlin. You know how lonely it is to go to a fresh place. She happened to say how desolate she should feel at first in Berlin. I remarked that I knew the city well, and then she wished we were going. I pledge you my honor that she said 'we.' Never dreaming that you would make any opposition, I said that I should be very glad to spend the next few weeks in Berlin. I cannot tell how it really was, but I found that it was all settled and arranged almost before I knew it. Now, you would not surely wish me to draw back? Come with me to Berlin, and I will show you how happy I will make you."

"No," she replied; "I will share your heart with no one. Unless I have all I will have none. I will not go to Berlin, and you must give up Madame Vanira," she continued; "Lance, you cannot hesitate, you must see your duty; a married man wants no woman friend but his wife. Why should you spend long hours and whole days *tete-a-tete* with a stranger? Of what can you find to speak? You know in your heart that you are wrong. You say no. Now in the name of common sense and fairness, let me ask, would you like me to make of any man you know such a friend as you have made of Madame Vanira?"

"That is quite another thing," he replied.

Lady Chandos laughed, sadly.

"The usual refuge of a man when he is brought to bay," she said. "No words, no arguments will be of any use to me; I shall never be really friends with you until you give up Madame Vanira."

"Then we will remain enemies," he replied. "I will never give up a true friend for the caprice of any woman," he replied, "even though that woman be my wife."

"Neither will I consent to go to Berlin," she answered, gravely.

"Then I must go alone," he said; "I will not be governed by caprices that have in them neither reason nor sense."

"Then," cried Lady Marion, "it is war to the knife between us!"

"War, if you will," said Lord Chandos; "but always remember you can put an end to the warfare when you will!"

"I shall appeal to Lady Lanswell and to the Duke of Lester," said Lady Marion, and her husband merely answered with a bow.

With them it was indeed "war to the knife." Such was the Gordian knot that Lady Lanswell had to untie, and it was the most difficult task of her life.

On the same evening when that conversation took place, Lord Chandos went to the opera, where Leone was playing "Anne Boleyn." He waited until she came out and was seated in her carriage; then he stood for a few moments leaning over the carriage door and talking to her.

"How you tremble, Leone," he said. "Your face is white and your eyes all fire!"

"The spell is still on me," she answered. "When I have thrown my whole soul into anything, I lose my own identity for many hours. I wish," she continued, "that I did not so thoroughly enter into those characters. I hardly realize this moment whether I am Anne Boleyn, the unhappy wife of bluff King Hal, or whether I am Leone, the singer."

"I know which you are," he said, his eyes seeking hers with a wistful look. "All King Hal's wives put together are not worth your little finger, Leone. See how the stars are shining. I have something to say to you. May I drive with you as far as Highgate Hill?"

The beautiful face, all pale with passion, looked into his.

"It is against our compact," she said; "but you may if you wish."

The silent stars looked down in pity as he took his place by her side.

"Leone," he said, "I want to ask you something. A crisis is come in our lives; my wife, who was told about that day on the river, has asked me to give up your acquaintance."

A low cry came from the beautiful lips, and the face of the fairest woman in England grew deadly pale.

"To give me up," she murmured; "and you, Lord Chandos, what have you said?"

"I said 'No,' a thousand times over, Leone; our friendship is a good and pure one; I would not give it up for any caprice in the world."

A great, tearless sob came from her pale lips.

"God bless you a thousand times!" she said. "So you would not give me up, and you told them so?"

"Yes; I refused to do anything of the kind," he replied; "why should I, Leone? They parted us once by stratagem, by intrigue, by working on all that was weakest in my character; now we are but friends, simply honest friends; who shall part us?"

She clasped his hand for an instant in her own.

"So you will not give me up again, Lance?" she said.

"No, I will die first, Leone. There is one thing more I have to say. I said that I would go to Berlin, and I have asked my wife to go with me; she has refused, and I have said that I would go alone. Tell me what you think?"

"I cannot—I think nothing; perhaps—oh, Heaven help me!—perhaps as your wife has told you she will not go with you, your duty is to stay with her."

"My duty," he repeated; "who shall say what a man's duty is? Do you think I have no duty toward you?"

"Your first thought should be—must be—your wife. If she would have countenanced our friendship, it would have been our greatest pride and pleasure; if she opposes it, we must yield. She has the first right to your time. After all, Lance, what can it matter? We shall have to part; what can it matter whether it is now or in three months to come? The more we see of each other the harder it will be."

A flush as of fire came over his face.

"Why must we part?" he cried. "Oh, Heaven, what a price I pay for my folly!"

"Here is Highgate Hill," said Leone; "you go no further, Lord Chandos."

Only the silent stars were looking on; he stood for a few minutes at the carriage door.

"Shall I go to Berlin?" he whispered, as he left her, and her answer was a low, sad:

"Yes."

CHAPTER LVI
AN APPROACHING TEMPEST

The Countess of Lanswell was in despair. Any little social difficulty, the exposing of an adventuress, the setting aside of a marriage, intrigues, or a royal invitation, "dropping" people when it was convenient to do so, and courting them when she required them, to all and each of these deeds she was quite equal; but a serious case of cruel jealousy, a heart-broken, desolate wife on the one hand, an obstinate husband on the other, was past her power of management. Lady Chandos had written to ask her to come to Stoneland House that day.

"I have something of the greatest importance to say to you," she wrote. "Do not delay; to-morrow may be too late."

Lady Lanswell received this urgent note just as she was sipping her chocolate, luxuriously robed in a dressing-gown of silk and softest velvet, a pretty morning-cap of finest Mechlin lace on her head. Her handsome, haughty face grew pale as she read it.

"It is a wretched piece of business from beginning to end," she said to herself. "Now here is my peace of mind for the day gone. I was to have seen Madame Adelaide soon after noon about my dresses, and the dentist at three. I know absolutely nothing which I can say to a jealous wife, I know nothing of jealousy. Most of the wives whom I know are pleased rather than otherwise when their husbands are away from home. Marion takes things too seriously. I shall tell her so."

But any little speech of that kind she might have tried to make was forgotten when she caught the first glimpse of Lady Marion's white, tragic face.

"My dear child, what is the matter? What a face! why, you have been crying for hours, I am sure," said the countess. "Marion, you should not go on in this way, you will kill yourself."

"Lady Lanswell, I wish that I were dead; my husband has ceased to love me. Oh, God, let me die!" cried poor Lady Marion, and the countess was seriously alarmed.

"My dear child, pray be reasonable," she cried; "how can you say that Lance has ceased to love you?"

"It is true," said the unhappy wife; "he refused to give up Madame Vanira, and what seems to me more dreadful still, she is going to Berlin, and he insists on going also. I cannot bear it, Lady Lanswell!"

"We must reason with him," said the countess, grandly, and despite the tragedy of her sorrow, Lady Marion smiled.

"Reason with him? You might as well stand before a hard, white rock and ask roses to bloom on it; you might as well stand before the great heaving ocean and ask the tide not to roll in, as to try to reason with him. I do not understand it, but I am quite sure that he is infatuated by Madame Vanira; I could almost fancy that she had worked some spell over him. Why should he care for her? Why should he visit her? Why should he go to Berlin because she is there?"

The countess, listening, thanked Heaven that she did not know. If ever that secret became known, it was all over with the House of Lanswell.

"I have said all that I can say," she continued, rising in great agitation; "and it is of no use; he is utterly shameless."

"Hush, woman! I will not have you say such things of my son; he may like and admire Madame Vanira, but I trust him, and would trust him anywhere; you think too much of it, and you make more of it than you need. Let me pray of you to be prudent; want of prudence in a wife at such a juncture as this has very often occasioned misery for life. Are you quite sure that you cannot be generous enough to allow your husband the pleasure of this friendship, which I can certify is a good one?"

The countess sighed; the matter was indeed beyond her. In her artificial life, these bare, honest human passions had no place.

"Over the journey to Berlin," she said, "you are making too much of it. If he enjoys madame's society, and likes Berlin, where is the harm of his enjoying them together?"

So she spoke; but she shrunk from the clear gaze of those blue eyes.

"Lady Lanswell, you know all that is nonsense. My husband is mine, and I will not share his love or his affection with any one. Unless he gives up Madame Vanira, I shall leave him. If he goes to Berlin, I will never see him again."

"You are very foolish, my dear. I heard yesterday, on very good authority, that my son, Lord Chandos, will be offered the vacant Garter. I believe it is true, I feel sure of it. I would not for the world anything should happen now, any disgrace of any kind; and these matrimonial quarrels are disgraceful, Marion. You should trust your husband."

"I have done so, but he does not love me, Lady Lanswell; my mind is quite made up. If he goes to Berlin, I shall never see or speak to him again."

"But, my dearest Marion," cried the countess, "this is terrible. Think of appearances, think of the world—what will the world say? And yours was supposed to be a love-match. It must not be. Have you not the sense to see that such a course of proceeding would be simply to throw him into Madame Vanira's hands? You will be your own worst enemy if you do this!"

"I shall do what my own heart prompts," she said; "no matter what the world says; I care nothing for the world's opinion. Oh, Lady Lanswell, do not look so angry at me. I am miserable; my heart is broken!"

And the unhappy girl knelt at Lady Lanswell's feet, and laid her head on the silken folds of her dress.

If there was one creature in this world whom Lady Lanswell loved more than another, it was her son's wife, the fair, gentle girl who had been a most loving daughter to her; she could not endure the sight of her pain and distress.

"I have made up my mind," sobbed Lady Marion; "I shall appeal to the Duke of Lester; he will see that justice is done to me!"

"My dearest Marion, that is the very thing you must not do. If you appeal to the duke, it becomes at once a serious quarrel, and who shall say how such a quarrel may end? If you appeal to the duke, the whole thing will be known throughout the land; there is an end to all my hopes of the vacant Garter; in fact, I may say there is an end to the race of Lanswell. Think twice before you take such an important step!"

"No one thinks for me!" cried Lady Marion.

"Yes, I think of you and for you. Give me your promise that for a week at least you will say nothing to the Duke of Lester. Will you promise me that, Marion?"

"Yes," said Lady Chandos, wearily; "I promise you that, but not one day longer than a week; my heart is breaking! I cannot bear suspense!"

"I promise you that in a few days there shall be an end of all your trouble," said the countess, who had secretly made her own resolves. "Now, Marion, put your trust in me. You have had no breakfast this morning, I am sure."

Raising the delicate figure in her arms, the countess kissed the weeping face.

"Trust in me," she repeated; "all will be well. Let me see you take some coffee."

The countess rang and ordered some coffee; then, when she had compelled Lady Marion to drink it, she kissed her again.

"Do you know how it will end?" she said gently, "all this crying and fasting and sorrow? You will make yourself very ill, and then Lance will never forgive himself. Do be reasonable, Marion, and leave it all with me."

But after the countess had left her, Lady Marion still felt very ill; she had never felt so ill; she tried to walk from her dressing-room to her bedroom, and to the great alarm of her maid, she fell fainting to the ground.

The doctor came, the same physician who had attended her for some years since she was a child, and he looked very grave when he heard of the long deathlike swoon. He sat talking to her for some time.

"Do you think I am very ill, doctor?" she asked.

He answered:

"You are not very well, my dear Lady Chandos."

"Do you think I will die?"

"Not of this illness, please God," he said. "Now, if you will promise me not to be excited, I will tell you something," and, bending down, he whispered something in her ear.

A flood of light and rapture came in her face, her eyes filled with joy.

"Do you mean it? Is it really true?" she asked.

"Really true; but remember all depends on yourself;" and the doctor went away, leaving behind him a heart full of emotion, of pleasure, of pain, hope, and regret.

Meanwhile, the countess for the second time had sought her son. Her stern, grave face, her angry eyes, the repressed pride and emotion that he saw in every gesture, told him that the time for jesting or evasion had passed.

"Lance," said my lady, sternly, "you are a man now. I cannot command you as I did when you were a boy."

"No, mother; that is quite true. Apropos of what do you say that?"

"I am afraid the sin of your manhood will be greater than the follies of your youth," she said.

"It is just possible," he replied, indifferently.

"You have heard that you have been mentioned for the vacant Garter, and that it is highly probable you may receive it?"

"I have heard so," he answered, indifferently.

"I want to ask you a straightforward question. Do you think it worth your while to risk that, to risk the love and happiness of your wife, to risk your fair name, the name of your race, your position, and everything else that you ought to hold most dear? Do you think it worth while to risk all this for the sake of spending three months in Berlin, where you can see Madame Vanira every day?"

Lord Chandos looked straight in his mother's face.

"Since you ask me the question," he replied, "most decidedly I do."

My lady shrunk back as though she had received a blow.

"I am ashamed of you," she said.

"And I, mother, have been ashamed of my cowardice; but I am a coward no longer."

"Are tears and prayers of any avail?" asked Lady Lanswell; and the answer was:

"No."

Then my lady, driven to despair between her son and his wife, resolved some evening to seek the principal cause of the mischief—Madame Vanira herself.

CHAPTER LVII
A PROUD WOMAN HUMBLED

The Countess of Lanswell had never in all her life been defeated before; now all was over, and she went home with a sense of defeat such as she had never known before. Her son refused not only to obey her, but to listen to her remonstrances; he would not take heed of her fears, and my lady saw nothing but social disgrace before them. Her own life had been so crowned with social triumphs and success she could not realize or understand anything else. The one grand desire of her heart since her son's marriage had been that he should become a Knight of the Order of the Garter, and now, by the recent death of a famous peer, the desire was on the eve of accomplishment; but if, on the very brink of success, it were known that he had left all his duties, his home, his wife, to dance attendance on a singer, even though she were the first singer in Europe, it would be fatal to him. It would spoil his career. My lady had carried herself proudly among the mothers of other sons; hers had been a success, while some others had proved, after all, dead failures; was she to own to herself at the end of a long campaign that she was defeated? Ah, no! Besides which there was the other side of the question—Lady Marion declared she would not see him or speak to him again if he went to Berlin, and my lady knew that she would keep her word. If Lord Chandos persisted in going to Berlin his wife would appeal to the duke, would in all probability insist on taking refuge in his house, then there would be a grand social scandal; the whole household would be disbanded. Lady Chandos, an injured, almost deserted wife, living with the duke and the duchess; Lord Chandos abroad laughed at everywhere as a dupe.

My lady writhed again in anguish as she thought of it. It must not be. She said to herself that it would turn her hair gray, that it would strike her with worse than paralysis. Surely her brilliant life was not to end in such a fiasco as this. For the first time for many years hot tears blinded those fine eyes that had hitherto looked with such careless scorn on the world.

My lady was dispirited; she knew her son well enough to know that another appeal to him would be useless; that the more she said to him on the subject the more obstinate he would be. A note from Lady Chandos completed her misery, and made her take a desperate resolve—a sad little note, that said:

"Dear Lady Lanswell,—If you can do anything to help me, let it be done soon. Lance has begun to-day his preparations for going to Berlin. I heard him giving instructions over his traveling trunk. We have no time to lose if anything can be done to save him."

"I must do it," said the countess, to herself, with desperation. "Appeal to my son is worse than useless. I must appeal to the woman I fear he loves. Who could have imagined or prophesied that I should ever have been compelled to stoop to her, yet stoop I must, if I would save my son!"

With Lady Lanswell, to resolve was to do; when others would have beaten about the bush she went direct.

On the afternoon of that day she made out Leone's address, and ordered the carriage. It was a sign of fear with her that she was so particular with her toilet; it was seldom that she relied, even in the least, on the advantages of dress, but to-day she made a toilet almost imperial in its magnificence— rich silk and velvet that swept the ground in superb folds, here and there gleaming a rich jewel.

The countess smiled as she surveyed herself in the mirror, a regal, beautiful lady. Surely no person sprung from Leone's class would dare to oppose her.

It was on a beautiful, bright afternoon that my lady reached the pretty house where Madame Vanira lived. A warm afternoon, when the birds sung in the green shade of the trees, when the bees made rich honey from the choice carnations, and the butterflies hovered round the budding lilies.

The countess drove straight to the house. She left her carriage at the outer gates, and walked through the pretty lawn; she gave her card to the servant and was shown into the drawing-room.

The Countess of Lanswell would not have owned for the world that she was in the least embarrassed, but the color varied in her face, and her lips trembled ever so little. In a few minutes Leone entered—not the terrified, lowly, loving girl, who braved her presence because she loved her husband so well; this was a proud, beautiful, regal woman, haughty as the countess herself—a woman who, by force of her wondrous beauty and wondrous voice, had placed the world at her feet.

The countess stepped forward with outstretched hands.

"Madame Vanira," she said, "will you spare me a few minutes? I wish to speak most particularly with you."

Leone rang the bell and gave orders that she was not to be disturbed. Then the two ladies looked at each other. Leone knew that hostilities were at hand, although she could not quite tell why.

The countess opened the battle by saying, boldly:

"I ought, perhaps, to tell you, Madame Vanira, that I recognize you."

Leone looked at her with proud unconcern.

"I recognize you now, although I failed to do so when I first saw you. I congratulate you most heartily on your success."

"On what success?" she asked.

"On your success as an actress and a singer. I consider you owe me some thanks."

"Truly," said Leone, "I owe you some thanks."

The countess did not quite like the tone of voice in which those words were uttered; but it was her policy to be amiable.

"Your genius has taken me by surprise," she said; "yet, when I recall the only interview I ever had with you, I recognize the dramatic talent you displayed."

"I should think the less you say of that interview, the better," said Leone; "it was not much to your ladyship's credit."

Lady Lanswell smiled.

"We will not speak of it," she said. "But you do not ask me to sit down. Madame Vanira, what a charming house you have here."

With grave courtesy Leone drew a chair near the window, and the countess sat down. She looked at the beautiful woman with a winning smile.

"Will you not be seated, madame?" she said. "I find it so much easier to talk when one is seated."

"How did you recognize me?" asked Leone, abruptly.

"I cannot say truthfully that I recognized your face," she said; "you will not mind my saying that if I had done so I would not have invited you to my house, neither should I have permitted my daughter-in-law to do so. It has placed us all in a false position. I knew you from something my son said about you. I guessed at once that you must be Leone Noel. I must repeat my congratulations; how hard you must have worked."

Her eyes wandered over the magnificent face and figure, over the faultless lines and graceful curves, over the artistic dress, and the beautiful, picturesque head.

"You have done well," said the countess. "Years ago you thought me hard, unfeeling, prejudiced, cruel, but it was kindness in the end. You have achieved for yourself fame, which no one could have won for you. Better to be as you are, queen of song, and so queen of half the world of fashion, than the wife of a man whose family and friends would never have received you, and who would soon have looked on you as an incumbrance."

"Pray pardon me, Lady Lanswell, if I say that I have no wish whatever to hear your views on the subject."

My lady's face flushed.

"I meant no offense," she said, "I merely wished to show you that I have not been so much your enemy as you perhaps have thought me," and by the sudden softening of my lady's face, and the sudden tremor of her voice, Leone knew that she had some favor to ask.

"I think," she said, after a pause, "that in all truth, Madame Vanira, you ought to be grateful to me. You would never have known the extent of your own genius and power if you had not gone on the stage."

"The happiness of the stage resembles the happiness of real life about as much as the tinsel crown of the mock queen resembles the regalia of the sovereign," replied Leone. "It would be far better if your ladyship would not mention the past."

"I only mention it because I wish you to see that I am not so much your enemy as you have thought me to be."

"Nothing can ever change my opinion on that point," said Leone.

"You think I was your enemy?" said the countess, blandly.

"The most cruel and the most relentless enemy any young girl could have," said Leone.

"I am sorry you think that," said my lady, kindly. "The more so as I find you so happy and so prosperous."

"You cannot answer for my happiness," said Leone, briefly.

"I acted for the best," said the countess, with more meekness than Leone had ever seen in her before.

"It was a miserable best," said Leone, her indignation fast rising, despite her self-control. "A wretched best, and the results have not been in any way so grand that you can boast of them."

"So far as you are concerned, Madame Vanira, I have nothing to repent of," said my lady.

Leone's dark eyes flashed fire.

"I am but one," she said, "your cruelty made two people miserable. What of your son? Have you made him so happy that you can come here and boast of what you have done?"

My lady's head fell on her breast. Ah, no, Heaven knew her son was not a happy man.

"Leone," she said, in a low, hurried voice, "it is of my son I wish to speak to you. It is for my son's sake I am here—it is because I believe you to be his true friend and a noble woman that I am here, Leone—it is the first time I have called you by your name—I humble myself to you—will you listen to me?"

CHAPTER LVIII
"BEHOLD MY REVENGE!"

Even as she spoke the words Lady Lanswell's heart sunk within her. No softening came to the beautiful face, no tenderness, no kindliness; it seemed rather as though her last words had turned Leone to stone. She grew pale even to her lips, she folded her hands with a hard clasp, her beautiful figure grew more erect and dignified—the words dropped slowly, each one seeming to cut the air as it fell.

"You call me noble, Lady Lanswell! you, who did your best to sully my fair name; you call me your son's best friend, when you flung me aside from him as though I had been of no more worth than the dust underneath his feet!"

Lady Lanswell bent forward.

"Will you not forget that?" she said. "Let the past die. I will own now that I was harsh, unjust, even cruel to you; but I repent it—I have never said as much before—I repent it, and I *apologize* to you! Will you accept my apology?"

The effort was so great for a proud woman to make, that the countess seemed almost to struggle for breath as she said the words. Leone looked on in proud, angry scorn.

"You apologize, Lady Lanswell! You think that a few words can wash away the most cruel wrong one woman did to another? Do you know what you did?—you robbed me of my husband, of a man I loved as I shall love no other; you blighted my fair name. What was I when that marriage was set aside? You—you tortured me—you broke my heart, you slew all that was best in me, and now all these years afterward you come to me, and think to overwhelm me with faint, feeble words of apology. Why, if you gave me your heart's blood, your very soul, even, it would not atone me! I had but one life, and you have spoiled it! I had but one love, you trampled on it with wicked, relentless feet! Ah, why do I speak? Words are but sound. No, Lady Lanswell, I refuse your apology now or at any time! We are enemies, and shall remain so until we die!"

The countess shrunk from the passion of her indignant words.

"You are right in some measure," she said, sadly. "I was very hard, but it was for my son's sake! Ah, believe me, all for him."

"Your son," retorted Leone; "you make your son the excuse for your own vanity, pride, and ambition. What you did, Lady Lanswell, proved how little you loved your son; you parted us knowing that he loved me, knowing that his whole heart was bound up in me, knowing that he had but one wish, and it was to spend his whole life with me; you parted us knowing that he could never love another woman as he loved me, knowing that you were destroying his life, even as you have destroyed mine. Did love for your son actuate you then?"

"What I believed to be my love for my son and care for his interests alone guided me," said Lady Lanswell.

"Love for your son!" laughed Leone. "Have you ever read the story of the mother of the Maccabees, who held her twin sons to die rather than they live to deny the Christian faith? Have you read of the English mother who, when her fair-haired son grew pale at the sound of the first cannon, cried, 'Be brave, my son, death does not last one minute—glory is immortal.' I call such love as that the love of a mother for her son—the love that teaches a man to be true, if it cost his life; to be brave, if courage brings him death; to be loyal and noble. True motherly love shows itself in that fashion, Lady Lanswell."

The proud head of Lucia, Countess of Lanswell, drooped before this girl as it had never done before any power on earth.

"What has your love done for your son, Lady Lanswell?" she asked. "Shall I tell you? You made him a traitor, a coward, a liar—through your intrigues, he perjured himself. You made him disloyal and ignoble—you made him *false*. And yet you call that love! I would rather have the love of a pagan mother than such as yours.

"What have you done for him?" she continued, the fire of her passion rising—"what have you done for him? He is young and has a long life before him. Is he happy? Look at his face—look at his restless, weary eyes—listen to the forced bitter laugh! Is he happy, after all your false love has done for him? You have taken from him the woman he loves, and you have given him one for whom he cares so little he would leave her to-morrow! Have you done so well, Lady Lanswell for your son?"

"No, indeed I have not!" came with a great sigh from Lady Lanswell's lips. "Perhaps, if it were to be—but no, I will not say that. You have noble thoughts and noble ideas—tell me, Leone, will you help me?"

"Help you in what?" she asked, proudly.

The countess flung aside the laces and ribbons that seemed to stifle her.

"Help me over my son!" she cried; "be generous to me. Many people in my place would look on you as an enemy—I do not. If you have ever really loved my son you cannot be an enemy of mine. I appeal to the higher and nobler part of you. Some people would be afraid that you should triumph over them—I am not. I hold you for a generous foe."

"What appeal do you wish to make to me?" asked Leone, quite ignoring all the compliments which the countess paid her.

Lady Lanswell looked as she felt—embarrassed; it was one thing to carry this interview through in fancy, but still another when face to face with the foe, and that foe a beautiful, haughty woman, with right on her side. My lady was less at ease than she had ever been in her life before, her eyes fell, her lips trembled, her gemmed fingers played nervously with her laces and ribbons.

"That I should come to you at all, Leone, proves that I think you a noble woman," she said; "my trouble is great—the happiness of many lives lies in your hands."

"I do not understand how," said Leone.

"I will tell you," continued the countess. "You are going to Berlin, are you not?"

She saw a quiver of pain pass over the beautiful face as she asked the question.

"Yes," replied Leone; "I have an engagement there."

"And Lord Chandos, my son, has said something about going there, too?"

"Yes," replied Leone; "and I hope he will; he knows the city well, and I shall be glad to see a familiar face."

There was a minute's silence, during which Lady Lanswell brought all her wit and courage to bear on the situation. She continued:

"Lady Chandos does not wish my son to go to Berlin. I suppose it is no secret from you that she entirely disapproves of her husband's friendship with you?"

Leone bowed her proud, beautiful head.

"That is a matter of little moment to me," she said.

My lady's face flushed at the words.

"I may tell you," she went on, "that since Lady Chandos heard of this friendship, she has been very unhappy."

"No one cared when I was unhappy," said Leone; "no one pleaded for me."

"I do plead for Lady Marion," said the countess, "whatever you may think of me. She has done you no harm; why should you make mischief between her and her husband?"

"Why did you make mischief between me and mine?" retorted Leone; and my lady shrunk as she spoke.

"Listen to me, Leone," she said; "you must help me, you must be my friend. If my son goes to Berlin against his wife's prayers and wishes, she has declared that she will never speak to him or see him again."

"That cannot concern me," said Leone.

"For Heaven's sake listen, and do not speak to me so heartlessly. If he goes to Berlin, Lady Chandos will appeal to the Duke of Lester, who has just obtained for my son the greatest honor that can be conferred on an English gentleman—the Order of the Garter. In plain words, Leone, if my son follows you to Berlin, he will lose his wife, he will lose his good name, he will lose caste, his social position, his chance of courtly honors, the respect of his own class. He will be laughed at as a dupe, as a man who has given up all the honors of life to dance attendance on an actress; in short, if he goes either with you, or after you, to Berlin, he is, in every sense of the word, a ruined man!" and my lady's voice faltered as she said the words.

"Why not tell Lord Chandos all this himself, and see what he says?" asked Leone.

Perfect desperation brings about perfect frankness—my lady knew that it was quite useless to conceal anything.

"I have said all this and more to my son, but he will not even listen to me."

A scornful smile curved those lovely lips.

"He persists in going to Berlin, then?" said Leone, quietly.

"Yes," replied my lady, "he persists in it."

"Then why come to me? If your son persists in a certain course of action, why come to me?"

"Because you can influence him. I ask you to be noble beyond the nobility of women, I ask you to be generous beyond the generosity of women, I ask you to forget the past and forbid my son to follow you to Berlin. You know the end must be a bad one—forbid it. I ask you with the warmest of prayers and of tears!"

It was then that Leone rose in righteous wrath, in not indignation, in angry passion; rose and stood erect before the woman who had been her enemy.

"I refuse," she said. "Years ago I went to you a simple-hearted, loving girl, and I prayed you for Heaven's sake to have mercy on me. You received me with scorn and contumely; you insulted, outraged, tortured me; you laughed at my tears, you enjoyed my humiliation. I told you then that I would have my revenge, even should I lose everything on earth to obtain that revenge. Now it lays in my hands, and I grasp it—I glory in it. Your son shall follow me, shall lose wife, home, friends, position, fair name, as I lost all years ago at your bidding. Oh, cruel and wicked woman, behold my revenge! I repay you now. Oh, God," she continued, with a passionate cry, "I thank Thee that I hold my vengeance in my hand; I will slay and spare not!"

Then she stood silent for some minutes, exhausted by the passion of her own words.

CHAPTER LIX
USELESS PLEADINGS

"You cannot possibly know what you are saying," said Lady Lanswell; "you must be mad."

"No; I am perfectly sane; if I am mad at all it is with delight that the very desire of my heart has been given to me. Do you forget when you trampled my heart, my life, my love under your feet that day? Do you forget what I have sworn?"

"I have never thought of it since," said the countess, trying to conciliate still.

"Then I will remind you," said Leone. "I swore to be avenged, no matter what my vengeance cost. I swore that you should come and plead to me on your knees and I would laugh at you. I do so. I swore that you should plead to me, and I would remind you how I pleaded in vain. You wrung my heart—I will wring yours, and my only regret is that it is so hard and cold I cannot make you suffer more."

"You are mad," said my lady; "quite mad."

"No," said Leone, "I am sane, but mine was a mad love."

"You cannot know the consequence to yourself if you persist in this conduct," said my lady, serenely.

"Did you think of them for me when you set aside my marriage with your son, because you did not think me good enough to be a countess?" she asked. "Lady Lanswell, the hour of vengeance has come and I embrace it. Your son shall lose his wife, his home, his position, his honors; I care not what," she cried, with sudden recklessness—"I care not what the world says of me, I will do that which I shall do, less because I love your son than because I desire to punish you."

Lady Lanswell grew very pale as she listened.

"Yours is a terrible revenge," she said, gently. "I wish that you could invent some vengeance that would fall on my head—and on mine alone, so as to spare those who are dear to me. Could you not do that? I would willingly suffer anything to free my son and his fair, loving wife."

"No one spared me, nor will I in my turn spare," she said. "You shall know what it means to plead for dear life and plead in vain."

"Can I say nothing that will induce you to listen to me?" said the countess, "will you deliberately persist in the conduct that will ruin three lives?"

"Yes, deliberately and willfully," said Leone. "I will never retract, never go back, but go on to the bitter end."

"And that end means my son's disgrace," said Lady Lanswell.

"It would be the same thing if it meant his death," said Leone; "no one withheld the hand that struck death to me—worse than death."

"You have nothing but this to say to me," said Lady Lanswell as she rose with stately grace from her seat.

"No; if I knew anything which would punish you more, which would more surely pay my debts, which would more fully wreak my vengeance, I would do it. As for three lives, as for thirty, I would trample them under my feet. I will live for my vengeance, no matter what it costs me; and, Lady Lanswell, you ruined my life. Good-bye. The best wish I can form is that I may never look on your face again. Permit me to say farewell."

She went out of the room leaving the countess bewildered with surprise and dismay.

"What she says she will do," thought Lady Lanswell; "I may say good-bye to every hope I have ever formed for my son."

She went away, her heart heavy as lead, with no hope of any kind to cheer it.

Leone went to her room, her whole frame trembling with the strong passion that had mastered her.

"What has come over me?" she said; "I no longer know myself. Is it love, vengeance, or jealousy that has hold of me? What evil spirit has taken my heart? Would I really hurt him whom I have loved all my life—would I do him harm? Would I crush that fair wife of his who wronged me without knowing it? Let me find out for myself if it be true."

She tried to think, but her head was in a whirl—she could not control herself, she could not control her thoughts; the sight of Lady Lanswell seemed to have set her heart and soul in flame—all the terrible memory of her wrongs came over her, the fair life blighted and ruined, the innocent girlhood and dawning womanhood all spoiled. It was too cruel—no, she could never forgive it.

And then it seemed to her that her brain took fire and she went mad.

She saw Lord Chandos that same evening; they met in a crush on the staircase at one of the ducal mansions, where a grand dinner-party preceded a *soiree*, and the crowd was so great they were unable to stir. It is possible to be quite alone in a great crowd, as these two were now.

Leone had on a dress of white satin trimmed with myrtle, the rich folds of which trailed on the ground. They shook hands in silence; it was Lord Chandos who spoke first.

"I am so glad to see you, Leone; but you are looking ill—you must not look like that. Has anything happened to distress you?"

He saw great trouble in the dark eyes raised to his.

"Is Lady Marion here?" she asked.

"No," he replied. "She was to have come with my mother, but at the last moment she declined; I do not know why."

She was debating in her own mind whether she would tell him about his mother's visit or not; then she decided it would be better. He bent over her.

"I came," he said, "in the hope of seeing you. I heard you say last night that you should be here."

In a low tone she said to him:

"Your mother has been to see me; talk about dramatic scenes, we had one. Has she told you anything about it?"

"No," he replied: "she does not speak to me; I am in disgrace; my lady passes me in silent dignity. She was just going to Lady Marion's room when I came away, but she did not speak to me. What was the object of her visit, Leone?"

"It was about Berlin," she said, in a low voice.

He started.

"Has she been to you about that?" he asked. "I thought she had exhausted all the remarks she had to make on that subject."

The green foliage and crimson flowers of a huge camellia bent over them. Lord Chandos pushed aside the crimson flowers so that he might more clearly see his companion's face.

"What has my mother said to you about Berlin, Leone?" he asked.

"She came to beg of me to forbid you to go. She says if you go either with me or after me you will be a ruined man."

"It will be a most sweet ruin," he whispered.

"Lance," said Leone, "do you know that while Lady Lanswell was talking to me I went mad—I am quite sure of it. I said such dreadful things to her; did I mean them?"

"How should I know, my—Leone; but we will not talk about it; never mind what my mother says, I do not wish to hear it. She came between us once, but she never will again. She parted us once, she shall never part us again—never. There can be no harm in my going to Berlin, and there I shall go—that is, always with your consent and permission."

"That you have. But, Lance, is it true that Lady Marion does not wish you to go to Berlin, and threatens to leave you if you do—is it true?"

"Let us talk about something else, Leone," he said. "We have but a few moments together."

"But I cannot think of anything else," she said; "because my heart is full of it."

What else she would have said will never be known, for at that moment there was a stir in the crowd, and they were separated.

She took home with her the memory of his last look—a look that said so plainly, "I love you and will go to Berlin for your sake." She took home with her the memory of that look, and lay sleepless through the whole night, wondering which of the evil spirits had taken possession of her.

The countess had gone in search of Lady Marion. She found her in her boudoir—the beautiful room she had shown with such pride to Madame Vanira.

Lady Chandos looked up eagerly as the countess entered.

"Have you good news for me?" she cried, eagerly.

And my lady could not destroy the lingering hope she saw in that fair face.

"Not yet," she cried, "but you must be patient, Marion."

"Patience is so difficult when so much is at stake. Tell me—you had some plan, some resource; I saw that when you left me. Have you tried it?"

"Yes, I have tried it," replied Lady Lanswell, sadly.

"Has it succeeded or failed?" she asked, eagerly.

"It has failed," answered the countess, dreading to see the effect of her reply.

But to her surprise, a tender, dreamy smile came over the fair face.

"Why are you smiling, Marion?" she asked.

"Because I, too, have a plan," she replied; "one quite of my own; and I pray Heaven it may succeed."

"Will you tell it me?" asked Lady Lanswell.

And the fair, young wife's answer was a quietly whispered:

"No."

Late that night, while the London streets were darkened by the cloud of sin that seems to rise as the sun sets; while the crowded ballrooms were one scene of gayety and frivolity; while tired souls went from earth to Heaven; while poverty, sickness, sorrow and death reigned over the whole city, Lady Marion, with her golden head bent and her white hands clasped, knelt praying. There was peace on her face and holy, happy love.

"God help me," she said; "I will put all my trust in Him. My husband will love me when he knows."

She prayed there until the sun rose in the morning sky, and she watched the first beams with a tender smile.

"It will be a day of grace for me," she said, as she laid her fair head on the pillow to sleep.

CHAPTER LX
"THIS WOMAN SHALL NEVER KNOW"

Leone stood alone in her pretty drawing-room, the room from which she could see the hills and the trees, and catch glimpses of pretty home scenery that were unrivaled. She stood looking at it now, her eyes fixed on the distant hills, her heart re-echoing the words: "In the grave alone is peace." In her heart and mind all was dross; she seemed to have lost the power of thinking; she had an engagement to sing in her favorite opera on the evening previous. Hundreds had assembled to hear her, and at the last moment they were compelled to find a substitute. Leone could not sing; it was not that her voice failed her, but to her inexpressible sorrow, when she began to tell the woes of another her mind wandered off into her own. In vain she tried to collect herself, to save herself from the terrible whirl of her brain. "Surely I am not going mad." She bent her head on her hands, and sighed deeply; if she could but save herself, if she could but tell what to do. The night before, only a few hours previous, it seemed to her her heart and brain had been on fire, first with jealousy, then with love, then with anger. By accident, as she was going to her wardrobe, her hands fell on a large, beautiful copy of the Bible. She opened it carelessly, and her eyes fell on the words: "For the wicked there shall be no abiding-place, neither shall they find rest forever."

Rest, that was what she wanted, and if she were wicked she would not find it for evermore. What was being wicked? People had behaved wickedly to her, they had taken from her the one love that would have been the stay of her life; they had made her most solemn vows nothing. She had been wickedly treated, but did it follow that she must be wicked?

"I could never be a sinner," she said; "I have not the nerve, I have not the strength. I could never be a sinner."

Lightly enough she turned those pages; she saw the picture of Ruth in the corn-field—simple, loving Ruth, whose words have stood the finest love-story ever written since she uttered them. There was another picture of Queen Esther fainting in the awful presence of Ahasuerus the king; another of a fair young Madonna holding in her arms a little child; another of the Magdalen, her golden hair wet with tears; another of a Sacred Head bent low in the agonies of death. She looked long at that, for underneath it was written, "For our sins." Wickedness meant sin. Standing there, her hand resting on the page, all the truth seemed to come home to her. It would be a sin to cause disunion between husband and wife; it would be a sin to cause the husband of another woman to love her; it would be a sin to give way to the desire of vengeance that was burning her heart away, and these words were so pathetic, "For our sins." She had laid her face on that picture of the Crucifixion, and burning tears fell from her eyes over it.

"God have mercy on me," she had prayed, "and save me from myself."

Then she had slept, and here was the morrow, a lovely summer day with the air all fragrance, the birds all song, and she was still doing hard battle with herself, for, as she had said to herself, hers was "a mad love—a cruel, mad love."

And as she stood watching the distant hills, wondering if in the blue sky that hung over them there was peace, a servant once more entered the room, holding a card in her hand.

"Lady Chandos," said Leone, wonderingly; "ask her in here."

She looked in surprise, almost too great for words, at the little card. Lance's wife, who had refused to speak to her, who had disdained to touch her outstretched hand—Lance's wife coming to speak to her.

What could it mean? Were the whole race of the Lanswells coming to her?

The next moment a fair, sweet face was smiling into hers, a face she had seen last darkened with anger, but which was fair and bright now, with the light of a holy love.

Leone looked at her in amaze. What had happened? It looked as though a new life, a new soul, had been given to Lady Marion. And hush, she was speaking to her in a low, sweet voice, that thrilled through the great singer like the softest cords from an Eolian harp.

"You are surprised to see me," Lady Marion was saying, "yet I have done right in coming. All last night, while the stars were shining, I prayed Heaven to tell me what it was best for me to do, and I shall always think that the white-winged angels, who they say carry prayers to Heaven, sent me to you. I refused to touch your hand the other day. Will you give it to me now? Will you listen to me?"

Leone's whole heart and soul had risen in hot rebellion and fierce hate against the Countess of Lanswell. They went out in sweetest love and compassion to her fair faced rival now. The sweet voice went on:

"I cannot tell why I have come to you—some impulse has sent me. Another woman in my place would have looked on you as a successful rival and have hated you. I cannot. The soul that has stirred other souls cannot be base; you must be noble and good or you would not influence the hearts and souls of men. Oh, madame, I have come to you with two lives in my hands. Will you listen to me?"

The dark, beautiful head of the gifted singer was bent for a few moments over the golden head of her rival. Then Leone raised her eyes to Marion's face.

"You are trembling," she said; "you shall speak to me as you will, but you shall speak to me here."

Some warm, loving irresistible impulse came to her; she could not hate or hurt this fair, gentle lady whom the countess had put in her place, and whom her husband did not love; a great impulse of pity came over her, a sweet and generous compassion filled her heart.

"You shall speak to me here," she repeated, clasping her arms round the trembling figure and laying the golden head on her breast. She kissed the fair, sad face with a passion of love. "There," she said, "Lady Marion, if I had wronged you even in the least, I should not dare do that. Now tell me what you have come to say. Do not tremble so," and the tender arms tightened their clasp. "Do not be afraid to speak to me."

"I am not afraid, for Heaven sent me," said Lady Marion. "I know that you will tell me the truth. I am as certain of that as I am of my own life. I have been very unhappy over you, Madame Vanira, for my husband seems to have cared more for you than for me."

"Has your husband ever told you anything about me?" asked Leone, gently.

And the answer was:

"No, nothing, except that, like everyone else, he admired you very much."

"Nothing more?" asked Leone.

"No, nothing more."

"Then," said Leone to herself, "the secret that he has kept I will keep, and this fair, tender woman shall never know that I once believed myself his wife."

Lady Marion wondered why she bent down and kissed her with all the fervor of self-sacrifice.

"I have been very unhappy," continued Lady Marion. "I loved and admired you. I never had the faintest suspicion in my mind against you, until some one came to tell me that you and my husband had spent a day on the river together. I know it was true, but he would not explain it."

"Let me explain it," said Leone, sadly. "I trust you as you trust me. I have had a great sorrow in my love; greater—oh, Heaven!—than ever fell to the lot of woman. And one day, when I saw your husband, the bitterness of it was lying heavily on me. I said something to him that led him to understand how dull and unhappy I felt. Lady Chandos, he took me on the river that he might give me one happy day, nothing more. Do you grudge it to me, dear? Ah, if I could give you the happiness of those few fleeting hours I would."

And again her warm, loving lips touched the white brow.

"I understand," said Lady Marion. "Why did my husband not speak as you have done? Does he care for you, madame? You will tell me the truth, I know."

And the fair face looked wistfully in her own.

Leone was silent for a few minutes; she could not look in those clear eyes and speak falsely.

"Yes," she answered, slowly; "I think Lord Chandos cares very much for me; I know that he admires and likes me."

Lady Marion looked very much relieved. There could surely be no harm in their friendship if she could speak of it so openly.

"And you, madame—oh, tell me truly—do you love him? Tell me truly; it seems that all my life hangs on your word."

Again the beautiful face drooped silently before the fair one.

"It would be so easy for me to tell you a falsehood," said Leone, while a great crimson flush burned her face, "but I will not. Yes, I—I love him. Pity me, you who love him so well yourself; he belongs to you, while I—ah, pity me because I love him."

And Lady Marion, whose heart was touched by the pitiful words, looked up and kissed her.

"I cannot hate you, since you love him," she said. "He is mine, but my heart aches for you. Now let me tell you what I have come to say. You are good and noble as I felt you were. I have come to ask a grace from you, and it is easier now that I know you love him. How strange it seems. I should have thought that hearing you say that you loved my husband would have filled my heart with hot anger, but it does not; in some strange way I love you for it."

"If you love him, madame, his interests must be dear to you."

"They are dear to me," she whispered. "How strange," repeated Lady Marion, "that while the world is full of men you and I should love the same man."

"Ah, life is strange," said Leone; "peace only comes with death."

CHAPTER LXI
A SACRIFICE

Lady Marion raised herself so that she could look into the face of her beautiful rival.

"Now I will tell you," she said; "you are going to Berlin; you have an engagement at the Royal Opera House there, and my husband wishes to go there, too. But we all oppose it; his parents for social reasons, and I—I tell you frankly, because I am jealous of you, and cannot bear that he should follow you there. I have asked him to give up the idea, but he refuses—he will not listen to me. I have said that if he goes there, I will never see him or speak to him again, and I must keep my word. So, madame, I have come to you; I appeal to you, do not let him go: you can prevent it if you will."

Leone's dark eyes flashed fire.

"There is no harm in our friendship," she said; "would you take from me the only gleam of happiness I have in the world?"

But Lady Marion did not seem to hear the wild words; the same raptures of holy love had come over her face, and she blushed until she looked like a lovely, glowing rose.

"Think how I trust you," she said; "I have come to tell you that which I have told to no one. I have come to tell you that which, if ever there has been any particular friendship between you and my husband, must end it. I have come to tell you that which will show that now—now you must not take my husband from me.

"Bend down lower," continued the sweet voice, "that I may whisper to you. I have been married nearly four years now, and the one desire of my heart has been to have a little child. I love little children so dearly. And I have always thought that if I could give to my husband children to love he would love me better. I have prayed as Rachel prayed, but it seemed to me the heavens were made of brass—no answer came to my prayers. I have wept bitter tears when I have seen other mothers caressing their children.

When my husband has stopped to kiss a child or play with it, my heart has burned with envy, and now, oh, madame, bend lower, lower—now Heaven has been so good to me, and they tell me that in a few months I shall have a darling little child, all my own. Oh, madame, do you see that now you must not take my husband from me; that now there must be no mischief between us; that we must live in peace and love because Heaven has been so good to us."

The sweet voice rose to a tone of passionate entreaty; and Lady Marion withdrew from the clasp of her rival's arms, and knelt at her feet. The face she raised was bright and beautiful as though angel's wings shadowed it.

"I plead with you," she said, "I pray to you. You hold my life in your hands. If it were only myself I would be glad to die, so that if my husband loves you best he might marry you, but it is for my little child. Do you know that when I say to myself, 'Lance's little child,' the words seem to me sweeter than the sweetest music."

But the beautiful woman who had been no wife, turned deadly pale as she listened to the words. She held up her hand with a terrible cry.

"For Heaven's sake, hush," she said hoarsely, "I cannot bear it!"

For one minute it was as though she had been turned to stone. Her heart seemed clutched by a cold, iron hand. The next, she had recovered herself and raised Lady Marion, making her rest, and trying to still the trembling of the delicate frame.

"You must calm yourself," she said. "I have listened to you, now will you listen to me?"

"Yes; but, madame, you will be good to me—you will not let my husband leave me? We shall be happy, I am sure, when he knows; we shall forget all this sorrow and this pain. He will be to me the same as he was before your beautiful face dazed him. Ah, madame, you will not let him leave me."

"I should be a murderess if I did," she said, in a low voice.

Her face was whiter than the face of the dead. She stood quite silent for a few minutes. In her heart, like a death-knell, sounded the words:

"Lance's little child."

Whiter and colder grew the beautiful face; more mute and silent the beautiful lips; then suddenly she said:

"Kiss me, Lady Marion, kiss me with your lips; now place your hands in mine. I promise you that I will not take your husband from you; that he shall not go to Berlin, either with me or after me. I promise you—listen and believe me—that I will never see or speak to your husband again, and this I do for the sake of Lance's little child."

"I believe you," said Lady Marion, the light deepening in her sweet eyes and on her fair face. "I believe you, and from the depth of my heart I thank you. We shall be happy, I am sure."

"In the midst of your happiness will you remember me?" asked Leone, gently.

"Always, as my best, dearest and truest friend," said Lady Marion; and they parted that summer morning never to meet again until the water gives up its dead.

Lady Marion drove home with a smile on her fair face, such as had not been seen there before. It would all come right.

She believed in Madame Vana's simple words as in the pledge of another. How it would be managed she did not know—did not think; but madame would keep her word, and her husband would be her own—would never be cool to her or seek to leave her again; it would be all well.

All that day there was a light on her face that did one's heart good to see; and when Lady Lanswell saw her that evening she knew that all was well.

"Lance's little child!" The words had been a death-knell to Leone. She had seen his wife and lived—she had seen him in his home with that same fair wife by his side, and she had lived; but at the thought of her rival's children in his arms her whole soul died.

Died—never to live again. She sat for some time just where Lady Marion left her, and she said to herself a thousand times over and over again those words—"Lance's little child." Only God knows the anguish that came over her, the piercing sorrow, the bitter pain—the memory of those few months when she had believed herself to be Lance's wife. She fell on her knees with a great, passionate cry.

"Oh, Heaven," she cried, "save me from myself!"

The most beautiful woman in Europe, the most gifted singer on the stage, the idol of the world of fashion—she lay there helpless, hopeless, despairing, with that one cry rising from her lips on which a world had hung:

"Heaven have mercy on me, and save me from myself!"

When she woke, the real world seemed to have vanished from her. She heard the sound of running water; a mill-wheel turning in a deep stream; she heard the rush and the foaming of water, the song of the birds overhead, the rustle of the great boughs, the cooing of the blue and white pigeons. Why, surely, that was a dream of home.

Home—the old farmhouse where Robert Noel lived, the kind, slow, stolid farmer. She could hear him calling, "Leone, where are you?" and the pigeons deafened her as they whirled round her head. She struggled for a time with her dazed, bewildered senses; but she could not tell which was the real life, whether she was at home again in the old farmhouse, and had dreamed a long, troubled dream, or whether she was dreaming now.

Her brain burned—it was like liquid fire; and she seemed to see always a golden-haired child.

"Lance's little child." Yes, there he was holding mother and child both in his arms, kissing them, while she lay there helpless and despairing.

"Mine was always a mad love," she said to herself—"a mad love."

Then she heard a sound of music—softest, sweetest music—floating through the room, and woke to reason with a terrible shudder to find that she was singing the old, sweet song:

"I would the grave would hide me,
For there alone is peace."

"I have been mad," she said to herself; "those words drove me mad, 'Lance's little child.'"

She went to her room and bathed her head in ice-cold water. The pain grew less, but not the burning heat.

The idea became fixed in her mind that she must go back to the old mill-stream; she did not know why, she never asked herself why; that was her haven of rest, by the sound of rushing waters. Within sight of the mill-wheel, and the trees, and the water lilies, all would be well, the cloud would pass from her mind, the fire from her brain, the sword from her heart.

She had two letters to write, one to the manager with whom her engagement expired in two nights, telling him she was ill and had gone away for her health, and that he would not probably hear of her for some time; and another to Lord Chandos. It was simple and sad:

"Good-bye. I am going—not to Berlin—but away from Europe, and I shall never return; but before I leave I shall go to the mill-stream to look at and listen to the waters for the last time. Good bye, Lance. In heaven you will know how much I have loved you, never on earth. In heaven you will know why I have left you. Be kind, and true, and good to all who are dear to you. Lance, if I die first, I shall wait inside the golden gates of heaven for you."

She did one thing more, which proved that her reason was still clear. She paid off all her servants, and to the most trusted one left power to give up her house in her name, as she was leaving it.

And far off the mill-wheel turned in the stream, and the water-lilies stirred faintly us the white foam passed them by.

CHAPTER LXII
"THE GRAVE ALONE GIVES PEACE"

The sun was setting—the western sky was all aflame, great crimson clouds floated away with vapors of rose and orange—crimson clouds that threw a rosy light on the trees and fields. In the distance stood the old farmhouse, the light falling on the roof with its moss and lichen, the great roses and white jasmine that wreathed the windows, the tall elms that stood on either side of the fertile meadows, the springing corn, the ricks of sweet-smelling hay. The light from the western sky fell on them all. From beneath the tall elms with the trailing scarlet creepers came a tall, graceful woman, whose face was covered with a thick veil; she stood for some time watching the farmhouse, her beautiful face white and set as the face of the dead; she threw back her veil as though she was gasping for breath, and then she stood still and motionless as a marble statue.

The blue and white pigeons were cooing loudly, as though they would tell each other it was time to rest, the birds were singing their vesper hymn, the cattle had all been driven to rest, the laborers had ceased their toil, in the garden the white lilies had opened their cups to catch the dew; it was all so sweet and still, as though a blessing from Heaven lay on it.

The silent watcher stirred when she heard the baying of a hound.

"That is Rover," she said to herself, "and he would know me. What would Uncle Robert say if he knew his lady lass was so near?"

She walked on through the green lane, where the hedges were one mass of wild rose bloom, through the fields where the clover lay so sweet and fragrant, until she came to the mill-stream. Her heart gave one bound as she saw it.

The picturesque old mill, half hidden in foliage, and the great round wheel, half hidden in the clear stream. There were the water-lilies lying quite at rest now; there were the green reeds and sedges; the nests of blue forget-me-nots; the little water-fall where the white rock rose in the middle of the stream, and the water ran over it; the same green branches dipped in the water, the same trees shaded it. She sat down in the same spot where she had last sat with him. She remembered how the ring had fallen into the little clear pool and he had found it. The same, and yet how different. And sitting there, with the wreck of her life round her, she sung in a low voice the words that to her had been so full of prophecy:

"In sheltered vale a mill-wheel
Still sings its tuneful lay.
My darling once did dwell there,
But now she's far away.
A ring in pledge I gave her,
And vows of love we spoke;
These vows are all forgotten,
The ring asunder broke."

How true and how cold the prophecy had been. As she sat there she saw a light in the mill, and the wheel began slowly to turn.

Foaming, laughing, singing, the water ran away shining in the red light of the setting sun, golden in the little wavelets that kissed the banks. Slowly the falling water set itself to music, and the rhythm was always:

"I would the grave could hide me,
For there alone is peace."

Shine on, setting sun. Sing on, falling water. There is no peace save in death and in heaven. Sing on, little birds, throw your sweet shadows, dewy nights; there is no peace but in death.

She lay down on the green bank and the water foaming by sung to her—it was all so sweet, so silent, so still. One by one the little birds slept, one by one the flowers closed their eyes, the roseate clouds faded, and the gray, soft mantle of night fell on the earth.

So sweet and still—the stars came out in the sky, in the wood a nightingale began to sing; the fire went out in her brain; the pain ceased; she grew calm as one on whom a dread shadow lies.

The lovely, laughing water, with the gleam of golden stars in it, falling with the rhythm of sweetest music. She drew nearer, she laid one hand on the little wavelets, and the cool, sweet touch refreshed her.

The night, so sweet and still, with the gray shade of the king of terrors rising from the mill-stream. The water-lilies seemed to rise and come near to her, a thousand sweet voices seemed to rise from the water and call her.

"There alone is peace," sung the nightingale; "There alone is peace," sung the lilies; "There alone is peace," sung the chiming waters. She drew nearer to them. Heaven only knows what ideas were in that overbalanced brain and distraught mind. Looking in the clear waters she saw the golden stars shining; perhaps she thought she was reaching to them. A little low cry fell on the night air. A cry that startled the ring-doves, but fell on no mortal ear.

"Mine was always a mad love," she said to herself; "a mad love," and the voice that had gladdened the hearts of thousands was heard on earth no more.

A mad love, indeed; she went nearer to the gleaming waters; they seemed to rise and infold her; the water-lilies seemed to hold her up. It seemed to her rather that she went up to the stars than down to the stream. There was no cry, no sound, as the soft waters closed over her, as the water-lilies floated back entangled in the meshes of a dead woman's hair.

In the grave alone was peace. So she lay through the long, sweet, summer night, and the mill-stream sung her dirge.

Was it suicide, or was she mad? God who knows all things knew that she had suffered a heavy wrong, a cruel injustice, a martyrdom of pain. She had raised herself to one of the highest positions in the world and there she had met her old love.

Only Heaven knew what she endured after that, when she saw his wife, when she saw him in his daily life, yet knowing that he was lost to her for evermore.

Then the climax came when his wife spoke of "Lance's little child." If those words drove her to her death who shall wonder?

She saw the stars in the water and thought she was going to them; and perhaps, on the Great Day, that thought, that imagination may plead for her.

It was a mad love, a cruel, mad love.

Some instinct came to Lord Chandos when he read that letter that all was not well. He started at once for Rashleigh.

The morning sun was high in the heavens when he reached there. Going at once to the mill-stream, he had seen the body of the woman he loved floating there, her long hair tangled in the water-lilies, a smile such as comes from perfect peace on her face.

He did the wisest thing he could have done—he brought Farmer Noel to the spot, and told him the story, while she lay with her face raised to the morning skies—the story of a mad love.

Farmer Noel uttered no reproaches.

"I never thought she would live a happy life or die a happy death," he said—"it was written so in her face."

They two kept the secret. In a small place like Rashleigh such an occurrence is a nine days' wonder; every one believed that the hapless lady had fallen into the stream as she was passing to the woods. Although the farmer grieved sorely after her, he never told any one that she was his niece, and no one recognized her.

There was a verdict of found drowned, and every one thought the farmer very generous because he undertook the funeral expenses.

How Lord Chandos grieved, no words could tell—it was as though the light of his life had disappeared; he never spoke of his sorrow, but it made him old in his youth and killed the best part of his life in him.

No one, even ever so faintly, connected the inquest at Rashleigh with the disappearance of Madame Vanira. The world went mad at first with anger and disappointment, then a rumor was spread that madame had gone to America, and had married a millionaire there.

The world recovered its good temper and laughed; then another grand singer appeared on the scene, and Leone was forgotten. The only person to whom Lord Chandos ever told the truth was the Countess of Lanswell, and it shocked her so greatly that she gave up all society for a few days, and then, as the world had done before her, forgot it.

Lord Chandos never forgot; the world was never the same to him. His wife's words came true; he was kindness itself to her, and she was very happy. She never even heard of Madame Vanira's untimely end, nor did she ever know who Madame Vanira was. She always respected her, because she had kept her word, and had gone out of her husband's way. As time passed on she, too—forgot.

Lord Chandos never forgot.

Fair daughters and stalwart sons grew around him; he was kind, cheerful, even gay, but in the depths of his heart he mourned over her. To please him Lady Chandos gave to one of her daughters the name of Leone, and it was pitiful to hear the pathos with which he used the name.

Of all his children he loves Leone best. In his dreams he sees the golden gates of heaven, and the other Leone watching for him there.

While she sleeps in peace by the mill-stream, and as the water runs by, it sings:

"A mad love—a mad love."

But "the mill will never grind again with the waters that are past."